Second Sight

Second Sight

Neil M. Gunn

Whittles Publishing

Published by
Whittles Publishing,
Dunbeath Mains Cottages,
Dunbeath,
Caithness, KW6 6EY,
Scotland, UK

www.whittlespublishing.com

Foreword © 2002 Dairmid Gunn
Reprinted 2006

The publisher acknowledges subsidy from the Scottish Arts Council
towards the publication of this volume.

ISBN 1-870325-89-3

Printed by 4Edge Ltd, Hockley, Essex, SS5 4AD

FOREWORD

The writing career of Neil Gunn, one of Scotland's greatest and most imaginative authors of the 20th century, spanned thirty years, ending in 1956 with the publication of his so-called 'spiritual autobiography', *The Atom of Delight*.

The early years of his writing saw his strong association with a Scottish movement in creative writing, which came to be known as the Scottish Renaissance. For him the main significance in the movement lay in the belief that Scotland possessed a national identity of its own, distinct from that of England, and had something to offer the world in terms of its historical and cultural experience. Gunn's own experience was firmly rooted in the Highlands of Scotland, an area where the vestiges of an ancient Celtic culture were still to be found. His sympathies lay with his own people and their way of life and he was at his most persuasive and strongest as an author when writing about them in the context of both the present and the past. Such books as *Morning Tide* and *Highland River* bear witness to this. Through a thoughtful awareness of his own origins, he was able to identify certain values and beliefs that had relevance to contemporary life.

It seems, therefore, like a departure from the normal when he writes a novel set in a shooting lodge, where the main protagonists are a group of people from England, whose visit to the Highlands centres round the excitement of the hunt in a remote deer forest. Is this novel, *Second Sight*, written in 1940, really such a 'departure' for Gunn?

With such a setting and such characters, the reader can be excused for thinking that Gunn has abandoned his concern for the Highlands in favour of a deer forest thriller on the lines of John Buchan's *John McNab*. The ingredients are certainly there; a shooting lodge party of wealthy English people, a team of Highland stalkers, a legendary stag to be hunted and a background of glen and corrie, shrouded from time to time by impenetrable mist. It is the title *Second Sight* that hints that this is no ordinary deer forest thriller. This psychic gift, or curse, is a phenomenon that is closely associated with the culture and history of the Highlands. This ability on the part of some people to foresee events introduces in the novel an extra dimension that dominates the plot and influences the ambience in which this exciting story takes place.

The principal character, Harry Kingsley, is a sympathetic stranger to the Highlands; through mixing with the local community in an easy and pleasant manner, he becomes aware of some of the intricacies of Celtic attitudes and culture. He also becomes aware that one of the stalkers possesses the so-called 'second sight' and has foreseen an incident of immediate relevance to the occupants of the lodge. This local prophesy colours all actions and conversations within the story, either directly or indirectly.

Kingsley's positive and sensitive approach to the local people is counterbalanced by that of one of his companions at the lodge. Geoffrey Smith, who dislikes and distrusts the local community, despises any belief for which there is no rational explanation. The clash between Kingsley's tolerant and enquiring attitude and Smith's intellectual arrogance provides an important motif for this novel of suspense, or 'inverted thriller'.

A derivative of Smith's contempt for belief in 'second sight' is an obsession to kill the much vaunted stag, King Brude. Smith's hunt is tinged with a desire to prove that his rational approach to life is superior to that of a culture impregnated with superstition and ignorance. His approach is gloomily negative. In contrast, Kingsley's approach is more in accordance with the wonder of a landscape of moor and hill, magically transformed from time to time by sunshine and mist. He also has the advantage of being in love with laird's daughter, Helen Marway. She too can transform the landscape. 'For here was Helen Marway, in the bright sun, running with the invisible deer, running beyond men, in the light.'

Landscape is always important to Gunn and is the backdrop to most of his novels. In *Second Sight* it virtually assumes the role of one of the protagonists. The atmosphere enveloping the land—be it light and shadow, swift transitions from light to half light, mist, rain, tones and flowing lines—contributes to the dramatic essence of the novel. All the characters are aware of it in one way or another, but Harry Kingsley, in particular, is affected by it. 'The cone of Benuain was islanded before them to the north-west, and mountain tops and long skerries floated on that white sea as far as the eye could travel. A feeling of the marvel of the first creation came upon Harry in an atmosphere not productive or hectic, but timeless and still. A creation not being created but creating itself from within.'

The theme of second sight is continually present throughout the novel; after setting the scene for the development of the plot, it lingers on in various guises and is particularly evident in the deeper conversations among the inhabitants of the lodge and their friends. It stimulates a clash between spiritual and material values and brings to mind T. S. Eliot's concern over the emotional and spiritual sterility of Western man in his great poem, *The Waste Land,* popular in the 1920s, the period in which the novel *Second Sight* is set. Despite its Highland setting and the exquisite descriptions of that most beautiful part of Scotland, *Second Sight* is not the most 'Highland' of Gunn's many novels in terms of writing from the 'inside' or 'within'; it gives, however, a Highland landscape a symbolic significance and sets the perceptive reader off on a hunt for renewed vision.

DAIRMID GUNN

Chapter One

With the lighting of the lamps came a slight uneasiness into the sitting-room of Corbreac Lodge. Upon the hollows and passes of the deer forest, darkness would be settling down, and though there was no need for anxiety, still there was always that odd chance of an accident, of the unforeseen.

There was, of course, a far greater chance that Harry Kingsley had been led over the hills and far away by the elusive King Brude, whose "wind-blown" antlers were becoming a legend of the forest. Disturbed by an involuntary vision of Harry's triumph, Geoffrey Smith got up and moved restlessly towards the bookcase. As it was not a vision he wanted to believe in, he tried to ease the stress of the moment by making a jocular reference to Harry's usual luck.

Sir John Marway, a tall lean man, with a head of strong dark-grey hair, stood with his back to the fire, smiling at the cannibal trout (12 lb. 2 oz.) in the glass case over the door into the hall, for his daughter, Helen, had promptly dropped her book on the couch and accused Geoffrey of being jealous.

"Well, obviously!" replied Geoffrey. "Wouldn't you be?"

"And to confess it, too!"

"How often have I warned you", said Geoffrey, "of the importance of keeping at least the mind clean?"

Helen's bright hazel eyes opened wide. "But what can you know about the mind? You may know about green germs on little glass slides—but the mind?"

1

"Ah, ze mind! ze mind! What a thing it is!"

"And what a thing it isn't!" said Helen, who was twenty-one.

Geoffrey had a hard, loud, but real laugh, for he was a practical fellow, who could enjoy a practical joke when not directed against himself. Thirty-four years of age, he was tall and straight in build, with a square fair head, light-blue eyes, and the set figure some men have at forty.

Lady Marway, busy over her work-basket, let the talk go on, for she knew the value of a chance interesting discussion or game sufficiently well, in so remote a spot, not to interrupt it unless she had to. She was a sensible, gracious woman, with hair that would presently be quite white. Many years of her life had been spent in India, where her husband had followed his profession of civil engineer with such admirable purpose and sympathetic understanding of the native mind that he was still consulted on engineering projects in the East.

Suddenly Marjory Warrington, the fifth person in the room, hushed them to silence. Geoffrey looked at her. He had of late unconsciously developed the habit of looking at her. She was taller and eight years older than Helen, very fair and with a mild expression that suited a figure which, though generous, did not suggest stoutness. Distantly related to Lady Marway, she had not a little of her quiet poise and efficiency.

Voices outside, the rattle of the gun-room door, and footsteps coming in. Then Harry's voice: "Never mind the rifle. Wait till I get you a drink." Followed by the voice of the stalker: "No thank you, sir. I'm all right." And Harry's swift: "Wait a minute." The door from the gun-room opened and Harry appeared.

His dark hair and eyebrows emphasised the pallor on his face. The pallor might have suggested exhaustion, were it not for the glitter of life, almost excitement, in his eyes. There was ability in the sensitively cut features, and at the moment—perhaps because of something boyish in the suppressed excitement—his slim figure hardly looked its twenty-eight years.

"Frightfully sorry," he said to Lady Marway. "We had a tough passage, and there was the usual accident to the flask!"

He smiled with a quick humour and turned to the drink cabinet that stood against the back wall near the window, for the Lodge was of modest dimensions and the service in keeping. When he had half-filled a tumbler with neat whisky he went to the door he had left open, saying, "Here you are!" and then, as he raised his eyes, cried sharply, "Alick, wait!" They heard the outside door of the gun-room being shut.

"Gone! the silly fellow!" Harry came back, closing the door, his face netted with concern. To cover up the concern, he looked humorously at the size of the whisky. "This will do me for the rest of the night, sir."

"What happened, Harry?" Lady Marway asked.

"Angus thought he saw you after King Brude," said Sir John expectantly.

"Yes." Harry smiled. "I say, that Alick is an extremely intelligent fellow. Quiet, but effective. Quiet humour, too. It grows on you. I don't think I have ever enjoyed a day so much. I'll never forget it." And murmuring "Thank you" to his host and hostess, he drank to them.

"So I presume we must congratulate you?" said Geoffrey.

"How noble of you, Geoffrey! Only your voice is just a little bit lacking in enthusiasm."

"I think I can honestly say that I almost do not grudge King Brude to you," and Sir John prepared to shake hands.

"How splendid of you, sir! But alas! I must decline the honour. He still lives."

"Not wounded?" Sir John's concern was sharp.

"No. But he might have been. That's where Alick comes in. After climbing to the east corrie on Benuain, we got about two hundred and fifty yards from him. Alick slid the rifle into the heather in front of me. 'Our only chance,' he whispered. And then, as I was getting my elbows fixed, he added, 'Do you think you can do it?' It meant: Unless you are sure, don't. And I wasn't sure."

"So you didn't? How noble of you!" exclaimed Marjory.

And Sir John, with a touch of mock ceremony, shook his hand. "Now I do congratulate you."

"So you didn't feel equal to it?" said Geoffrey drily.

"For one thing, I hadn't the heart to disappoint you, Geoffrey. And for another, while I was still swithering—with my heart going like a clock that has dropped its pendulum—you know the feeling? Alick said: 'The light is beginning to fail'!"

"How dramatic!" said Helen.

"And was it?" Geoffrey asked.

"How nasty!" said Marjory.

Geoffrey laughed heartily, for he could not help feeling relieved that Harry had not got King Brude.

"He's a good stalker, Alick," said Sir John thoughtfully.

"So you had no luck to-day?" Lady Marway got up.

"Not a single shot."

"I thought you said it was the best day ever you had." She stood smiling.

"In a way it was. I really can't tell you how much I enjoyed it. I don't know what it was about it. The stalking was excellent, exciting. Real artist's work. But also—somehow—I got in touch with—the environment. You will think it absurd, but I got in touch in a way that I never did before. Direct touch. See it, feel it, smell it."

"*Commune* with it?" suggested Geoffrey.

"Pretty nearly," said Harry, frankly. "In fact it became so real, so natural, it was as if——"

He hesitated, and Helen, who had been following him with fascinated interest, said, "As if scales had come off your eyes."

Geoffrey let out a roar of laughter and turned away.

But Harry, looking at Helen, was not affected by the interruption. "Precisely." He nodded. "I found I could focus directly and the naturalness of everything was enchanting. I know it sounds nonsense. I can't really explain it."

"Didn't you also feel like that the day you were fishing with Alick?" Marjory asked Helen. "I'm afraid the child has had a small crush on him ever since," she explained.

"I have not," replied Helen promptly; then, imitating Marjory's cool, amused manner, "in any case, not to any marked degree."

"I don't want to hurry you, Harry," said Lady Marway, "but, as you know, dinner is already——"

"I know. I'm frightfully sorry. I'll rush."

"Well, for our sake, don't get enchanted in your bath!" called Geoffrey.

Harry turned and looked at him "Five minutes in your sane, scientific company, Geoffrey, and all enchantment vanishes—poof! Had a good day?"

"Oh, so-so. Eleven-pointer. Seventeen stone, clean. And the best balance of a head and spread yet. And a nine-pointer, over fifteen. That was all."

"You glutton! And you, sir?"

"We followed a nice beast," said Sir John, "until he lay down. But we couldn't get near enough. And then they were disturbed."

"By Geoffrey?"

At which point Marjory, who had been watching Harry all along with the closest interest, said to her hostess: "Do you know, Aunt Evelyn, I am quite certain Harry has something on his mind. In addition to enchantment."

"Aren't the others back yet?" Harry asked Lady Marway, ignoring Marjory.

"No. Not yet."

"Why?"

"Why?" repeated Lady Marway, looking at him. "Well, if the loch wasn't up to much, they were both going on to Dingwall. Joyce wants to see some tweeds."

"And see what Greta Garbo looks like in a little country picture-house. She thinks she will look different. Do you?" asked Helen.

"She might, you know," Harry replied. "Things *can* look different."

"Why do you ask?" Lady Marway was still looking at him.

"Oh, nothing." Harry smiled. "Only, George was doing a flat fifty over the wooden bridge at Clachvor. I got him with the glass."

"But that's his normal pace," said Helen.

"Oh, of course."

"Come on!" said Marjory. "No side-tracking. Out with it!"

"With what? I'm off!"

"Frightened to pull the trigger—for the second time!" Geoffrey gave his short, sharp laugh.

"No—not exactly *frightened*," replied Harry, pausing reluctantly. "And yet——" he gave a chuckle at himself— "there is something. It was so extraordinary. And coming on top of such a day. Perhaps it is no more than that I can hardly resist having one at the scientific mind, personified in Geoffrey." He looked at Lady Marway. "Perverse of me, isn't it?"

"What was it, Harry?" When Helen's face grew interested, her eyes shone with light. A vivid, virgin face, very alive.

Geoffrey was now delighted at Harry's reluctance. "Don't be shy! We all love the romantic."

"He doesn't want to tell us now!" cried Marjory.

"And now you have made us all curious," smiled his hostess.

"Oh, look here, this is absurd. I apologise. I shan't be two shakes." Harry turned for the door.

"Coward!" called Geoffrey.

As Harry grasped the knob he appeared to get a shock, as if he had been stung. His head came round slowly. "The knob turned in my hand!" They saw his mind lost in fear. Then swiftly he turned the knob and flung the door open. And faced round again. "No-one!"

It was so well done—for he was good at these little entertaining surprises—that for the moment he held them. Then Geoffrey laughed. "So it was spooks, was it?"

"You must tell us now," said Helen. "You must."

"I'm sorry for you, Harry," smiled Marjory. "The whole atmosphere is wrong. You've done your best to create a feeling of the unusual, and it has fallen flat."

"I know. Don't you think I should wait to see if I can't get the right atmosphere? It was a pretty dramatic happening— but quite short. Pity to waste it."

"I know. I sympathise."

"It's the presence of an unsympathetic mind," said Helen.

Geoffrey chuckled. "The medium cannot get in touch with the unseen."

Then quite simply and directly, Harry said, "It *was* the unseen."

"Was it?" asked Helen.

Harry nodded to her. "Yes."

"Where?"

"On the way in—with Alick."

"What happened?"

Again reluctance got hold of Harry, and he looked with an uncertain smile at his hostess.

"Is it worth spoiling the meat for?" she asked, and there was meaning in her quiet tones.

Geoffrey gave a scoffing chuckle.

"Mother!" exclaimed Helen.

"Very well," said Lady Marway.

But Harry still hesitated.

"Go on," said Sir John, and instantly his quiet voice sanctioned the situation.

Harry went on quietly: "Alick and I were coming along the path up there—just as you round the fir wood and see the house. We had been walking for some little way in silence. There was nothing on my mind at all. I was certainly thinking of nothing. In fact I had that pleasant tired feeling that often follows a perfect day. You know—pleased with myself and everything. My mind felt free and happy. It sort of floated along with me, if you understand."

"Like the scent of a flower on the wind," suggested Geoffrey solemnly.

"Precisely," said Harry. "I am trying to tell you that any thought of tragedy was utterly absent from my mind. Certainly I could not have suggested to Alick anything like what he saw. Now the next odd thing is that I feel sure that Alick had enjoyed his day, and certainly had no reason to begin imagining gloomy or deathly things. Quite the reverse. We had been friendly—in that pleasant way, without class-consciousness and what-not. And to prove that that is true, when Alick did see what he saw, he put his arm out across my

7

chest, pushing me back off the path—like that. 'Stand back,'
he said quietly but intensely. The moon was just up. A perfectly clear but black sky. It is really a lovely night outside.
You can see a mile. Well, I thought he was seeing something
coming out of the wood—some animal or bird or something—for he has an extraordinary knowledge of their
queerer habits—but though I stared where he stared, I could
see nothing. And his arm was still out. Then a cold shiver
went up and down my spine."

"You saw nothing?" asked Marjory.

"No, I saw nothing. But I could see that he was seeing
something—and that it was no bird or beast or any natural
thing. Whatever it was, I *felt* it—perhaps from him—coming
towards us, passing us, and going on. It was a very vivid experience. For I don't know how many seconds I was really held—
like that." Harry closed his right hand. "He edged me back a
bit on to the heather as it passed, and his head slowly turned
after it. He had gone quite stiff and once you looked at him
you had to look where his eyes stared. I've never had any
experience like it. You had no time to think. You were caught.
And for a moment or two it was—anything but pleasant."

As Harry paused, Sir John said, "I did not know Alick was
affected that way. A funeral procession, was it?"

"Yes."

"You did not question him?" Though in the form of a
question Sir John's words held half a warning—if need be.

"I did, of course," said Harry, showing Sir John by his eyes
that he understood him. "But he obviously did not like to be
questioned, so I did not pursue it too far."

"But surely you asked him what he saw?" demanded
Geoffrey.

"Naturally. He saw some persons carrying a dead body."

"The phantom funeral," explained Sir John. "It was not
an uncommon experience in the old days in the Highlands,
if we believe the old tales. But with the advance of science it
is getting rare."

"Naturally," agreed Geoffrey. "But it's an interesting form
of delusion or hallucination. And Harry was obviously

impressed!" He looked at Harry. "Can we really take your word for it that you are not spoofing us?"

"Geoffrey!" exclaimed Helen, shocked.

"You can," said Harry.

"You mean you are satisfied that the man did actually imagine he was seeing something?"

"It is not the sort of thing a man would make up, is it?"

"I merely asked you a question."

"And I have answered." Harry regarded Geoffrey drily. "This is not a court of law—with the dead body as exhibit number one—not *yet*".

"Now don't get fantastic. That's the worst of you romantic people. You see something—or at least *someone else* sees something—or imagines he sees something—and then you all promptly develop a situation. Good Lord! you don't mean to say you are serious about this?" Into a chuckle Geoffrey could contrive to put a considerable amount of complacent sarcasm.

"It isn't a question of being serious or otherwise," replied Harry, for he could not stop himself reacting to Geoffrey. "You flatter yourself you are the modern, unprejudiced, scientific mind, yet here you are, bung-full of prejudice before you have even approached—a certain definite experience which I have laid before you. That experience may be susceptible of a perfectly rational explanation. An effort at sarcastic laughter explains nothing."

"Touch!" said Marjory.

"'Experience which I have laid before you' is good." Geoffrey was tickled by it. "You have laid nothing before us except a sort of vague situation. This sort of situation: a man sees something—which isn't there. You were there. You saw nothing. Yet you are now prepared to create a situation about it. Don't you know anything about delusional psychology?"

"Not much," said Harry.

"And you wondered why I laughed!"

"I still do," said Helen.

So Geoffrey laughed again, and the others smiled.

"I'm afraid I cannot help you," said Geoffrey.

Helen raised her eyebrows. "But that's nothing to be superior over."

"Now, Helen, child, it's time——"

"But, Mother, I'm not a child. I'm twenty-one and fit to be the 'father' of a family. What I object to is this. Geoffrey uses a big word as if it were a stick. That stick may beat me—but it will never make me believe. He thinks it will. The materialist is always a bully."

"Oh, bravo, Helen!" cried Marjory.

"You mix up two things, my child: reason and belief," Geoffrey explained. "You emotionally want to believe in something. My reason is not impressed."

"My lamb, neither is my belief impressed by your reason," retorted Helen.

Sir John chuckled, as he nearly always did when his daughter spoke in this way, for he was fond of her. Lady Marway smiled and was just about to order Harry off, when Geoffrey replied:

"That may be. But again it proves nothing. Let us agree that this man Alick did have his delusion, that he genuinely imagined he saw things. Well, we all know about that. Our asylums are full of people who see queerer things than funerals. The things they see never take place—except inside their own heads."

"Yes—but—but that's not the same." Helen was rather stumped, until she had the bright idea: "Do you mean that Alick should be in an asylum?"

Geoffrey just laughed.

"I think Geoffrey is probably pretty near the truth of the matter," said Sir John, pleased, with his wife, to leave the matter there.

But Harry could hardly leave it there. "I merely notice that Geoffrey has explained nothing—in his usual adroit way. The people inside asylums, as far as I know, have delusions about themselves. They do not have delusions about specific happenings in the future divorced from themselves. People in asylums are obsessed. Alick is not obsessed. The delusion, as you call it, was quite involuntary. He has had it very seldom. Only once or twice in his life. He dislikes it. Hates it. I was sorry for him."

"Well?" Helen challenged Geoffrey.

"How, for example, do you know he dislikes it, hates it?"

"From the evidence he led," replied Harry.

"You mean," said Geoffrey ironically, "he *told* you he hates it?"

"Oh no; he never told me he hated it."

"The evidence, then?"

Harry hesitated. "He began to tremble—when they had passed."

"Nothing more?"

"Then—he was sick."

"Sick?"

"He vomited—in the heather."

There was a very distinct pause.

"You asked him what he saw?"

"I asked him what was wrong with him. He muttered that he had seen something. I asked him what it was. He would not speak. I could see a tremendous reluctance upon him. But I begged him to tell me. I was friendly. I wanted to help him. He said at last: 'Four men carrying a dead body.'"

"Did you ask him", probed Geoffrey, "if he recognised the dead body?"

"I did." Harry's eyes were coldly on Geoffrey. They all waited for his next words. Tonelessly they came. "He said: 'No'."

Lady Marway drew in a full breath, but Geoffrey was in pursuit at once. "There you are! Why is it that he did not see the one fact, the one piece of evidence, by which his so-called vision could be checked?"

"I can't tell you, I'm sure," replied Harry. "Possibly it is rather a good thing he doesn't."

"There you go! Anything, so long as it is beside the point! Here's what is reputed to be a vision of the future. Yet the one most important thing in the vision itself—and the only thing by which the vision could be checked—is not recognised. In any detective story, whether the author plays honest or dishonest, at least you are always told who the dead man is."

"There's something in that," Sir John nodded. "In all these phantom funerals, the person who sees it never seems to know the dead body, now that you mention it. He sees the procession winding along a path——"

"And afterwards," interrupted Geoffrey triumphantly, "when a funeral procession does wind along that same path—as funeral processions must at some time wander over every human path there is—the people shake their heads. Ah, three days ago—or three years ago—or three centuries ago—Alick Macdonald, the stalker at Corbreac, foresaw this death. Ah—mysterious!… Now, I mean to say, isn't it absurd? All joking apart."

"I think so, Geoffrey," agreed Lady Marway. "I think you have made it perfectly clear. And now——"

"But, Mother, he hasn't!"

"No?" Geoffrey raised amused eyebrows.

"Has he?" And Helen turned to Harry.

They were all amused, including Harry, who said to her, pleasantly: "I agree, Helen. He hasn't. Let us assume that when you go back home you go bang into a funeral and pull your car up to let it pass. You are presently alarmed to find a great number of your friends there. You wonder who can have died. But you cannot tell. Why? Because you cannot see through the coffin."

"Phew!" breathed Marjory. "We are getting gruesome, aren't we?"

"What have you to say to that?" Helen asked Geoffrey.

"May I inquire of your counsel if the medium in this particular case recognised the four men who carried the dead body?"

"Did he?" asked Helen.

"He did," said Harry.

"He mentioned them to you by name?" challenged Geoffrey.

Harry took a moment, then said, "He did."

They all looked at him. No one asked for the names. At last he continued, "There is no reason why I should not give you the names. It has nothing to do with—uh—anyone in particular." (They felt that he was deliberately reserving at least part of the truth). "In Alick's interest, I don't want to be more definite. He felt the experience so much that I shouldn't like him to run into any gossip about it. I hope you see what I mean. I had an unusual experience and I was full of it, I admit. But"—he began to smile in his entertaining way—"it's gone far enough. And now——"

"One minute," said Geoffrey. "Are you prepared to write down the names?"

"Yes," said Harry, now smiling cheerfully, "and sign, seal, and deliver them to your banker."

"And you didn't see—or hear—anything yourself?" Helen asked.

"Not a thing! Though—now you mention it," and he laughed, "I did *hear* something. It was just as the procession had passed. I heard the deep ringing of a ship's bell in my ears."

At that moment, the dinner-bell, a rather slow deep-noted one, began ringing. By the way Harry's head jerked up and his eyes opened—obviously involuntarily—they all saw at once that that was the bell he had heard. But he let the smile come on his face very cunningly. "Of course, as Geoffrey knows," he said, "a bell ringing in one's ears is quite a common experience. Usually something to do with the liver, hasn't it? But it was my conscience—for being late." He bowed to his hostess. "I do most abjectly apologise. Please don't wait for me."

"They must have heard you come in and assumed you would be dressed and in your right mind." She smiled. "I shall try to forgive you."

"It would take more than a ghost", said Helen, "to stop Cook having the bell rung when she is ready."

"And now I feel like a school boy!" Harry rushed out.

They had all got up, and, as they went towards the door, Lady Marway said: "At any rate, he does contrive to keep us alive."

"Barely," answered Marjory. "I'm famished. But he stood up to you, Geoffrey."

"Yes, didn't he?" Half-closing her mouth, Helen could coo in her throat like a pigeon.

"He did his best," said Geoffrey. "But you haven't heard the end of all this yet. You wait!"

"Don't you think you should let it rest?" suggested Lady Marway.

"Let it rest! Now that I have him and can document the case? We'll have some fun out of this. I see it coming. Harry's ghost!"

Helen turned in the door of the dining-room and in a deep, slow voice said, "What if it's *your* ghost?"

She said it very well, and there was just a second before Geoffrey laughed.

Chapter Two

While they were at dinner, Mairi, the parlour-maid, came into the empty sitting-room with a duster in her hand. As she faced the room, listening, she closed the door behind her very softly. The air of tension in her attitude heightened the colour in her cheeks. She was dark, with brown eyes. "A dark, pretty country girl," was how a visitor remembered her in London. She was twenty-one, the same age as Helen. But where Helen might fly, Mairi would dive. She now listened naturally, every instinct alert, and not for one thing but for everything.

Opposite her, across the room, was the gun-room door, with the fireplace to the right of it. The wall on her left hand was to the back of the house, and through its window, which faced north, could be seen in daylight the green-painted larder where the stags were hung up, a corner of the garage, and the "back road" that gave on pony tracks into the forest. A brown curtain, hanging to just below the sill, covered the window at the moment. Mairi's eyes rested on it, then she began gathering the glasses and cleaning up the ash-trays.

The room was furnished simply and in good taste, with some comfortable armchairs, a writing-desk, and a mahogany bookcase—the bottom half with doors. A bracket lamp in the wall by the bookcase was usually turned low—until required in that part of the room for reading or writing. It was of the same kind as the standard lamp, which with its incandescent mantle and bulbous opaque white globe stood over towards the fireplace. The antlers above the gun-room door and the spotted cannibal trout in its glass case above the hall door somehow did not obtrude. A spray of red autumn berries in a brown earthenware jar suitably suggested the time of year.

Mairi moved about deftly, but she still kept listening, and at last, hearing a sound in the gun-room, she stood still so suddenly that her very nostrils seemed to scent the sound, like a hind's. It came nearer. She glanced away from it towards the hall door, then, going to the gun-room door, calmly opened it.

"Oh, it's you," she said coolly.

"Yes," said Alick.

As he approached her, she stepped back. "What do you want?"

He came into the doorway, a rifle and an oiled rag in his hand, glanced round the room and then looked at Mairi.

"Anything wrong?" he asked.

The dry searching satire came out of an expressionless face, except for the eyes, and they were, for so big a man, rather small. He was as tall as Geoffrey, but with the powerful shoulders and lean flanks of the "heavy" athlete. He walked lightly and could probably be as quick on his feet as a cat. His face was full, without being fleshy, and his eyes, of a greeny blue, could be penetratingly steadfast, as indeed they were now. This still waiting quality in him defeated Mairi, and despite herself concern crept into her voice when she repeated, "What do you want?"

"To tell the truth," he said, "I was wanting a drink."

He said it so simply that she was shocked. Her voice was a note lower and more intense when she replied, "You know I would never give you or anyone else a drink out of their private decanter." Then she looked around as if she might have been overheard.

"I know that," he answered, in a voice light in tone, like his fairness. "But, you see, Mr. Kingsley promised me a drink."

"Well, he can give it to you. I can't."

He glanced at the decanter, still on top of the cabinet, and entered. "I see I'll have to help myself."

"No, you won't!" and she faced him, her back to the decanter.

"Going to stop me?"

"Yes." She was breathing rapidly.

"Good for you! I have always admired your spirit, haven't I?"

"Go away! Go out!"

He looked about him. "Mr. Kingsley poured some whisky into a glass for me. I didn't want it then. But I want it now. Did he pour it back?" He smiled at her. "Why this sudden opposition? It's not your whisky. And I'll tell Mr. Kingsley to-morrow that I took it."

"No!"

Then he looked into her eyes.

"Has Mr. Kingsley been talking?"

"Yes."

"You listened at the door?"

"Yes."

"The whole story?"

"Yes."

"I see!... In that case you must know I need the whisky. It's two miles home. Why refuse me a drink?"

"It's Sir John's whisky."

"No, it's not that. It's not because it's *his* drink, in spite of your honesty. The queer thing is—you don't know why you're doing this yourself. Isn't that so?"

"Go away!" she said to his eyes.

"You are vexed that it happened. And you are frightened... of what?"

"I don't know."

He dropped his eyes to the rifle barrel and smoothed it with the oiled rag. He had seen her body quiver. "Be sensible, then." The easy-going good nature in him gave a twist to his smile. "You know they come to the Highlands to be entertained. You know that. Well—we must do what we can. They expect to see ghosts and queer things. All part of the environment. Someone must play up."

She was now staring at him, herself forgotten.

"You don't believe me?" he asked, raising his eyebrows.

She gulped. "You wouldn't—dare——"

"What?" His smile searched her out and its good nature terrified her. "Frightened I'm daring the Black Place, down below." And then on the same tone: "If you don't give me the whisky, Mairi, I'll raise Satan himself."

"Alick!" There was horror in her voice.

"You see? You really want to save me. But you don't know from what. It's not because you're afraid of the Devil. Not a bit." Then quietly, with a penetration that hurt her: "You hate—in your heart—that I should have let him see—that I should have let them in on me. Why?" Slowly his smile came again. "Lord, Mairi, one would almost think you were in love with me! Stand aside now, like a good girl."

"No."

"No? You'll be wanting a good old flare up—so that all your bits will crash together. Is that it? It gets like that." His left eyelid quivered in humour, as he laid the rifle and the rag on the floor. Then he straightened up and faced her; but obviously in no hurry. "I love your spirit, Mairi, me darlin'. It's a pity that you hate those tricks of mine."

They were words he would never use normally. The clairvoyant, underlying-bitter mood in him began to have a disintegrating effect upon her. As she filled her lungs, her whole body trembled. He saw she could not stand it much longer and he put his arms about her to lift her aside. But as they lifted they embraced her, and at that her spirit was released. She struggled with such startling violence that they overbalanced against the cabinet and sent the decanter flying to the floor, where it crashed into pieces and scattered the whisky.

So appalled was Mairi that she still gripped his jacket with one hand as she listened. Then she came to herself. "Quick! Out before they come! Quick! Quick!"

But he stood unmoving. There was the sound of a door, of footsteps.

"Quick, Alick! Get out!" Madly she pushed him towards the gun-room door, but his body resisted. She was too late anyway. The hall door opened and Geoffrey's head appeared, duly followed by his whole person.

"What's—happened?"

"It's—it's the whisky, sir," said Mairi. "It fell. I pushed it over. I'm sorry." The gulp in her voice kept back the flood of tears.

But Geoffrey was watching Alick slowly picking up the rifle and the rag. "It's whisky all right." He sniffed audibly. "And it's you, Alick."

"Yes, sir," said Alick calmly.

"Were you helping her to push it over?"

For Mairi had clearly been in some sort of struggle. She started mopping up the whisky with her duster.

"I'm afraid I was."

"Afraid you were, what!"

Helen entered, followed by Marjory.

"I say!" said Marjory, sniffing.

"What's happened?" Helen stood still, fascinated.

Sir John and Lady Marway came in, but Harry remained in the doorway, his eyes on Alick.

"They pushed the whisky over—accidentally," Geoffrey explained. His humour was hard and sarcastic, for Alick's unyielding eyes had angered him.

Mairi leaned back on her heels. "I'm sorry, ma'm," she said in deep distress, to Lady Marway. "It fell off—there. I hit against it. I'm very sorry."

"Was that the way, Alick?" Lady Marway asked calmly.

"Yes, ma'm," said Alick.

Lady Marway surveyed the floor. "You'd better get another cloth."

Carrying the broken pieces and her sopping duster, Mairi withdrew.

They all looked at Alick, who seemed to be waiting for what they had to say. He stood extraordinarily still and expressionless. A solid opaque body, vaguely ominous.

"Well, I think we may finish our dinner." Lady Marway regarded Alick with a certain level humour. "You promise no more distractions?" Then, as he did not answer: "Very well, you may go."

Without a word he turned and went out at the gun-room door. At the same moment, Harry withdrew from the hall door.

"Rather sinister figure, don't you think?" said Geoffrey.

"Oh, Geoffrey!" Helen looked at him. "Didn't you see the sweat on his forehead."

"Can't say I did. But possibly you're right. They had a bit of a struggle."

"Struggle?" Sir John's brows wrinkled.

"Yes. The rifle was on the floor. And she was somewhat deranged. Didn't you notice?"

"Do you mean he was trying to take the whisky from her?"

Geoffrey's smile grew more sarcastic. "Possibly he was trying to do that, too! In fact——"

"Hsh!" said Helen, as Mairi came in with a dry cloth.

When Lady Marway had sent them back to finish dinner, she inspected the floor and for a moment watched Mairi at work.

"I am very disappointed about this, Mairi."

"Yes, ma'm. I am very sorry."

"Was it entirely an accident?"

"Yes, ma'm."

"Alick was not to blame—in any way?"

"No, ma'm. He was cleaning Mr. Kingsley's rifle and—and just came in to speak to me."

"I see."

"I hope, ma'm, you don't think Alick had anything to do with it?" Her lips quivered.

"All right, Mairi. I'll try to forget it."

"Thank you, ma'm. It won't happen again."

"I hope not. You can open the window for a little."

"Yes, ma'm."

When Lady Marway had gone, closing the door behind her, Mairi finished her mopping, then went to the window, held the curtain aside, and heaved up the lower half. She was wondering whether she should draw the curtain open, when a step startled her and she swung round, letting the curtain fall over the open window.

"All right, Mairi! Don't be frightened." Harry stood in the gun-room door. "He seems to have gone."

She stared at him, speechless.

He entered, hesitated for a moment thoughtfully, then gave a half-shrug and, about to go, paused and smiled to her. "Tell me," he said in a kindly way; "do you believe in second sight?"

Out of her dark eyes came glancing shafts of fear. She did not speak.

"You don't care to answer, perhaps?...Uhm. Difficult, I suppose." He looked away from her. "Do you—then—like the idea of it?"

"I hate it!"

The words came with surprising force. Harry nodded, not looking at her. "I understand. Tell me—do you think he will go straight home?"

"I don't know." From being intense, her voice had become completely non-committal.

"What do you think?"

"I don't know."

Harry nodded. "He must have hated being caught out here, like this. It was bad luck. But—don't you fret. He'll be all right." Then he turned his head, let the friendly smile in his eyes speak for him, and made for the dining-room.

She looked after him, and, as the door closed, her face came alive again. Listening, she heard the sound of the wind rising. The window curtain fluttered out, then fell back and remained still. She heard the sound die over the fir wood. Lifting her wet cloth and the tray of glasses which she had placed on the writing-table, she went out hurriedly.

In a little while she came back with the coffee tray and, when she had disposed it properly, gave a swift look around to satisfy herself everything was in order. When she heard voices coming from the dining-room, she immediately started for the gun-room door, her fingers already unfastening her white apron. She gave the impression of one about to hurry into the night.

Helen and Marjory entered, discussing the manner in which a dinner can be ruined.

"I think your mother is marvellous, she's so patient," said Marjory. "They'll crack nuts now, to ease their excitement! I must say I think Harry is provocative."

"Harry? Surely it's Geoffrey."

"No. It's Harry—and you. Geoffrey is merely like that. True to himself. He must expose superstition."

"Surely, Marjory, that's absurd—anyway, about Harry and me?"

"Not a bit. You are creating a situation, as Geoffrey said. Can't you feel it being created, with the horrid underfeeling that one of us is about to die? Ugh! there's positively a chill in this room already. I think your mother would like to stop it. I think she is right."

Helen, who had lifted a coffee cup and saucer, stood looking at Marjory as she went towards the fire. She forgot to pour coffee into her cup, so arrested was she at the *spoken* thought of death. The death of one of themselves here. *One of themselves!* She moved away a pace or two, but the thought went with her. There *was* a chill in the room. Marjory got down on her knees before the fire.

"You feel that?" asked Helen in a small voice.

Marjory looked over her shoulder at her, then with a shrug prepared to stir the fire. "I feel the chill in the room anyway."

There was a low whine of wind outside. Helen gave an involuntary shiver, as if an unearthly chill had touched her. And at that moment the curtain behind her, fluttering inward, did touch her, with such soft caressing movement that she gave an abject scream and the coffee cup and saucer shot out of her hand, the saucer landing on the carpet unbroken, but the cup smashing to bits on the polished surround. She was in the middle of the room before she stopped herself and, turning, saw the curtain smoothly falling back.

Marjory saw it, too; got up off her knees and approached it carefully; then, grabbing it, pulled it aside—and exposed the open window. Letting out a heavy breath, her left hand on her chest, she dropped into the nearest chair and began to laugh, as the others hurried in.

Helen met them, still panting. "I—I'm sorry. I dropped my coffee cup."

Marjory interrupted her laughter. "We're all going daft!… Who opened the window?"

"I told Mairi to open it to let out the smell," said Lady Marway.

Marjory laughed again. "We felt the chill in the room. Unearthly presence. Then the wind whined up in the pine wood—hsh! there it is again…only it was a much better theatrical effect than that. Helen was standing with her back to the window. Out came the curtain about her—feeling her. Ooh! If she hadn't a good heart she'd have dropped dead."

Geoffrey joined in her laughter, obviously delighted.

Helen, gone very pale, was about to stoop to pick up the pieces of the broken cup, when Harry forestalled her. "You sit down. I'll pick it up."

She sat and dropped her head back. Lady Marway rang.

"Feeling all right?" asked her father.

"Yes." She tried to smile. "I did get a fright. I am certain my heart stopped for a second. Silly of me. I am ashamed."

"Nothing to be ashamed about," he explained. "It's the most terrifying thing on earth—to be touched, when you feel there is nothing *can* touch you. The leap of the beast out of the dark." He patted her head affectionately, then went and closed the window. "Now, that will keep the jungle out."

Lady Marway poured the coffee and Geoffrey, as he handed Marjory her cup, remarked, "An object lesson in the occult!"

"Did you say object—or abject?"

"Or both," suggested Geoffrey, in good form.

"I think," said Marjory, still inclined to laugh, "I think abject is the word. When fear gets you it is rather horrible. Ugh."

"What's happened to Mairi, I wonder? I rang. We're a cup short." Lady Marway looked slightly annoyed.

"I'll get it," said Helen.

"No. Wait."

"Please." And Helen got up and walked out before anyone could stop her. Harry looked after her, then back at Lady Marway.

"It really was nasty for a moment," said Marjory, a sensible girl. "I was at the fire. Felt the chill in the room. Then Helen screamed and there was the curtain feeling around her. It should have been obvious to any sane person that it was nothing, but———"

"But for that one moment," said Geoffrey, "you are not sane. There's the rub. And she only *felt* the thing. If for that moment she had imagined she *saw* the hidden thing as well, she might easily have been really sick." He glanced slyly at Harry, to whom he offered a cup.

"Thanks," said Harry. "You are coming on."

Geoffrey laughed, then in a loud whisper to his hostess: "He refuses to be drawn!"

"Perhaps he is learning wisdom," she said.

"No," replied Geoffrey, shaking his head. "Only a safe reticence. You can see there's nothing in all this so-called occult or second-sight business but can be explained. But your devotees of the cult—they don't like it explained. They don't like to be told—it was only a window curtain moved by the wy-ind. Poetic, what!" He was delighted with himself.

"Have a cigar?" said Sir John.

"What's your opinion about this occult business, Sir John—your frank opinion?" Geoffrey lit his cigar, prepared for pleasant discussion.

"Well, I don't know," said Sir John. "I must admit that, in India, some of these native fellows do queer things."

"Yoga and so on?"

"Well, yes; there's that, too."

"But that's understandable enough. Control of the body by the mind—beyond what we can do. That's all right. But have you ever seen anything that to all appearances could not be explained—like, I mean, well, like Harry's experience?"

"I wonder what's keeping that child?" said Lady Marway. She stood for a moment thoughtfully, then walked out.

Before she had quite closed the door, Marjory got up and followed her.

"Uh—what was that?" said Sir John, his eyes on the door.

"Have you ever seen anything that could not be explained—anything *super*natural?"

"Well, I have seen the rope trick," said Sir John.

Harry's private concentration broke on an ironic sniff.

"The rope trick. A trick. Yes." Geoffrey smiled.

"It's mystifying all the same," said Sir John. "You simply see the rope rising up into the skies and then you see the boy climbing it away up out of sight. There is no preparation or stage apparatus. They can do it anywhere at all—outside on the bare earth, or beside your own bungalow. Anywhere at all. It beat me."

"But you never believed it to be a manifestation of the supernatural—something outside natural law?"

"We all say it is a trick, of course. A conjuror's trick. Very clever."

"Exactly. You know that if it was anything more than that, if it was a real rope and a real boy climbing it—the whole order of life would suffer a vast change."

"Yes, but——" began Harry.

"There would be no need," continued Geoffrey, "for Mr. Gandhi or passive resistance. There would be no poverty—and *you* know the incredible poverty one can meet in India. All the deserts would blossom into orange groves."

"I don't quite follow," said Sir John.

"Doesn't the same fellow who sends the boy up the rope—or someone like him—also put a seed in a pot of earth? You see the seed buried in the pot. You see it come sprouting through the earth. You see it growing into a small tree. You see the fruit forming—before your very eyes—and all in a few minutes. Then he plucks off an orange or a mango or whatever it is and presents it to you. And behold! it is a real fruit. And you eat it."

Sir John smiled. "I see."

"Yes, but you say: a manifestation of the supernatural— something outside natural law," remarked Harry. "What you should say, I think, is—something outside natural law *as we know it*."

"Well, certainly; that's obvious!"

"But it makes a difference."

"How?"

"By its implication that there may be laws which we do not know."

Geoffrey gave a half-impatient shrug. "Oh—yes—of course!"

"Assuming", said Harry, "a law which we do not know——"

"Excuse me," said Sir John, and he walked out of the room.

They looked after him.

"Dammit," said Harry, "I hope there's nothing wrong."

"Good God!" said Geoffrey.

"Think we're going soft?"

"Think? You can *see* it."

"Of course it does not get really bad until you can *smell* it."

"What are you getting at?"

"Merely half-suggesting that you might blow your nose hard."

"And the idea?"

Harry smiled. "That you might get some of the more positive noises out of your head."

Geoffrey gave a short laugh. "Where there is a touch of humour there is still hope. Uh—you were going to assume something, weren't you?"

"Nothing much. The rather vague assumption that some of us may not know everything."

"So I gathered—vaguely."

"Uhm."

Geoffrey turned on him. "Hang it, if you have anything to say, why not say it? Why this—this creation—of—intangible nonsense?"

"You know quite well what I have to say," Harry replied reasonably. "It is simply that there may be in existence a relationship of time and space which we do not normally apprehend. An exceptional mind at an exceptional moment *may* apprehend it—quite involuntarily—in what we call vision or second sight. Do you say that is impossible?"

"It is not impossible to say that the moon is made of green cheese. Because of our astronomical and physical knowledge, however, I deny it, confidently."

"That's merely flippant. That's the worst of you fellows, you hate your old methods and convictions being upset. In that respect, your orthodox scientist is just like your orthodox religious leader or art academician—he has no time for the new. Even in a common-good, solid thing like medicine—become unorthodox, introduce chloroform, or anything really new and helpful, and the head witch-doctors are after you. In short *you* are in the mind *not* to believe beforehand."

"The usual twaddle. There may have been instances, as in the case of a stuff like chloroform, where——"

"There were. And one instance is always sufficient—scientifically. It could happen again."

"You do not know what you are saying, or anyway, you cannot know what scientific method means."

"You're sliding again, aren't you? Scientific method—yes. But destructive disbelief, before you have applied the method—no."

"But, heavens!" exclaimed Geoffrey, "don't you see I *have* been applying the method, trying, in your particular case, to discover any tangible basis in fact—without the slightest success?"

"Do you mean you doubt the happening I related?"

"Not at all. *Your* version of the happening I accept. But you yourself have no facts. You were merely *told.*"

"Lord, are you trying to tell me that the fellow acted all that? With no aim, no object, obviously hating it?"

"I am not saying he acted it. Though even that could be possible."

"Oh!" Harry turned away impatiently.

"Wait," said Geoffrey. "I'll even suggest a reason. Assuming he is a sinister type, preparing, let us say, to do someone in. The little piece of acting by the roadside prepares you, and such as you, to expect death, death in unusual circumstances, even violent death—as 'natural'."

Harry regarded him sarcastically. "If you were going to murder someone, I take it you would rehearse the murder publicly beforehand?"

Geoffrey tried to cover his anger with a more biting sarcasm. "Whatever I might do, I certainly wouldn't be fool enough to say I saw something which *wasn't there*; not to mention that I saw a happening before it happened, which wasn't there!"

"Ah, but you're an acute fellow."

Geoffrey's look concentrated; then he shrugged. "I'd rather be an acute fellow than a fool."

Harry did not answer, and Geoffrey went on in lighter, but no less taunting, tones, "So you think someone is going to get killed here?"

"It is possible that someone may die."

Geoffrey laughed. "Of course! Almost certain, I should say!"

"In this house—within two weeks."

"Oh?" Geoffrey concentrated again.

"And that the odds are in favour of its being *you* or *me*."

There was silence for quite a little while.

"Good God!" gasped Geoffrey. "You don't mean to say you believe that?"

But Harry had heard footsteps. "Hsh! Shut up!" he said quickly.

Helen came in, followed by Marjory and her mother, declaiming, "Dramatic entry of missing body!"

Geoffrey laughed. "Thank goodness! A certain young man here was almost out of his wits."

"Things are coming to a pretty pass", declared Helen, "when a child can't lie down to twiddle its thumbs without the whole family attending the cradle."

Sir John came in, with folded newspapers under his arm. "A paper, anyone?"

Harry took one. "Ah pictures! Here you are, Marjory!"

"How clairvoyant of you, Harry!" and she graciously accepted the *Bulletin*.

Geoffrey got hold of the *Manchester Guardian*, while Sir John settled down to wipe his glasses, light a fresh cigar, and go through *The Times*.

Harry, with a smile for Helen, drew some papers from a long envelope. He was an engineering architect in a business allied to Sir John's.

Lady Marway got in touch with her work-basket again. She was a very neat needlewoman and found a close concentration on exact stitching soothing and restful. She had done some quite useful tapestry work in her time, though at the moment her concern was to arrest a ladder in her daughter's stocking.

Helen collected the coffee cups and rang. The room was so pleasantly and softly bright that she looked at both lamps to make sure the mantles were all right. The bracket one, an older type, was inclined, particularly on a windy night, to burn up and blacken its mantle and fill the room with soot. But now it was behaving excellently. In fact, the whole room was behaving excellently; because, as she realised, it was behaving normally.

She got hold of her book again. It was one of those sixpenny novels, which travellers nowadays are inclined to buy at railway stations instead of the old, popular magazines. She had long meant to read this book because it dealt with the English countryside in that slow, wise way which has so often been a characteristic of the best writers of her race and which she loved (once she had made the effort to get into its mood). Sometimes she had the uneasy feeling that this was not being modern. So she tried to make up for it by reading the most advanced modern stuff at other times. But now she was on holiday.

As she settled down in a corner of the couch, she looked around at the heads that had so recently been disturbed by Alick's experience of the occult. That uncanny Highland irruption might never have been, so decorously did it appear to have been smoothed away. She could almost find a small place in her heart for regret—now that the tumult was over! Her eyes rested on Harry's dark head, and remained there unconsciously.

Until, outside the gun-room door, quite distinctly, she heard a small sound. It struck right on her heart. The rattle of the gun-room door followed. Marjory showed she heard it, then Harry. Footsteps in the gun-room now—slow—uncertain. Lady Marway frankly lifted her head. Each one in the room grew extremely still and silent. There was the soft thud of something falling, and a high-pitched smothered exclamation. But the footsteps drew nearer—slowly—and, after what seemed a very long time, there were fingers against the door, finger-nails scratching the door. They saw the knob rattle and turn. The door opened—and Joyce appeared, blinking in the light.

"Pitch black in there. Ooh!" She was a geranium-lipped, blonde young woman of the world and rubbed her elbow.

"Where's George?" asked Lady Marway.

"Putting the car away. Why? Anything wrong?" She stared from one set of eyes to another.

"No, no!" said Lady Marway quickly.

"Pff!" said Joyce. "Gosh! Talk about a battery of eyes! You make me feel like a disembowelled spirit."

Geoffrey laughed. And Marjory. Laughter became infectious. Sir John joined in.

Joyce looked at them. "I suppose you put out the light on purpose? You are a bunch of toughs."

They laughed on, heartily.

Chapter Three

The following morning Sir John, Geoffrey, and Harry were up early, according to plan. George Marway, Sir John's nephew, was not a natural hunter of wild game, his inclinations running rather towards racing engines and racing skis, so he lay abed, to breakfast later with the ladies and, in due course, act as their chauffeur.

When Sir John left the breakfast table and went out to consult with Maclean, the head gamekeeper and his own personal stalker, he found that grey-bearded tough-fibred man of sixty with a concerned expression. Alick had not turned up. "It is unlike him to be late," said Maclean.

Both men stood silent for a little, in a way characteristic of them. "Do you think he'll come?" asked Sir John, without any impatience.

"I'm hoping so," said Maclean. "It's not like him to sleep in. Angus has gone over to see if he can see him. He shouldn't be long."

Geoffrey and Harry came out and joined them. Sir John explained the position and then asked Maclean what his plans were. So they all looked at the sky, and saw the slow carry of the clouds over its blue field, and nodded as Maclean mentioned this hill and that corrie and the next pass. This was part of the game that the two younger men enjoyed, particularly Geoffrey, whose eyes grew so animated and lively that sometimes he could not help outrunning Maclean and describing conditions in a certain place before the wise old hunter had arrived at it. "That's so,"

Maclean would say, and then Geoffrey would nod quickly, delighted.

It was characteristic of Geoffrey that his eye and his intelligence should be on the hunt, with a hope already growing in him that he would be given a certain stalk (even expressing his hope in such a remark as, "*That* should be good to-day"), while Harry was moved more by the general feeling that here was a new morning, with sky and wind and moor and pass and mountain forming a realm into which he was about to adventure for a whole long day. He usually stood on the edge of it, a faint smile on his face, not made any less pleasant in its expression by a cunning consciousness of what was moving in Geoffrey's mind. The rivalry, the eagerness, in Geoffrey distilled its own sort of humour—for those who understood and appreciated it, and could ask themselves what would sport be, anyhow, without those keen qualities in some form or other.

But this morning Harry was not listening very well, and smiling not at all. And when he saw Angus, Geoffrey's stalker, appear round the corner of the garage, alone, his look concentrated upon him as if to search out his mind before he spoke.

Angus was sandy-haired and freckled, with a generous mouth, a loose-jointed body, and shy manners. Geoffrey and he got on very well together, for on the hill each was as keen as the other (to be keener being impossible) and Angus would cheerfully have endured through day and night and any privations so long as the hunt was on. He stayed with his mother, and in the garden of their cottage he grew a heavy crop of weeds.

He now faced Maclean solemnly and said, "There's no sign of him."

"Were you at the house?"

"Yes. He was out very early in the morning."

"What's keeping him, do you think?" Maclean's tone was sharp.

"I couldn't say," replied Angus.

"Oh, never mind," said Harry. "He'll turn up all right. You go ahead. And whenever Alick comes along, we'll follow to our own stalk."

"Well, it's whatever you say," Maclean answered. "But I am
annoyed with him. If I had known—I might have made other
arrangements."

"He may turn up," said Sir John. "If you care to wait?"

"Certainly," said Harry. "Please carry on. Do." He smiled
good-naturedly, his manner urgent, and so persuaded Sir
John.

"In that case, perhaps," Maclean suggested, addressing Sir
John, "Mr. Smith could take the Rock Corrie beat. It should
be good to-day. You and I perhaps could take the car round,
and go in over the flows for the west side of Benuain. That
would leave the Home Beat for Mr. Kingsley, so that if Alick
does turn up late they wouldn't have so far to go."

Geoffrey was smiling. The wind where it was, he had the
stalk he wanted. And it had been his turn for the Home Beat.
Lunches, rifles, ammunition were got together and a move
was made towards the garage.

"Hard luck on you," said Geoffrey, as Harry walked along
with him. "But if you will let your stalker dabble in the
occult!" He bravely restrained his laugh.

"What do you think has happened to him?" Harry asked.

"Happened? I should say he went and got blind drunk."

"Why?"

"On the basis that any excuse is good enough for a man
constituted like him—to put it nicely."

"Still feeling a bit sore?"

"Me sore?" Geoffrey's astonishment broke on a laugh.
"Now in the light of this bright morning, weren't you—to put
it very mildly—a bit fantastic last night? Own up, now!"

"I wonder," said Harry.

"That's right. You keep on wondering!"

The cocksure, complacent element in Geoffrey's manner
irritated Harry, though he was used to it, but now they had
overtaken Sir John.

When they had gone, Harry turned back to the house,
quite certain of two things: that Alick would not turn up and
that Angus knew more than he had said. I shouldn't mind
laying a bet that he didn't even go to Alick's home! he

thought. Though all there might be in that thought, he couldn't fathom.

But it made him very uneasy. The loss of the day's stalking he did not mind—even if Alick might have had a little consideration for him! And then his conscience was suddenly struck: What if Alick had found out that his ghastly experience had become a whole night's debating topic in the Lodge? Damn that! said Harry, experiencing a hot sting of vexation and shame.

He didn't want to engage in talk with any of the others at the moment, and they should be appearing soon. Helen was often up before all of them. But perhaps she hadn't slept too well last night! Would he chance ringing for Mairi? He rang.

She appeared and when he had greeted her he asked:

"You haven't any idea why Alick didn't turn up this morning, I suppose?"

"No, sir."

"You didn't happen to see him last night—afterwards?"

"No, sir."

"You have no idea—where he could have gone?"

"No, sir."

He gave her a moment. "What do you think has happened to him?"

"I couldn't say, sir."

She was pale and strained, but cool.

"Excuse me asking you," he exclaimed, with his quick friendly smile, "but I feel worried a bit. It's all right."

She hesitated for about two seconds, then turned and went out.

They are a communicative people! he thought, picking up a walking-stick by the gun-room door. He would scout around a bit and give himself time to think it over.

Corbreac Lodge faced slightly west of south, and from its front door the brown gravel road, after a preliminary curve, ran fairly straight and only slightly downhill, before it dipped out of sight and, about three-quarters of a mile away, merged in the main east to west highway, which was narrow enough to require poles at intervals to mark "passing places". This prospect of moor and distant peak in front of the house was extensive, and on suitable evenings provided some exquisite light effects.

Harry looked along its farthest prospect now and thought of Helen.

More than once in the last four years, Helen, when alone at the hour of sunset, had had to turn away into the house and up to her room. Not the beauty, not the loneliness, not the stillness...she did not know what it was affected her so strongly, and never quite let herself find out. He remembered, not what she had said, but the look in her eyes.

If there was nothing much to be seen except moor and mountain from the south, west, and north sides of the Lodge, on the east side (on which the gun-room door gave) the ground, after a level hundred yards, dipped fairly steeply down a short hill-side of birch and hazel by the Corr River. This small river made a winding wooded glen of intimate beauty, full of bird life and fresh scents and some obscure element of secrecy.

Less than two miles farther down, it flattened out for a space into what was the old crofting township of Clachvor, now derelict, while about the same distance up stream, where it curved eastward, there were the cottages of Corbeg, from which the Lodge drew its necessary labour.

As he went down the serpentine path the scent of birch and bracken drew his eyes to first traces of autumn colour in their greenness, to faintly stirring movements of the wind amongst them, and all at once his disappointment at not being on the hill passed from him. He got the feeling of being on holiday and all by himself; and something deep in him quietly exulted in this. He had had the experience once or twice before. You get away from everyone, not purposefully or by desire, but by what seems an unlucky chance, and then suddenly you find you have wandered right into yourself, and there you are standing upright, amused and pleased at finding yourself alone.

He knew on the instant that he needed this holiday, and being in no hurry he would make the best of it. A fellow can be so long away from himself, he thought, that he loses the feeling of being an individual and in the round.

The freshness, the fragrance, the ease.... It was a cloudy morning, with no blue opening showing, the sort of morning that in the Highlands can be grey and incommunicably sad, until, by looking at growing things near you, particularly after rain or mist, you get a vivid apprehension of colour and scent, a small delicious shock. Harry approached the bank of the small river and stood looking into a pool.

The water was low and clear, with long fingers of greenish slime telling their tale of a dry summer. Salmon came up here to spawn, and for a day or two, after the height of a flood, the fishing was often excitingly good. But when the floods had gone down the salmon lay in deep rock pools and refused to come to any lure. How Maclean managed to get one now and then for the table was supposed to be a mystery.

Of course, in a real sense, thought Harry, it is a mystery; and standing there by the pool he involuntarily visualised the rites. Cook—a woman of strong character and slightly deaf—informs Maclean on Monday that he must get a salmon for Wednesday's dinner. After a certain interval of silence, Maclean solemnly replies that he will see what can be done about it, but that it might be as well if she did not rely on getting it, for the river is low and no fish are running. As she is not interested in the height of the river or the habits of salmon, she says no more on the subject, and they part like two Covenanters who have adequately encompassed the doctrine of predestination, Cook unswerving, Maclean's bearded countenance gravely covering his annoyance.

Then at daybreak on Wednesday, before anyone is astir, Maclean goes down to one of the rock pools on the Corr with his salmon rod, game bag, and book of flies. He selects a "Black Dog" of enormous size from which the dressing has been almost entirely worn away. Having set up his rod and line, he attaches the fly directly to the end of the line, dispensing with the refinement of a gut cast. Thus equipped, he approaches his pool with care, knowing precisely where a certain fish will be lying. It may be that he casts his fly out over the water—and over the fish—but as the fish won't come to the fly he has perforce to make the fly go to the fish. Which indeed it does quite naturally by sinking, guided by the rod, down beside the salmon. The fish may now technically be said to have stopped the fly, whereupon Maclean, in the ritual of fishing, "strikes".

At first Sir John had been astonished at Maclean's mysterious skill and asked him what fly he had used.

"Oh just a 'Black Dog'," said Maclean.

"Surely a *very* small size?"

"Indeed, sometimes it seems small enough," replied Maclean gravely.

Sir John, in his innocence, had been deeply interested and had pressed the matter to the point of getting Maclean to accompany him during a whole day's fruitless fishing in clear pools. "There was maybe just too much sun," said Maclean at the end of the day, "and not enough wind."

As Harry pursued his way up the river path, he thought to himself what a torture that day must have been to Maclean. For he dared not tell his new employer of his unorthodox methods. Sir John, the Cook and Maclean. He began smiling to himself, seeing their personalities moving before him, in a grave elderly drama. Sir John innocent, Maclean with a scar on his conscience, the Cook dominant.

It was a pleasant but somehow dark humour, as if there were in fact something of ancient ritual in it, and at the next pool, when he stopped to look into the water to see if he could see a salmon, he gave an involuntary shudder, for it suddenly came upon him that what he might see would be Alick's drowned body.

He actually had to visit the five deep pools to make sure that the body was not in any one of them, his legs dragging him, tremulous, to the last rocky ledge.

It was rather a horrid experience and he did not like it, because it pierced his detachment. And when he stood back, there were the birches, with a drooping yellow streak here and there, and the dark mature green of the bracken, so graceful, so beautiful—so still.

How swift the change in a mood from delight to fear! And back again—or half-way, holding consciousness of both! As if, in truth, there were some panic something or other inhabiting this half-mile of narrow wooded glen and rock-pool.

Harry turned his face to the widening valley and presently saw the half-dozen houses of Corbeg on the other side of the stream on comparatively flat ground. They, too, seemed very still, with some motionless cattle and sheep dotted here and there on the slow-rising slopes behind. Two of the outlying houses were thatched, their humped roofs outgrowths of the landscape. The scene was more lonely than anything he had yet seen in this lonely country—until a movement in the river a little higher up arrested him. The head of an otter? he wondered. Some tilted flagstones and boulders made a perfect hiding-place. As he approached them stealthily, a little boy darted away on the other side, splashing through a yard or two of shallows, and was up the short slope and into the shelter of some stunted birches before he had quite seen him. Poaching! Hunting one of Maclean's sacred and nominated beasts! The young rascal!

Harry's smile broke into a soft friendly laugh. These two young eyes would now be watching him with the glancing lights he had once seen in the clear, frightened eyes of a fawn. Lord, this sort of life did produce a capacity for sensitive vision! He had better look out or he might presently be seeing through things! That moment by the rock-pool he had seen exactly what Alick's body would look like drowned in the pool. In fact, if they found the body so drowned....

But this was getting fantastic, so he lit a cigarette and went on to the swing-bridge that spanned the stream. As it heaved with him he held on to the two wire ropes, the boards coming up to meet his drunken feet. This put him into normal good humour, and when he met a tall man whose reddish hair was turning sandy-grey, he greeted him in a friendly way. Immediately the man answered, in his quiet voice, he knew he was Alick's father. There was the same stillness of the body, the slow movement, the friendly yet reserved expression. Very courteous, very dignified, but with that tendency to turn the shoulder, to look away, which was new to Harry. He had seen it in Maclean, but there had thought it the natural habit of a man used to consulting sky and hill for indications of weather.

"You are Mr. Macdonald, I think," Harry said, smiling. "I should know you from your son, Alick."

"Yes, I am," replied Mr. Macdonald, looking at him.

"My name is Kingsley. Your son and I stalk together."

"I am glad to meet you, sir," said Mr. Macdonald and shook Harry's extended hand gravely and yet with a curious inherent warmth that touched Harry's heart.

"Thinking of tackling your corn?"

"Well, I was thinking of putting an edge on the old scythe." Harry followed the downward glance and saw the long, sinewy forearm with its covering of reddish glistening hairs and the powerful tough hand. As he looked up again, he caught the head of a woman drawn rapidly back inside the front door, less than twenty yards away, for they were standing by the old thatched barn.

"A good crop this year?"

"Yes. We have no complaints. It was a good summer."

"For once!"

"Well, perhaps, yes." His smile had a shy humour. "It is not always so good indeed."

"Better than last year, anyhow!"

They went on talking for a little time, Harry wondering how he could ask after Alick. Mr. Macdonald gave an opening by saying, "You are not on the hill to-day?"

"No, I thought I'd better have a day off. I think you appreciate the hill better by having a day off now and then."

"Perhaps you will then," said Mr. Macdonald politely.

"Yes. So I thought I'd have a stroll round your country instead."

It was going to be difficult, because he had the clear feeling that Alick was not here and that the father was wondering how he, Harry, came to be here, seeing Alick was supposed to be on the hill with him.

He was deciding to move on, and had actually taken a tentative step or two away, when the head appeared at the door again, and was in a hesitant and yet impulsive manner followed by the whole woman.

She was if anything under middle height, dark, with dark eyes, and stout. She glanced at Harry once, then spoke to her husband: "Won't you ask the gentleman in for a glass of milk?"

Something in her approach, in the way her expression seemed to melt in kindness, decided Harry to accept at once. "Thank you very much," he said, with his quickest smile. Merriment edged his voice. He told how dry he was, making a joke of it.

She showed him into the parlour, and this he regretted, not merely because it was small and crammed with awkward bits of furniture and photographs and smelt of Sunday clothes, but because he wanted to be in the ease of the kitchen with its peat fire. He took off his cap, and presently Mr. Macdonald took off his cap too, while Mrs. Macdonald came with a jug and a glass on a round metal tray. The milk was creamy and delicious and he paid no attention to remarks he had once heard (though he involuntarily remembered them) about dirt and insanitary conditions.

In the dim light (there were flower pots inside the small window) and stuffy air, with Mr. Macdonald sitting awkwardly upright on a cloth-bottomed dining-room chair and Mrs. Macdonald at first standing and then sitting on the edge of a similar chair, Harry lolled in the hair-bottomed arm-chair with an almost exciting sense of discomfort, his face to the window.

There was a tremendous contrast between husband and wife, both of whom were probably over sixty (the man possibly nearer seventy). The woman's hair, combed smoothly from a middle parting, was still quite black. Harry, out of a natural interest in his sporting ground, had read a bit about the racial history of the Highlands, and some tentative thoughts were suggesting themselves automatically when the woman said, "We felt sure you would have been on the high ground to-day, seeing Alick did not come home last night."

"No," Harry replied, smiling, and drank again. "This is delicious milk. No, thanks—really, I couldn't take any more. Thank you ever so much. No, I didn't go to-day. I took a day off. The others left quite early. They are going far in."

"Didn't I tell you?" said Mr. Macdonald drily.

"Does he not come home at night sometimes?" Harry asked conversationally.

"It's very rarely indeed he stays away," she replied. "Sometimes, if they are late on the hill at night or want to make a very early start, he sleeps over at the Lodge. But he hasn't done that"—she looked at her husband—"for three years, isn't it?"

"About that." He smiled with a humoured knowingness. "She does not get to sleep very well until she hears him coming in!"

Harry laughed.

"I don't mind him being away at night at all—so long as I know not to expect him. Last night I got—I don't know." She looked confused for a moment and then smiled, asking Harry to excuse her. She was full of those quick tentative kindnesses and emotions.

"Well, if you don't mind my saying so, I am very happy to have your son's company. We get on extremely well together. And he has taught me to use my eyes—and perhaps my mind—better than any teacher I can think of. He is really a fine fellow."

"That is very kind of you, Mr. Kingsley," she said, her voice pitched low and quick in gratitude, in pride, her eyes on her knees where her hands were.

"It's only the truth," he said, getting up. "Well, that was a very pleasant rest." And, after unhurried farewells, he turned his back on Corbeg, his brows immediately wrinkling, his voice coming audibly, "Now where in the name of God can that fellow have gone?"

For he had not slept at the Lodge and he was not on the hill. A real concern touched Harry now, a waking fear—not unlike the fear he had had in that wretched dream last night.

Manifestly something had gone wrong, or Alick wouldn't have put that mother of his to such concern. And by not turning up at the Lodge this morning the silly ass was simply asking for it, for was it not inevitable that someone should go to his home and spill the news? It's a search party he's asking for! thought Harry angrily. And then his mounting fear was suddenly allayed by remembering Angus's return that morning with the information that Alick was not at home. For it was now perfectly obvious that Angus had not gone near Alick's home. Why? Because he knew beforehand that Alick was not there. Which implied that he knew where Alick had been last night. Which further implied—that there was no need to contemplate tragedy quite yet!

Harry smiled to himself. These intricacies of the mind! The fact that one could depend on the other like that, to understand and cover up! Typical of them somehow. And probably they had cursed each other as well.

Out of sight of the cottages, he pulled up and was gazing in front of him when Geoffrey's words came loudly into his mind: "Blind drunk!"

And there it was, no doubt of it! Geoffrey had cut clear to the truth. Which was annoying to Harry at that moment. Alick had been after drink, had tried brutally to force Mairi to give him drink, had failed, and so had gone and got blind drunk. The process was clear enough to Geoffrey. No doubts or refinements needed. Swept all feelings and emotional difficulties and fears, all the dark or tragic patterns of mind, into the dustbin. An apprehension of the overpowering force of Geoffrey's complacency swept Harry's mind so strongly that it left behind it for one moment a wrung-out, dry hatred.

Then he went automatically towards Corr Inn, which lay over three miles to the north-east, at a road junction.

It looked a lonely enough place, as he saw it from a last low hill-crest. Any sort of revel could be carried on there at night. And drunk men could sing and stagger around it and lie and get up and fight or mutter their inmost thoughts to each other and sleep or disappear into the moor, and no one in the wide bright world be a bit the wiser. When Harry saw it, its dark-slated roof lay low upon it, and no life moved about it.

No life moved over all that vast landscape of moor and hill, flowing in lines of smooth beauty. If beauty was the word? If beauty could lie at ease beneath these lines, could inhabit such barrenness? If beauty, then beauty with a bowed head and an empty mind, the wind whistling through its vacant mind, and dying away in a sigh. The wind came in a soft eddy, warmed from the lower ground, and his vacant mind was filled with the fragrance of wild bee's honey. It was the heather, of course, which was everywhere in full bloom. Leagues of purple under the grey sky, mounting to dark horizons. Harry dropped in the heather and lay flat out and closed his eyes and let the wind pass over his face and through his hair.

He did not actually fall asleep, but lay on that borderland where all is ease and a quiet forgetting, where to forget is to be full of peace, of release, of a wandering like the wind that wanders and yet never goes. It was a trick from the sunny meadows of southern England he knew as a boy, and from one place in particular, where the wind came blowing from a distant common of gorse, golden flaming gorse, whose too-near scent could almost make him sick or make him swoon.

Ten minutes and he got up, completely emptied of all humours, and then down he went until he got by the bank of the small and almost dried-up stream, which he followed with his boyhood's eyes, noting chance wild flowers and once or twice being startled to a standstill at the brilliant enamels of vagrant beetles.

So that he approached the inn with open frank eyes, remarking to himself conscientiously that what he desired now was a mug of good beer.

The place appeared tidy enough, if bare and unused looking. A few vegetables in the garden, but more weeds, with straggling unpruned currant bushes against a low dry-stone wall. And the usual rank-looking rhubarb. He tried the door but found it locked; knocked; and waited some time before it opened and disclosed a strongly built man of middle years with thick black hair neatly combed, an unshaven but ruddy and fresh face, and eyes that were taking him in completely while the mouth said "Good morning!" and the whole man waited.

Harry returned the greeting and asked if he might have some beer.

"Well," said the landlord, with a friendly, even an engaging smile, "we haven't opened yet. Eleven o'clock is opening time, you know." He looked at Harry.

Harry looked at his watch. "It's after ten now," he said, "and I think I'm slow."

"Well, now, perhaps you are. But have you come far?"

"I have come from Corbreac Lodge. And that's far enough, surely."

For one instant Harry thought the dark eyes winced, but in the next he decided he must have been deceived for the man's expression had merely become astonished.

"On foot?"

"Yes."

"Please come in."

Chapter Four

Harry was late for lunch, and still later he found Helen in the sitting-room.

"Hallo!" he exclaimed, his eyes brightening at sight of her. "You didn't go with them?"

"No," she said, leaning back in her chair and letting her arm fall by her side in a characteristically frank gesture.

"I say!" He was still looking at her.

"I somehow didn't feel like it—not a whole day of it," and she stirred and sat up.

"No, not a whole day," he said, as he pushed round the leg of the neighbouring armchair with a lazy foot and sat down. "Have one?" And holding the light to her cigarette he murmured, "I was glad to see you," as though some sort of explanation of the way he had looked at her was necessary.

"Well, I'm glad to see you, I don't mind confessing."

"And here we are!"

"Like conspirators."

"Exactly. I wish I had known you weren't going with them." He tried to speak casually, but it was difficult to subdue the note of excitement that had come from nowhere. She was really very good-looking at the moment, very vivid, with a warmth in her skin and a depth of brightness in her clear eyes.

"If I had been up as early as usual, I might have caught you. But I overslept."

"Did you?"

She smiled. "You're astonished! You haven't found out anything about Alick?"

"No. Can't trace him at all. I don't know what to make of it." He smiled. "I really had a rotten night last night. Quite abysmal."

"I know." She nodded. "I had a nightmare."

"Had you?" He laughed. "There is something in what Geoffrey says: you can work up a situation. You know, there was a moment during the night when I became so sensitive that I heard the wind crying round the house and crying away out on to the moors." He shrugged. "It's not exactly that you hear *voices* in the wind, but that you *hear* the wind itself—as if you were a small boy, listening to it, with a strange dread, in a lonely country house. But I can't explain."

"Do you have that feeling, too?"

"Why, do you?"

She nodded. They both smiled.

"Do you ever feel," she asked, "a gust of wind going away up into the sky—and curving over—into a sort of dome— like a vast parachute—going away up—and you hold down— you snuggle down into your bed? It's not altogether unpleasant—if you have nothing on your mind. But if you wake up out of a horrid dream and hear it...."

"What was your dream about?"

"Oh well—pretty complicated—and pretty awful."

"Was it?"

"Uhm." She nodded.

"Why won't you tell it? Was I in it?"

"As a matter of fact, you were."

"Was I horrid?"

"No."

"Purely as a matter of research, what was I?"

"Purely as a matter of fact, I hung on to you. But then—I was beside myself with terror."

"I happened to be a handy sheet anchor in the wind?"

"You *can* be helpful."

"Good! And—purely in the dream of course—how did I take your hanging on to me?"

"Again, as a matter of fact, you took it very well. You were really very nice indeed."

"That's a relief."

"Why?" Her glance was quick.

"Well—you wouldn't have liked me to be nasty to you—in such circumstances."

"You mean—when you might naturally have been?"

"Not *me* naturally. It's *you* who dreamed, remember."

"I don't—quite see—"

"Never mind—so long as I was nice to you. Was I very nice?"

She found she could not quite carry off this persiflage, and, in a slight embarrassment, got up. "Oh, you were quite all right, quite helpful. I then looked at the time." She looked at her wrist-watch. "It was three o'clock."

"That was when I looked at the time." Harry got up. "We must have been singularly in tune."

"To the same idea, perhaps—not necessarily to each other."

"Oh, naturally. I should not presume for a moment to go outside the idea."

They both laughed, excitedly. They had often pulled each other's leg, but never quite to this extent.

Then Helen's expression became serious, as a shadow follows light. "Was Alick in your dream?"

"Yes," responded Harry quietly. "Was he in yours?"

She nodded. "Yes. His face—looking back over his shoulder—as he went away into the night...awful—it tore my heart."

"Did it?"

"Yes." She took a restless step or two. "He has a strange gift—when you think of it afterwards—of making you see things." She looked at Harry with all her natural frankness. "I understood you so well when you said that about enchantment last night. He points to something in the grass—a moment—and goes on. Or he stops and you hear a bird. 'Chaffinch,' he says, and goes on. Time and again, with such ease, such a feeling of leisure, as if time had no end, until...."

"The scales fall off your eyes."

"That was a dreadfully hackneyed thing for me to say, wasn't it? And before them all, too. It made me squirm in bed. But that's exactly what happens all the same, isn't it?"

"Yes. And scales off your ears."

"Yes. Do you know"—and her voice caught a note of wonder—"I do believe there is enchantment. I mean—really enchantment. And the best of it all is that you *know* it isn't a delusion. On the contrary, you know that it is *the* real thing. That it is exact and real—where before everything was vague or blurred. You…oh, I can't explain. Imagine someone, colour-blind, suddenly seeing all the colours—the real colours, vivid and lovely—growing—in sunlight. Like that—only, too, it's somehow full of fun and—and you find yourself having a small laugh to yourself." She looked at him as if she were going to have a small laugh to herself. "Or have I gone too far for you?" And her smile held the sound of a small, secret laugh.

"You *have* gone too far," he said solemnly.

"It seems," she said thoughtfully, "that when I go as far as Alick I go too far for you." It was a pity.

"You are enchanting me."

She opened her eyes on him. "I'm what?"

"I accuse you of enchanting me."

"Harry, how horrid of you!"

They faced each other, challengingly, until her expression ran into a rare smile and her splutter of laughter broke through. She turned away and, as he followed her, got a chair between them.

"No horse-play, please. Remember we are grown up."

"Hmf!" He shrugged, and his voice thickened in harsh satire. "Fancy having all the tricks—at your age!"

"Tricks!" She flamed upon him. "What do you mean? How dare you say that to me?"

"Well, it's true." Even the twist of his lips looked ugly. "You are an enchantress—with all the tricks."

"Tricks!" She was hurt to the quick and made to walk past him, but he got in her way.

"Don't be a fool," he suggested. "What on earth do you expect me to say?"

"Certainly nothing but what you believe to be the truth. I will thank you to get out of my way."

"Going all dramatic?"

"I am not dramatic. I am hurt."

"Sorry." And then he smiled. "Hang it all, Helen, there's a limit to what you can do and what a fellow can stand. And anyway you must understand that you can't go on talking about enchantment like that, about colour and bird-singing and enchantment. It's simply not done. You forget that we are English. We keep that for books on bird life and plants." He paused. "Perhaps that is why the English write the best books in the world on birds and wild flowers and—and rock gardens. It is a profound thought."

"You're being pretty clever," she said doubtfully, her eyes on him.

"No." He shook his head. "Simple truth. Think it out. This affair here has set me thinking. You see, a fellow like Alick does not get his kick out of *reading* about—well, all this rather magnificent environment of bens and glens and so on. He gets the kick direct. And we needn't go out of our way to misunderstand or sentimentalise the folk hereabouts. That's an old romantic trick. They are realists—with a feel for what is real in life like the feel of earth in your hand. I mean, the actual business of living, of being alive, in all its hidden twists." He shrugged. "Oh, I don't know."

She still had her eyes on him, for he had taken a step or two in the difficult labour of definition, and after a moment she asked directly, "What do you think has happened to Alick?"

He looked at her frankly. "I just don't know. That's why I know I can see only a very little way into this." Then he remembered Geoffrey. "But Geoffrey was quite sure. He said Alick went and got blind drunk."

Her face cleared. "How characteristic of Geoffrey!"

"I hope Geoffrey was right," he said quietly.

"What?"

"If Alick only got blind drunk, he'll turn up."

"Harry. Do you think he might have——" Her voice sank.

"God knows," said Harry. "I went over to Corbeg this morning to see if I could spot him. I ran into his father by an old outhouse, carrying his scythe, like old man Time. A quiet-spoken old fellow, keeps his head up, eyes steady and looking beyond you, and that grave rather attractive dignity. Sort of puts you on your best manners. Then the mother came out: short and stout and dark, but busked all tight and hardy, like one of the really old inhabitants, Iberian or something. Actually they were two pretty good samples of the small dark and tall fair. Have you ever read anything about the ethnology of the Highlands?"

"No."

"Oh well, you see——"

"Tell me—what happened?"

He chuckled. "Well, she had those dark, shy, half-embarrassed eyes—as if she were so full of kindness that she was frightened to intrude it upon you. But you won't understand that."

"Go on," said Helen.

"So in I went and had her glass of milk and right creamy it was. I had completely forgotten how good milk tastes. Have you? But of course not—you're young enough to remember. Well, we talked and I casually found out that Alick had not slept there last night. She had been a bit alarmed, but he said to her 'I told you so', for apparently Alick has been known to sleep in the Lodge here, when there is a very early start. Very rarely, of course, but it's happened."

"Didn't they wonder why you——"

"I told them I was having a day off. But not the others—who were having a long day."

"He didn't sleep here?"

"No. So remembering Geoffrey's 'blind drunk', off I set for Corr Inn. I wish I could tell you what happened there, but I can't because it's only still working itself out in my mind. In the cleverest way the landlord made me tell him I was staying here and had walked on foot to the inn and so on. An extremely engaging fellow, simple as the black water you see in some of these tarns on the high-ground moor, anything but translucent, yet really clear enough. How astonished a fellow must be who drowns in one of them! I feel like the fellow who has just managed to crawl out."

"I say, you are getting deep!"

"Bogged is the word. He played me like a trout. But once—twice—I hit him."

"Your metaphors are obscure."

"You would hardly notice it. I was on the way home before I completely noticed it myself. I could not ask for Alick directly, so very cleverly I began asking if the stalkers and gillies came to this inn of his for a jollification, as it seemed an excellent place for it. Have you ever touched a snail when its feelers are out? Well, something in his expression, his eyes, went in like that. Momentarily isn't in it, of course. But there it was—and in that moment he not only knew who I was, but what I was after, and I know quite positively that by this time he has contrived to warn Alick of my spying. Even at the time, it made me feel uneasy and mean. Remarkable, isn't it?"

She nodded. "I do understand that. I have had that sensation of their mind feeling you."

"Invisible feelers. Yes." His smile took a thoughtful twist. "Now normally one of two things may happen—though I don't know quite how I know this—when you hit the mind and it goes in like that: either the body may lash out at you dangerously *or* the body may go opaque and stupid-looking. And it is inclined to go stupid—to its superiors. We are its superiors."

The quiet irony excited Helen and she moved about restlessly.

"Not that that happened," Harry explained, "in the case of the landlord, of course, because he could cover up, not being personally involved. But—I know I'm right, exactly as if he had demonstrated."

Helen stopped. "And what are you going to do next?"

"Just wait. You cannot go against destiny."

"You are not growing fatalist, are you?"

"No. I merely have an intuition that I should do nothing."

"An intuition?"

"I am beginning to go like that. Pretty bad, isn't it?"

She turned away to the window and stared out.

"There's Alick," she said quietly.

"Is it?" He did not move.

"And there's Father and Geoffrey.... A pony with a stag."

"Only one stag?"

"Yes."

"Geoffrey's?"

"I don't know."

"Then it's your father's. Is Alick with them?"

"No, he's gone. Maclean is weighing the stag."

Harry walked over to the window.

"Yes, your father's. Geoffrey has manifestly had no luck. Which way did Alick go?"

"Round that way," and she indicated the right. Then she left the window and Harry slowly followed her. "Well, that's a relief, isn't it?" she said.

"Yes."

But the brightness in her question was artificial and Harry did not respond to it. He stood preoccupied. It was a mood utterly unaccountable to him, in which there was no relief.

He said vaguely, "I wonder what's happened?" And she answered, "I don't know."

The figures of Sir John and Geoffrey passing the window and their voices as they came in at the outside door to the gun-room stirred them reluctantly. Their eyes met in a glance, in a half-rueful smile. Had they been children they might have taken hands and fled.

But Geoffrey's loud, "Hallo, you two!" brought the real world into the room, and Harry asked, "What luck?"

"Rotten!" said Geoffrey, rubbing his palms audibly and sending currents of fresh air about the room. "We had a magnificent stalk into the Rock Corrie. The last bit I had to do all on my own. The stag could see me. So Angus stayed behind. I crawled flat out. When the stag's head went up, I lay still. Oh, devilish tricky. But I did it! And then—I don't know what happened. Hang it, I was mad! It was not that the shot was too far. I should have done it. Only I was firing downhill."

"And you fired over his back?"

"No," said Geoffrey. "No. That's the cursed thing. You are told that you are likely to fire over his back, downhill. So I tried to correct it. And I am now quite satisfied I was *too low*. If Angus hadn't whispered, 'Remember it's downhill', I'm certain I'd have got him."

Harry laughed, and Helen went to meet her father quickly, implanting a swift kiss on his cheek. "Because you deserve your luck!"

"Thank you, my dear. And Maclean was so good——"

"Oh." She flew to the drink cabinet.

"So you had all the luck to-day," Harry greeted him.

"I'm afraid so," said Sir John. "But—one minute."

"My sympathy, Geoffrey," said Helen.

Geoffrey, who had hardly ceased talking, turned to her. "Yes, rotten luck, wasn't it? Dash it, and I wondered to myself even as I was pulling—what if I'm too low? And quite a good head. We had come to the top of a little watercourse, and now there was the curve-over of the ground which brought me into sight. The stag could see me. So it was inch by inch, pulling with my fingers and pushing with my toes, stopping when he raised his head—and then waiting a second to see he did not raise it quickly again—and then wriggling on. And all the time in my head"—Geoffrey attempted Angus's accent—" 'Remember eet's downhill'."

"Did you tell him about it afterwards?"

"I did. Not unpleasantly, of course. Still—I admit I was a bit put out."

"You didn't swear, I hope?" Helen asked.

"No no," said Geoffrey. "Not that you would notice." And he laughed. He seemed in such good form, considering his trials and the blank day, so excitedly taken up with the sport—which, after all, was the reason for their being here—that Harry remembered his dark moment or hatred with some uneasiness.

Sir John came in again, his gaunt, smileless face saying quietly, "Sorry about your lost day, Harry." He set down the decanter on top of the cabinet. "If I had been sure, when we

left, that Alick would not turn up, we could have fixed you up
with Andrew all right. Maclean was saying that Andrew did
some good work with the hinds last winter."

"Oh, it was quite all right. I really enjoyed the lazy day.
Besides, I thought it would give Geoffrey the whole field
for—uh—King Brude."

"When did Alick actually turn up?" Sir John asked.

"As a matter of fact, I went for a long tramp and haven't
yet spoken to him."

"Oh," said Sir John thoughtfully. "I saw him meet Maclean
some way back. I took it for granted you had sent him. Too
bad of him. Really too bad."

Geoffrey chuckled heartily. "He'll have squared Maclean
first! I say, would it not be fun to ask him point-blank what
excuse he has? The trouble is"—and he smiled to Sir John
with a certain sly amusement—"that you would not push the
matter to a relentless finish: too considerate, if you can
pardon my saying so. And as for Harry here—he'd be made
to *see* an excuse. Now if you'd let me have a few simple words
with him—I shouldn't miss a second time!"

"I could hardly——" Sir John smiled.

"Merely just to demonstrate," suggested Geoffrey. "To my
mind, he'll either tell the truth or he'll tell a whacking lie. I'll
give you twenty to one now that he'll tell perhaps an elaborate, even an artistic, but still a whacking lie. And I'll expose
it by simple question and answer. I shan't rub it in or anything."
Geoffrey was in ruthlessly good form. "I mean I shan't make it
uncomfortable for the—uh—more sensitive minds present."

"Geoffrey, how could you think of such a thing!" said
Helen.

"There you go!" And Geoffrey had his laugh.

"I'm agreeable," said Harry. "And as for the bet, right.
Twenty to one in what?"

"My feet are sodden," said Sir John. "Shall I leave justice
in your hands, Harry, seeing you lost your day? And do you
mind my having the bath first, Geoffrey? Thanks."

When he had gone, Helen turned on the two men. "I
think this is grossly unfair."

"Why?" asked Harry.

"Why?" she repeated, looking at his set face with some astonishment. "Because you obviously have him at a disadvantage."

"So you know he would lie?" Geoffrey smiled dryly.

"I never said that."

"No?" Geoffrey raised mock eyebrows. "I must be getting dull. Or is the light beginning to fail?"

The daylight was in fact beginning to go, and Helen's face seemed to gather a paler glow. "You can be maddening."

Geoffrey laughed again.

"I'll get hold of him," said Harry casually.

"What?" demanded Helen.

"Well, why not?" asked Harry, facing her. Though he did not show it, he was stung by Geoffrey's attitude, and suddenly annoyed that Alick had not reported to him first. It was the very least the fellow might have done. "He deserves all he'll get."

"Having him cornered, you'll both proceed to hit him. In that case, don't you think it would be better to do it as his superiors—not as his friends?" She went to the bell-pull. It slapped back firmly. They kept looking at her, but she ignored them. The door opened and Mairi appeared. "Is Alick about, Mairi?"

For a fraction of a second Mairi's eyes went blank, evasive. "I think so, ma'm."

"Would you mind asking him to come here?"

"Yes'm." Mairi withdrew.

"Well, I'm damned!" Geoffrey enjoyed the moment. "But you're quite right. We've got to go straight about this."

"Do you suggest someone was going to go crooked?" Harry asked.

Geoffrey caught the dry inflection. "Oh, you know there's no offence. You are, you know it, sympathetic—and, to that degree, not the best person to draw out the brutal truth."

"I see."

"Now, look here, Harry," and Geoffrey's tone tried to be reasonable. "You just watch what happens. If the fellow confesses right away—that's one up for you. If we find him in an involved lie, then you may be better able to understand my scepticism, not only of this affair which, if you like, is unimportant, but of last night—which you contrived to make us think *is* important."

"Very good," said Harry, tonelessly.

There was silence. Geoffrey glanced from one to the other, but they were not looking at him or at anything in particular. He had difficulty in keeping his peculiar humour in control. Then Helen's head went up, listened, and she strolled to the bookcase. To the knock on the door, Harry called "Come in!" and Alick entered a pace or two and stood still.

He was without any trace of self-consciousness. His face was quite expressionless, yet not wooden. He looked levelly across the floor at Harry, awaiting his question or humour.

In the involuntary silence, Helen, lifting her head from the book she had picked up, glanced at him from under her lashes and was thrilled, for she realised she might have been guilty of commanding a presence that would have been awkward, dourly self-defensive, intolerably painful to her. Neither a duke nor a butler could ever have been so naturally there! And though the moment was not one for a smile, a slight warmth did steal over her body. She found herself tremulous with excitement, as Harry's voice came without any stress: "You didn't turn up to-day, Alick?"

"No, sir."

They waited until it was quite clear that no excuse was to be given.

"I thought at least you might have come and told me—and so saved me hanging on here."

"I'm sorry," said Alick.

"What happened?"

Alick gave no response of any kind.

"You do not care to say?" Harry pursued him.

"No, sir."

"Was it so very private?"

No answer.

Geoffrey stirred. "In fact," he said, "you refuse to discuss the matter?"

Alick looked at him.

"Is that it?" asked Geoffrey with his driest smile.

"No," said Alick.

"Good," said Geoffrey. "Where did you go last night?"

"I think, what I do at night, is my own concern," said Alick without any stress.

Geoffrey's lips parted for an astonished moment. "Oh, I see! Well, what did you do with yourself this morning, which, I trust you will agree, is our concern?"

"I was on the hill."

"On the hill! All alone?"

"Yes," said Alick.

"And what were you doing on the hill, all alone?"

No answer.

"Stalking?" suggested Geoffrey.

"Yes," said Alick.

"Very interesting," said Geoffrey. "From pure love of it—or were you trying to get a beast for someone—as a present, let us say?… Can't you answer?"

"I was not poaching."

"Stalking just for fun like." Geoffrey nodded. "I see. Was it a good beast?"

"It was King Brude."

Which silenced the room, until Geoffrey, with a small secret smile to himself, blandly asked, "Did you get him?"

"I had no rifle."

"Go on," said Geoffrey.

"Last night, he headed out of the forest—so I thought I'd turn him back."

"And did you?"

"Yes," said Alick.

Geoffrey regarded him for a few moments in silence. "Why didn't you say so at once—or did you require time to develop this story? I ask—because you said at first you would rather not tell. Was the good deed for the forest, then, something to be ashamed of?... I must be frank. In a word, how can you expect us to believe you?"

"I'd rather not say," replied Alick, his eyes levelly on Geoffrey.

With a dry smile, Geoffrey responded, "I appreciate the difficulty. However, I'm sure we'd all like to have the details of your story. By the way, had you any witness?"

"Yes."

"Who?"

"Yourself," said Alick.

"I beg your pardon," said Geoffrey.

"You didn't see me. You were stalking at the time."

"I happened to be stalking all day. Whereabouts *exactly* did you see me stalking?"

"In the Rock Corrie."

Geoffrey's eyes narrowed on him. "And what was I doing?"

"You were stalking over the brow of the corrie—in sight—all alone."

"You mean, you have been talking to Angus?"

"Angus was not with you *then*."

"Really?"

"You crept along——"

"Oh, look here," said Geoffrey, impatiently interrupting him, "the only place you could spy into the Rock Corrie from was Benuain. Isn't that so?"

"Yes."

"And do you mean to ask me to believe you could pick me up, crawling, from that distance, even with a telescope?"

Alick went on as if Geoffrey had not spoken. "Twice the stag you were after raised his head and looked towards you. You lay still until he started to feed again. When you got into position, you saw another stag—*a very particular stag*—at what you said to yourself was *over three hundred yards*. Will I go on?"

"Oh, good heavens," said Geoffrey, throwing his hands up with a harsh laugh, "this nonsense is just too much!" Then he rounded on Alick. "Will you answer this one question sanely? If you had been on top of Benuain—how on earth could you have performed the feat of being back there at the Beallach before us—unless you flew?"

They watched Alick in what became a tense silence, for into his eyes, as they remained on Geoffrey, came a light that communicated hidden knowledge, an assured and intolerable knowledge. Helen stopped breathing. Alick's words came slowly:

"I was not on Benuain."

Even Geoffrey was held, as one is held in a nightmare, until he broke out, blustering, chuckling raucously. "Oh, but this is the sheerest utter nonsense."

"Will I go on?" Alick asked him.

"There is a limit—even to my patience," said Geoffrey, stamping about.

"But why not let him go on?" Helen asked Geoffrey.

"Go on," said Harry to Alick.

But Alick kept his eyes on Geoffrey, who clearly had had enough of them. "I'm used to dealing with evidence—not fairy stories," he was saying, heaving his shoulders, and blowing his wind through closed lips, "pfff!" as if the chill of having been on the hill was at last getting at him and it was high time he was doing something sensible, like getting into a hot bath, instead of listening to this trickster and his manifest nonsense.

Alick looked at Harry. "I am sorry I could not turn up."

Harry answered as quietly: "All right, Alick. You may go. To-morrow morning sharp."

Geoffrey could not resist a parting shot: "You did not manage to follow the bullet in its flight, by any chance?"

Alick turned at the door. "The bullet *was* low. You should have raised the sight—*as you thought of doing in your mind*—another hundred yards." Then he went out, quietly closing the door behind him.

Geoffrey, staring at the door, became aware that Harry and Helen were looking at him.

"God, he has all the tricks of the business," said Geoffrey, laughing blusteringly rather than with his usual hilarity. "He has practised his stuff. Yes! I don't quite get the trick of it.

Hm! But leave it to me. I'll get at it. Yes, I'll get him! I'll go into this. I'll expose him. You wait. Pfff!" He poured himself a whisky and, just about to drink it, paused as if a sudden thought had occurred to him. "Perhaps—uhm." His eyes seemed to light up. He drank. "Well, I'm getting out of these cold togs." He was smiling. "You wait, That's only the first move." But feeling he was not acting very convincingly he could hardly go, and when at last he went it was awkwardly, helped by the entrance of Mairi to light the lamps.

"Phew!" whistled Harry softly to Helen.

"I wonder?" breathed Helen.

"Heaven knows!" said Harry, shaking his head.

They were both charged with wonder, thrilled by the end to the strange encounter. And though Mairi's back was to them, as she unscrewed and lifted the chimney and mantle of the bracket lamp, preparatory to lighting it, they felt constrained in her presence. They expanded their chests, too, as if they were being choked.

"I feel I could do with some fresh air," said Helen.

"Yes." Harry nodded. "What about a stroll out to meet the car coming back? We could crowd in."

"Oh splendid! Wait till I get on some shoes."

As they went out, their faces were eager and excited.

Mairi looked after them, the white glass shade in her hand, and listened, her tongue-tip against her top lip. Then she put the bulbous shade down over the chimney and turned up the light just far enough to do away with the flickering sound. With the standard lamp, she went through the same performance, but raising the light until the mantle was fully incandescent; then she went to the window and, before drawing the curtains, stood a few seconds staring out into the rapidly gathering dark. Anyone interested in the house could not fail to see her. When there was a noise at the outside door of the gun-room, she rapidly drew the curtains and became the efficient maid. The light must not burn too high. She put one or two things straight in the room, hesitated, listened, looked at the gun-room door and went towards it. As she opened it, Alick said, "Hallo!"

"It's you, is it?" she remarked coolly.

"More or less," he said, coming towards her.

She backed a pace into the room before holding her ground.

"What do you want?"

"What about a drink—to begin with?"

"I should have thought you had enough of that last night. You can't come in here."

"Why not? I can't see you in the kitchen alone. Where am I to see you?"

Before his advance, she backed a few paces, saying intensely, "You ought to be ashamed of yourself!"

"You think so?" he asked lightly, looking around. He saw the decanter. "Now if you had only given me a drink last night."

She appeared desperate but kept control. "You can't stay here. They may come in." She listened, the blood burning in her cheeks.

He smiled sardonically. "I've given one of them enough to keep him out for a few minutes. He thought himself very clever—so I went one better."

"If I give you a drink, will you go home?"

"All right."

"You promise?"

"I'd promise you anything," he said, smiling to her with a measuring humour.

"You'll get the sack—that's what you'll get."

"If you come with me, I shouldn't mind."

She ignored him, listened a moment, then went quickly to the decanter and was about to pour some whisky into Geoffrey's glass, when Alick suggested, "What about a clean glass?"

It was no time for argument. She tried to replace the decanter quietly, and as her hand lifted a clean glass, it shook. She was breathing in little gulps. The decanter's neck was clinking against the glass, as the door opened hurriedly and Harry came in.

But Mairi miraculously saved the decanter from falling, and Harry, taking in the unexpected situation in one swift glance, went towards her, saying in a pleasant voice, "Good! I'm glad you held that one!" He took the decanter from her and the glass. "I'm sorry I did not think of this before, Alick." He poured out a stiff drink and went over with it to Alick, in his normal friendly way.

Alick took the glass automatically, looking not so much confused as darkly angry. He stared at the glass but made no effort to drink.

"All right, Mairi." Harry nodded to her, indicating that everything was all right and that she could go.

She hesitated, then went out at the hall door and drew it shut behind her.

"I suppose you feel like a good one—after last night," said Harry in the tone of one man to another. "I know the feeling. Drink up."

Alick's eyes narrowed on the glass. Harry saw he was in a dangerous mood. Without word or look, Alick got up, set his glass on the cabinet, and turned to walk out.

"No need to take it like that," said Harry.

Alick turned. "No?"

But Harry went and companionably poured himself a small whisky. "Like some soda in yours?…No?" Then he faced Alick and said frankly, "Well, here's *slàinte!*"

It was the friendly courtesy of the flask and the hill. His dangerous humour recognising its naturalness, Alick dropped his eyes, flushed a trifle, and, with a touch of awkwardness, took up his glass. Harry drank. "*Slàinte!*" muttered Alick, and drank his off neat.

"You'll feel the better of that. And—don't take it amiss, Alick, if I say you were on my mind last night. It is difficult to talk about. When I couldn't find you to-day, I went along to the inn. I never mentioned your name, but I could see the landlord thought I was doing the detective. Gave me rather an unpleasant feeling for a minute."

"I heard you," said Alick.

"How—do you mean?"

"I was there."

"Oh!"

"I went there last night. Then————"

As he hesitated, Harry said, "You need not tell me anything, you know, unless you like." He finished his drink. "It's entirely as you like. I myself didn't want to————" He put his glass away.

Alick's manner eased. "Early this morning, I found myself on the hill. It was the first grey of the dawn, and, when my eyes opened, ten yards away from me was King Brude, looking at me. I believed it after a moment or two, for when I sat up he trotted back to our forest. It brought me to my senses and I found my way back to Corr Inn." The faint smile faded and he said in an almost natural voice: "Don't know what he was doing so low down. Hope he's not in the mind to leave us so soon."

"That would be a pity," said Harry. "Sit down." And as he motioned Alick to a chair, he sat down himself.

"Oh, I'll be going," said Alick, taking the chair reluctantly.

"So you were on the hill this morning?"

"At that time, yes. But not later."

Harry looked at him.

Alick's smile became faintly confused and he swung half round as if for his glass.

"Just a tiny spot more," said Harry, jumping up.

"No, please!"

"It won't do us any harm." And he also poured a small one for himself.

"I didn't mean that," said Alick.

"I know. Reflex action," and Harry smiled companionably.

"Thanks very much," said Alick. "I—I'm afraid I played a bit of a joke on Mr. Smith."

"You what?" Harry sat up.

"A bit of a joke on him."

"Really!... You did it pretty efficiently!"

"Oh well, it was easy."

Harry laughed abruptly. "Excuse me, but—he is not the one who would think it easy."

"I could see that. So I thought it wouldn't matter."

Harry laughed again. "Tell me. Go on."

"Oh, I was just talking to Angus for a few minutes on the way in. Mr. Smith had said a word or two to Angus, after he missed. He did not mean them against Angus. He was just upset. Angus had remained behind the ridge, because there was no point in two of them crawling in full view. Angus said he would wait for him. And when Mr. Smith came back, right enough he found Angus where he had left him. So naturally enough Mr. Smith thinks that no one in the world could have seen what he actually did—except from Benuain opposite—and that of course was out of the question. Now what happened was that Angus decided to crawl a little bit forward to get his glass on the stag and see what the shot did, for sometimes a man will wound a beast without knowing it. Then as he felt Mr. Smith was taking a bit too long, he crawled a yard or two more—and saw him aiming at another beast over four hundred yards away."

"Four hundred!" exclaimed Harry. "Impossible!"

"Angus was very astonished, too," said Alick. "So when Mr. Smith fired, Angus doubled back at once to the place he had left, because he knew fine Mr. Smith would hate to think that anyone had seen him fire at a living beast over such a long range."

"King Brude, was it?"

"I wasn't there," said Alick.

Harry, appreciating this reticence, nodded to himself in thoughtful astonishment. Then he looked at Alick again. "Explain this. You told us what passed in Mr. Smith's own mind—about the distance. How could you know that?"

"I had a glance at his rifle. I noticed the sight was still at over three hundred. Angus, as I say, had let drop that the distance was over four hundred. Mr. Smith has a good eye. He would have been troubled."

"I—see! So having sighted for three hundred, he was bound to be low."

"It was very likely, I think, because he is a good shot."

Harry's eyes glimmered, for it was a humour too deep for laughter. Then he impulsively got up. "Have another drink." He began to chuckle as he got hold of the decanter.

"Please, I don't think so, honestly."

But Harry was saying to himself, "Well, I'm blowed!"

Alick stopped the flow of whisky into his glass.

"You don't want to start off again, eh? Had a heavy night at the inn."

Alick gave a shake of his head. "It was pretty thick," he confessed.

"Was it?" Harry laughed softly. "I caused some trouble here myself last night. I hadn't meant, you know, to say a word—but, well, I did. Geoffrey—Mr. Smith does not believe in what he calls 'superstition'. So it was a temptation. Just as you were tempted by him when you came in here. You can understand?"

Alick nodded, withdrew his eyes to his glass, and then drank.

Harry's eyes narrowed on his face secretly, then he looked away. "To tell the truth," he said, "I can't quite forget it. I could wish—it had not been quite so real."

His eyes on his empty glass, Alick said quietly, "You don't wish it as much as I do. If you hadn't been with me——"

"Yes?"

"No one would ever have known."

Harry looked at him keenly again. Alick, lifting his eyes, met the look and gave a wry smile, then removed his eyes, wearily.

Harry stirred, uncomfortable. "Couldn't we—can't we—do something?"

"Against what?"

"Oh, I don't know. Fate, if you like."

"You could try," said Alick sardonically.

"I can't help thinking about it. I wish you could help me. Really I do. Supposing one of us went away from here—so that the vision you saw could not be—could not take place. You know what I mean. Which one of us would you suggest?"

"I think I'll be going," said Alick, after a small gulp from the stomach. He got up.

"Not feeling sick, are you? Sit down."

"Too much drink likely," said Alick, with a tired humour. "I'll be going." He stopped near the door, but did not turn round. "Thank you for your kindness," he said. "I cannot answer your question surely—but I don't think it was you."

"Was it Mr. Smith?" The words came from Harry before he could stop them.

Alick stood silent, until his body gave a short convulsive heave, and he went through the gun-room like a half-drunk man making for discreet refuge.

As the outside door slammed, Harry damned himself, and felt a trifle sick out of his own excitement. He was still staring into the unlit gun-room when the door behind him opened and Helen entered, saying, "Is he gone?"

"Yes." Then he realised she had her coat on ready to go out. "Oh, I'm sorry. Have you been waiting for me?"

"I thought you had gone outside. So I went out, and met Mairi, and she told me you were in conference."

"Forgive me, Helen. But I'm hanged if I know where I am or what to do. I somehow feel rotten about it. He's a queer chap."

"Anything more happened?"

"Bagfuls. You felt, didn't you, that there was something supernatural in the way he shut up Geoffrey? It was a pure leg-pull."

"No!"

"Yes. And when I think it out, he never even told a direct lie. Sheer detective work. And Geoffrey must have felt filthy. You see, Geoffrey tried a long impossible shot at, of all beasts, King Brude. He should never have done it, should never have fired over two hundred yards, because of the danger of wounding the beast. It's simply not done. Over four hundred yards! He was just caught in temptation and—now he knows it. Hence all the eager talk about downhill, for Geoffrey is a good shot and had to justify missing the stag they had been stalking, which wouldn't have been more than a hundred and fifty yards away. And he had to keep on talking, keep the thought of it away from himself—and vaguely frightened, too, possibly as one is when one has done something wrong—and he found a diversion in the idea of baiting Alick! And he found it, by heaven!"

But Helen was smiling. "Dear old Geoff! Human of him, wasn't it? And to think I got the ghostly shudder when Alick said, you know, that he hadn't been there! Yet he didn't rub it into Geoffrey. Rather delicate of him wasn't it?"

"Particularly when you think how Geoffrey rubbed it into him! By the lord, Geoffrey must not know we know!"

But Helen was thinking again. Out of a pause, she said, looking at Harry, "Were most of our sympathies misplaced last night?"

Harry shook his head. "When he had told me how he had hoodwinked Geoffrey, I did have one minute's profound doubt, and looked at him, and gave him an oblique opening, and he looked back and saw what was in my mind—and only smiled as if he were tired."

"Where did he go last night?"

"To the inn, and, as Geoffrey forecasted, got blind drunk. Then he found himself somewhere on the hill, wakening in the cold dawn, with King Brude calmly inspecting his exhausted corpse. I doubt if the Devil knows what moves in the haunted abysses of that mind. And, by Jove, he could be dangerous!"

"I'll tell you one thing that moves in his mind," said Helen practically. "Mairi is in love with him. She doesn't like him having this gift. Anyway, I think she hates that we found out." Then she added simply, and profoundly, "And so I know—beyond any evidence of yours or his—that what he said he saw to you, he did see."

Harry nodded slowly, trying to take it in. "That—I think—is important."

"Think? You're taking a risk."

"Is Alick in love with her?"

"I'm afraid so."

"Ah-h."

"Never did have much luck, did I?"

"And yet your hand is stacked with trumps—every one a trick. It is tough."

"Perhaps if I really tried enchanting him—with the wild flowers and the birds and——"

"And yourself. Perhaps. Only—answer this one. Would you like to be married to a man with that gift?"

"I—wonder?" said Helen thoughtfully.

"If Alick could tell you your future now *beyond any doubt*—would you ask him?"

"People go to crystal-gazers and palmists."

"So would you or I to see how we'd fare in love or war or fortune or how many children we'd have."

"Why shouldn't I ask?"

"Because of one thing—the one only thing—that is certain."

"You mean?"

"Death."

She looked at him steadily and in silence.

"I'm glad", said Harry, "that you didn't say the obvious thing: that that's morbid. Though they say that when you're young you can talk of death because it seems so far away; and when you're old because it is so near. It's the great middle-aged crowd, busy with success and——"

But Helen, hardly listening to him, interrupted directly: "Did he say who the dead person was?"

Her searching manner and the sound of the car scattered his wits for a moment. "Not really," he said.

She went towards him. "Harry, tell me."

"I can't. I don't know."

"Harry!"

"And in any case, don't you see I couldn't tell——"

"Is it you?"

"No."

"Father or Mother?"

"Good heavens, no."

"Geoffrey?"

"Oh, come now, Helen, play fair." He heard voices.

But she had him by the lapels of the coat. Clutching them tightly, she breathed—"Geoffrey!"

And to confound him fully, the memory of Alick's silent pause came upon him.

"You can't jump to conclusions like that. You mustn't! Oh, hang it!" He did not know what to do and, in the madness of the moment, faced by Helen's burning beauty, he caught her in his arms, crushed her, found her mouth and crushed his own upon it, with a roughness, a brutality he certainly had never shown before. Under this completely unexpected assault, Helen collapsed and lay passive in his arms.

They did not hear the opening of the door, and Geoffrey stood and stared, then turned his back to them, rattled the door handle and coughed loudly. When he faced the room again, they were standing apart, breathing heavily, stupidly flushed. He began to laugh.

Marjory came in and Joyce and Lady Marway, with motoring coats on.

"What's the joke?" asked Marjory. "We're dying for a good laugh." The bright eyes of the women rested on Helen and Harry.

"I've got it!" cried Geoffrey and laughed again. "I have solved the whole mystery! And it was clever! By gad, it was clever!"

"I love detective stories," said Joyce.

"Out with it, Geoffrey!" called Marjory.

Geoffrey had had so bitter a time with himself when dressing that he was prepared to be more than merciless. In a blinding sustained spasm of anger against Alick's eyes and the watching faces of Helen and Harry, he had disrupted the bath-sponge—and when he saw what he had done, he had groaned: irrational behaviour that he utterly detested, that debased him.

"For a reason", he began, with elaborate humour, "which—uh—I need not specify, Harry did not want to go to the hill to-day. So with his well-known genius for invention he worked out an ingenious excuse, complete with ghostly procession and consequent absence of stalker. A first-class frame-up. All for our entertainment and—*and* the aforesaid unspecified reason. Congratulations, old man!"

"You look a bit flushed, child," said Marjory to Helen.

Joyce, with the frank if slow-witted innocence of her kind, said solemnly to Harry, who was easing his collar with two fingers, "You seem hot about the collar, Harry."

"Not specially," said Harry, continuing to ease it.

Geoffrey half-turned away in an excellent effort at suppressed laughter. Marjory began to chuckle softly. Lady Marway smiled. Suddenly Joyce emitted a few throaty notes, open-mouthed, "Ha! ha! haw!" feeling clever at having tumbled to so subtle a situation.

"Now, now, everyone," said Lady Marway, "no cold dinner to-night! Come along!" And she shepherded Marjory and Joyce outside. But in a couple of seconds the door re-opened. Marjory put her head round it and in a high small voice, as if from a distance, cried :

"Hel—en!"

Helen faced her, her back to the men, and, after her lips had cursed Marjory in two soundless words, she stuck out her tongue to the root. It was wild anger, it was physical assault, but Marjory merely smiled and in an intimate way beckoned her with her head. Then she pushed her head further to one side until she commanded Harry's face and in a low gruff voice said:

"Harry, you young dog!"

Helen advanced upon her. Marjory's head popped back and the door closed. Helen stared at the door. Impulsively, without looking back, she opened it and went out.

"Satisfied?" His face white with wrath, Harry stood dead still, staring at Geoffrey.

"Uhm, yes," said Geoffrey, taking a step or two in his humour.

"I think it was a bloody witless thing to do."

"Well, of course."

"You damned fool!"

Geoffrey paused and regarded him with a considering smile. Harry looked intense as any murderer. "You must learn, my dear fellow," said Geoffrey, not dissatisfied, "to take the joke when it is turned on yourself."

"You call that a joke?" Harry's body was quivering.

"From our point of view, it had its amusing aspect."

Harry's mouth shut tight, and his breath came in a gust through his nostrils.

Geoffrey lit a cigarette and strolled towards some papers on the writing table. "You cannot spoof us—and expect us not to retaliate."

Harry had not moved. And now it came slowly: "You think I prepared all that—so that you could have a four-hundred-yard shot at King Brude?"

Yesterday's newspaper crackled in Geoffrey's fist. He dropped it and came towards Harry.

"What's that?"

Harry did not move. "Spoofing you, what?"

There was a tense moment before Geoffrey controlled himself. He succeeded and nodded slowly. "So that's what the fellow was getting at?"

Harry kept his eyes on him.

Geoffrey turned away. "Yes," he said. "I knew he was a sinister figure. But by God"—and he swung round swiftly—"I'll let him—and you—know something before I'm done with you."

Harry had never seen Geoffrey roused like this before and his own bitter state of mind eased a little.

"You must learn", he said with satire, "to take the joke when it is turned on yourself."

Geoffrey glared at him. "You call that a joke!"

"From our point of view, it had", said Harry, "its amusing aspect," and he strolled out of the room and up to his bedroom, where the hand-lamp, with its red glass bowl, was lit.

As he entered and stood in the silence he caught a face looking at him from a little distance. It was his own face in the mirror, of course, but it was considering him in a detached way, the features a trifle darker than they should be, as if with dark blood. Harry's mouth twisted to one side. So did the mouth in the glass.

Long ago in Lewis a man was haunted by a spirit in every respect like himself. This spirit accompanied him out into the fields and, while mimicking his every act and gesture, would sometimes ask very impertinent questions. He turned up at night in the house, but sat silent, invisible to everyone except the man himself. The story came into Harry's mind, and he turned his head slowly and looked at the mirror. Reflected in the glass was the top edge of the door slightly ajar. He could have sworn he had closed the door when he entered the room. He got up and closed it, but omitted to contemplate himself in the mirror, as he returned to his seat on the bed.

He knew he was occupying his mind with trivialities. The truth was that there had been a moment when he could have sprung at Geoffrey. Many a time in his boyhood he had been ferocious enough. But somehow it had been of the flesh. The desire had been to hit and smash. He could see there might be a desire, springing out of some primeval evil, to tear asunder.

He saw how a man could be murdered.

The evil knowledge sickened him a little, sent weakening tremors over his flesh. Oh, but this is damned fantastic! he thought, moving restlessly from hip to hip.

For the real truth of the whole thing was that what would get torn asunder would be the peace of the house. And to help to that end in any way would be utterly and absolutely swinish. Oh God yes! he cried inwardly, twisting on the bed.

That moment when Geoffrey had turned on him, there had been something in his face while he yet struggled for control that had been really dangerous. And not only Geoffrey's face but his chest and arms, which had snake-writhed in a spasm of impotence.

How drastically Geoffrey would have dealt with the King Brude accusation had it been untrue!

Hell, I've been making a mess of things! he thought. I must stop this.

But he couldn't cover the real hurt to his mind much longer, and suddenly he threw himself face down on the bed. "Helen," he said, "it came over me. I didn't mean to do it—there—like that. I'm sorry." The shame seeped into him bitterly.

Chapter Five

The following morning, Harry saw that Geoffrey had had a bad night. His effort at being agreeable showed it. The skin over his face seemed stretched a little more, his eyes goggled slightly, and his laugh in restraint tended to become a giggle. It was a curious old-maidish expression flickering over the real force of the man beneath. In some obscure way it made Harry feel ashamed.

For he did see now that if the peace of the house was not to be damaged beyond repair he would have to subdue himself and give in to Geoffrey, by degrees, but starting from this very moment.

"You have that beat, Geoffrey."

"Not at all," said Geoffrey. "You have it."

"Oh, go on!" said Harry. "You have it. You know you're the better shot."

Geoffrey looked at him.

Harry's tentative smile grew awkward despite himself. He had never intended any reference to Geoffrey's markmanship of the day before. It was the last thing he would want to do. But apparently Geoffrey did not think so. In a sudden fear lest Sir John and Maclean should feel there was something wrong, he accepted the beat when Geoffrey refused it.

But for a long way it irritated him, and only when Alick and himself were at last alone did the tension in his mind ease.

For it was absurd to him, amid this peace of the hills, that human beings should behave to each other in so childish a way. And surely extraordinary, that out of such behaviour could be distilled a real venom. A thin dark poison that seeped in about the roots of the mind. Lord, it made one think!

For in one's own mind one could feel what the cumulative effect of it might be. Between individuals and peoples and everything. This dark poison distilled out of the ego.

Harry had a vision of it world-wide. Or, rather, an apprehension, for he saw nothing very distinctly, and thought nothing very clearly; yet the truth of this apprehension was so powerfully in him that he experienced the illusory feeling of holding the round dark world in the eye and thought of his mind.

Which softened his smile in humour as his carnal eye took in the smooth round of a slope, a suave timeless shoulder of a hill. For here was a thing he was noticing now: that from an intricate vision of the poisons of life he could lift his eye to such a slope and experience a feeling not only of exquisite relief but of sheer positive happiness.

And as he went plodding on, ordinary words like *release*, *freedom* were overtones from bells struck beyond the range of the ear.

Geoffrey could crawl down in his valley bottom. What was that to him? Why should he worry his head about it? Which showed that he did worry his head about it. Which showed that he would take Geoffrey to the mountain-tops, if he could. And everyone. And he had to admit, with a confused smile, that that is precisely what he would like to do at this moment—always assuming it could be done inadvertently, don't you know!

What else had one to think about, following a fellow like Alick? What other sort of thought could one indulge in, with that tall solid figure in front, stepping so quietly, with easy poise, that opaque body—with its deathly visions?

Alick stopped, laid down the rifle, and silently took the hazel crook from Harry. After he had stuck it in the ground, he withdrew the spy-glass from its slung leather case, adjusted it to his own marks, and, supporting it against the stick,

directed it at once into a distant corrie. "There are a few of
them there. One good beast, I think," he said quietly, hand-
ing the glass to Harry. Harry sat down and steadied the telescope against the stick, leaning back like Alick in what always
seemed a difficult posture.

He had to glance once or twice along the top of the
telescope before he could make sure he was aiming at the
right corrie and then could find nothing. "A little more to
the left...not so far," said the voice above him.

"I've got them!" said Harry.

It always gave him a thrill of pleasure when he picked up
the distant quarry with the glass. Something about it of the
magic eye, annihilating distance, bringing the remote and
secure and unsuspecting quite close for him to look at and
study. A godlike intrusion, with omniscience somewhere.

"See the beast to the left—a little above the others?"

"Yes."

"That's him."

Harry eased his neck and sat forward. "King Brude?"

Alick smiled, his keen eyes on the corrie. "No."

Harry had another look, but could not see any marked
difference in the beast from some others. Then Alick took
the telescope again, slowly went over the wide areas in front
of them, shut it up and returned it to its case.

"Nothing else?" asked Harry, appreciating, as he always
did, this sure display.

"No. It will make a good stalk. They're eating over
towards that broken rocky ground to the right of the corrie.
They've come across from Benuain way, and, with any luck,
by the time they come within range of the outcrop we should
be in position. But it's a long stalk, because we'll have to
circle down and round and the wind may be faulting just on
the crest there. There's not much of it and it's going to die
out. In fact I don't like the look of the day very much."

"Why?" said Harry, scanning a cloudless sky, glittering
high rock faces under a hot September sun, and moors so
stretched out and at peace that surely bad weather would
never visit them again. On the far horizon towards the sea,

there was a soft haze, that at evening would turn opalescent and——

"Mist," said Alick. "There will be mist to-night. You will see it coming over the moor, solid and white as a cloud, and Benuain will draw it up like a blanket. Anyway, I hope it will be no worse."

"Why?"

"Angus is inclined to forget the weather—and they will go far."

"Do you mean that he and Mr. Smith might get caught in the mist on Benuain?"

"They might. I've been caught once or twice myself. It just means patience—if you do lose your way. But perhaps we'd better be going."

They dropped down below the level of the distant corrie and then walked on at a steady pace.

"There's no danger in it really?" Harry asked presently.

"In the mist? Oh no. You just lose yourself, and when you know you are lost, if you're wise, you find the best shelter you can at once before the night comes."

"But surely a man used to these hills would know at least where he was. I mean when he came to a burn, for example, wouldn't he be bound to know it and then follow it, until it went into the Corr, say, and then he could follow *that*?

"Yes," said Alick politely, "he might do that."

Harry laughed. "If he was lucky, you mean?"

"Well, he wouldn't be lost then."

"But I mean he could go on until he struck something he knew, couldn't he?"

"Oh yes. Only he mightn't find it. He might even know that it's within a hundred yards of him and yet not find it. It's a queer feeling when you discover that you have lost your direction. The mist is all around you. The heather roots are smoking with it. The place you stand on goes strange. But you know that the track is only a hundred yards away. And you are quite sure you know the way to it. So you go for a hundred yards. And then you go a bit farther. But there is no track. You still do not believe you are lost. So you try again and again until suddenly you just know you are lost. It is an eerie feeling."

"But if you go on, I mean a man like you who knows the forest, you are bound to strike something you know, and so get your bearings, aren't you?"

"You would think so. But you may not. You will come on a little lochan and it is quite strange to you. The ground is boggy and when you begin to go over the boots, you pull back. You circle it, and go on. You can spend hours like that, getting nowhere; and always you are mocked by what you feel is something familiar here or there. Then you get to know that these are deceptions. And all the time the mist is about you, surrounding you in the same way wherever you go, like a cage or prison whose walls you can never touch. Queer shapes come out of it. And its silence is the most complete thing you ever heard. Perhaps then you will come on a burn. And, ah yes, you know the burn, and you will see by how relieved you are how panicky you must have been getting. Yes, this is the burn at the back of so-and-so, and you follow it. It has small features you never seemed to notice before, but then how little we do notice exactly. So you go on—and on—until you no longer are sure if it is the burn. The moment comes when you are sure it is not the burn, and you stand and try to think. First you try to work out where you might be if you had gone the wrong way. You are angry at the mist. You could cry out. Perhaps you do cry out. And that's a queer sound, too. Then you see that the mist is getting thicker, that you can hardly see one step in front of you. And suddenly you realise that it is not the mist that is getting thicker: it is the darkness that is falling."

He spoke with such ease in his quiet, rather small, and toneless voice, that the words might have come out of the mist he was describing, without the least emotion or force, yet with a friendliness, a curious intimacy, that made of time itself a legend. It was not a thing you could intrude upon, yet it was very companionable.

It was at this moment that Harry realised he could not question him again on the second-sight episode. Several times he had thought to himself, particularly in bed, that he would get hold of Alick and put the whole thing before him in all its bearings, sensibly, man to man. With an odd feeling of the strangeness, the isolation, of human personality, he realised it could not be done.

"There is no real danger of course?"

"Not if you keep your head," said Alick.

"A fellow like Angus would keep his head, wouldn't he?"

"Oh yes."

"But you are not so sure of Mr. Smith?"

"I feel that Mr. Smith is not the sort of one that would like to be beaten by mist."

Harry laughed and fell in behind Alick in a short, steep climb. That hit Geoffrey straight down the fairway! There is no time when a man can be more free with himself than when climbing behind another. The fellow in front has all the responsibility, and concentration limits him, but the fellow behind is free and can indulge in the most wayward thought.

And Harry's thought was extremely wayward. From Alick's solid back it slid sideways over the hill-face, over the moors, to a hazed horizon, between one step and the next, and an airy smile would in as short a time pass to a pressure of teeth and to knuckles that blenched as he gripped the heather. For he simply could not look at Helen, could not contemplate what happened last night. And yet she was behind his mind, behind the airy smile and this incommunicable happiness coming out of the world around him.

Not that it mattered a damn kissing anyone. He had kissed more than he could remember. He had pecked at Helen more than once, for they had been normal companions from her childhood. There was a time when he had kissed her to make her mad. So what was all the fuss about and the teeth-grinding?

When the real stalking began, his mind drew to so fine an edge that Alick's abdominal curves and hobnail boots held a gargantuan humour, full of warmth and friendliness. Close to the ground, they wriggled on in front of him, with a noble earnestness. Harry wiped the sweat out of his eyes. This was noble living; keen and clean as the tang of the heather in his mouth and behind his nostrils. The hunter's instinct, direct and quivering and true.

Alick paused, and crept a foot or two, and paused, and crept, and steadied, and slid slowly back. Then his head turned and beckoned Harry, who noiselessly drew up beside him.

"He's there," whispered Alick, a faint smile on his face, a glimmer in his eyes.

"Is he?" whispered Harry.

Alick nodded slowly.

He was there! No need for hurry now. The ultimate moment was at hand. For a few seconds they lay without moving, lost in this first stage of accomplishment. Alick's duty was done. Harry's was to begin, and already the excitement of it was about his heart, weakening him a little, and searching out a flat and empty stomach.

Alick's soft whisper went on: "About one hundred and eighty yards—the nearest beast. A twelve-pointer—a royal. A really fine head."

"A royal!"

Alick nodded, the glimmer in his eyes again.

There is a communion in which minds do not meet or commingle but merely look at each other with all the strangeness of personality behind. Nothing is given away, but something is glimpsed, friendly and timeless.

"Take your time," said Alick.

Harry pushed the rifle ahead of him. He was on his mettle now. To fail would be to lose something more than the stag. It was Alick's turn to watch the body in front, and his appreciation hung for a moment on the quiver of an eyelid, a faint satire, detached, considering, but not unfriendly. From the cylindrical leather case he withdrew his spy-glass.

When Harry saw the stag, he had to take a deep breath to ease his lungs. The stag was quietly eating, as were four others farther out. He waited a moment, then pulled up against the rifle stock, and at that moment the stag raised his head and, turning it over his shoulder, looked directly at him.

Another head went up, another...until they were all looking at him.

Normally Harry had a short secret ritual that he went through at this particular moment. After taking careful aim, he would withdraw his eye from the sights and say to himself, "No need to be excited;" then go through the process a second time, before putting gradual pressure on the trigger.

But now he had an intuition that the stag was on the very point of swinging his head back again and trotting off. He got excited. He sighted midway down the body, behind the shoulder, where the heart is. The outline of the stag against the sparse heather and the brown burnt tips of the bent was anything but clear. At this distance there was no need to worry over elevation or shifting of the sights. The trajectory of his modern rifle was straight up to about two hundred yards. The point of his rifle was fairly steady. The stag's head swung away. He pulled.

The stag leapt, and head up, began scrambling away.

"Got him through the spine," said Alick, on his feet.

He found himself leaping after Alick, his eyes on the stag. He fell, head first, but was on his feet in an instant. The stag, head up, antlers sweeping the air, was going very slowly, as if pulling an invisible weight. Then Harry saw that the hind legs were paralysed, that he was dragging them.

A pang struck him; he groaned and stood still as the royal head, at bay, turned and faced them.

But Alick kept up his swift assured stride, the walking-stick in his hand, straight for the head. Oh God! cried Harry, feeling beforehand the lengthy fumbling bloody business of killing with a knife. The eyes of the brute, the soft deep liquid eyes, the dumb eyes, in the magnificent head, the proud wild head. Quick! quick! his spirit cried. Quick!

At his last stride the antlers lowered in combat, but before Alick had yet drawn both feet to a pause, the crook of the staff was in the air. It came down with what seemed no more than a firm rap fair on the forehead and the stag fell over as if it had been pole-axed.

The relief of that moment was one of the most exquisite Harry had ever experienced. Alick took out his knife at once. Harry lay down.

"That was the neatest thing I ever saw," he said.

"What was?" Alick asked, at the stag's throat.

"The way you hit him."

"Oh that," said Alick. "An inch higher and you'd have missed entirely."

"He was just going to move."

"So you pulled instead of pressing?"

Harry smiled. "I think so. Was he going to move?"

"Yes. His body was swaying to the first step."

"There is that pause—just before the move—a lovely sort of suspense it is. It excites a fellow, I think."

Alick began cleaning the stag.

"Did you ever use your stick like that before?" Harry asked.

"No, I don't think so." said Alick, his hands red.

Harry lay back and looked up at the sky, whose blue was swathed in a diaphanous milky film. There was a remarkable competence in this fellow Alick, an all-round sureness in the open. A mysterious affinity in some way between him and the stag! Harry could not fathom it, but some dim understanding of such a relationship moved him.

Alick cleaned his knife by stabbing the blade in a tussock of bent. The gralloch had rolled over beside a boulder.

Now they could examine the head at leisure, and it was a noble head of a deep amber-brown colour and bold sweeping curves, the tines long, elegantly shaped, and white-tipped. With his flexible steel tape, Alick took quick measurements of length, beam, span and extreme span.

"To tell the truth," he said, "he's better than I thought he was."

"Have you ever seen a finer head?" Harry asked.

"Well maybe not very often," replied Alick politely.

Harry laughed, but the head fascinated him. Something in its wild beauty touched his heart, struck some primal chord in him. With a quick embarrassed sincerity he said, "I'm very grateful to you, Alick. Oh hell, come on and have a drink. What time is it?" From his watch, he looked up in amazement. "Quarter to four!"

"Yes," said Alick. "I thought if we stopped for lunch, you might miss your chance, and I didn't want you to do that. You see, by the way the stags were feeding——"

He was being apologetic! Harry interrupted him with a laugh. "There will be the usual accident to the small flask at one fell swoop. Come on!"

There was nothing that Harry enjoyed more than the delicious languor that followed a long and successful stalk. An utter and benign irresponsibility washed softly through the flesh, the soft wash of warm fulfilled blood, half-drugged by the whisky. And it didn't require much whisky. The milky veil over the blue had deepened. The air was cool, was growing cold. He always hated to hurry away after eating. In any case, there was nothing more to do. And it was delicious to let oneself sink down through the heather. On such an occasion he was always sure he never quite fell asleep, even if he completely let go for a second or two, though often he had to confess he was surprised at the speed with which a half-hour could slip past. He became aware of the pony, of young Donald and Alick talking together, of the stag's neck bent back so that the tilted head looked across at him tragically. Through his lashes, he recognised the Landseer composition, toned down, less dramatic, but with some intimate quality added, as if with the beginnings of understanding he was in truth penetrating into the strange and wild.

Alick turned away from Donald with a little upward nod of the head, and came across towards Harry. Harry closed his eyes to get the full savour of his last minute. He heard Alick's boots in the heather, then silence. He opened his eyes and saw Alick staring into the distance like a seaman. He watched him for a few seconds, then got up.

"The mist," Alick said. "It's coming."

The horizon had bulged out, had drawn nearer, was lying in a hazed bank on the moor.

"I didn't think it would come like that. We'd better go."

After his warm nest, Harry felt the chill in the air and shivered.

"How did you think it would come?"

"I thought it might come in patches, white blankets of it, local. This is not that sort of mist. It will be thick about us long before we're home."

And so it happened. They were following a rivulet down a hollow in the hills when Alick turned and said, "Look at that!" It came in a billowing cloud down upon them, filling the valley, something ghostly about it, fearsome a little, especially where it grew ragged and curled over in fantastic whorls. Its cold breath touched their cheeks, and it was about them, thinly, not nearly so thick as it had looked, and passing on.

They could see things in the immediate vicinity quite well. There was no difficulty at all in walking.

"You and I could push on ahead, if you like?" Alick suggested.

"Not at all," said Harry. "There's no hurry."

"All right, then," replied Alick at once. "We'll keep by the pony for a bit anyway."

The track was clear and made walking easy, even if the surface was rough and here and there water-scored. Harry commented on this and Alick explained it was part of their duty, before the season came on, to see that all tracks and culverts were in a proper state of repair. Harry took out his cigarette case and held it to Alick. When they had lit up, he turned towards Donald to find that he and the pony had vanished. He hurried forward a step or two and they loomed upon him so like mythical figures that he involuntarily hesitated before calling Donald and offering him a cigarette.

"It's mist all right!"

"Ay," said Donald. "It's getting thick." He was a shy lad, dark and sensitive. His gratitude for the cigarette showed in his smile. He went on at once. Harry knew that neither of them would have lit a cigarette in his presence without permission—and they would never ask permission.

Donald's smile remained with him. "Full of charm," he said to himself; "crawling with it."

He began to wonder about this, to try to understand it. Often the most charming were the least trustworthy, like the inn landlord—who might cut your throat.

Now why had he thought that? And at once some part of him answered: The landlord would more readily cut someone else's throat for your sake. If you were his friend, that is. That sort of loyalty. But how do you know that? Harry asked himself. Heaven knows? was the reply. And the idea of loyalty hung about in the mist.

Neither of these two would care to speak to him the whole way home, unless first of all he spoke to them or unless practical advice or caution had to be volunteered.

That stoical quality! Donald and the pony and the beast on the pony's back assumed legendary shape, like what's-his-name, thought Harry, going down into Egypt! With Alick, the tribe's Seer, bringing up the rear! In the midst of this convoy, he felt himself a stranger, a visitor from another, more light-hearted clime. Light was the word, indeed; a light-weight.

Yet that was not true; not quite true, anyway. For he was getting an understanding of the background, and suddenly he remembered Alick's smile, the slow glimmer in the eyes, when he slid back and said, "He's there." That moment when their minds recognised each other, that evanescent moment of communion.

Moments. Well, of course.

The mist was smoking out of the heather roots by his side and the silence was really pretty eerie. Even their footfalls were muffled. He realised how utterly one could be lost in it. And he thought of Geoffrey—refusing to be conquered, making up Angus's mind for him—onward! He got some pleasure out of the thought, for there was no cause for alarm, no real danger. If Geoffrey had to spend a night on the hill, it might cool him a bit; and if he fell into a bog and got hauled out it might cool him still more! If only he had some ghostly experience to turn his fleshly assurance a haggard grey! But no such luck!

Soon the mist overcame these wayward thoughts and Harry sank down through his mind into the movement of his feet. This mindlessness, of which he was vaguely aware, held some bodiless quality of delight that he could not make an effort to grasp, and, not grasping, enjoyed the more. His dark-brown eyebrows were beaded with the mist, and when he looked up the rising ground on his left hand, his face was grey and damp, with the jawbone moulded more firmly and the eyes almost black.

Chapter Six

"Listen!" said Helen.

Sir John slowly lowered his newspaper and removed his glasses. Lady Marway listened without moving. Marjory's head went up. As Harry's pipe left his lips they remained apart.

Yes, it was a car.

Helen dashed to the window and drew the curtain aside. Marjory followed her, and Harry. They stared at the fogged lights that glowed white, like shrouded eyes, and swung away and vanished, to a muffled roar and fade-out of mechanism.

"George and his ghost-train!" cried Helen. Everyone smiled.

"Thank goodness!" exclaimed Lady Marway. "I felt George might have been trying to break a record in the mist or something."

"He probably has," said Marjory.

As the talk went on they became aware that George and Joyce were taking an unduly long time to come from the garage, but no one quite liked to say so. At last Helen, because she was excited by the new strange coldness between Harry and herself, dramatised the affair by standing forth and saying in hushed tones:

"What if it *was* a ghost car?"

But it did not quite come off. And when her mother gave her a pointed look, Helen's cheeks caught a slight flush. She knew she had lost some element of self-confidence, was not perfectly sure of herself, inclined to that overstress at the wrong moment that was very annoying. Harry got up and smiled, without looking at her; which annoyed her intensely. "George will be tinkering at something just to know why it didn't do it quite right," he said, and closed the gun-room door behind him.

They listened to his footsteps; they heard the outside door rattle open. They continued to listen, as if waiting for something to happen.

It happened so dramatically that the high-pitched woman's scream lifted Lady Marway to her feet. The scream cracked into a harsh squawk and died. The terror in the scream made their skins crinkle. Sir John swung open the gun-room door and hurried outside.... They could hear voices, the broken voice of a woman. It was Joyce.

"Joyce!" called Lady Marway, making into the gun-room. "What is it, child? What is it?"

Sir John was bringing her in. "Oh!" she was crying brokenly. "Oh, what a fright I got!" She flopped into a chair, her ghastly pallor emphasised by smudged geranium lips.

"Where is George?" Lady Marway asked.

But Joyce did not hear her. She was trying to laugh. "I was coming—feeling my way—my hands out. Something moved near me. My hand touched—a hand—in the air." Her laughter was growing hysterical.

Lady Marway spoke soothingly to her, but Sir John in sharp cold tones said, "Now, Joyce, steady up!"

Lady Marway at once stopped caressing her.

"Joyce!" called Sir John peremptorily.

Joyce made a real effort. "I'm sorry," she spluttered on the verge of a breakdown.

"Where is George?"

Joyce gulped. "In the garage."

Sir John ignored her, speaking coolly to his wife.

Harry and George came in.

"I'm frightfully sorry," Harry said, looking at Joyce. They noticed there was blood on his cheek. Sir John looked at Joyce's hands. But George was the real attraction, for his make-up of oil, grease, and earth was quite striking.

"Wherever have you been?" Marjory asked.

"In the ditch," said George. He glanced at Joyce, then brought all attention on himself by launching into a graphic account of their mishap in the mist. Though driving at a walking pace, with the utmost care, he had ditched the off front wheel on the narrow road where it bends at Clachvor. He had stopped instantly, of course. Then he described a manoeuvre by which he had hoped to drive the wheel out and had all but succeeded, when the front and rear wheels slithered on the grassy verge and both slid in. "I passed a few remarks to Joyce and she passed a few to me, and there we were. Looked pretty hopeless, didn't it? But I said to Joyce it was a pity to give in on this, and she was sporting enough to agree. I crawled about and underneath and tried to think, and Joyce said there isn't even a bally stone. And that gave me the idea. I thought what if we get some tidy-sized stones and jack her up on 'em, first one wheel and then the other, you see the idea?"

"Phew!" said Joyce, getting to her feet. "I feel all trodden on and filthy. Excuse me." She wavered a step or two, but walked fairly out of the door, which Harry held open, murmuring to her, "I was a fool."

"You're telling me," drawled her voice with surprising verve, and she departed, making it clear she required the help of no one, so that Helen and Marjory looked after her but did not move.

"She's got a bit of a jolt," said George.

"She took hold of herself remarkably well," said Sir John.

Whereupon George grew exuberant. Now that he had his audience on a familiar topic, he could enjoy himself in a general show of exaggerated action and speech that was right in character.

"You know the story of the huge stone by the roadside at Clachvor?"

Marjory didn't and George explained, "Well, once upon a time, that stone was over in the field, two or three hundred yards away, this side the first ruined cottage. The fields were tiny in those days and this stone took up a jolly lot of space. The fellow who lived in the cottage, he had *whoo!* the second sight. Went about mooning to himself and they all knew he had this power. Well, one morning when the people of Clachvor woke up, they found the stone gone from the field and resting in its present position by the roadside."

"And he couldn't have rolled it there because it must weigh a ton?" said Marjory.

"On a conservative estimate, it weighs twenty tons," said George. "Am I right?"

"Near enough," said Sir John.

"Well, I mean to say, there you are," said George. "The folk were astonished, of course. Who wouldn't be? However, the important thing for us was that we remembered the ruined cottage whenever we saw the stone, for I barged into the stone when scrounging around. So I said to Joyce I know where we'll get tons of stones, and she said where, and I said over at the dear old cottage of the what's-his-name. Now it's pretty thick outside and I said to Joyce, you wait here in the car, and I'll scrounge over, and you can give me a shout if I'm wandering off the straight and narrow. But Joyce said she would rather be doing something instead of sitting and doing nothing, so I said if she felt like that all right. So off we goes and sure enough we finds the ruined cottage—first shot. Extraordinary luck, wasn't it? Though I only appreciated that afterwards."

"Unless, of course, you were drawn," Harry suggested.

"How do you mean drawn?" asked George. Then he laughed. "Oh, I see! That's a good one. Dashed good! Because, you see, here we were at the ruined wall and I was keeping in touch with Joyce with my elbow and voice and what not, for of course you could not see your own nose. Slice it, wasn't in it. I was tearing a nice flattish stone from the wall, when something hit Joyce's foot and she said *Ouch!* and she stooped down and while she was in that position something solid hit her on the top of the head and knocked her clean on her beams. She gave a yelp naturally, and I let out a blood-curdling cry at the thing, to frighten the life out of it, for I heard it quite distinctly. It all happened so quickly that you didn't know quite what was what for a second, if you understand me."

"A sheep," smiled Sir John.

"I said sheep, but Joyce said the thing was solid and hard, so we pow-wowed and wandered hand in hand, and found that the thing had come out of the door of the old cottage. However, to cut a short story long, I got hold of some stones and Joyce insisted on hanging on to one too, and we started back—but instead of arriving at the road we arrived at another ruin. Which meant we were going the wrong way. So we dropped our stones and turned back, meaning to pick up some more at the first ruin, though Joyce had no particular desire to see it again, I may say. Well, we went farther this time—or at least so it seemed—for we were going pretty carefully now. And once or twice I got down on all fours with Joyce driving me by the coat tail. Simply had to because of the awful feeling we were going to step over. How long we did our babes in the wood act I don't know, but I estimate it at nearly two hours. We visited three more ruins. I was getting a bit desperate myself, and Joyce was nearly all in. I never experienced anything more utterly futile. It maddened you. And at last I got that awful feeling that we might wander right off the map the wrong way. A cold damp mist and Joyce's teeth were positively audible. I shouldn't like to spend a night in it myself. Really, it began to get serious. I felt that over a whole night Joyce might quite possibly pass out from exposure. And if we tumbled over something and broke a leg or anything, even the strongest man might give up without much fuss." From looking at their faces, a thought visibly struck him.

"Where's Geoffrey?" he asked.

"He hasn't come back yet," said Sir John.

"I say!" said George, quickly glancing at their faces again. "I *have* been working up the horror!" He laughed with exaggerated exuberance.

"And what happened then?" Helen asked.

George described how he found stones in the ditch itself and jacked up both wheels and at the second attempt got free, but the exhilaration had noticeably declined, and quite frankly he asked, "So old Geoff is caught out in it?"

"It looks like it," said Sir John. "I'm afraid it's going to mean a pretty cold wait for him."

"It sure will," said George. "Won't he be hugging himself at this moment! Sorry I stayed so long in the garage, but I bumped, and did want to make sure if I had bent something underneath. Sorry and all that."

"You go and wash your face," said Lady Marway.

"Righto!" and he swung away hurriedly.

Marjory turned to Harry. "And what were you trying to do?"

"It's so thick," he explained, "that you can only walk with your hands out in front of you. Joyce must have heard me and stood still. I heard absolutely nothing—until my hand caught a cold hand suspended in mid air. I had to hold on to it. Then she lost her head for a second. I thought she was all right, when I handed her over. I wondered if something had happened to George. Joyce drives as you know. And when I got to the garage, sure enough mysterious grunts came from under the car, as if George were bleeding to death. It was merely his difficulty with language."

This was more like the normal Harry and Lady Marway turned to her tapestry frame and Sir John to his *Times*. Helen and Marjory were too excited, however, to concentrate on anything, and, on an impulse, they both left the room.

Harry tried to read, but after half an hour could hardly sit still. His mind, too, would not focus. He arose and went up to the bathroom and studied his cheek in the glass and wiped it clean of blood. Then, on a thought, he dabbed the scratches with Milton, for Joyce's finger nails were long and varnished and dirty. She had struggled in his arms with quite amazing fury. A dissolving, ugly, fleshy, warm, terrifying performance. Had had to pin her arms and get his mouth in her ear: "Joyce, Joyce, it's Harry!" And then the sag, and her forehead against his neck.

Strange beast, the human animal. He corked the Milton and shut the cupboard and wondered what he would do next. Marjory and Helen would be talking away somewhere, that odd woman's excitement on them, like the excitement on birds gathered together.

One thing was quite clear: Helen was hurt right to the root over the kissing business. It was not the act itself, he agreed, sitting on the edge of the bath, but something damnable and shattering in the public way it was done. A silly little rotten act like that has often the effect of putting one dead off something that had loomed quite big or important; suddenly tires one of the thought of it, and there it is! Helen, he saw, just meant nothing to him really. Not a thing; and as his face lifted and stared at nothing, his mouth twisted into little ugly shapes. Amusing to think how among the high hills she had been behind his mind like beauty behind the world! And he had been half-conscious of this as a strength in himself, so wonderful that it was a secret mirth! Ye gods! he muttered, and rubbed finger-tips upward against his jaw-bone. What the hell was he sitting in here for? As he closed the door behind him, he stood and listened. There were two corridors of five or six bedrooms each. The girls' corridor was on the other side of the stair-head. He heard nothing, and went into his own room, where it was pitch black. He groped his way to the bed and sat on it.

Annoying experience, this, of not being able to get hold of your mind. Sort of diffused, disgruntled blank into which a picture comes entirely of its own volition—like the way he now saw the three girls in Joyce's bedroom, their heads inclining to one another, Helen with her feet tucked under her on the edge of the bed. They did not interest him, and Helen's veiled excitement was nearly an offence. Geoffrey's face came up at him, like a drowned face up through water. Grey it was, and pallid, but by no means drowned when it looked at him. The eyebrows strained together, intolerant and angry. It's going to take a lot of your mist to trap me! it said. Harry turned away from it. Served the blighter right!

At first he had thought it rather fun having his mind sharpened in this penetrative unusual fashion. He was by no means so sure about it now.

All through that damned fellow Alick, with his thick, solid, opaque body. He was built to be a chucker-out in a pub. That was the job for him. His eye would know at once the dangerous drunk, and his body would find relief in action. Here he wasn't getting a real outlet. That was what was wrong with him. He was moving in a lost world.... George and Joyce, the babes in the wood, wandering hand in hand, terrified, through the Celtic mist—from ruin to ruin. Ruin to ruin! Lord, what a picture of historic significance! He began to chuckle, and the perverse humour easing his mind a little, he got up, with the queer, but not unpleasant, feeling that he did not know himself. He overtook the three girls going downstairs.

"Am I forgiven?" he asked Joyce.

"No," she said. "I'll never forgive you for making me make a fool of myself."

"Oh, if that's all, I don't mind."

"Clever boy!" said Marjory.

George and Joyce went to eat, for they had had nothing since lunch and it was now nine o'clock. Joyce seemed even more than her old self, as if she had got wearied out of every humour. Nothing more was going to upset her. George was solicitous and attentive, capable of an exuberant gesture, when required. He could be relied on to play his part. When they had left the sitting-room, they were missed.

For folk could not go on talking about Geoffrey, however his absence pervaded the room. And Harry knew by the way in which not the slightest reference had been made to the second-sight incident that it was in every mind.

Lighting his pipe, he glanced across at Lady Marway. Coolly and quietly she worked, without a suggestion of unusual preoccupation. Just normal and cool—the wise woman. Then as she turned over the small tapestry frame, Harry saw her give a quick look at her husband, who seemed happily absorbed in the Editor's letters, before going on with her task.

The wise mother! Her chair and tapestry spread out like a hen's wings. Then he glanced at Helen—and found her looking surreptitiously at Marjory, who was staring over the top of her book at nothing. This picture so arrested him that he contrived a steady look at it, for clearly here was a new hidden situation of which he had no understanding. Helen's eyes came upon him so completely that for a moment he could not turn away. When he did he felt uncomfortable, as if he had been caught prying. In a moment or two he was even angry, and looked back again deliberately. She was still contemplating him, with the absent expression a woman directs towards a playing child or towards the thought of a person. Then she saw him, regarded him for a moment calmly, and got back to her book.

As he tried to read he was painfully aware of the beating of his heart. He realised he had no control over that wayward muscle. He felt its flushes in his hands. For the awful, the terrifying, thing—it came upon him like revelation—about Helen was that she was alive.

Presently Joyce and George came in, but very soon the room settled down upon them again, and all was quiet until the outside door to the gun-room rattled.

The only one who stuck to a chair was Marjory. George had the inside door open in a moment.

"I thought I would just look round," said Maclean. At the sound of his voice, expectancy died.

"Very good of you," Sir John welcomed him. "No word of any kind, I suppose?"

"No," said Maclean. "They would surely have been in by this time, if they were coming to-night. So they'll just be settled down somewhere. There's no need to worry about them. They'll be all right."

"Thank you. I hope so."

"There's nothing we can do but wait for daybreak. Mist or no mist, we'll be off then to meet them. So we just can settle down for the night. I thought I would tell you so because there's no need for worry."

"Will they find good shelter?" Lady Marway asked.

"Oh yes, ma'm," Maclean answered. "You search about until you find a heather bluff of some kind. It will be colder than being in your bed, maybe, but you can always get up and take a little dance to yourself. I've done it more than once."

"Have you?"

"Och yes." His grave smile was infectious. "The wife was saying to me how anxious you would be, so I just thought I would come over."

"That was very good of you." She looked at Sir John.

"Come and have a drink, Maclean," said Sir John.

"No no, indeed, sir—thank you very much. I'll just be going to my bed. Good-night all."

Everyone called good-night and Sir John accompanied him to the outside door. "You took a risk, coming in this."

"Maybe I've come too often for that," said Maclean. "Good-night, Sir John. I hope it will be a better morning."

"Isn't he a dear?" cried Helen, as Sir John came in.

"Don't forget the wife," Lady Marway said.

They all laughed. Maclean had carried away the burden of the room on his back.

George ventured upon "a No-play of Geoffrey taking his little dance to himself". From a curled-up position on the floor, where things tickled his neck and bit his thighs, he pushed himself laboriously erect, and with a face of wild solemnity, puffing, shivering, and blowing, did a flat-footed war-dance to a No-tune of barbaric rhythm. There were exaggerated gestures in which could just be traced some of Geoffrey's mannerisms. No one could help laughing. "You're sure there's not a drop left in that flask, Angus?" "No, sir, there eesn't wan drop eetself."

Lady Marway smiled upon George.

At eleven-thirty, she said, "Bed."

There was some protest. Obviously there would be no hill to-morrow, but Marjory, stooping, kissed her hostess good-night. At once Joyce followed suit. Helen shrugged and, about to stoop, paused.

"I thought I heard footsteps," she said.

"Helen, child, you mustn't——"

"There!" said Helen.

"There's something," Harry murmured. The room became a listening ear on which the fumbling at the outside gun-room door struck loudly. Sir John opened the inside door and, staring before him, said:

"Angus!"

The muddied bedraggled figure stared back at Sir John. "Mr. Smith has come home, sir?"

"No."

"Hasn't he?" said Angus. "I thought I heard his voice—through the window."

"No," said Sir John.

"Hasn't he?" said Angus. Harry saw the protective dazed look come down over his face.

"Come in," said Sir John. Angus followed him reluctantly and Sir John made him sit down, then went to pour out a tot of whisky. Angus blinked in the strong light and smiled awkwardly, not meeting any of the faces concentrated upon him. His face was smudged; his hair in wet disorder; his brow glistened from wiped sweat. His large loose mouth kept forming a foolish smile. He was intensely nervous.

"Drink that," said Sir John.

He drank it at once. "I thought I heard his voice," he said, "through the window."

"Where did you leave him?" Sir John asked.

"On the hill—Benuain. I missed him. He didn't wait for me. I asked him to be sure to wait. He didn't wait. I thought maybe he was in front of me. I didn't know what to do." He smiled foolishly.

"What happened exactly? Take your time," said Sir John, in a quiet kindly voice.

"The mist came down on us."

"Where?"

"On the other side of Benuain, near the march."

"The march!" exclaimed Sir John.

"Yes. We were following a beast. Mr. Smith was anxious to get him. I thought the mist...but he was very anxious to get him. So the mist came down, just before we got to the spot. So we started for home."

"Take your time," said Sir John.

"It was very thick, but I had seen how the wind was carrying the mist. The wind gave us a direction. And we would have been all right, but we came to a place where there was no wind. We kept going. It was a very thick mist. Then we got the wind again and we found we were off our way. So we altered our way, but we were never coming to the black-water burn."

"I see. Take your breath. Don't hurry," said Sir John, aware of the terrific internal effort that kept the simple expression on Angus's face.

"We came to a place I didn't seem to know. Everything was strange in the mist. I did my best, but in the end I had to tell him we were lost, and the only thing we could do was to find the best shelter we could, till the mist lifted."

"Quite," said Sir John. "That was right."

"Mr. Smith wasn't pleased, and said we must keep going. It was very thick. I thought by the ground that we were still about Benuain, and it is not easy going there. Then I thought it was dangerous to be walking on, for I could feel the daylight going and—and—so I asked him if he would stay and—and—I would search out from him. And when I had quartered the ground, we could go on and try another place. At last he said all right. I had a feeling the wind had changed. The wind blows different ways in the hills. But I had a feeling it had changed round. I half-faced it and went three hundred and twenty three steps straight and came to a burn. I didn't know it at first, so I decided to follow it to see if it was one I knew."

He was now getting better control of the way his breath tended to ball up in his chest.

"I put three stones on the bank to mark the place. Then I followed it some way but could make nothing of it until suddenly I came to a place on the bank, and I knew it at once. It was a place that Alick had taken me to once when he was setting a trap. I knew it at once. I knew now where we were. The only thing was that the place seemed to be on the wrong side of the burn to my memory of it. I sat down to get hold of it, and then I saw I had come at the burn the opposite way to what I thought I had." His brows gathered up and he glanced at Sir John.

"I know that feeling," said Sir John.

Angus was relieved. "I turned the whole place about, and got it clear in my head. So I knew where I was. And I was very glad. And I went back up the bank until I came to the three stones, and then with the wind half in my back walked three hundred and twenty three steps. I called, but Mr. Smith did not answer me. I kept shouting and found the spot where I had left him. But he was gone." His brown hands were still wringing his cap, twisting and wringing it.

"How long were you away from him?"

"I couldn't say. It didn't seem very long to me."

"Would it be half an hour?"

"No, no," said Angus positively.

"Think," said Sir John. "How far did you go down the bank? Another three or four hundred yards?"

"Not more, I'm sure."

"Say eight hundred yards altogether—and back. The better part of a mile. Very bad ground and thick mist. You sat down. It couldn't have been anything short of half an hour, could it?"

"It didn't seem anything like that to me."

"No. And even if it had been more, Mr. Smith should have waited. For you did your quartering very intelligently. He would have grown impatient. To him ten minutes would have seemed a very very long time. He probably thought *you* had got lost."

"Perhaps he did," said Angus. "If only I had gone back when I found the burn! But I wanted to make sure of it. I kept calling and whistling as I came on."

"How did you possibly manage back here?"

"I don't know," said Angus. "When I thought he might be in front, I kept going as fast as I could by the burnside. Then I climbed up the hill-face and got on to what I thought was the north shoulder of Benbeg. I was trying for the pony track but I couldn't find it. I kept going. I kept going a long time. I came to a dry water-course. I came to a place of great stones. Then I came to the ruins of the Picts' Houses and I knew where I was."

"The Picts' Houses!" said Harry. "Right off your course."

"Yes," said Angus. "I was lucky. I sat down and thought it out. Then I struck through the moor for the Corr. And at last I came to it."

"Could you see at all?" George asked him.

"Oh no," said Angus. "I couldn't see a foot before me."

"Jehosaphat!" said George.

"What do you think Mr. Smith did?" Sir John asked him.

"He would go on for a bit maybe, but he was bound to know that he was lost, and in a short while he could not go on, for the light went. He will be in the best shelter he could find. There is no danger within miles of him."

"There's nothing more we can do to-night?"

"No, sir. But I'll start back after a little while."

They looked at him. He got to his feet and visibly swayed, smiling; turning for the door, he staggered. Harry caught his arm. "The whisky has gone to my head!" he said in a thick voice.

"Wait, Angus," said Lady Marway.

"No, I'll be going," and he made out, Harry hanging on to him. He wanted to get to the old loft over the garage. He wanted to lie down. He could not stand their faces any longer, could not stand any more. But Harry hung on to him, and, outside, was beginning to reason with him, when Alick's voice said, "Is that you, Angus?"

"Yes," said Angus; "is it yourself, Alick?" Harry felt Angus's voice and body tremble with relief. Their tones were intimate with companionship. "I'll see to him, sir," said Alick's voice.

"Good," said Harry. "Where are you going?"

"We have shake-downs in the loft for to-night."

"But, look here, what about something to eat? You must——"

"Oh, it's all right, sir." They were moving off.

Harry came back into the sitting-room, and met the eyes Angus had met. No wonder his head had finally gone round a bit! Marjory's dumb, tragic expression was potent enough in itself!

"He'll need something," Harry said. "He's pretty well all in. I should say tea. I suppose Cook has gone aloft?"

"Yes," said Helen. "But I'll make tea. You could take it out to him." She got up at once and went to the kitchen. Harry followed her.

But already there was a light in the kitchen, a hissing which turned out to be the small primus stove in action. Mairi looked at them as they entered.

"Good, Mairi!" said Harry.

Mairi did not speak. There was a confusion of colour in her cheeks and her dress was in slight disorder. In the indifferent light of the handlamp, she looked very attractive.

"You are making tea?" Helen said.

"Yes, ma'm. I'm waiting for the kettle to boil."

There was nothing for Helen to do, and she suddenly realised it.

"You needn't bother waiting," Harry said to her. "I'll take out the tea."

"Oh," said Helen and paused; "all right," and she walked out.

Dismissed! thought Harry, and felt the swift hurt in Helen's mind. He had never scored so directly over her, so cruelly. He heard her footsteps pause and go on. Pulling herself together!

He smiled. "You heard Angus coming in?"

"Yes, sir," said Mairi.

"Couldn't sleep?"

"No, sir."

Why, he wondered, didn't she question him about what had happened? Or did she know? She must, of course. She seemed indeed full of warm, secret, and desperate conspiracies—but with the powerfully attractive innocence that springs out of real feeling. He watched her move about, swill at the tap a teapot that had obviously been swilled before, for there were no leaves in it. She never looked at him. Her face was dumb with the oppressive consciousness of his presence. As the hum rose in the kettle, she stood patiently by the primus, her back to him.

A thought struck him. "Perhaps you could take it out yourself?" he suggested.

She hesitated.

"It is so pitch black that I thought perhaps I could do it for you. But if you can manage all right yourself?…"

"I should be thankful if you could take it out," she said in clear but low tones.

"Certainly. And, look here, what about buttering some biscuits or something?" He followed her to the cupboard and was slicing the brown loaf she gave him when Lady Marway came in. Mairi turned out the primus and put the full teapot on top of its hot ring.

"A good strong cup, Mairi?"

"Yes, ma'm. It's nice and strong."

"Will you fetch him in or what?"

They both looked at Lady Marway. Then Harry looked at Mairi.

"I thought of taking it over," said Mairi.

"I'm taking it over," said Harry. "He's tired—and might not care to——"

Lady Marway agreed.

Mairi got a milk pail to carry the tea, but Lady Marway made her fill two thermos flasks and put them, together with the sandwiches, into a small basket, which swung lightly from Harry's hand as he set out on the hundred yards or so to the garage.

It was on this short trip that he began to understand the incredible nature of Angus's feat. If he had not had the edge of the road to guide his toes, he might quite easily have missed the garage. As it was he struck his waving hand sharply against the lime wall. Then he crept along it to the off gable-end, where an outside stone stairs went up to the loft floor—remains of an earlier age, when the garage had been a stable.

He heard their voices as he went up, feeling his way. They were loud and unguarded, charged with a life their employers never or rarely saw. It was their laughter that hit Harry, that brought him to a standstill, deliberately listening.

"God, I fell twenty feet if I fell an inch," said Angus. "I thought it was all up. And, do you know, even as I was falling,

I was mad! It was the damnedest funniest thing you ever knew." He laughed.

"It was the hell of a place to attempt, that," said Alick.

"I know. I knew that. But it's a queer thing that happens to you. You start off, with every muscle strung up, feeling, feeling out, until you're trembling like a held horse and you know you'll never do it. Then you get wild and curse the mist and the night and everything You could have heard me far enough!... Then you get past that. You don't give a tinker's curse. You go like a drunk man. Remember the night at Corr Inn when Sandy Innes, full as a piper, crossed——"

"Yes."

"There should have been death that night."

"There should. But tell me, didn't you see the mist coming? Why didn't you at least cross over until you got on the near side so that——"

"I know. I said that. But would he listen? Damned the bit! Look here, he has offered me two pounds if he gets King Brude! Don't say a word, for heaven's sake. He's going to get him or die. Do you know that we were making for the march *beyond* Benuain? I said to him. 'That's the farthest point of our march.' 'Is it?' he said, like that. What's a march? He's a b——r to go! That's the only thing that's frightening me now. Lord, I am tired. Look at my bloody legs jumping!" He laughed.

Harry hit the stone steps with his toes and then shouted, "Hallo, there!"

There was silence until he got to the top, then the door was pulled open and quickly closed behind him to keep the mist out. A single candle was burning on the floor, between two floor beds, with pipes and matches about it.

"Don't move," said Harry, as Angus sat up. "I've brought you some tea."

"Oh, that's too much, sir," said Angus in his quiet polite voice.

"I've brought two flasks, so you can have some too, Alick. And some sandwiches. Here you are. I hope you're feeling all right?"

"Yes, thank you," said Angus. "It was just in the warm room, after the drop of whisky—I got light-headed a little." His eyes were glittering.

"I know, very annoying," said Harry. "You've got a real robber's cave here," and he looked around into the shadows at vague junk.

"It serves a turn," Alick said.

"I bet you there's been many a good night here," Harry suggested.

"Oh well," said Alick, smiling also.

There was silence. "I don't know how on earth you managed to get here, Angus. I hope I hit the house going back!"

"It's very thick," said Angus, holding a fistful of the bedclothes.

"Well, wire into it. Good-night."

"Good-night, sir."

Alick came after him. "Watch your feet on the steps," he said.

"Oh, that's all right."

Alick was at his side at the foot of the steps. Harry protested but Alick walked beside him, until they felt the bulk of the house loom against them. Harry stopped.

"What are we going to do, Alick?"

"Maclean will be here with the first of the daylight. You should have a rest until then, sir. Sleep if you can."

"There's nothing can be done?"

"Nothing. I may take a bit of a walk around, myself, but——"

"Where will you go?"

"Oh, nowhere much. Angus and I were talking it over. I know the ground well. It's a question of wondering what Mr. Smith might do. But Maclean will arrange everything that's proper."

"Look here," said Harry, "have you told Maclean?"

"Not yet. I'll have to go over. I'll tell him you've all decided to go to bed. Angus is very worried."

"Is he?"

"Yes. He's a little beside himself."

"Oh." Harry stood in the silence. Then it began to come out of him. "Look here, Alick, I'm desperately worried myself. It's—it's—you know. It's at the back of my mind, that vision you had. I'm sorry to—to bring it up again. But I wish I could get my mind quite clear on it. You see, I must, not only for my own peace of mind, but because——" The silence struck him. "Alick!..." There was no answer. He plunged forward a step or two and felt the air where Alick's voice had been. But Alick himself was gone.

For a moment or two Harry was madly angry. He even started for the loft. He would have shouted Alick's name peremptorily, if it hadn't been for those in the house who might hear. But after a few quite reckless paces, he stopped.

Like fate, the silence seemed adequate to the occasion!

His sharp irony bit into him. For he realised what he had been on the point of doing. Once or twice in a day-dream, he had thought: Assuming it was Geoffrey, would it not be possible so to arrange affairs that Geoffrey could be recalled to London urgently and thus destroy any possibility of the vision's being fulfilled? Seemed a simple way out. He even arranged how it might be done. If only he could be dead sure it was Geoffrey's funeral! Was Alick himself absolutely dead sure?

All in a moment again, he had wanted to know with an intense urgency. Deep in some primal part of him, he believed in the vision!

Talk about the grip of superstition! Geoffrey was right.

He stood there, unable to go either to the loft or into the house.

He could feel the mist searching out his ear-drums. His face turned in the direction of the forest, and he thought of Geoffrey impotently squirming in the clammy stuff, getting colder and colder till the marrow grew cold and the teeth clattered, and his face grew death-grey. If only his impatient spirit would keep him to the one place. "I fell twenty feet if I fell an inch." But would it? Was he that kind?

Or would four men carry him home?

He turned to the house, angry with himself, deeply angry. He did not mind being fantastic or cynical with himself or with anyone else, but there was a limit!... And all the time further back in his mind he knew that a man did die, that every man died; apprehended it with the awful solemn simplicity of a child.

He struck the kitchen door and went in. Mairi was still here, and though she pretended to be doing things, he knew she was merely waiting.

"They're all right," he said cheerfully. "I think the feed should do them good."

"I'm glad of that," she answered simply.

"Yes. No need for worry." There was a human silence for a little. "You go to bed, Mairi, and get some sleep."

"All right," she said.

A fine girl, with a shy, real woman-warmth. The sort of companion a man wanted at such a moment. Game to the last, self-forgetting, and always there. He found himself lingering. He wanted some of that warmth, wanted its understanding, its comfort. So he said at once, "Good-night, Mairi. Go to bed now!" and walked out of the kitchen and into the sitting-room, where they were all waiting for him.

"Angus is pretty done up, feeling bad about having come home." He was smiling, almost casually.

"Has Maclean been told?" Sir John asked.

"Alick is going over to tell him. They'll start out at the dawn. I think we should get some sleep."

"Will they come here?" George asked.

"I should think so," said Harry. "You and I should be ready, anyway."

"Goodo!" said George.

"Bed it is, then," said Lady Marway. "Come on, girls. Off you go." Her firm good sense was appreciated, and within a quarter of an hour, the room was dark.

Harry got entangled in his sleep with a shroud, and when the vivid experience awoke him, he imagined a perceptible greyness in the direction of the window. He listened but heard no movement—though a ghostly populous movement still went on in his mind. He struck a match and found it was five o'clock. The dawn should be coming.

He lay back, wide awake, with that early morning consciousness which can be so bodiless and sensitive and often full of optimism. The shroud he had seen was still almost tangible, its white folds between the outer and the inner eye, to be ignored or focused.

Yes, that's it! he thought, remembering how Alick had muttered about four men carrying a dead body "in its shroud". That was what Alick had said, when the vision had passed and he had questioned him. But now Harry began to wonder if he had not actually heard the words "in its shroud" for the first time in his dream. This effect of double-consciousness, of hearing something and imagining he had heard it before in the same circumstances, was common enough—particularly in the shape of seeing things, like new places. Yet, of course, he knew Alick had said it—though exactly how, in what specific sentence, he could not be certain.

The disquieting thing, behind it all, was—that the business of a shroud was to cover things over. The shroud in his dream with its stream-lined folds was like something painted by a Watts to cover over the beauty of the world. It enshrouded a figure, who was the beauty of the world. There is never anything sentimental in a dream. Harry would see the figure when the shroud was drawn back from the face. Alick's hand began to draw back the shroud. He wanted to stop him—yet could not move, held in such a horror that it awoke him.

So he actually had not seen Helen's dead face under the shroud, but he must have imagined it, at that moment or some other, in a half-legendary, Rossetti-like death beauty, for the pale image of it swam in upon him now.

Supposing it was not Geoffrey at all, but Helen?

In the extreme stillness of the morning, he heard a movement downstairs, and at once swung out of bed, lit a candle, and dressed.

Cook, Mairi, and the kitchen-maid, Ina, were in the lamp-lit kitchen when he entered. No one else was downstairs. He addressed Cook and asked her if Maclean had called.

"No one has called," she answered, "but someone threw up pebbles at the girls' window." She was a dark-haired medium-sized woman of nearly sixty, capable, and domineering, but "good-hearted enough when it comes up her back", as Ina had once put it grudgingly. Ina had lank fair hair, and rather angular gestures, could make a moody mouth and flash blue eyes, looked brainless when sulking, and could play with children for long enough. Mairi was making sandwiches, and as she glanced up at him, Harry gave her a smile and a nod. Cook noted it. It was always useful, she found, to have a few disciplinary observations up one's sleeve.

Harry went up to George's door, opened it, and entered. George stirred and shot up in bed, staring at Harry's face behind the light he carried. "I say! Have I slept in?"

"No," said Harry. "But the maids are getting stuff ready in the kitchen. Maclean or someone has been along."

"Goodo! Hanged if I could get to sleep—and then wasn't I sure to pop off at the psychic moment!" He was getting into his trousers by the time Harry had lit his candle. "I won't be a shake."

"No hurry at all. Do you think we should waken the Chief?"

There was the sound of a door and footsteps. Sir John, in his dressing gown, looked in. "Oh, you're getting up, are you?"

They talked together for a little, then Sir John went back to his room and Harry downstairs, where in the sitting-room he found Marjory fully dressed.

He whistled. "What are you doing up at this unearthly hour?"

"Why shouldn't I be up as well as you? Do you think women feel such an occasion less?" It was the usual raillery, but with an edge to it, a real edge.

"Suppose not. But what can you do?"

"Men have that advantage: they *do* things, don't they?"

"I say, Marjory, being clever at this hour! Breakfast is bad enough, but this hour! Have a heart!"

She smiled. "Not much good lying in bed if you're wide awake. So I thought I might as well come down to see what was doing. I even thought I might help somehow—though I can't quite see how."

Harry removed his eyes, suddenly and unaccountably moved.

Marjory had, if not an over-generous, certainly a sound figure. She was the last person to suggest the word ethereal. So Harry decided it must be the extreme fairness of her skin at this early hour. Her eyes, too, were larger than he had thought. Was he developing a habit of seeing women at their unusual best or what? "I suppose the other two young females are pounding their ears good and hard," he said, in an amused voice.

"I listened at Joyce's door. I think she is. I hope she is."

"Hope so, too. Who's this?"

It was George, and Harry immediately felt he had to protect Marjory from George's astonishment at seeing her, so he at once sent him to the window to study the light.

Maclean was heard in the unlit gun-room. As they got him into the room, Sir John appeared.

There were quiet greetings. The mist was very thick. Maclean had seen it last for two or three days, but that was unusual. "If an air of wind springs up it'll go. And it may go now any time for the sun is up. Though more likely it will be eleven or twelve o'clock." There was obviously something on his mind. And at last he said, "I am sorry about Angus coming back. He shouldn't have done that."

"We quite understand. He did it for the best."

"He should never have left Mr. Smith alone. His duty was to stay by him—or take him with him—but never to leave him alone."

"That's all right, Maclean. Don't worry about that. Angus found himself in a new position where he had to make a decision. It's a moment that comes to us all."

"Oh well, perhaps it is as you say, Sir John," he answered politely, but clearly not believing it. Then he went on to tell them of the arrangements he had made, and presently they stood before the plan of the forest in the gun-room.

Maclean had thought out all the probabilities, but Harry also found himself listening to the Gaelic voice in its pronunciation of the corries and sgurrs and burns and slopes and passes; the liquid *l*, the aspirated guttural—that utterly un-English sound far back in an open throat—the broad, the narrow, the gliding vowels, the lazy hang-on to diphthongs as the voice rises against a hard consonant,—and falls over, like water over a boulder. Now and then it went harsh and croaked like a raven.

"I could go with Alick's party," Harry said.

Maclean looked at Sir John. "I am sorry, sir, but Alick has not turned up yet. He came over and told me about Angus last night. Then it appears he went back to the loft and saw Angus to sleep. When Angus awoke he was not there." Maclean's brows furrowed. He was being sorely tried by his staff. Harry could see a deep, suppressed annoyance.

"Did he go home?" Sir John asked.

"No," said Maclean. "I have made sure of that. However, we can do without him. Indeed I am beginning to think perhaps we could do without him permanently."

"Perhaps we need not go so far as that," said Sir John with his smileless humour.

"It's as you say, Sir John. But—I don't know."

Three parties were formed, and Maclean explained their respective routes, their rate of progress, and how they would try to get in touch when Mr. Smith had been found. A thermos flask was missing, but Angus contrived, through Mairi, that the others should not hear of this.

Maclean's party, including Sir John, took the Home Beat, with its direct low-ground approaches to the Lodge. Andrew, with George and three others, set out leftward for the Benuain Beat. Angus, with Harry and Donald, took the right-hand stretch of the forest, bounded by the Corr.

It was seven o'clock before they got properly under way, for Maclean was obviously in no hurry. "We don't want to miss him," he said, "if he's walking home by himself." The mist was now all white again, but there was no suggestion of wind. It hung about them, dank and heavy.

"Do you think it will lift?" Harry asked Angus.

"I don't know," said Angus, "but I think it will."

Harry could see how keen he was, how internally alive. And he had learned his lesson, for he saw that Harry did not wander far from his side! His voice became confidential, too, and he explained to them how they must cry or whistle to each other to keep in touch at all costs. Harry responded with such understanding that he eased Angus's responsibility.

Once the early morning malaise had passed and his body had warmed up, Harry found their expedition full of the weirdest elements, of bodies disappearing and suddenly re-appearing like tall tree trunks, of voices answering out of the mist, smothered and ghostly, of a sudden hill-bird's cry, high-pitched and anxious, falling away and drowning. Now and then the three of them would stand together and Angus, with fingers in mouth, would let out a prolonged whistle. As they held their breaths, the silence was the silence of death, of an utter nothingness, and once Harry felt it as the primeval silence before life was.

Progress was slow, for Angus had detours to make to likely spots and shelters, and every burn or watercourse received faithful attention. As time went on, his energy increased, and Harry, trying to keep up with him, often found his brow prickling with sweat and his breath laboured. Once as he pitched over a tussock and his shoulder took the soft moor, he lay for a moment and laughed at himself, a slaver of saliva dribbling over his lower lip. Out of the mist Angus came and picked him up anxiously. Harry, the laugh still on his face, gave him the sort of look Alick had given him yesterday when at last they had come within range of the stag.

For there was a companionship in all this, something fine and good and full of a friendly humour. The mind was purged and freed. Even tragedy could be felt only as a passing out into freedom. What more could a man expect? We don't live for ever.

"All right, Angus," said Harry. "We're doing fine."

Angus responded with a quick glance, before his eyes moved off and a confused smile came over his own face. So that he became more alive than ever—and more anxious.

"I'll tell you what," he said, with the natural eagerness he might have directed at Alick. "It's now after ten o'clock. If it's going to lift to-day it should soon be showing signs. Away up on our left here is the shoulder leading to Benbeg. Now, what I think is that we should take the slope in front of us at an upward slant. But you, Donald, could go straight ahead until you come to the Hags. From there you will follow the old watercourse, with the hollowed peat-banks—you know?—until you come, right up on the far shoulder, to the well. You'll stop there at Toberuain, whatever happens, until we reach you."

As Harry went on with him, he explained that he would like to make sure whether the mist was going to lift or not, and, besides, a man under the impression that he was going the right way was as likely to climb as not. He did not speak again until he stood on the crest of the shoulder, then he turned his damp freckled face with its loose generous mouth on Harry and smiled. "It's brighter here."

It was undoubtedly brighter. One could see farther. The mist was thinner. Beyond this world of spectral gloom, the sun still shone!

"This way," and Angus was off.

The shoulder dipped before it rose again into the fairly steep final slope of Benbeg. Harry could have done with a rest on that shoulder, but he never thought of stopping the anxious tireless figure in front, now climbing as if hot on a trail. Presently he lost sight of him, but the mist was thinning, growing irradiated, warm, and then a voice cried from above:

"The sun!"

Harry emerged into pure sunlight, under a blue tall sky, on the wide rounded table-top of Benbeg.

There was a shout of delight in him, but wonder held it in check, for the scene was of unusual beauty. The cone of Benuain was islanded clear before them to the north-west, and mountain-tops and long skerries floated on that white sea far as the eye could travel. A feeling of the marvel of first Creation came upon Harry in an atmosphere, not productive or hectic, but timeless and still. A Creation not being created, but invisibly creating itself from within. Eternity hung over that white sea, hung over all the world, let it dissolve or move as it may in temporary form and formlessness.

And Harry knew what was under the sea; valleys, roads, transport and houses; Helen looking into the mist, and Marjory with her new ethereal expression looking and wondering, like life in some underground aquarium, their faces against the dim glass.

"It looks well," said Angus.

It was the first time he had ever known a gillie or stalker express appreciation of his surroundings. It was not their business of course! And Angus's voice was practical enough, adding:

"It will lift soon."

It would lift beyond doubt. It would lift!

"If you feel tired, we could rest for a bit here by the cairn," said Angus. "There's no great hurry now."

There was no hurry at all. Harry stretched out his legs, lay full on his back, and stared up at the blue sky. "People look at natural scenery," he said musingly, "but they forget to look at the sky. Do you ever look at the sky?"

"Oh yes," said Angus, taking out his telescope. "One has to, often, for the weather." Then fixing his telescope against his stick, he began to study Benuain.

Nothing could be more perfect than such a moment, more divine. Harry did not listen to anything any more. The sun warmed him, dried the sweat in his hair. His wet feet were in a glow. He could hardly remember having looked at the sky himself before—not certainly since he was a boy…perhaps on some drowsy common, with the scent of broom in the air. He was suddenly that small boy and an obscure instinct made him want to move his head and say "Ah-h-h" under his breath.

The "ah-h-h" of wonder, of drowsiness, of being impersonally alive; wariness forgotten, the everyday self gone, and the happier, simpler self come up to take the air.

All life had been a training to get him away from that diviner self. Exactly why? Something touched him stealthily.

"Hsh!" said Angus, in the softest whisper. "Don't move. Just turn your head slowly."

Harry turned his head slowly and saw a remarkable sight. The leading stag, a magnificent beast, had come clear of the mist and stood with head thrown up, staring directly at him, full in the sunlight. Harry remembered him as some legendary beast out of a dream, for he had only vaguely seen him before in a half-light. Three other stags stood on the edge of the mist, wholly visible, while between those beasts and behind—or below—them, heads, grey-dark as old bog oak, stared unmoving. As Harry's eyes roved they caught ever more heads, shadowy ghost heads, until he got the impression of a vast herd.

"King Brude," whispered Angus. "Don't move."

No legendary beast could have chosen a more suitable moment for his advent! Some wild humour in this touched Harry to a thrilled solemnity. He counted the tines—twelve. He had seen many famous royals on the walls of shooting lodges, but never one like this, carrying in the sweep of its antlers so pure an inspiration.

No wonder Geoffrey had been led astray!

And the heads never moved. They stared as if they had been transfixed by a weird charm. The complete absence of movement became uncanny. Harry began to stare himself and his muscles to cramp unnaturally. His mouth grew dry, his throat uncomfortable. He was hardly breathing through an open mouth.

"Don't move."

From far away came the faint sound of a whistle. King Brude turned his head and sniffed the air, but in a second was looking at them again. He turned his head towards his other shoulder, and looked back once more. Then, his antlers riding high, he bore away into the mist and in a moment all were gone, as they had come, noiselessly.

"A great beast, isn't he?" said Angus.

"I'll never forget that sight", said Harry, "until I die."

Angus looked pleased. "They have been disturbed", he explained, "by the whistling and cries. In some forests, they tell me, gillies are sent out round the boundaries to drive the deer into the stalkers. We don't do that in this part of the country."

"Thank God", said Harry, "for this part of the country."

"That was Maclean whistling. They are away off down there in the mist."

"Are they?" said Harry, hardly listening, staring out over this strange world.

Angus indicated a shoulder of a hill coming into view and called attention to the distinct "air of wind". "It will clear quickly now, except for the lowest places." His voice sounded eager, but with that undernote of concern which made him wrinkle his eyebrows. "Perhaps we should be going," he said hesitantly.

Harry looked at him. "You're not sure?"

"If it lifted quickly, we could spy all round us with the glass. But perhaps we should be going on?"

"In that case, we'll wait for a little."

"Do you think we should, sir?" He was full of indecision and eagerness. Harry could see the excitement in his hands.

"Yes," said Harry.

"All right, sir," said Angus. But with the mist obviously beginning to lift, he could not rest. "I'll go along and give a shout to Donald at the well."

"Do," said Harry.

Angus started off but after going twenty yards came back. "Ach, it doesn't matter," he said. "Donald can wait."

"You're not going to leave *me*," said Harry.

Angus smiled and flushed.

"Sit down," said Harry, "and let us watch the world being born."

He was in the mood for a spectacle of the kind. If Geoffrey was dead, he was dead. Nothing more could be done about it now. Nothing more could be done about anything. God sat on his creative hill-top, and inside his immutable laws things happened thus and thus—as they happened to gnats before the eyes, pursuing and pursued, round the tiny heather trumpets blowing their purple colour, blowing their honey fragrance, round the green stalks, the dark stalks, to the roots, where the damp rotting moss and mire made a soft swarming breeding bed. The eyes watched the gnats with understanding, with gentleness, with detachment—with no need or desire to interfere.

A movement came upon the face of the mist. The top fins, the long black ridges, of the backs of primeval beasts cut the upper surface of the white sea. The rock of Benuain grew taller. And rocks far away. And rocks close at hand, down which the mist-cataracts poured into seething cauldrons. The white tide ebbed from the distant reefs. The valleys were being born. The glens. The corries. The passes.

Known places—born out of memory—out of…. A surge of feeling came over Harry drowning something he could not grasp, could not know, and leaving him quivering like an instrument struck by a beauty that was triumphant and somehow poignant, too….

Angus, with his glass, let out a low, Gaelic exclamation.

Harry turned on his right side and looked at him. Angus brought his eye from the glass and, in a gulp, said, "They're coming."

"Who?"

"Mr. Smith and Alick." He was trembling. "Look!"

It took a little time before the two figures walked into the round eye of the telescope. But there they were, unmistakably, and, oh sweet heaven, how characteristically! Geoffrey in front, limping steadily on, staff in hand, doggedly, and Alick a good six yards behind. There was no intercourse between those two figures! Harry could feel Geoffrey's mood.

He brought his eye from the glass, his whole face shining. "Yes, there they are!" He began to laugh.

Angus laughed, too, and jumped to his feet and waved his cap and shouted. It was a spontaneous action, and he covered it by saying, "You never know: some of them may have a glass on us." Then he controlled himself and, putting four fingers in his mouth, let loose three piercing whistles, in quick succession. Whereupon he got hold of his telescope again and directed it at the two figures.

"Will you move about and wave a hand?" he said to Harry.

Harry did this, shouting and jumping and moving his hands. His teeth were clicking. He had not realised how cold he had got. "Hurrah!" he shouted. "Good old Alick! Stick it, Geoff!" I'll soon get warm at this rate! he thought, and laughed all over again. Then he saw Angus, while still contriving to look through the telescope, make a formal salute of recognition.

"They've seen us," he said. "It's all right." A treble whistle reached them, like a far echo of their own. "That's Maclean, away under the shoulder of the Druim."

"What about the other party?" Harry asked him.

Angus took a thoughtful moment.

"I think," he said, "that I better cut across and—get in touch with them."

Now that Mr. Smith had been discovered, Angus had no desire to be in at the rejoicings! His look was so innocent, that Harry could not help smiling. "All right," he said, "You don't mind my smiling, do you?"

Angus's brows wrinkled. "Someone must stop them."

"Of course," said Harry. "I was only pulling your leg."

"We can go down towards the well and pick up Donald, if you like," said Angus in the same tone. "It's——" Donald came up over the crest and joined them, saying, "I heard you."

Angus told him the good news.

When they reached the path, down in the base of the glen, they paused. They could see Geoffrey and Alick coming slowly on about three-quarters of a mile back. Angus said, "I think I better whistle again." This time response from the Maclean party sounded much nearer. Angus continued to listen. There was no third response. Harry saw that he was waiting for orders and discussed the matter solemnly with him. "Very good, sir," said Angus, and started off to find George's party.

Harry looked after him. The relationship between gillie and gentleman had been restored! A likeable fellow, careless probably in the smaller things of life, generous, and touchy, too! With great drive and strength, for so lean a body.

"We'd better go to meet them," he said to Donald.

Harry became a trifle self-conscious as he drew near Geoffrey, for he was not at all certain of his humour. He hailed him from a little distance, but beyond pausing for a moment, Geoffrey did not respond.

"Congratulations!" he said, and shook Geoffrey's hand with a genuine warmth.

Geoffrey smiled and said, "Thanks," drily. Pardonably enough, he was not in a hilarious mood. His face was grey and puffy-looking, his brows drawn.

"Nothing serious, I hope?" Harry regarded his limp.

"No, nothing much," said Geoffrey. "One of a search party?"

"Well, we thought we'd come out to cheer you home!"

"Other parties also?"

"Well——"

"Good God!" said Geoffrey, going on determinedly.

"Good morning, Alick!"

"Good morning, sir."

Harry saw the missing thermos flask sticking out of Alick's pocket. Donald went up to Alick and they stood together until Harry and Geoffrey drew some distance ahead.

"You must have had a rotten night," Harry said.

"It was bitterly cold," Geoffrey acknowledged indifferently, and Harry saw that he was in a vile humour and did not want to be questioned.

"That fellow Angus got back apparently?"

"Yes," said Harry. "Late last night."

"Hmff," said Geoffrey.

"What happened?"

"Didn't you ask him?"

"We did. He seemed very upset at losing you."

"Losing *me*! Pretty good I must say!" He laughed a harsh note or two. "The damned fool! What excuse did he give for clearing out and leaving me?"

"He says he went back to where he had left you, but you were gone."

"Same story as he gave to Alick. It positively tallies."

117

"What actually happened?"

"He lost his way in his own forest, and kept me going round in circles before he admitted it. Then he said, 'You stay here and I'll go out for a little way and come straight back.' He went out. He never came back. I must have waited an hour. I shouted. Then I struck out, thinking he had fallen and broken his neck. He apparently took care to avoid so drastic a step. Logic is not their strong point."

"He said——"

"Is that some of them?"

It was Maclean's small party, with a pony. Harry nodded: "Yes."

"Good God!" said Geoffrey. He deliberately sat down, and, lowering a stocking and pulling up his breeches, examined his flesh as far as possible. The skin was not broken, but it was discoloured, and he probed the knee-cap.

"You got a toss," said Harry.

"Looks like it, doesn't it? However, there's nothing broken. And there might have been." He felt his hip-bone, and then his shoulder. "God, I'm tired," he said, with dry malevolence.

"What about a small tot?"

"A what? Why didn't you——" He bit off the sentence, took the flask, and drank. Then he shuddered. "No water in it." He eased his throat harshly.

"Sorry," said Harry. "Have a cigarette?"

"No, thanks. I wish you had told me there was no water in it."

"We don't usually carry water in it."

"My throat." It was obviously tender. "Thanks." He looked towards the approaching party: Sir John, Maclean, and a lad with a pony. "Where are all the women?"

"Waiting anxiously to receive you at home."

Geoffrey gave him a glance, but was beyond comment. Harry's dry smile irritated him acutely.

Harry saw the slow, deliberate effort with which he pulled himself together to greet Sir John and Maclean. But these two experienced men soon realised his mood and sympathised with it. "Get up here," said Sir John. "We can talk later."

The young man led the pony that Geoffrey bestrode. Sir John and Maclean fell in behind. The most comfortable going was in single file.

Walking alone, Harry felt relieved, as if his own company were better than Geoffrey's any time! He smiled at the dry touch of spite. But it was odd how a mood like Geoffrey's could blast the morning sunlight. Didn't, of course, affect the sunlight at all—only his own mind, inducing in it a mood somewhat like Geoffrey's. And Geoffrey had obviously the greater cause to feel disgruntled!…

But deep in him, Harry knew that all this arguing was beside the point. The glory of the hill-top had been destroyed. And that, he thought—lifting the argument from the personal—is what tends to happen so often in this old life. The glory of the hill-top was far back in his mind— a sheen of memory—a divine stillness and loveliness. He lowered his head, wondering about it, idly, without concentration, as one wonders in a day-dream, and presently the irony lingering about his mouth faded out and his face became expressionless, like a face asleep, except for the eyes that gathered a sheen of their own, a steady glimmering.

He came out of this vague mood, this half-lost region, without any distinct consciousness of coming out of it, to find his mind quite calm, as if it had been washed clean. His body felt cool, too, and clean. He looked at Geoffrey on his pony. Was he a conqueror, leading the silent cavalcade? Or a prisoner, being led?

The prisoner—of what and towards what?

Harry glanced at the sky—and then at Sir John's tall gaunt figure, obscured, except for the head, every now and then by the broad set figure of Maclean. Glancing behind, he saw Donald come next at a respectful distance and then Alick, expressionless as ever.

A thought struck him sharply: how *exactly* had Alick found Geoffrey? In the relief of first seeing Geoffrey coming under his own steam, he had taken it for granted that Alick was just the sort of person who would find him.

But—how? Alick must have lifted the second full thermos flask, after he had deliberately put Angus to sleep, walked from the garage direct into the centre of the hills in a darkness black as pitch, gone up to an invisible but real Geoffrey and said, "I've brought some hot tea for you."

The thing was just too utterly incredible for any sort of belief. The chances were infinity to one against. Not merely a miracle, but a fantastic one.

Soft gusts of humour came through Harry's nose. For he knew in his bones that there had been no miracle. What, in any case, is a miracle but a happening whose laws we do not know?

And then one further thought struck Harry: what exactly had happened at that miraculous meeting? Geoffrey had made no reference to Alick. He was in a vile mood.

You pays your money and takes your choice! thought Harry in a wild amaze.

At which moment, the track widened into a bay where a car could turn, and continued in the shape of a narrow gravelled road. Sir John went up and spoke to Geoffrey, walking by his side for a little, then dropped back and spoke to Maclean. Harry wanted to wait for Alick, but felt he dared not, lest Geoffrey look round. So they came down on the bridge and saw the women, four to the front of the house and three—Cook, Mairi, and Ina—to the rear.

Harry's face began to twitch. Pretty tough on poor old Geoff! he thought.

But Geoffrey bore up very well. The laugh had gone out of him. He could not say, "See the conquering hero comes!" His mind was too grey for that, too wearied and angry and exhausted. And because he could not say it, a deep spite came upon him. But he smiled with a wry mouth, when Helen whooped a welcome.

"I feel pretty done up," he said to Lady Marway. "You'll excuse me if I get to bed?"

They saw he did not want to speak to them, that all this attention annoyed him. Only Marjory seemed calm and unperturbed.

"I should hop off at once if I were you," she said.

"I think I will, if you'll excuse me?"

"Certainly," said Lady Marway. "You're sure you don't want something to eat or drink?"

He shook his head. "No, thanks." His leg had gone very stiff. He nearly fell. "Nothing," he said. He was very grey.

"Come along," said Sir John and gave him his arm, and they walked to the stairs.

"He's had a bad night," said Lady Marway to Harry in a low voice. "Did he tell you much?"

The four women stood around him. Their profound relief at finding Geoffrey safe was seeking outlet in a natural curiosity. They talked in quiet voices.

And Harry told them all he could, even more than perhaps he quite knew. "Though, as you can understand, he was not in the mood to talk and I did not press him. We must give him time."

"Who found him?" Joyce asked.

"Alick," said Harry.

Lady Marway looked at him. "That's one good thing about Alick—he does know the forest."

"But I thought Alick could not be found this morning?" Joyce went on.

"He left earlier, by himself," Harry said.

"But—do you mean—he went away in that fog—and found him?"

"Apparently," said Harry.

"You mean in that utter darkness that George and I——" Harry nodded.

"No, I don't believe it," said Joyce. "I just don't believe it. It couldn't humanly be done."

"Where did he find him?" Helen asked calmly.

"We got to the top of Benbeg, before the mist lifted. When it did lift, we saw them coming, between us and Benuain."

"As far as that?" murmured Lady Marway. "Of course they do know the ground marvellously. Just as we could get about this house in complete darkness, if we had to."

"Where's George?" Joyce asked.

"I sent Donald away to whistle them back. They shouldn't be long now."

"Is Geoffrey's leg really bad?" Marjory asked.

"Not really. The flesh is discoloured, but the bones are absolutely all right."

"No need, of course, to get a doctor?" Lady Marway looked at him.

"No, no!" said Harry quickly. "For heaven's sake, no!"

"Well, for anyone who hates a fuss—to have to come riding in like that—I mean——" Marjory shrugged in understanding.

Quite! They all agreed.

Sir John came in. "I'll say a word of thanks to the men," and he passed out through the gun-room. Lady Marway set off to see about lunch at the earliest moment, and Marjory immediately followed her, asking Ina in a quiet aside if she had actually put the hot bottle in Mr. Smith's bed.

Joyce went out to look for George's party.

"Suppose you all had an anxious morning," Harry said to Helen casually, as he poured himself a small drop of whisky and plenty of soda.

"Naturally," said Helen.

"Uhm," said Harry, and drank off the lot. "A fine day now, isn't it?"

"Very excellent day indeed."

"I hope it keeps up," said Harry. "It's nice when a good thing keeps up," and he dropped into an arm-chair.

Helen walked over to the window.

"Though not so nice," said Harry vaguely, "when it doesn't keep up."

"Are you trying to be smart or what?"

"Not smart. I wouldn't say smart exactly."

"No?"

"No."

"Oh."

"Uhm."

Helen could not very well now leave the room, so she walked to the bookcase.

"Been reading a lot lately?" Harry inquired.

"Quite a bit."

"Any more dreams?"

She shut the book with a snap and swung round on him.

"I had a dream about you," he said, without looking at her. Suddenly remembering the dream, he did look at her. Heaven knows why he had mixed her up with the Rossetti type—she was so uniquely, so vividly, so angrily—she was, oh lord, he didn't know what she was, with the whirl and disturbance going on inside him. He strove to keep casual, rubbed his jaw, and smiled towards the cannibal trout.

She simply stopped looking at him and walked out.

His head fell back, his eyes closed, he breathed like one exhausted. I am really pretty tired! he thought, and gripped the arms of the chair, and in a moment was on his feet. But not to do anything. Just to stand. While he was still standing, Helen came back. It was clear that she had thought out the proper thing to say and was now in the mood to say it. She met his face, and saw that it was quite naked. This knocked the beginning of the words out of her head and she stared back at him as she might in a dream or a half-nightmare. Sir John's footsteps came into the gun-room. She looked sideways, towards the window with a strange glancing expression, then turned and left the room for the second time.

Chapter Seven

That afternoon, after tea, Helen walked down the winding path towards the river. No one even suggested going with her, for the Lodge itself lay heavy and inert after the night's adventures.

She did not mind this. She was indeed glad of it. Every now and then, after longer or shorter intervals, hours or weeks, she had this impulse to slip away into some place where she had herself for company.

And she was in for it now! She knew it whenever she sniffed the birches. The thrill of the scent went right through her body, quickened her sleeping heart, and so up to her head, where it brightened her eyes, enriched the skin, and lightened the grey matter so notably that the heels had an urge to rise above the toes.

The brown note in her dark hair seemed more pronounced; her lips looked soft and warm. Her skirt, all neat and simple, hung to just below her knees, so that her ankles and sufficient of her legs could be seen to enhance the suggestion of upflowing curves, suave and taut, and really there seemed no reason why she shouldn't stretch out her arms and take off down the waves of hazel leaves!

Yet nothing would come quite right. She would be on the point of becoming her old simple self, when she didn't know what happened but she had to move on; move on, not merely in her mind but in her physical body, getting up to take it from one spot to another.

Something had invaded her secret place. It was not a person. She could talk to persons, hold long, eye-bright conversations with them. As she had done, for example, many a time with Harry—particularly when she had been at the age to make Harry her husband. She had worked out house, furnishings, and social affairs for Harry and herself more than once. And she hadn't to go back an endless period for the last time!

But that had been a pure game, with Harry the necessary pawn or king. At the back of things, she knew it might very easily not be Harry, almost certainly would not be Harry—if the *mysterious something* happened to her. At which apprehension of the ecstatic unknown, a hush came upon her heart and a gulp into her throat. Once or twice she had got up and run away.

But this present feeling could clearly have nothing to do with all that. For it was not a person but a form of malaise that had invaded her, so that she couldn't get the old harmony, the bright fun of being totally herself. She was not afraid, not in a panic: she was—oh she didn't know what she was. And, the most extraordinary thing of all, she had never, never apprehended the scent of the birches, the beauty of the glen, as she did now.

Ah, it was this beauty that was getting the better of her, the sheer loveliness of the birches, the splashes of autumn colour, golden flotsam on the billows of green, the bracken, the bronzes, the rowan tree, the blood-red berries, the blackbird with the brilliant orange beak, harebells—"the Scottish bluebells"—and scabious, the taste of wild raspberries, the lines and the depth—and the scent of it all, with that pervasive under-scent of the earth itself, that quickening and terrifying scent.

Blowing into her stone circle, about its ultimate altar stone, on the wind's breath.

That was what her growth had been towards, as the growth of the compact bud to the blown rose.

She was being invaded, her own beauty by the strange beauty in the world. Not of the world. In the world. In the world.

She wanted to shut it out, and she didn't want to shut it out, and so she wandered on in her strange sweet misery, sometimes on the path, sometimes on a stone by the bouldered river—until the sound of the water, the meandering infinite rhythm, caught a cry in the heart of it, and she had to get up and go. From the wooded path to the bank, and from the bank—

> *Fra bank to bank, fra wood to wood I rin...*

The words came into her mind like a cry, from that haunting old Scots sonnet, repeated to her so often by her schoolgirl friend, Maisie, and surely the most beautiful ever written:

> *Fra bank to bank, fra wood to wood I rin*
> *Ourhailit with my feeble fantasie*
> *Like til a leaf that fallis from the tree*
> *Or til a reed ourblawin with the wind,*
>
> *Two gods guides me, the ane of them is blin,*
> *Yea, and a bairn brocht up in vanitie,*
> *The next a wife ingenrit of the sea*
> *And lichter nor a dauphin with her fin.*
>
> *Unhappy is the man for evermair*
> *That tills the sand and sawis in the air,*
>
> *But twice unhappier is he, I lairn,*
> *That feidis in his heart a mad desire*
> *And follows on a woman throw the fire*
> *Led by a blind and teachit by a bairn.*

The lightness, the dolphin ease, the fin—moulded like her own body, her breast, her arms. *And follows on a woman through the fire.*
Follows on...
Fra bank to bank, fra wood to wood...
Till her feeble fantasy quite overcame her, and she suddenly sat down beneath the birches, and drooped her head, and burst into tears, pressing her hands up against her face, hiding it in shame and in sorrow.

Shame at her own weakness, this vague woman weakness, arising out of nothing—oh, out of nothing.

Loving her weakness, seduced by it, giving in to it—but aware, behind the forgetfulness of her tears, of the peril and the panic, of the noiseless beat beat, of feet...

Like a beat out of the heart of the earth. The noiseless beat of feet—coming——

Her heart leapt within her, and past the near tree trunks came a man's legs and feet. Alick!

He saw her, but never paused, as if he had not seen her.

"Alick!" she said, getting up, half-turned away from him, drying her tears, then turning to him with a confused smile.

From looking at the ground near his feet, he looked past her, with no expression on his face, waiting.

"Where are you going?" she asked.

"To see about the morning."

"Are you in a hurry?"

"No, ma'm."

"Well—wait a bit," she said slowly, awkwardly. "I don't know what came over me. Must be the strain." Her smile was friendly, softly confused.

He waited, his eyes touching her for a moment.

"I suppose I must look a bit of a sight. But—I don't know. It's rather lovely here." She racked her brains for something to say. "I should like, sometime, when you are not on the hill, to have another day's fishing. Do you think that would be possible?"

"Oh yes," he said in his quiet voice. "Though the only place at the moment is Loch-an-eilean."

"The loch with the little island! That would be lovely."

"It's getting a bit late in the year. But there are good trout in it."

"Well—the next time you are free?"

"Very good, ma'm."

"Ah—as you know—we have had an anxious time. It was marvellous of you finding Mr. Smith. We—tell me, how did you manage it?"

"Oh well, it just happened."

"I wonder! Tell me how. Or do you mind?"

"There's nothing to mind," he said simply. "I just thought he might go the way he went—and found him there."

"But——"

He waited.

She looked at him directly. He was looking past her, politely. It was difficult to be friendly with this man—unless the relationship was the impersonal, normal one of a fishing expedition. Then he would talk and tell you things and even smile. At the moment he might be anything— inimical, wary of intrusion, suspicious, or bored. There was some queer force in his body, a pent-up force, that would stand at ease like this for an indefinite time. She always felt it, it always excited her, and she slightly feared it, except when it was impersonally friendly, and then it was alto- gether pleasant and lovable, communicated the sense of freedom, the feeling that it was good to be alive in the open air.

She gave a small shrug. "I shan't question you," she said, with a touch of humour, smiling to him.

The slight characteristic smile came to his face.

"The first day, then, that you are free?" she said.

"Very good. This hill weather won't keep up for ever," he volunteered.

"Let us hope not! Thank you, Alick. Good-bye."

"Good-bye, ma'm."

My tears are safe with him! she thought. But within a few paces she wondered, and within another few was uncertain, with spasms of painful doubt.

For what did she know about him really?

That force within him; it was strong; it might be brutal— given the occasion. He would never mention anything about her tears to her own people. But to his——?

Perhaps make a joke about it, an innuendo.

Hateful to think about. The implication that she had been making advances—conveyed by the mouth in a fleshy twist of sarcasm.

128

For—such things did happen—were happening more and more. And she remembered Mrs. Matheson's story to her mother. The Mathesons had a forest over towards the seaboard. And Mrs. Matheson told of a neighbouring estate where the daughter of the shooting tenant, in her early twenties, selected each year a different gillie for her amorous needs. Quite openly. Everyone knew about it. The best-looking, most virile type, don't you know.

And the story about the local dance—told by an English chauffeur who had been present, to a gillie when he came back, who told it to the keeper, who told it to the cook, who told it to the lady's maid, who told it to her lady. The poor chauffeur had suffered from an *embarras de richesses* amongst some of the local beauties that could not be experienced, he reckoned, outside certain places in Paris. And so on.

That suggestion of the beginning of demoralisation, perhaps quite localised, perhaps spreading, but in the air. The possibility of that rotten section of London society finding here for a short while a keener air, a more complete irresponsibility. Odd stories even from the Isles, not so much of intromissions with the native stock, as of promiscuities and perversions amongst themselves.

And not all rumours. Quite definite facts. Known facts. That sort of thing—that she knew of in London, that accompanied its social life, like a miasma about decay. What socialists called the canker at the decaying root of capitalist civilisation. And the feeling that haunted her more and more that the socialists were right.

You had to be modern and emancipated and talk about those things in London, of course....

Alick was bound to know about that!

She found herself walking quite quickly.

Sex accompanied a young woman's life, sometimes in a rosy cloud, sometimes as a fire, but sometimes shameful and hateful like *that*. It is her fate! Helen supposed, a flick of angry colour in her cheeks.

Why so annoyed, why so angry?

Her own young body was virgin enough. So virgin that it might be glass. Was that it? A consciousness that she was inexperienced, adolescent? Like that recent quoting of poetry and tears! To-day! Like a Victorian girl with the vapours!

Poetry, old poetry; love, that follows on a woman through the fire! How certain girls she knew would laugh—so sure of themselves, so experienced, so expert in the realities!

A school miss, smiling through her tears at her father's gillie! These girls with their knowing eyes, their conspiracies, their intimacies, their fingers of bright gossip tap-tapping against her breast—with an odd one drawling out a wearied oath or two. Little regard for the men except as puppets in the game, necessary to the game, and therefore to be intrigued about or quarrelled over. And the men...

If the men were real men the women wouldn't...

Stop it! she cried inwardly to herself. Oh, stop it!

For she knew the nature of this attack. She had had it before. It was not that she minded about morality and virtue, she believed. It is not that one should be correct and proper, she passionately alleged to herself. For the appalling thing was that the cry came out of her the more wildly the more it was smothered: I want poetry, love, fire!

She had been in a mood when she could investigate an attack of this kind, turn over its mess with the fingers of her mind, pry into it, and even know a doubtful fascination. Then move out of it, alert a little, but whole and stronger.

Now, however, she felt dispirited, unclean, and could not become her normal self. The inner cry was quite silent.

As she climbed from the river path to a track on the brow of the declivity, she began to feel tired, too, in her body—reaction from the tiredness in her mind. She went in over the grassy bank and lay down, for she had sometimes found that by lying on her back and looking up between leafy branches at the sky her troubles would lift away in forgetfulness. She went, however, reluctantly, for she did not want her misery to be lifted. Her misery was the truth of living, the reality.

The truth is, said a voice far within her, your pride is hurt! She squirmed, under the leaves, shutting her eyes to the sun, to the airy communion of leaves and sun…and heard again the beat, beat in the earth. She peered through the fringe of grass and bracken. Angus was coming along the path, with every sense alert, stealthily. At the bend in the path, opposite to her, he paused, to see round it, then with a quick backward glance went on. She saw that what he was trying to hide was a rifle.

On hands and knees, she crawled a yard or two to the right. He was making for the Lodge.

She found her heart beating painfully, her tiredness gone. Before she knew what she was doing she was following through the trees as swiftly and quietly as she could, until she had to stop or emerge into the open. While she hesitated, Alick came round the larder towards the garage. The two men met, spoke for a few moments, then looked around them with elaborate carelessness, and—there was no one about—went up the stone stairs to the loft, closing the red door behind them.

At once Helen left the trees and went towards the Lodge. This had to be told at once to someone, and the only one was Harry. Otherwise there would be talk, alarm, heaven knew what—as if the whole Lodge were waiting for just some such happening.

She assumed a casual air as she entered at the front door. She went into the sitting-room. Only her mother and father and Marjory were there. Humming, and with a smile for Marjory, she picked up a book and went out—and upstairs. On the landing, she paused. Could Harry be in his bedroom? Listening all ears, she heard nothing, and went along to her own room. She must find Harry and find him alone. She did not care to go to his bedroom, not of course that it mattered a hoot, for she must find him. She looked through her window and listened.

Her heart was beating too strongly. If she went to his bedroom, she might not be able to speak. Besides, she would have to knock.…

A door! She went tip-toe out at her own and saw Harry as he reached the landing. She beckoned him. He stood for a moment, then came towards her. Without a word, she ushered him into her bedroom, and closed the door with such care that it took her a few seconds.

As she turned round, he gazed at her hot, confused expression.

"I—I have something to tell you I don't want the others——" She listened. Then she told him what she had seen.

He whistled softly, looking past her, for he had seen the beat in her throat.

"There's nothing in it, is there?" she whispered.

"No. I shouldn't think so. No." He was trying to collect his wits. It couldn't be that they were secreting a rifle to poach? Obviously not in the daylight. Besides, these fellows never poached—no point in it—and would not from such a centre anyhow. Nothing like that. No.

Helen caught his wrist. The steps came softly along the carpet and into Marjory's room. They smiled to each other in a strained way, then listened without breathing. Marjory's door closed again, and, outside their own door, Marjory paused and said, "Helen?" Helen's grip tightened in the tense silence. Marjory went away.

Helen dropped his wrist, and filled her lungs slowly, and wet her lips. She looked pale, a trifle giddy.

"I didn't want her to know," she said. "She's—I think she's very fond of Geoffrey."

Harry looked at her, his own lungs swelling up.

"Is she?" he muttered.

She nodded, not looking at him. "Now you can go," she said and, opening the door, held on to the knob.

"But—Helen——"

"Go now," she said. "Please."

He breathed heavily, and shrugged, "Oh, all right," and went, forgetting to tread discreetly.

She threw herself on her bed, feeling quite exhausted, and slightly sick.

But the relief of being alone was sweet, oh it was sweet and precious. She felt she could easily go to sleep. But then she had had very little sleep last night. Few of them had had sleep. The whole place was getting a little overwrought. For a few seconds, perhaps minutes, she did lose hold of everything, but very soon she was on her feet again, looking out of the window, fixing her hair, powdering her nose, feeling obscurely happy.

If she met Marjory going downstairs, she could say she had been in the bathroom? A faint humour came into her eyes, as she took the stairs with a cautious carelessness. Out by the front door, and to the right, so as not to pass the sitting-room window. And now it was Harry's turn to beckon—from the fir plantation.

She went with such outward appearance of aimlessness that Harry's smile to her as she arrived was a pleasant tribute. He was quite cool now and friendly. She smiled back, widening her eyes frankly in the inquiring expression of younger days.

"Come here!"

She came quite close to him.

"When I left you," he began, in an amused whisper, "I went down and into the gun-room. An idea had struck me. I looked along the rack for Geoffrey's rifle. It wasn't there."

Her expression opened uncertainly. "You mean—it's Geoffrey's rifle?"

He nodded. "Must have been left on the hill. When Angus didn't come back with George's party, I thought it was because he was frightened of what Geoffrey might say to him. Angus never mentioned the rifle to me—or to anyone. But all the time he knew! So you must have seen him coming back—right from the head of the forest."

"I say!"

He nodded. "That was all that was in it."

"Oh!" Colour came to her face.

He chuckled softly.

"But how was I to know? It looked—so desperate——"

"Quite." He was teasing her in the old way and she felt like giving him a punch in the ribs, but couldn't.

"Go on," he said.

She looked away, with that brilliant glancing expression in her eyes—and put out a hand. He followed her eyes and saw Alick coming down the stone stairs from the loft alone. At the corner of the garage he stood still, and then Angus came down the stairs and walked past him in the direction of the gun-room. They could see only in snatches between the tree trunks, but Angus became clearer as he approached the house, and they observed that the rifle was upright against his off side. Alick began to walk towards the fir wood as Angus disappeared—and reappeared in half a minute without the rifle.

Harry lifted his forefinger, a glimmer of humour in his eyes. "Hsh!" Angus came towards the wood, following Alick. Harry looked about him, caught Helen by the elbow, side-stepped very softly behind an up-rooted pine, and drew her close.

"Shouldn't like Alick to think we had seen them."

She nodded, full of the conspiracy. He kept hold of her elbow, the better to make them both listen.

"That's that!" came Angus's voice, clear in its relief. "Man, wasn't I lucky to find it!" He laughed.

Alick said something they didn't quite catch. But the voices were approaching, and Harry's expression showed apprehension. The two men came to a standstill, secure in the shelter of the plantation, less than a dozen yards away.

Angus was full of the merriment of relief…"the cover was on the rifle, so I laid it against the peat bank behind us and said to him quite distinctly, 'I'll leave the rifle here.' There just is no doubt he knew it was there…. But what's the good of talking? He's that damned thrawn and cocksure. If I had lost the rifle, it was the boot without the option!" He laughed and presently was asking Alick how on earth he had found Mr. Smith.

"I began thinking the thing out. When you lost him, I suppose you whistled?"

"Yes," said Angus.

"After you whistled, you listened. And when you heard nothing, you went on again."

"Yes."

"Supposing he heard your whistle—well, he couldn't whistle back. He doesn't know how to put his fingers in his mouth and whistle. All he could do was shout. And in his rage, he would have shouted so hard the first once or twice that he would have hurt his throat without making much in the way of a carrying sound. After that—it would have been little more than a croak—that fifty yards of mist would have smothered."

"I—see. But——"

"You would have been a peewit, crying in the mist, leading him on—until even your whistle faded out, with no direction in it, or the wrong direction. Leading him on, almost certainly to his death."

"You mean I should have stood?"

"Yes. Whistling from the one spot—until time made you certain he was not hearing. And if you had done that at once——"

"What a fool I was! Lord alive, what a fool! Of course! I see it now!"…

They could hear Angus's feet trampling the pine needles.

"To give him his due, you gave him little chance," said Alick.

"I know." Angus groaned and laughed and swore at himself. "Go on! For heaven's sake, go on and let me forget it!"

"So I saw him setting out after your whistle—the whistle that always went away from him. Would he be angry? Would he follow on blindly, cursing you? But—your whistle would have given him a certain direction. That was something. I tried to see the thing happening. I followed him in my mind…. Our forest is simple enough in its lay-out. You started off from here and came so—and so—until you left the burn that drops into the main glen there, then climbed up to the shoulder here…" Alick was obviously plotting the route. "Very good. He starts off after your whistle. He at last gets a grip of this burn. He is certain that it is going to take him into one of the home glens. He follows it—until he comes here. Then he falls over."

"Did he tell you that?"

"Not he! It's a nasty toss. He decides to lie. There are boulders and tufts of long heather, as you know. Well, he lies. Time passes. He gets very cold. Right to the marrow. He gets afraid—afraid, let us say, of pneumonia. Have you ever listened to a burn in the darkness? The queer sudden belches of sound. Moans and groans."

"Often! Lord, yes! I thought no one had heard it but myself."

"But surely you have heard old hill men talk of the 'hill voices', the voices that no one has ever been able to explain. You hear them coming up, passing you, and going away, quite distinctly—especially in mist."

"Yes," said Angus. "I have heard them myself."

"Well, supposing *he* heard them? The burn beside him goes tumbling past boulders, and then—sheer over—far below him. He decides to climb up again. Madness, of course. Madness for anyone to move in a darkness like that, except perhaps ourselves, who know that the lay-out of our forest is very simple. Except for some corries and all the west side of Benuain, we have no sheer rocks or precipices much. However, there are some nasty corries, and one of them is just there. He climbs up. He comes on and on. Very slowly. Hands and knees, like an animal, cursing occasionally to drown the noises—until at last he comes round the shoulder of Coirecheathaich, under the impression of course that he is giving a wide berth to the falls of the burn, for he has a confused picture of the main glen in his mind. But he has been keeping too far up. He's afraid of another fall. And he's in pain. Well, in time he hits the small stream in the foot of the corrie. Now as you know, if he had gone up the stream, he would have come right out over the top, quite smooth and clean, then downhill anyway he liked until at last he would fetch the path by the Corr. Nothing but soft bog holes and muck to trouble him. He could have rolled down half the way. But he's not going to do that. Why? Because he has found a stream and a stream now must flow homewards. Sound reasoning—which the short-cut that the stream takes over the cliff wall at the foot of the corrie does not affect, of course."

Angus laughed.

"So I decided," said Alick, his unhurried voice quiet and dry as when he began, "to head him off. I took the long shepherd's crook and had to fumble often enough. But there's no danger on the Corr route. The only difficulty was in getting into the corrie. I was lost once completely, I thought. However, it turned out I wasn't. I took up my position some little way back from the cliff and beside the burn."

"And he came?"

"In time, yes. If I hadn't been expecting him, God knows I would have been frightened enough. I don't blame him for the sounds that came from him now and then. And to have come so far, he had real guts. He had to keep going, to fight things back, keep them off. The thought of death rode him."

Harry and Helen glanced at each other.

"You mean—he was——"

"He was frightened, anyway, and all jumpy, and angry—regular bad mix-up. When he was so near that I heard the gasps of his breath, I thought it was time to say something. So I addressed him quietly by name."

"Lord almighty!" said Angus.

"He let out a squawk. Perhaps I should have shouted to him earlier. I don't know. If I had, he might have turned and made off. If it had been your voice, it would not have been so bad. Any voice but mine. I had to touch him—to show him I was real. He gave a yell and let out. He hit me there—in the neck—and all but knocked me out. I sagged, like a shot stag. But I gripped him before he got much farther. 'Don't be a bloody fool!' I yelled at him. I was very angry and had him on his back before it dawned on him that I was there in the flesh. So he came round to common sense. But it was not pleasant for a little while after that."

A wild chuckle came out of Angus.

"I knew it couldn't be far from the dawn. So I made him lie down. He did not speak for a long time. Then he asked if you were home. Then he cursed you—and was silent. Out of him I felt an awful hatred coming towards me. To tell the truth, I did not care for him much myself. I began to feel I could throw him over the cliff. So I went a little bit from him and lay on my back. The dawn came in and I made no move. Neither did he. After that, both of us may have dozed off a bit—or got into that state, you know, where you're cold and miserable and think you're awake all the time, but maybe you're not. Anyway, the time came when we started. We hardly spoke. He was very stiff and could hardly walk. We got over the off side of the corrie. I saw it would be easier for him to slide on his bottom down the very steep slope beyond the rocks into the main glen, than tackle the climb and the soft ground down to the Corr. And once he was on the track, I could leave him to get on with it. He was in no hurry, I tell you! We never spoke—not even when the mist rolled away and you whistled."

"He must know you saved him from certain death?"

"I doubt it."

"But if you hadn't been there and he had gone on, he would have gone over the lip with the long heather, head first, and could never have saved himself. Never, absolutely."

"And you would have been to blame!"

"Ay," said Angus, soberly. "You saved me that, I know."

"Hmf! I don't know what it is. In many ways he's a decent fellow. Not caring for your feelings and jealous and all that— but still, more decent than most of them. I've had army bullies and slave-drivers and bastards of one kind or another who treat you like dirt. Oh I don't know. That fellow will never like me now."

"I wouldn't say that. When things are going his own way, he'll crow; and when he's sure that you see he's right and you're wrong, he's all right again. Then he laughs. It's a great joke!"

"He'll carry a joke too far—one day."

There was silence for quite a time. Helen and Harry felt this silence coming out of Alick's quiet voice, like some moody conviction of fatality.

"Ah well, to hell," said Angus, "it's all over. I was talking to Lachie from Screesval. They're going over to dinner there to-morrow night. So Lachie was saying what about the lads from Screesval and Corbreac and anywhere else meeting at the inn for an evening of it. What about it?"

"I'll see," said Alick, in a moody tone.

"Oh, come on! Why not? Take your fiddle, too. Damn it, we need something now and then...."

But Alick did not answer and their footsteps and Angus's eager voice died away.

Harry and Helen glanced at each other.

"They have him taped," said Harry.

"What an awful scene that must have been in the corrie!"

"Bit gruesome, what!" Harry's lips twisted. There was a strange light in his eyes as they roved between the tree-trunks.

Helen's whole body gave a spasmodic shudder.

"When you think that Alick must have remembered—his own vision!" said Harry. "Talk of the possibilities of automatic, hypnotic action! The deadly hatred. And he saved his life!"

"You still believe in that vision?"

"Looks to me as if we're going to be forced to believe in it. It's an extraordinary thing that's taking place. It's something in Geoffrey's spirit—I don't know what it is—something that disintegrates. I saw its effect last season on Alick once. His may be the advanced sort of analytic mind that we're not ready for. He disintegrates—without integrating. But ordinary human nature—cannot stand much of it. Oh, that may be all rot, but I'll tell you a thing I was reading in that deer-forest book the other night. I had heard of it before. But the other night I saw something in it, saw it suddenly illuminated—in a way the writer never thought of, I bet!"

"You know the old stuff about how the people were cleared out of their homes all over the Highlands, to make way for sheep that paid the landlords better? Then Scrope and Landseer and Charles St. John and these boys got going and advertised deer-stalking to such an extent that deer-forest rentals rose to three times the sheep rentals. So exit sheep—which was a good thing for landlords, as the sheep-racket had begun to go bankrupt. In course of time the deer forests began to deteriorate, too. *Nouveaux riches*, annual rentals, shooting of best heads, of young stags not mature, leaving the wasters and the rubbish and so on— which is the position to this day. However, some time ago there was great concern about this and a few landlords thought, why not bring back virility to these poor Highland red deer, bring back heavy bodies and good heads—particularly, good heads, by introducing some English park deer. So they tried, and it was a ghastly failure."

Helen looked at him. "Why?"

"In the first place, the whole idea was wrong. The Highland red deer has a noble history direct from palaeolithic times. He has fended for himself in the wilds, without artificial feeding or help of any kind from man. He has indeed lived through ages of being hunted by man, adapting himself to every change. Deer are naturally woodland animals. So were the old red deer. They love woods yet. But when the woods that covered all this land were destroyed by man, the red deer took to the open, to the hills. That's the type of the beast. Sensitive, quick, swift like the wind, living by the wind—he'll smell you a mile off; in and out the mist, like an apparition, proud and game to the last gasp when he's cornered. Oh I saw him this morning on the top of Benbeg. He was beautiful, Helen. O God he was! I'm talking too much. Let us sit down."

They sat down on the bare trunk near the upended root. "Am I talking too much?" he asked, without looking at her, an awkwardness in his voice.

"Please go on," she said quietly.

"We had come up out of the mist—all that horror of the night's mist—right into the sunlight, pure sunlight under a blue sky. It was the most beautiful emergence into light— that I have ever known. And I have this strange sort of feeling about it, too, that I'll yet see it still better—I somehow even feel it more at this minute than I did.... I'm getting muddled. Forgive me. We lay down to rest there. Angus touched me with his hand. I turned my head and there was King Brude—standing just clear of the mist, in the sun. Stags on each side of him on the edge of the mist, and heads—heads—back into the mist, staring out of it like ghosts. An extraordinary sight. I'll never forget it."

"This morning?"

"Yes. But it was King Brude that—that gave the whole thing—I don't know what. Distinction, nobility—in the wild native state. Impossible to explain. It's not so much his size or weight. He's certainly not twenty stone. But the throw forward of his power from his haunches to his breast and neck and head; the magnificent poise of his head, and—crowning all—the antlers. I have seen, I should think, pretty nearly all sorts of heads—royals and imperials of every formation. But I have never before seen a head that gave me so direct a thrill. In my royal, one of the second or bay tines is missing. Authorities say that the loss of the bay tines shows decline from perfect form. Perhaps they're right. And bay tines are far more often missing than not, in the Highlands nowadays. I'm coming to that. But King Brude has both bay tines. The balance of the head is superb, the black colour, the sheer arching loveliness of the span—the most thrilling example I have ever seen, in any collection or book, of what is called "wind-blown". For when you come to the last fork in each antler, and the last two tines reach over to the other two and yet up—long delicate points 'blown', as it were, by the wind—Lord, it puts the heart across you. It's pure creation of the mountains and the hill winds—or am I talking balderdash or what?"

"You make me see it," she said softly. "Please go on."

"Where was I?" He smiled. "I was going to make a point or something—but the antlers seem to have knocked it out of my head. What was I talking about?"

"You were talking about deer forests and their deterioration and——"

"Yes. I remember. Only—I don't know that I want to make it now. It seems so damned priggish."

"Please do. I think I'll understand."

"Well, it was this deterioration. Introduction of English park deer. Had to be hand-fed in the winter. Then hand-feeding of native stock to keep the numbers of rubbish up. Stalking and

141

shooting hand-fed beasts. And so the rot went on—and goes on. And suddenly my mind switched over and applied all this to the native human stock—to a fellow like Alick who is, spiritually, the king of his kind. Now I know we English are capable of the most appalling complacency. For heaven's sake, don't misunderstand me. There is a social life in London that you and I know is rotten beyond all redemption. Some of its elements come here and spread the plague about. And there are always the well-entrenched slave-drivers, the pukka bullies, for whom killing as a sport is everything all the time. I'm not referring to all that, nor to degenerate Cockneys or Highlanders. It's to something far less obvious than that, something infinitely more subtle. It's awful when a thought is biting you and you can't grip it. I'm talking an awful lot. But what I'm trying to say is that—that in a fellow like Alick—oh, I know he's moody and could be brutal and dangerous—but still there is in him, in his spirit, a quality, a delicacy, a vision, that is the counterpart of the wind-blown antlers on King Brude. Not many of them have it, let us say. There are not many King Brudes. Dying out. The bay tines are going. And in the end—King Brude will go into the mist for ever, and Alick will be driven forth."

Harry shut his mouth, for the last words had come from him in a way that stopped any self-excusing addition of talking "awful rot". His face was serious, with something of sadness and irony and intolerance, as Helen glanced at it—and glanced away at once. Out of the silence she said simply:

"I'm glad you spoke like that, Harry. I'm very glad."

"Oh, well—perhaps it's this place. I don't know. But sometimes—I feel it sort of getting me. Dashed if I can understand it. Do you think it's the place?"

"I think so," she said slowly. "I think it must be."

"Sort of puts one on edge somehow. I'm not given to analysis and that, normally. I mean I detest the morbid. Heaven save me from anything of the kind. I should loathe——"

"Naturally. But you're not fair there."

"How do you mean?"

"Well, you know quite well it's not morbid. You know it's the very opposite of morbid. You said, for example, that your mind was illumined. You talked about emerging into the light. It's light. Light—in which you see things."

"I say, that's pretty clever, Helen! Really—pretty clever. Uhm." Eyes in front, he nodded, a trifle excited. "You know, when you're stalking, this business of light is quite remarkable. You're spying out a corrie that's in shadow—glassing the whole place with the greatest care—not a living thing. Then the shadow passes, and the light comes, and there are stags and hinds, amongst the boulders, the clumps of heather, with the light on their brown coats turning them reddish, all alive. You would hardly credit it unless you had actually done it."

"I wonder," she said, after a moment.

"What?"

"Is it my turn for getting light? I suddenly have the idea that perhaps all this Celtic business—you know—the Celtic mind—is an affair of the atmosphere over this land: light and shadow, swift transitions, mist and rain, tones, such soft lovely tones, and flowing lines."

"Not Gaelic or Celtic so much, you mean, as a property of the atmosphere over this land? Like the atmosphere over the peat-bogs of Ireland or the Connemara hills? It's so like the thing, that I doubt it. But—it's exciting! There's something there!"

"I do feel excited," said Helen.

"Do you? So do I."

"It's this *seeing*…"

"Uhm. Sort of second sight all on its own!"

"Yes."

He turned his head and looked at her. But she did not meet his look. Her eyes were so brilliant that the points of her lashes seemed dark and wet. Her skin was very vivid.

A surge came into his throat that stopped him speaking. The sound of his swallow was quite audible. She jumped to her feet, "Come along," and walked away.

He could not move. From a little distance, she turned half-round. He got up, but she did not wait for him till she was out of the wood.

Chapter Eight

"Mr. Smith has just rung, ma'm. He begs to be excused for not coming down to dinner."

"Oh. All right, Mairi. You will see that his dinner is properly served in his room."

As Mairi withdrew, Lady Marway turned to her husband. "I think you had better go up and see him. Ask if there is anything in particular he needs."

In a very short time, Sir John was back.

"Says he is feeling very tired. Didn't sound as if he wanted to talk much."

"Anything really wrong with him?"

"He assured me there is not. Said he fell on his right side and hurt it a bit. Purely muscular."

"A bit moody, is he?"

"Well—I don't know. He's just in the mood not to be bothered. Natural enough."

Lady Marway sat thoughtfully silent.

Sir John gave her a side glance, and then looked at the old cannibal trout in its glass case.

"Nothing worrying you, is there?" he asked.

"No, not exactly. What makes you think so?"

"Nothing. Only I suppose it is natural enough that we should have been worried over Geoffrey. He's all right now, however. Feeling a trifle sorry for himself, perhaps."

"I know. Geoffrey is like the boy who must harry a thing to death—or at least break it up to prove to you that what is inside is not what you imagined. In that respect he has never quite grown up. What date is it?"

"It's the nineteenth, I think. Yes."

She sat quite still. "He goes at the end of the month. Then Ernest and Betty come up. I like Geoffrey, but this time I shall be rather relieved when he goes."

"I hope you haven't been really upset."

"Not really. It's—rather vague. But I just feel that way."

"You are not", he said in an expressionless voice, "getting tired of this place?"

"No."

"You're quite sure?"

"Yes." There was silence for a time. Then she said. "It was my idea as much as yours—more than yours, perhaps. All that happened to us happened in India. All that was exciting in our lives—in my life certainly. When we got back to London, I thought—now life at last can be secure. Then I began to miss India, especially the nights, and particularly—how strange human nature is!—the nights in which I had been terrified. Those nights up country are a very vivid memory. That night, with the cries in the forest and the servants prowling about outside. I was very frightened that night."

"You were quite certain I was not coming back!"

"I was. And it was that night I realised…. I could never quite tell you. A young wife is naturally enough in love, I suppose. And we have our emotions for expression. But it was more than that. It was a rather terrifying experience, inside me. The terror gripped me—gripped my bones—and it gripped me *with your fingers*. I can give you no idea of it. I do not know yet how I managed to control myself. For what I wanted to do was to catch up a spear and go away and find you and—and kill anyone who…. In a way I was mad—quite beside myself."

"Thank God, you didn't do that, anyway. And I had begged you not to come up on that trip."

"I suppose I was in love with you then. Or thought I was—until that night."

"You were very lovely, Eve. And you can have no idea—what a responsibility!"

Then he turned quietly to her, stooped, caught her right hand and kissed it, and, without a word, resumed his original position.

"The awful thing about you, Jack, is—that you could always—do a thing like that." She smiled, but her lips were pressed together and her eyes were bright.

"Fortunately for me, your fears were groundless."

"That is not quite fair. You know perfectly well there was deadly danger that night. You got through it because of your character—the image of you in the native mind. You may not understand that. I do. However, all that only came into my mind because of what you said about being up here. Far from being tired of this place, I love it. London, I'm afraid, would drag without the autumn here—somehow it is the true autumn to our summer. And it has, in a way, the same sort of strange foreignness."

"How well you do contrive to put a thing! You were always clever at that."

"About Geoffrey—I do not want to be unfair—but I wish sometimes he could contrive to leave a slightly different image in the native mind. That's all."

"But—I say—that's..." Sir John smiled. "I am just a little afraid that you are allowing your imagination, over a certain matter, to get the better of you—very slightly, of course."

"Possibly. And imagination, as Geoffrey might say, isn't a scientific entity."

"That's better!"

"You do me a lot of good, my dear, frequently—or at least, occasionally."

"I'm glad to be of service at any time."

"You can have no idea—no man ever has—the amount of good a little talk does a woman." She picked up her tapestry frame and regarded it critically. "I think now I can risk a slightly brighter shade of red."

"Don't plunge too rashly."

"Because you never plunged rashly, you mustn't come to conclusions on the matter."

"Agreed. My failing, but I never could plunge rashly."

"No. You just calmly plunged." She added quietly, "I like this break, too, for Helen."

"She does seem to enjoy it."

"Yes." She nodded. "I suppose you see what's going on."

"What do you mean?"

She turned the frame over and pulled the thread through, "With Harry," and tightened it.

"Oh—with Harry!" That was an old story. His concern eased, for he was very fond of his daughter.

"I would rather this background—if it's got to be—than London. Young women nowadays—they're very modern. Cocktails and midnight parties and so on. Quite different from our time. They are emancipated. Like Joyce."

"I like Joyce," he said. "I must say I do. I like her bright modern ways."

"So do I like Joyce. The open frank manner is a healthy advance. That's obvious enough. I still happen to think that too much drink and too many late nights aren't good for anyone, particularly for young girls. But it's not quite that that I mean. After all, no age ever has a monopoly of social looseness. There are decadent periods—always have been. Take India—away back nearly thirty years ago, when you and I knew it first—well, you know what went on. You knew one of the reasons why I wanted to be with you, if it was humanly possible. You knew all about it, didn't you?"

"Yes."

"Our experience of human nature has been too wide to leave us narrow-minded, at least I hope so. We had our own terrors and troubles—and tragedy—too."

"That's so."

It was friendly, talking like this. Such talk always happened quite naturally and at unpredictable times. Sir John experienced a curious sensation of the suspension of time while it went on, and his wife's speech flowed quietly and naturally, as if out of some wide, still lake of reminiscence.

Woman's talk, a form of remembering; and, listening to it, he felt lapped about.

"Well," said Lady Marway, "I don't know, but I should like to think that Helen—who must know far more about life than you imagine—I should like to think that Helen got some feeling about what matters, what really matters and what remains, when social fashions have come and gone, in the way I did. A little like that. Something she will be able to hang on to, when things begin sliding round about her, as they will, something that will keep her steady. Do you know a little thing that made an extraordinary impression on me? Remember your little pocket compass that you had fixed to the other end of your watch chain?"

"I remember how you laughed that first time—and how very even and white your teeth were."

"It seemed so incredible a toy. No matter how you turned it, the pointer always remained true to the north. It seemed pure magic. And to tell the truth, I still don't really understand how it does it, though you've explained more than once."

"But, my dear, it is so simple. The earth, you see, is a magnet. Now if you——"

The door opened and Helen and Marjory came in, ready for dinner, and listened to Sir John finishing his elementary explanation of the working of a compass.

"Perhaps so. But I still find it difficult imagining the earth as a magnet."

"But why bother imagining it?" asked Sir John. "It simply is so."

"I suppose so," said Lady Marway.

They all laughed. Harry came in, followed by George, and, a minute later, by Joyce.

The discussion on the compass became animated and exploded now and then in bursts of laughter.

Dinner was a pleasant affair, and afterwards the party were in such good spirits that, when the newspapers had been dealt with and comments on the international situation exchanged, Joyce suggested they should have a game.

Groans were immediately produced, but of such exaggerated a nature that Joyce took the floor. Lady Marway
looked at her in slight apprehension, for Joyce, with her
bodily exuberance and forthrightness, could be almost
alarmingly inept. She was quite capable without a thought
of suggesting the latest fashionable form of the murder
game.

But that night they did not learn the nature of the game,
for as Joyce was about to explain, the door opened and
Geoffrey appeared in a blue silk dressing-gown.

The hearty nature of the welcome he received clearly
took him by surprise. His face, though newly shaved, looked
pale and haggard. He smiled in that strained, slightly embarrassed way that goggled his eyes, and made his excuses to
Lady Marway for his dressing-gown, as, with the aid of his
stick, he came forward and let himself into a comfortable
chair. "I thought I'd try this side of mine by coming downstairs," he explained to Sir John. "But, I'm afraid, it's no use
for to-morrow."

"That's bad luck. You must have got rather a nastyone?"

"Yes, it wasn't too good. I fell sheer—I don't know how
many feet. However, it's nothing really. Merely bruised a
bit."

"You're quite sure of that, Geoffrey?" Lady Marway asked,
looking closely at him. "Now you'll have a drink," she said,
and at once got up and poured him a stiff whisky.

"Thank you very much," said Geoffrey. "Though it's soon
enough after food, what?"

"All the food you ate won't make much difference."

"I say!" Geoffrey protested.

"Merely an efficient staff. I was informed that you had
eaten hardly anything."

Geoffrey gave an echo of his old laugh.

The other faces sat around, with an unconscious smile,
looking at Geoffrey, who would now tell his story.

And he started in an off-hand manner, as if it hadn't
much importance, apart from one or two idiotic things that
were done. "What Angus wanted to stay away an hour for,

149

I don't know. I naturally thought he had fallen into a hole. I became concerned about him, and set off."

"Didn't he shout or anything?" George asked.

"I don't know if he shouted. But I did hear a whistle. I shouted back. No answer. Then I set off in the direction of the whistle. He might have been in difficulties or anything. The staff was very helpful, for you could see just absolutely nothing when it got dark. Then I heard the whistle again—but farther away than ever. It really did annoy me. I struggled on. I struck a stream. I thought it might be the upper reach of that tributary of the Corr where it swings in round towards Benuain. The going was painfully slow, of course. But you develop a way of poking your staff in front of you. You hear the water trickling. I was getting very tired— and careless, I suppose. Anyway, my staff poked into nothing and I went after it before I could stop myself. The fall badly shook me, and I decided to stick where I was until morning. I got frightfully cold. I was sure I knew where I was now because of the falls below me. There are no falls on the Corr. The weird sounds of the water came swirling up. I got desperately cold, and I reasoned that it would be better to move anywhere than sit until I got pneumonia. So I climbed back—a very ticklish job." Geoffrey paused and took a mouthful of whisky.

"Jove, you were plucky!" said George.

"In time I struck another burn. This troubled me. However, it was going in the right direction. But I had no staff now. I had lost it in the fall. You scramble about. The mind naturally gets strung up. My side was painful. And then, when I was feeling absolutely all in, a voice quite close spoke my name." Geoffrey eased himself in his chair.

"Alick?" said Sir John.

Geoffrey nodded, and looked at Sir John with a hard glittering eye. "Would you have believed, in my position, that it could have been—that fellow, of all people? And if only the idiot had given me warning, anything! Instead, a hand came down on me! There was a bit of a struggle... However, it appears it was all right. So I decided to wait until the dawn came before going any farther. I was warm enough now." He gave a wry smile and finished his drink.

"Did you question him?" asked Sir John.

"A bit," said Geoffrey. "He said that if I had gone on another fifty yards I should have gone over a cliff or something like that. It was very kind of him, even if I had made up my mind not to go over any more cliffs."

"Wait a bit," said Sir John, and he went into the gun-room followed by all except Lady Marway and Geoffrey. Yes, the map made it clear. Geoffrey had gone round the slow slope and into Coirecheathaich. There was a cliff at the lower end of it, with boulders at its foot.

"But how could he possibly have known that Geoffrey would take that route?" Joyce asked as they left the map. "I mean—the thing is weird!"

"Beats Stanley in Africa hollow," said George. "If only he had had the wit to remark out of the darkness, 'Mr. Smith, I presume?' the thing would have been complete."

"I think he's uncanny," said Joyce. "Pfoo!"

"I don't think so," said Geoffrey.

"But——"

"Surely the whole matter", said Helen, "is quite simple. I bet five bob I'll explain it to anyone's satisfaction in a few words."

"Done!" said George.

"Angus returned and told Alick the general lie of things." She tipped off her thumb. "Alick argues that if Geoffrey follows suit, the only real danger is this corrie with its cliff. He decides to go there to intercept him. If he doesn't come this way, it doesn't matter. If he does—he'll be stopped on the right side of death. O.K.?" And she tipped off her little finger.

They all gazed at her. It seemed so simple and reasonable.

"Oh, but look here," said George. "Geoffrey could have gone any way, any point of the compass. Let us be realistic. I am not satisfied."

"But," said Harry, "surely Alick was very realistic, for the chances were that Geoffrey would come this way."

"Now," said Geoffrey sceptically, "how exactly do you make that out?"

"Because", said Harry, "you did come this way."

"Isn't that", said Geoffrey, "a mere arguing after the event?"

"What else is the scientific determinism to which you pin your faith? Presumably the causal factors that combined to make you come the way you did were stronger than all other factors. Isn't that the idea?"

"I put it to the vote of the meeting," cried Helen. "Does George owe me five bob or not? I'll have a show of hands, please."

"I object," said Geoffrey. He looked hard at Helen. "Have you had access to special information?"

Despite herself, she flushed. "Special information?"

Geoffrey smiled with dry triumph. "It merely isn't supposed to be good sportsmanship to bet on a certainty."

"But—but," stammered Helen, "I spoke to no one about it."

"Did anyone speak to you?" Geoffrey asked.

"No."

"I smell a quibble," said Marjory.

Geoffrey laughed.

"You are not very good at dissembling, my child," said her mother. "Tell us about it."

"I merely overheard a few remarks, from which I saw what happened. I refuse to say any more."

"Do I owe you five bob?" asked George.

"If you are as mean as that about it, I wouldn't touch your filthy money."

"Loud and prolonged applause," cried George. "Hip-hip-hooray!"

Voices spoke at once, and Sir John's gaunt face smiled down upon them.

"There's Maclean, I think," said Lady Marway.

Sir John opened the gun-room door, greeted Maclean, and hoped he had not been kept waiting.

When Sir John returned and asked about the morning, George's voice rose above the others with the suggestion that,

Geoffrey being so inconvenienced, he was prepared to take his place, "Do or die!"

"And I'll be your gillie," cried Joyce. "What a splendid idea!" Immediately she became loud and enthusiastic.

George glanced at Sir John.

"And here, Helen—what about you accompanying Harry?" Joyce demanded. "Why not?"

Helen took a moment, then shook her head, smiling.

"But," said Joyce, "why not? Is it implied that women couldn't stalk as well as men? What's the big idea present?" And she looked round.

"The idea," said Geoffrey, "is that this is a deer forest, not a sea-side resort." Then his suppressed laugh came through, more loudly than it had done that night, as if he were beginning to be pleased with himself again.

"What an impertinence!" said Joyce.

"He's merely frightened," said George, "that I'll bag King Brude. He's afraid of beginner's luck. And I tell him now to his face, that I'll leave no avenue unexplored, no stone unturned, to achieve my ends."

This dramatic declamation was applauded.

Joyce went up to Sir John. "May I accompany George—for this one day?"

Sir John smiled to her. "I see no reason why you shouldn't."

"Helen—are you going to let your sex down?" demanded Joyce.

"I'm afraid so."

"Dirty dog. As for you, Geoffrey, I think you are a worm."

Sir John's smile broke into a soft laugh.

This sort of talk went on for quite a time, any uncomfortable suggestion being hilariously drowned, until Joyce said:

"Why surprised? Wasn't she prepared to take money under false pretences?"

"I wasn't, then," said Helen. "I gave you an explanation which you could not refute. And you wangled yourselves out of it."

"Really?" said Geoffrey.

"Yes, really," said Helen.

"I thought you admitted having overheard some remarks, by your local friends, who were privy to what happened?"

"I know what you thought," said Helen, "but you were wrong."

"Helen, child!" said her mother.

"Well, they are trying to make out that I was betting on a certainty."

"And weren't you?" asked Geoffrey.

"Yes," said Helen.

Loud laughter.

"Only," said Helen, "it was not *that* certainty."

The room grew quiet. Joyce scratched her head. "I'm bogged."

"Hush!" said George. "Dramatic pause."

"I think it's time," said Lady Marway sensibly, "that we were all in bed. Especially you, Geoffrey." She got up.

Geoffrey heaved himself to his feet, staggered, and gripped his side. "Phew, a stitch!" he exclaimed, and sat down. "Nothing at all. No. Please." After a little time, he got to his feet again. "That's better. Thanks," he said to George who picked up his staff. He wiped his forehead.

"Let us give you a hand," offered George.

"Rubbish. Sitting too long in the one position. Or perhaps", he said, turning his face to Helen, "I was pierced by a premonition of a forthcoming reference to second sight." His laugh was heard as a bark and he made for the door.

Harry found it difficult to get to sleep. The secret excitement that nothing could intrude upon, that nothing could damp, was still within him, and not only in his mind but running through his blood, in his hands, in his restless legs. I'll never get to sleep! he thought. And though he did fall asleep, he awoke with the same feeling of alertness, and when he was at last shaved and dressed, he stood quite still on the floor of his room, more uncomfortably in the grip of his excitement than ever.

Joyce's voice floated up from below.

He took a deep breath, gripped the stair rail, and, knowing he was behaving with madness, began tiptoeing towards Helen's door.

He arrived, choked with excitement, caught the knob. It made a noise, but his rigid grasp kept turning it. He pushed the door open and stepped into her room.

Helen was sitting up in bed, all eyes. He tried to smile as he approached her. It was a ghastly effort and for a moment he could not speak. Then he whispered, "Will you come to-day?"

He saw her breast heave. She nodded. At once he turned and left the room, drawing the door nearly shut, not closing it, went along the corridor, and ran down the stairs.

Out on the path to the Corr beat, this little incident afforded them considerable amusement.

"What really did you think when you saw me come in?"

"I was beyond thinking."

They both laughed as they strode side by side at some little distance behind Alick and Donald and the pony.

"I was frightfully nervous," said Harry. "I'm sure I must have looked an awful ass. I really didn't know what to do. It was on my mind—Joyce having asked you—and I never said a word. It occurred to me once or twice during the night. I wondered—what you thought."

"I—I really never thought," said Helen. Then her eyes sparkled. "I'm sorry your conscience was troubled."

"It wasn't my conscience," said Harry.

"No?"

"No."

They laughed.

"Isn't it a divine morning?" cried Helen. "Feel the touch of frost? And the mists, clearing off the tops, look! Do you think there's any place in the world so marvellous on a morning like this?"

"The colours."

"I know," Helen nodded. "The blues and purples and high-up greens in a suave wash—for miles. A colour photograph would look like a sentimental fake. Have you noticed that?"

"Yes. Like those postcards, the large coloured views, bought in bookshops in little Highland towns. They look fantastically unreal."

"And they're not. Extraordinary. Except, of course, that they don't give you the sense of breadth and strength. This—this exhilaration," said Helen.

"Do you feel it tingling through you?"

"Yes. Do you?"

"Yes."

They laughed.

"Look at that," said Harry, as the mists curled away from the throat of Benbeg. "Does look like lace round a throat, doesn't it? Sort of night-dress effect."

"I think that's a trifle far-fetched."

"Is it?"

There was silence for a moment; then their eyes met and glanced away.

"You looked pretty well really," said Harry.

"Did I? When?"

"This morning."

"Oh. I say, look at the perspective opening up off there. Into infinity. Withdrawing the curtain—to reveal what?"

Harry did not speak.

"I think autumn is the best time, the most lovely time," Helen prattled on. "It *should* be spring. But there is something in autumn on a morning like this. A spirit moving somewhere. No, not moving; waiting and listening and—near. Do you feel something like that?"

"Yes."

"Jumps right on the heart—*quick!*—like that. And you could do anything; sing or—or cry. Have you felt it like that ever?"

"You're enchanting me again."

Helen kept her eyes in front. "Harry, don't spoil it."

"Sorry."

"Please—please don't spoil it." There was a pleading, passionate note in her voice.

"I'm sorry, Helen."

"Don't be sorry—like that."

"All right, Helen, forgive me. I merely have an urge to spoil it. I can't help it."

"Don't think me unreasonable."

"I can't think of you at all. I wish I could. I'll be more reliable if we're talking of something else."

"And that spoils it too."

"Does it?"

Their eyes met and they all but laughed.

"What did you think of last night?" Helen asked. "I mean about the bet. Did you think I was quibbling badly?"

"No. You were merely making a game of it. It was Geoffrey who tore it."

"I wasn't quibbling really. Did you wonder afterwards what I meant by saying it was not *that* certainty?"

"To confess the truth, I didn't. I thought about something else."

"Did you?" She looked round at him.

"Afraid I did." He smiled enigmatically.

"Oh," she said, and looked ahead. "I thought you might have wondered. What I meant was that Alick did not work out the factors quite in the way I suggested first. He *saw* the thing happening."

"You mean—he had second sight of it?"

"No. Something between. I can't express the state. A certainty so strong that it becomes visualised. I can only vaguely grasp it myself. But—oh it's no good trying to make sense."

"That's extremely interesting," said Harry. "I vaguely follow. Perhaps there are degrees in seeing. Although, wait! Can there really be degrees in seeing? Surely you must either see or you don't?"

"You can imagine you see?"

"Wait, again! You mean there may be different ways of arriving at seeing? That is, you can have an involuntary vision—the real second sight—like Alick's; or Alick might have sat there beside Angus, after he had put him to sleep, and by sheer concentration, in a half-dream state, have seen Geoffrey walking?"

"Yes," said Helen eagerly. "Something like that. Isn't it remarkable how one's mind develops an understanding of that sort of thing? You get a kind of light. And Harry, look!— look at the light on the water in the burn!… Do you know, sometimes I can sit by a burn like that and feel it pour past me and through me. I cannot describe the sensation of intimacy. There is a free fresh loveliness in it, a delight, full of light. And sometimes a cunning delight, full of fun. The bubbles sailing past, and the water, the clear or deep-brown warm and cool water, like velvet. See the bubbles, the little bright bubbles, being kicked up by the heels of something passing over that stone? See how they sparkle? Darlings, aren't they?"

"Of course, Helen, you'll have to be careful that you don't——"

Helen laughed outright. "Because I called the bubbles darlings!" Her mirth was delicious. She was so sane, so elusive, oh sweet heaven so attractive! Harry's heart turned over in him.

"Helen—don't spoil it."

"Sorry."

"Don't say you're sorry—like that."

"Harry," said Helen, "I doubt if there's one dancing bubble such a darling as yourself. However, that's by the way. What——"

"I have an awful feeling in me that you'll pay for this— and pay dearly."

"I've stopped betting."

"Humff!"

"Humff."

Suppressed noises came from her throat.

Harry looked grim.

"Oh Harry," said Helen, "isn't it just heaven to be alive?"

"You seem to forget hell."

"How divine of you to come for me! And you looked— such a frightened, awkward boy."

"I put the heart across you, anyway."

"Faith and you did." Nothing could subdue her mirth. "So please don't do it again."

"Don't worry."

"Not without warning, anyway."

He stopped and regarded her back, as she moved on humming an air. She stopped, turned, and raised her eyebrows. "Anything wrong?"

As he came on, she kept time to his deliberate steps: "Grumf! grumf! grumf! grumf!"

But what he was going to say or do was obliterated by a roar that came rumbling out of the hill-side. It was the forest roar of a lion, a deep-throated fearsome sound. Helen stood looking up at Benbeg. She knew what it was. It was the stag's challenge. The mating season had begun.

"What a terrifying sound!"

"Sounds as if he meant it," Harry answered. There was a disturbing male sarcasm in his voice. Helen ignored it. Alick and Donald were waiting for them. As they came up, Alick said, "It's the twentieth of September. In Gaelic they call it the Day of the Roaring." The quiet, half-humoured expression was on his face. They all stood together, looking up at the hills. From far in towards Benuain came another roar, much less in volume, but with an added impressiveness from distance. And then the first roar was repeated.

"I think", said Alick, "that he is in Coireglas. Hinds like that corrie for the flat of green grass in its lower end. You'll often find a few of them there in the morning and evening."

"Do you think we should make for it?" Harry asked.

"I think we should."

"Right!" He looked at the sky, but after the dispersal of the mist it was innocent of cloud. However, there was a distinct air of wind. "It should blow into the corrie from the main glen?"

"Yes," said Alick, "at a slant. Towards the middle of the corrie on the south side"—he drew the narrowed horse-shoe formation of the corrie with Harry's staff—"it is steep, with some rocks, just here. If the wind is coming at that slant, as I think it is, then it hits this steep point and swirls round the back of the corrie and along the north side—to meet the incoming wind again."

"Which means," said Harry, "that if we tried to do things along the north side we are liable to have our scent carried on the back eddy?"

Alick nodded. Harry explained to Helen how, though moving against the general direction of the wind, one can run into a betraying eddy going the opposite way—dead into the wind. "Interesting, isn't it?"

"Yes," she said. "Very. Are you going after the stag that roared?"

"Yes,—but, of course, you never know."

"Quite. I see."

They all moved on, until at last Alick stopped Donald and told him to wait with the pony for further directions to be given by signal.

"Aren't you coming?" Harry, turning round, asked Helen.

"I don't think I should. I'll just be in the way."

"No, you won't. This is your day."

"Oh, I don't think so. You have your stalk."

Harry looked at her. "You mean you would rather not?"

She nodded. "Yes." Harry still looked at her, uncertain of her motive, for she was capable of denying herself in any one's interest.

"Well—as you like. We'll be an hour or two in any case, and, if we wound the beast, any number of hours."

"I'll really enjoy myself here. I want to have a look around for any strange hill plants. Truly."

"As you say." Harry raised his cap. As he was turning away, she smiled.

"Please don't wound him."

He smiled back, but in a constrained way.

He's put out that I didn't go with him! she thought. Why didn't I? She knew she wouldn't like to see the stag actually being shot. She would hate it. Or so she imagined. But that did not interfere with her common sense....

She started talking to Donald, until she saw that though he spoke calmly enough and politely, he was really embarrassed by her presence. Besides, her only questions could be personal ones, and what right had she to inquire into his hopes or destiny? Yet she felt the seductive pleasure of talking to him, because of his dark eyes and black hair and dusky face and long eyelashes and an utterly indefinable quality of charm. Not exactly the shyness, the awkward grace, that flatters one's vanity, nor altogether the unselfconsciousness that enchants by its natural ease. Actually Donald was rather a gauche, slightly overgrown youth, well fleshed, with hair blue-black and surely too thick, too luxuriant. And then she would see the smile open in his face, like a dark rose, and there she was!

Unlike Harry, she was quite certain that this was not the charm that deceives. The charm that deceives is much franker, more ingenuous. It is not conditioned by anything, least of all by "morals". Its deceit has a child's face, a good man's kindness. It is forgiven over and over—until it is despised and loathed.

"Do you know anything about the plants that grow on the moor?"

He did not know much, he said. So she left him and began to wander around, until her mind became a maze of colours and marsh and peat-ooze. I could go poking about like this for ever! she thought. She was intensely happy. She found deer's grass crawling amongst the heather like green snakes. And once she lost herself in reverie, staring at the tiny flowers on a stalk of heath. So perfect they were, so beautifully formed, so rich in colour, and honey-fragrant. Her eyes caught a gleam of serpent humour as she found herself drawing the stalk slowly along her lips.

She gave a small smile to herself and remembered Harry. Her teeth gleamed.

That heavy man's sarcasm at the roar of the stag! That dumb brutal male humour of the flesh!

She was not letting it affect her much. She was too quick for that. Elusive as the wind! she thought.

It will overtake you yet!

Will it? she challenged.

But after a time, she confessed, apropos of nothing:

I shall go mad some time! I shall go clean mad!

And she lay down, and drew her knees up to her breast, curled under the sun, and crushed her madness slowly, and let her mind escape.

At the echoing crack of the rifle, her right hand clutched fiercely under her left breast. She felt a pain, no broader than a bullet, pierce her heart. She listened, mouth open. A second shot. She turned over, crushing against her elbows. Oh, Harry! she cried silently. Harry! And buried her face in the hard prickling heather. Then she got up, smoothed her face, and wandered slowly back to Donald.

That young man was eagerly watching the hill-tops and could not tell her what had happened.

"Did he miss the first time?"

"Yes." Then he added: "Or may be he tried for a second one."

They stood there for a long time, but neither Harry nor Alick appeared.

"Perhaps he wounded him," said Donald.

Helen's face winced, as she asked what that would mean.

"When you wound a beast, you have to follow him", explained Donald, "until you kill him!"

"Will that take time?"

"It all depends. If he is badly wounded it mightn't take so long, but sometimes you may have to follow him into another forest."

"But you must get him?"

"If you can."

Helen nodded. Pain and death, pain and death. From the hills, from the moors. The incoming surge hurt and frightened her. Not to-day! cried her spirit. Oh, not to-day!

"Does the wounded beast just run on?" she asked calmly.

"If he is badly wounded, he falls out soon. He tries to find a place. Then you stalk him there."

"And the others run on and desert him?"

"Not always. Often another stag or two will stay with him and keep guard."

"Do they?" asked Helen, heartened.

"Yes," said Donald.

They were silent for a long time. Running deer, lovely running deer. Her sympathies were with the deer and not with the hunters. This was like a betrayal, a betrayal of Harry, of all her men, the hunting men, the hunters that came over horizon after primeval horizon, through dark ages and medieval ages, into the September sun of this day she was alive in.

As she shifted her stance, she glanced at Donald. His eyes never left a certain point in the hills. He had the keen concentrated expression of the hunter, the eyebrows gathered a little over far-sighted eyes. Ruthless, she thought.

And all at once she was struck by something terrifying in the aspect of man, something she had never experienced before, that separated man from her, some dark force of the spirit, that could grip male flesh. Donald never moved. He looked as if he could stand like that for ever.

The moment's sensation carried within it its own visual image—an aspect of man, a man's questing head, potent and mythological. Deep in her it would remain for ever.

For here was Helen, Helen Marway, in the bright sun, running with the invisible deer, running beyond men, in the light.

Not pain, not death, not potent mythological faces—but light and the hooves of the running deer.

Until she felt in herself the dreadful cleavage, the awful balancing, pull and counter-pull, passion and ecstasy, between dark and light.

"There they are," said Donald.

"Where?"

He did not answer, looking into the hills. He gave a signal with his right arm. "They're not wanting me."

"Where are they?"

He tried to point them out to her, and when she said that she could not see them, he replied that it was impossible to see them now because they were against a dark hill-side. He obviously kept looking at them for a few more seconds, before suggesting, "Perhaps we should go to meet them. We have the lunch."

"What's happened, do you think?"

"I don't know." But as they moved forward, he volunteered the suggestion that there wouldn't likely be any more stalking. And when Helen questioned him, he explained that what with the good day that was in it, the deer would now be on the tops.

"Do you think they have got the stag?"

"Oh no."

"Perhaps it was wounded and got too far away."

"I couldn't say."

"What do you think?"

"I don't think it was wounded."

"Why?"

"Because if it was wounded Alick would get it."

"You have great faith in Alick?" She watched the smile dawn in his face.

"Yes, ma'm."

And Donald proved to be right. Harry gave Helen a wave.

"What luck?" she cried.

"Rotten!" And, as he came up, "I'm ashamed of myself. A really fine head. Ten pointer. And what a weight! I don't know what went wrong. An absolutely clean miss."

"But didn't you fire again?"

"Yes. Tried him on the run. Don't mention it, for heaven's sake. What a shot!" He sat down with a thump. "Let us eat and forget it. Where's the flask? Alick!"

"It was a long difficult shot." Alick explained to Helen.

"It wasn't. It wasn't nearly two hundred yards—and straight across—target practice!" Harry declared.

"It was the colouring behind. The outline was vague at the distance. A very difficult shot."

"Bosh! Drink this."

"Good health!" murmured Alick and drank. Then he turned towards Donald and the pony and they went away some little distance before Alick sat down, and Donald opened out the gillies' lunch. Their backs politely to the toffs, they ate and talked away together.

Harry talked, too, describing the stalk with animation. "I was so keen to bag a good head to-day. I did really want to

get you a fine trophy. I was so keen. That's the whole thing.
I'm mad at myself, really mad."

"I'm not."

"Very decent of you. You can be really decent. All the
same, that doesn't let me off. I wish I had that shot over
again. Here, eat some of these."

"Give me time. I'm ravenous."

"We could have gone much much farther. But we'd never
have got back in time for that bally dinner at Screesval. Hang
it! Oh never mind!" He shoved most of a sandwich into his
mouth, said, "George is certain..." and choked.

Helen laughed. "I have a confession to make."

He looked at her.

"I put a hoodoo on you."

He swallowed.

"I do not want you to kill the stag to-day."

His eyebrows gathered and he gazed at her with a male
penetrating expression.

Helen's eyes wavered, and she looked across the moor
with an enigmatic defensive smile.

"How do you mean?"

"Oh"—Helen lifted her shoulders—"just a joke." Then
she flashed him a smile. "Was the stag keeping company?"

"Regular old sultan."

"Poor old chap. Bit tough on him, I thought, on such a
fine morning."

Harry kept looking at her. Then he shrugged also and
smiled. "Oh, that."

"Pretty poor joke, Harry. I'm sorry."

He kept on eating. "Here, have some of these."

"Thanks. Been a gorgeous day, hasn't it?"

"Rather. It was a damned hind that spotted me and
barked."

"How mean of her!"

"You for a pukka sahib!"

"I do feel awful."

"Sentimental. You!"

"Go on, rub it in."

"Don't you see you're letting down your race?"

"Absolutely. I can assure you, however, that it was merely a temporary aberration." A danger flash came into her eyes. "I can assure you it shan't happen again. In these circumstances, perhaps you could strain your sahib's conscience to overlook it."

"No. Nothing will make me forget that hoodoo. The thing is too fundamental."

"Proceed. I'll observe the well-known process of self-flattery."

"It's not often you give yourself away, Helen."

"Will you be good enough to explain exactly in what way I gave myself away?"

"Well, you just gave yourself away." He shrugged. "I mean you just gave yourself away."

"I'm not ashamed of a thought directed towards the sparing of any life."

"What's that got to do with it?"

"With what?"

"With—with—the why and the wherefore?"

She regarded him carefully. "Are you trying to be funny?"

"Good lord, no. I was never more serious."

"Harry Kingsley?"

"Helen Marway?"

"I think you're a mean hound."

"My cup is full."

"It isn't. Hold it out." Coldly she filled it with hot coffee.

"Thanks." As he kept on trying to get the cup to sit on the heather, he said uncertainly, almost shyly, "Helen, do you mean you did not want me to kill *anything* to-day?"

She gave him a glance, then announced: "The discussion is closed."

"I am reconciled," he said. "The glory has returned unto the day. Allah is Allah."

A warmth suffused her face as she gathered the sandwich papers, crushed them into a ball, and poked them into the peat, but she gave nothing away.

He glanced at her. "How does it go?" he asked gently.

She apparently did not hear, but after a moment she looked up towards Benbeg and slowly intoned: "*Lâ ilâha illa'llâh....*"

He gazed at her.

She withdrew her eyes to her hands, which lay in her lap. "There is no god but God...."

He bowed his own head, still hushed by the vowelled liquid run of her voice. She was body and spirit—and all that time meant and could ever mean. He bowed down until his forehead touched the heath before her, like a Moslem at prayer.

She looked at him with a calm smile, and kept looking as he raised his head and met her eyes. The warmth was still in her face but she was not confused.

"You are the woman who sat among the rocks and dived in deep seas," he said, with uncertain humour.

She smiled upon him, poised and enigmatic.

He glanced towards the two gillies. Their presence made action impossible, and action was what he needed. He could not bear her any more. He must....

She met the swift return of his eyes, and began to laugh very softly, through her nostrils, until her lips parted and the deep cooing chuckle came through. In an instant her voice whipped: "Harry!"

The sound stopped his advance.

"You'll pay for this," he vowed. "You'll pay for it beyond anything you have ever dreamed." He tried to dissemble his heavy breathing, and so merely emphasised it.

"I wonder," she said, and began to collect the luncheon apparatus.

As Alick and Donald and the pony followed them on the way home, Alick said, looking at her ankles and the easy grace of her body, "How did you get on with her?"

"Oh fine. She's all right."

"A bit of a beauty, what?"

"Boy, isn't she!" said Donald.

"How would you like to have a girl like that?"

"Och, be quiet!"

Alick smiled. "What was she talking about?"

"I could see she didn't like the idea of the stag being wounded. She asked me if I knew about plants."

"What did you say?"

"I didn't know any plants. She wandered off by herself."

"Did she get any?"

"I kept watching her out of the corner of my eye. I don't think she got any. Then she lay down. She's queer in some ways, I think?"

"What ways?"

"Oh I don't know. Are there any plants?"

"A few. She didn't look for them very long?"

"I don't think so. I got a bit of white heather."

"Did you? And did you give it to her?"

"No."

"You should have given it to her. She would have been delighted. Why didn't you?"

"I didn't like," said Donald.

Alick laughed. "Have you got it yet?"

Donald did not answer.

"Give it to her."

Donald shook his head, embarrassed.

"Lord, man, you'll never get a girl if you behave like that. I do believe if she began to make love to you, you'd be frightened."

"Would I?" said Donald. "I'll soon let her see!"

"What?"

"Get up!" said Donald, and he hit the pony on the flank with his palm.

"I can see you have fallen for her a bit."

"Who? Me?" asked Donald. "Not on your life!"

"She's a beauty, though, isn't she?"

"Oh, she'll do."

"How would you like to be in a position, with the money, where you could walk in and carry off a girl like that?"

"I should like the money all right."

"Look here," said Alick. "If you had given her the white heather, I bet you she would have given you an extra good tip and perhaps squeezed your hand."

"You be quiet," said Donald. Then he added, "To tell the truth, I thought she might think that I—that I might expect a tip or something."

Alick looked at him, and, looking away, remarked, "The day will soon come when that won't bother you."

Donald glanced at him. Then they walked for a long way in a silence which Donald felt so much that his dark eyes caught a strange animal glimmer of pain.

When next Alick spoke, he referred to the projected meeting at Corr Inn that evening. "Would you like to come?"

"Yes," said Donald.

"So long as you won't get drunk."

"I can get drunk if I like."

Alick looked at him, a smile on his face, but Donald moodily refused his eyes.

As they approached the Lodge, they could see evidences of excitement.

"Angus has done it on us," said Alick.

He was right. George had shot a really good beast.

Joyce stalked about in great feather. Harry and Helen were getting details of the hunt. Geoffrey, leaning on his stick, waggled his head in ironic mirth over the mystery of beginner's luck.

"Let us go round this way," said Donald.

"No fear," said Alick.

They were hailed. Helen took her folded rainproof off the pony, though Donald clearly wanted to take it into the house himself. "Not at all," she said, giving him a bright smile. "Thank you, Donald, for a very pleasant day."

His face darkened, and he went on with the pony.

Alick found Angus in the gun-room, and as they cleaned their rifles Angus said, "Talk about luck!" and in a few words described how, while they were resting, he saw the stag coming towards them. "I think he had just come into the forest, on the rut. He began ploughing up a peat pool at fifty yards. I could have hit him with a stone."

"Mr. Smith will be delighted."

Angus glanced around and whispered, "Wasn't I a fool? I really meant to take Mr. Marway for a walk. I knew if we got anything good it would be against me."

"And why didn't you?"

"Because of the way it happened. And I got all strung up. I couldn't—I couldn't frighten the beast. Damn, it wouldn't have been fair. Ach, what the hell do I care?"

Alick smiled. "He'll take it out of you."

"Let him! A good head, isn't it?"

"Yes; fine span."

Geoffrey came in and walked past them into the sitting-room. He did not speak. When the door closed, Angus winked to Alick. "The b——r has the pin in for me!"

"You're not the only one," said Alick.

Angus looked at him. "He hasn't thanked you for what you did for him?"

"Only that deep, silent thanks."

"God, it wouldn't have cost him much to have said thank you, however he felt."

"I don't mind," said Alick.

"Perhaps not," said Angus. "All the same…"

"We can leave him to it."

"To what?"

"To his fate."

There was no emphasis in Alick's voice, but Angus suddenly felt uncomfortable. "Come on," he said. "Let's get out of here." Alick unhurriedly finished his job. Angus glanced at the tall big figure, so full-chested, upright, and at ease. There was something in Alick, some strange reserved element of personality, that could never be touched. A snatch of a pipe theme came hissing softly through his lips. He played reels and strathspeys on the violin, not with the fire, the "lift", that gives them life and rouses enthusiasm, but with an extraordinary purity of tone, a limpid small tone, that haunted the memory. A big man, playing quietly to himself. To dance to this music was, for some inexplicable reason, a memorable experience, an extra delight. The dancers would glance at Alick. He never danced himself.

They left the gun-room. "Coming in for a moment?" and Angus nodded sideways towards the kitchen door.

"No," said Alick.

They went on.

Joyce parted from Helen in the hall, her loud voice hurrying for the sitting-room. Before hanging up her rainproof in the cloak-room, Helen shook it out. From an internal fold something fell to the floor. She gazed at it. It was a piece of white heather.

Chapter Nine

Some two hours later, Helen sat beside Harry in the back seat of George's car. Darkness was falling and George kept in sight the tail light of the front car in which Sir John and Lady Marway, Geoffrey and Marjory, were leading the way to Screesval and dinner with Matthew Blair.

Screesval had a small salmon river of repute, which was its main attraction for the lessee. His grouse moor he let younger friends shoot over. Like Sir John, who had been at college with him, he could not consider himself one of the true sporting tribe. But he had always loved the Highlands in the autumn, and fishing was his mild passion, inducing the pleasant natural moods that assorted so well with his taste for classical literature and the attributes thereof, like simple, good food and good wine. The invitation to dinner always accorded with the arrival at Screesval of his friend, Dean Cameron, for a fortnight's fishing. The Dean and Mr. Blair contrived as far as possible to have this short spell to themselves, though it sometimes happened, as on the present occasion, that Mr. Blair had another guest.

But it was the thought of the Dean that tickled George, who was in remarkably good form after his successful day's hunt. "We'll turn him on to Geoffrey!"

"I say, wasn't old Geoff amusing over our stag?" cried Joyce.

"Can you blame him?" Helen asked.

"No, of course not! That's the joke!"

"But about the Dean," said George. "He's a dear old boy. And so is old Blair. But, it's just, you know, talk, and sometimes the smile sorta sticks on your face. And whatever you say about Geoff, he is never troubled with qualms in a fight. I should like to get Geoff all out on an argument."

"I'll tell you what," said Joyce. "We'll ask the Dean about second sight and that. You know, is it from on high or from on low? I must say Alick's feat of finding Geoffrey in the dark gave me the jitters. What was it you said about it, George?"

"Whoops!" exclaimed George. A wreath of mist came at them, glowed blindingly, and vanished. "Another!"

The heather and the bog and the narrow road were swept by the headlights. Helen peered out of the window and saw the hills. It was a mysterious land, so silent, so self-contained.

"There's Corr Inn," said Harry. Helen turned to his side and saw the solitary light. Their knees touched, their hands. Harry caught her hand. She squeezed his swiftly and withdrew her own.

"Isn't it weird!" Joyce exclaimed.

Helen turned to her own window and stared out. Driving at night in this country always affected her strongly. To-night there was something in it that hurt her. For it was not an objective beauty. Surely nothing had ever been devised by nature to prove more completely that beauty was an inward experience. And yet, in another sense, could anything in nature be more objective, with that added, almost terrifying suggestion of being withdrawn? Withdrawn and heedless— till the very quick of the heart shivered and the pressure behind the seeing eyes was like a pressure of tears.

She was going to have warned Joyce about not introducing the topic of second sight. It was essential that she should. Her mother had been worried enough about it. And Geoffrey would welcome it out of a feeling that he would like to make them all thoroughly ashamed of their sentimentalities—and so get some of his own back. But she could not draw her mind away to tackle the point. Moreover, she was becoming almost unbearably conscious of Harry's near presence. And there he was, touching her—gently, as if by the swaying of the car; and there again—the back of his hand against her knee—not finding her hand. She huddled herself over against her window. The sad beauty of the young night—she wanted to bury her head, to turn blindly to him and bury her head.

"Have you gone to sleep, Helen?" called Joyce.

"Not with George at the wheel."

"Oh, I say!" exclaimed George. "This funeral crawl. I can't help it."

"Don't worry," said Harry. "Yonder are the lights of Screesval."

As the car drew up, Harry turned to Helen. Her face, moon-pale in the shadows, smiled to him. He caught her hand to help her out but could not speak to her. Turning to George and Joyce, he said, "By the way, don't introduce that second sight business."

Joyce looked at him. "Why ever not?"

Harry shrugged and turned towards the rest of the party coming from the other car.

Screesval Lodge was larger and more solidly furnished than Corbreac. Corbreac was a shooting-box, a temporary home: Screesval had a library, dark panelling, and a cellar. The walls were rich with trophies and prints, and the corridor to the billiard room was panelled with carefully matched deerskins. In Screesval footfalls were softer and noise more distant. It was a home that Mr. Blair, except for the winter months, when he went to the Madeiras, tended to occupy almost continuously.

He was a little man, with a rolling gait, a rubicund countenance, and gay charming manners in company. He knew everything that went on about the house, brought presents to his headkeeper's children, interested himself in a choked ditch (when he could get thoroughly wet poking his walking-stick into the mud), a sick cow, or a mole trap. Anyone less like a classical student it might be difficult to imagine. But then Mr. Blair did not read a masterpiece for knowledge so much as for companionship and sustenance. He had the distinct impression of knowing Virgil personally. He had been a stockbroker.

His welcome was extremely bright. He bowed over Lady Marway's hand. "Ah, my dear!" he said to Helen, regarding a beauty that made him sigh. He turned to Sir John. "How you bring my bachelorhood home to me, Jack!" His laughter was cunning, his eyes full of merry glances.

The Dean was quiet, gentle-mannered, pale, with a smile that lingered on his face as he listened. There was a quality about him, immediately arresting, even forceful. Only after a time did one gather that it centred in the eyes.

Mr. Blair's second guest was Colonel Brown, a tall, strong-boned man of sixty, with the intelligent practical expression that has been used to directing the evolution and organisation of an army's mechanised units. Difficulties called out his ingenuity and a guarded sense of humour. His wife was to have been with him, but she had been caught into the social whirl of arranging for a daughter's wedding.

Thus Lady Marway became the hostess of the evening.

At dinner all their doings, their luck and mishaps at sport, the names of mutual friends, the usual topics, were touched upon. It was not until they were going to join the ladies in the large comfortable library that Mr. Blair, who loved his food and wine, became properly aware of Geoffrey's slight limp. "My dear fellow, you must tell us about that fall of yours. May I take your arm?"

"Not at all," said Geoffrey. "A slight muscular stiffness that will be quite gone by to-morrow, I hope."

"In the mist? Did I hear you say you were caught at night?"

"Yes."

"But—wasn't that extraordinarily dangerous? Shouldn't you have sat down until the morning?"

"By all the rules, yes."

"And you didn't? You——" He bowed to the ladies. "We could not leave you more than five minutes." When he had all his guests seated, he stood for a moment, saying, "We must hear about Mr. Smith's adventure in the mist. I once got lost myself. But, fortunately, never in the dark. I should be grateful for a few tips. Do you mind?"

"Not at all," said Lady Marway. "Even if—we don't want quite to have its anxiety again."

"Of course, you would have been anxious!" He turned to Geoffrey. "How *did* it happen?"

"Oh, simply enough," said Geoffrey, warmed by the good port. "In the rigours of the chase, my stalker and I got separated. The mist was thick and then the night came down—and there I was."

"You would be!" said Mr. Blair. "Jove, you would! And you kept going?"

Geoffrey described how he had kept going and fallen over.

"That was a narrow squeak," said Colonel Brown.

"And after that?" asked Mr. Blair.

"Oh, I lay for a bit, until I got too uncomfortably cold. Then I set off again. I was making fair headway, when Harry's stalker found me. We waited till the dawn."

"Did he have to go far to find you?" asked Colonel Brown.

"Right into the heart of the forest," said Geoffrey.

"That seems pretty miraculous, if it was dark as all that, doesn't it?" The Colonel kept looking at Geoffrey.

"Oh, it was," said Geoffrey, with solemn malice; "it was quite a miracle. But, as Miss Marway here will tell you, he has second sight."

They all looked at Helen.

"That is Mr. Smith's idea", she explained, "of making a joke."

Geoffrey's released laugh rattled out. Mr. Blair and his two guests smiled, looking from Geoffrey to Helen. Obviously here was a house joke, with some amusing personalities behind it. And presently the Colonel asked Geoffrey: "Purely as a matter of curiosity—for mist is one of our bogeys—how do you think the stalker found you? What is his technique?"

"I don't know," said Geoffrey. "I assume he worked out the way I should be likely to come and chanced it."

"George," said Helen, with a smile, "what about those five shillings?"

"I object!" said George. Then he rushed upon an explanation of the bet.

Geoffrey kept silent, enjoying himself.

"All the same," said Mr. Blair. "It was an extraordinary feat—however it was done. Really extraordinary." And he asked some more questions; until at last the Dean inquired in his clear, rather low-pitched voice:

"Had you any real reason to suspect second sight?"

At once there was complete silence, for as they looked at the Dean they came under the influence of his eyes. His pale skin had a faintly ivory pallor, worn fine, like old monastery parchment, as if the inner mind had worked outward upon it.

His question was directed at Geoffrey, who knew that his hostess would rather he let the subject lie, and yet who could not resist the temptation to score over certain others of his party by exposing their superstition.

"I don't know about real reason," he said, with apparent hesitancy. "The trouble is you never do get any reason from the inherently superstitious type of mind. You get statements, of course. However, I may go so far as to say that certain young members of our party are disposed to believe that the stalker in question has second sight."

The Dean smiled. "But surely not without some evidence?"

"Oh, I assure you the evidence was most striking," said Geoffrey.

The Dean looked along the young smiling faces and settled silently on Harry.

"He is merely trying to get one back on me for having had the worst of an argument over an experience I had alone with this stalker." Harry smiled. "The stalker's experience was certainly very striking. But if you don't mind, sir, I would rather not go into it again."

After a moment's silence, Mr. Blair said, "That seems quite the authentic attitude. You know old Farquhar—you've met him—with the long beard?"

Sir John nodded.

"Well, he's remarkably interesting on the subject. I've been trying to check up some of his stuff, but I can only find one or two Highland books dealing with the matter. He seems genuinely moved."

"Quite," said Sir John. "None of them means not to be genuine. There can, however, be self-deception—and a rumour can grow. In India, we had too often to deal with what was demonstrably, and in fact, superstition to permit credulity to move us unduly."

"I suppose you had," said the Dean. "All the same, we cannot quite dismiss a real spiritual or mental experience merely because it arouses dubious reactions in the minds of others, can we? In science, when you discover an exception to a law, you invalidate the law. But a superstition does not in that sense invalidate a spiritual truth. The difficulty here, of course, is extremely complex. But therefore to dismiss the difficulty is surely an over-simplification."

"I quite agree," said Sir John. "The difficulty is one of assessing the evidence. And it would appear to be almost insuperable."

"At any given moment a difficulty which cannot be surmounted, whether in physics or psychology, is in fact insuperable," said the Dean quietly. "But that does not deter either scientist or psychologist. Why? Because past experience has shown us that patient investigation tends to surmount the difficulty."

"But the only way that I know", said Geoffrey, "of surmounting the difficulty is by testing the evidence. If all the available evidence does not make a conclusive case, then you are compelled to dismiss the truth or reality of that which the evidence was supposed to prove."

"Granted, but only after assuming two things. First, that all the available evidence, all of it, is brought forward for test and, second, that those who assess the evidence are in fact competent to assess it."

"Granted," said Geoffrey.

The Dean smiled slowly as he looked at Geoffrey. "There is just one further point. All the evidence at present available may not be all the evidence available to-morrow or ultimately."

"I am afraid", said Geoffrey, meeting the smile, "that my interest is in physics rather than in metaphysics."

The Dean leaned back, enjoying the thrust.

"Now let us apply that", said Mr. Blair, with his jolliest speculative expression, "to this business of second sight. I have a feeling that in a moment we shall be in the region of intuition, when the ladies shall be able to lead our stumbling conclusions to esoteric heights."

"I wonder why", said Marjory, "there should be this flattering assumption on the part of man that women are not quite capable of the grave refinement of reason?"

"Oh, splendid, Marjory!" exclaimed Joyce.

Mr. Blair laughed and clapped his hands. "Bravo! But I refuse to retract. Why? Because, according to Colonel Brown, intuition is the process of reasoning in the fourth dimension." His face became portentously solemn. "He can explain it to you. You will appreciate it. Alas, it is too deep for me." And he wagged his rubicund face and bald head.

Marjory's assumed innocence collapsed graciously and a warmth came into the room, so that Mr. Blair insisted on pouring out glasses of port—it did not occur to him to pour anything else—with little exaggerated mannerisms and eye-twinklings. Joyce very nearly called him a dear, funny old thing as he filled her glass to the brim.

"Gentlemen, the ladies!"

Then, setting down his glass and still standing, he pressed his palms against his sides, lifted up his chest, and asked, "Now where were we?"

"Awaiting the evidence," said Geoffrey slily.

"Ha, you scientists," said Mr. Blair, wagging a finger. "It's not evidence you want of second sight: it's the fun of knocking it into a cocked hat."

There was a burst of laughter at this unexpected sally and Mr. Blair sat down, happy as a schoolboy to have brought ease and mirth to his guests. It was his experience that there is nothing like a "subject for discussion" to keep guests reasonably animated—the possibilities of variation in subjects and guests being, of course, infinite.

"Now would it be too much for me to ask you to assume", he said, addressing Geoffrey politely and pointing to the coal scuttle, "that this is the cocked hat?"

"I think so," said Geoffrey. "It's a bit too full to hold all the rubbish." And he laughed loudly.

"You frankly don't believe it?" asked Colonel Brown, with his guarded humour.

"No," replied Geoffrey. "Do you?"

"I am inclined on the whole to say yes. The evidence regarding prevision is pretty mixed, but there is evidence. It is not perhaps conclusive evidence, but still it is evidence. And mathematically once you admit dimensions beyond the third, the thing does at least appear to be feasible."

"I see," said Geoffrey, with the smile that implied he had heard that sort of reasoning before. "But I am inclined to be impressed only by evidence. We can say, of course, that anything is possible. That may be an inspiration to the scientist, but it is hardly anything more."

Colonel Brown smiled and nodded. "You are quite right. But still we have got to work with the tools we have. Like you, I prefer physics to metaphysics. But the possibility of the existence of second sight in no way interferes with physics. It is an interesting speculation scientifically because of the existence of certain evidence and of our power to bring mathematics to bear upon it."

"What form does this evidence take?" Geoffrey asked.

"Several forms. There is the evidence of what certain thinkers can do in the East; there is the evidence, never properly sifted, of second sight in the Highlands—and elsewhere; there is the recorded evidence of dreams, in which future incidents are foreseen; there is a tremendous body of miscellaneous evidence, dealt with by the Psychical Research Society and other groups or individuals. The persistence of the idea, together with these manifestations, is also something."

"Yoga, serialism, and all that. Quite." Geoffrey smiled sceptically. "As for the origin and persistence of the idea, any sound anthropologist can deal with it adequately and satisfactorily. Take something similar, like water-divining. It has had for itself an almost equal persistence and belief. In fact, the Government of India recently employed one of our most famous diviners, Major Pogson, to find drinking water in certain Indian villages. He divined one hundred and twenty-four villages and was successful in locating drinking sites for one hundred and two of them. That seemed good enough working evidence. Yet under laboratory tests in Cambridge, he failed."

"That is very interesting," replied Colonel Brown, "but hardly analogous. For example, if we took the diviner out over Farquhar's croft, he might divine water at a certain spot. We dig and find water. But if we dug at a dozen other spots we might also find water. We don't know—and could not know without digging the whole place up. That the diviner is extremely skilled in finding water is obvious from his results. But that skill *might* come from a fine co-ordination of the senses under a good geological eye. Much as a man has a good eye for a horse or for a—well, for something equally fast—or an unusual ear for music.

"There is another kind of evidence, however, in which one single instance proves a whole belief or hypothesis to be valid. Take Ross and his mosquitoes. Ross got the belief that mosquitoes carried the malaria germ. So back he went to India and began dissecting mosquitoes. Out of hundreds of species he first of all had to find the right species. The authorities were against him. The microscopic study of bacteria was regarded as a new fad. Authoritative opinion is very often against the pioneer. It was August and the weather was stifling. Ross had dissected in the course of time about a thousand mosquitoes. The mere dissection of each mosquito took at least two hours. Imagine the colossal labour; the amount of belief necessary to carry on; and nothing but failure a thousand times over. Then one day, the sweat running into his eyes, a crack in the eye-piece of his microscope, his sight badly strained, he is just about to give up work, when he sees the incriminating dark stain, and in that moment his whole case was established and humanity became his debtor for a supremely important scientific discovery.

"Similarly about this prevision. If I could assert, as the result of what I may call a vision, that something was going to happen to you in the future, involving factors of which I could demonstrably have no previous knowledge, and if such happening did take place, then I should be expressing a knowledge acquired otherwise than by means of my five senses. And such knowledge, whether we elected to call it second sight, clairvoyance, or any other name, would be a *fact*, calling, of course, for scientific investigation and, if possible, explanation. But that again, as Dean Cameron says, would require that the scientist investigating the fact, was, in fact, competent to assess it."

"You desiderate some special kind of scientist?"

Geoffrey's sarcasm was not lost on Colonel Brown, but he appeared to enjoy it rather than otherwise. "Well, I merely mean that a man, let us say, who is exclusively a chemist, would hardly be the right kind——"

"Hah-haw!" observed George, and amid the general merriment Colonel Brown looked blank, until, glancing at Geoffrey, he realised that he must have put his foot in it.

"I'm sorry," he said. "I'm sure I had no idea that I was intruding upon a real chemist," and was forced to laugh himself.

"It's all right," said Geoffrey, smiling, but flushed a trifle.

"It's the more absurd", said Colonel Brown, "because obviously you and I, trained to the scientific attitude, should be in league against the metaphysicians."

"But actually," said the Dean, "is it not true that practically everyone is on Mr. Smith's side? That there is an instinctive desire *not* to believe in second sight? That it arouses antipathy and fear? It is the unknown, and the unknown we dread. And when anyone can show that it is untrue, we are in our hearts relieved?"

By the nature of the silence that followed it would seem that this expressed a general truth.

Mr. Blair turned to Geoffrey. "How would you set about showing it was untrue?"

"Well, it seems to me simple enough," Geoffrey replied. "Second sight, like any other illusion or delusion, is due entirely to the mechanical condition of the brain. It results from certain physiological adjustments or maladjustments. It has no more to do with time or eternity than, may I say, an eructation produced by an internal stomachic condition. I would make the suggestion that currents of nervous energy get short-circuited in a temporary derangement or muddle of the brain paths along which they usually travel, and you get a spark at the wrong place. That's about all.

"Now consider. If you don't accept that, where are you? If the manifestation we call second sight is not the spontaneous product of the mechanical functioning of the brain, then it must be induced by some power or animus or spirit independent of the grey matter. An arbitrary and miraculous interference by an over-soul or something like that. Once you admit that special kind of interference where are we, and, in particular, where is science? And, in any case, why do it, why call in an hypothesis based on miracle, when we know that a mechanical interpretation can explain it all? Surgeons and psycho-analysts deal successfully with deranged brains in vast quantities daily. Economy is an important word for a scientist, and he has even made a scientific law called the Economy of Hypothesis."

Geoffrey had been speaking so forcefully that he wiped his mouth. Then he smiled and drank off his wine.

"Excellent," said Mr. Blair, filling up Geoffrey's glass. "To tell the real truth, that rather tallies with my own severely classical attitude. Could you also do a service to my mind on this matter of dreams? Who is the gentleman, again— Mr. Dunne?"

"As far as I have been able to gather," said Geoffrey, "a dream is quite an irrational performance. It may be good in parts, like the curate's egg, for those who are looking for marvels, but surely it hardly provides a basis on which to build a real scientific edifice."

"I think you are quite brilliant to-night, Geoffrey," said Lady Marway, with a friendly smile.

George asked if he might lead the cheers at the dispersal of the mist. There was laughter and cigarette-smoking and some more wine. Then Joyce said nonchalantly, "You have really got to get lost in the mist to appreciate decent head-lights." And was a little surprised, and secretly deeply flattered, at the reception her words got, for she had been thinking simply of her own experience. Long discussions usually bored her to tears. She now looked very animated.

The focus of attention had shifted from Geoffrey to Colonel Brown, who, before he drank, said with a smile, "I am inclined to be impressed only by evidence."

"Ha! ha! and so we come back to where we started from. Which is doubtless", said Mr. Blair to Marjory, "what you would expect?"

"You don't subscribe altogether to Mr. Smith's mechanistic theory?" the Dean asked Colonel Brown.

"I'm afraid not. In so far as it does not cover all the facts, it must be unsatisfactory. For example, I happened to mention the word serialism, and clearly Mr. Smith was not impressed, any more than he was by Mr. Dunne's dreams, wherein it is made to appear that Mr. Dunne foresaw the happening of certain events. Now Mr. Dunne is an army man like myself, obviously an able mathematician, and his attitude is self-evidently scientific. He is not concerned about inducing mystical states. He is a frank inquirer who takes you step by step in a very practical and logical and even humorous way. Just let us look for a moment at an instance of the sort of thing he presents in his *An Experiment with Time.* He had a dream, involving an argument with a waiter as to whether it was half-past four in the morning or in the afternoon. On looking at his watch in the dream he found that it had stopped at half-past four. He awoke, lit a match, hunted for his watch, found it on a chest of drawers, and discovered it was stopped at half-past four—and subsequently proved that it must have stopped just before he got out of bed, that is, at the actual moment of the dream. Thinking about this experience one morning later on in Sorrento, he wondered if it were possible for him to tell the time on his watch at that particular moment. He shut his eyes and concentrated, got into a half-doze, and presently the watch appeared in front of him, surrounded by a sort of white mist. The vision was binocular, upright, about a foot from his nose, and lit by ordinary daylight. The hour hand stood at eight o'clock. The minute hand swung between twelve and one. Dividing the arc of the swing, he decided that the time was two and a half minutes past eight. Having so decided, he opened his eyes, reached out under the mosquito curtains, got hold of his watch, pulled it in, held it up before him—and saw that the time on the watch was precisely two and a half minutes past eight."

"That sounds marvellous," said Lady Marway. "But what sort of relation has it to second sight?"

"Well, it would appear that he had had second sight or prevision of himself looking at his watch. The white mist was the mosquito netting outside the focus of attention. He had foreseen himself doing something before he had actually done it."

"And how does he account for it?"

"Ah, that's a long argument. Only he does attempt to account for it, not at all on the basis of miracle, but on a basis of mathematics and the existence of dimensions beyond the third. Now mathematics is the sort of thing that we all are prepared to pin our faith to. The absolutely pure science. Yet mathematics constantly deals with what should be to us—and are—quite fantastically imaginary things like, say, the square root of *minus* one. Consider, for example, such a simple thing as this: unless you can add something to less than nothing to make it equal to nothing, there would be no algebra. Do you remember the old school difficulty of trying to understand how two *minuses* make a *plus*? Mathematics also deals confidently with what are to us even more difficult to imagine, namely, dimensions beyond the third. Yet mathematics gets its marvellously valid and indisputable results."

"I wish I could understand the fourth dimension," said Helen.

To the smiling faces, Colonel Brown shook his head. "That is difficult. We can't make a mental picture of the fourth dimension, as we can of the first, second, and third dimensions. Just as we can't make a mental picture of a minus quantity. We can only sort of hint at it. The first dimension, as you know, is a straight line, without any breadth or thickness, just a pure line. The second is a surface, having length and breadth but no thickness. The third has length, breadth, and thickness—like all of us in this room, and of course like the room itself. Our physical world is entirely three-dimensional. Now try to imagine that this white square of linen—let me unpin it and spread it on the floor—is two-dimensional only. That is, it is a surface, with no depth. Now imagine an equally flat living creature, a two-dimensional bug, let us say. This then would be its whole world, its universe. It could not conceive, could not picture, anything outside it. But I, moving in three dimensions, can bend down and lift it off its world up onto another world. This action of mine would be to it a pure miracle. But to us—we merely smile. It's a common illustration. Do you get it at all?"

"I think I can imagine it, yes," said Helen.

"Now if you were capable of moving in the fourth dimensional world you would be able to interfere with the third, just as I in the third interfered with the bug in the second; that is, from outside you could suddenly appear in our midst, though doors and windows are all closed. But it would be no miracle to you or to any of your fourth-dimensional friends. You would all smile at our astonishment, at our terror—gently, let us hope."

Helen looked so thoughtful that some of the others smiled, and laughed when she said, "I thought for a moment I got a glimmer of it."

"To finish with it," said Colonel Brown: "you get the fourth dimension by adding to the dimensions of length, breadth, and thickness, the dimension of time. In the four-dimensional, you should be able to look along the dimension of time, just as we can look along the dimension of a straight line. If I put my finger there on the edge of the white cloth and call the spot *Now*, I can see not only the *past* part of the line extending up to my finger but the *future* part extending beyond it. In the same way, a person in the fourth dimensional world could not only see the *past* on our line of time up to *Now* but also the *future* beyond it. And I have only to lift the square of linen"—a twinkle came into his eye— "and place it over the slow curve of this arm of my chair, and we should be right bang into curved time. In short, what appears to happen in second sight is that you enter the world of four dimensions and so quite naturally see the future."

"But does that mean that the future is rigidly determined?" Harry asked.

"That is even more difficult," said Colonel Brown, as he blew out the match with which he had re-lit his pipe. "I cannot go into it. The mathematics of the situation, taking the serial, multi-dimensional view into account, would appear to permit of interference with foreseen events. Complete free will is as meaningless as complete determinism. Intervention in the limited sense that applies to all reality as we know it is possible to us in our dimension. I must leave it at that—or else borrow a blackboard and Mr. Dunne's diagrams."

"But does that mean that if I foresaw something that was about to happen, I could take steps to prevent its happening?" Harry persisted.

"It would appear that if you did your best, you might achieve a considerable degree of prevention."

Geoffrey laughed loudly and for quite a time.

"I admit," said Mr. Blair, "that is where I, too, get stumped."

Colonel Brown enjoyed the mirth, even if Geoffrey's appeared to be unduly excessive for a social occasion. He said to his host, "But we are always in the process of getting stumped. That's the normal condition in evolution. If you had said to a scientist before Röntgen's day that you were hoping to take a photograph in a dark room, he would have proved to you quite conclusively the impossibility of doing so—assuming he was tolerant enough not to suggest a mental home. Yet photographs are now taken in dark rooms. We can even photograph a pin inside your stomach without putting you to the trouble of taking off your clothes."

"But that's quite logical."

"Yes—*now that you understand the process.*"

"What do you think of all this, Mr. Smith?" asked Mr. Blair.

"I think it is the modern type of fairy story. Nothing more. The sort of pretty thing that looks valid to please our primitive appetite for wonders."

"I don't see anything very pretty about second sight," said Harry. "But apart from that—how do you explain the vision of the watch?"

"I should not think of attempting any explanation", said Geoffrey, "until I had an opportunity of testing such an alleged vision under laboratory conditions."

"But surely", said Colonel Brown, "it is clear that you cannot produce a psychical state and lay it on a bench as you would a lump of matter?"

"Manifestly," said Geoffrey. "You usually put it on a couch and psycho-analyse it."

George laughed. Old Geoff was doing damned well!

"Is it not possible that we are confusing two quite different things," said the Dean, "as different as physics and psychology? The one deals with matter; the other with mind. Each functions in its own way and has its own quite different conceptions and laws. Our *appreciation* of colour, of sound, of all sensory things, not to mention abstract things like love and hate, is not the concern of physics. For these things we have a separate science which we call psychology. There is a certain interrelation, inasmuch as the material body is an instrument for expressing psychical qualities. But no physicist could ever deduce from my grey matter my conception of beauty or horror or joy or pain. Yet these are precisely the qualities that are very important to me, to all mankind—and would be even if we were incapable of appreciating anything beyond sensual reactions. To us they are life and hope; they are *being.* Very well, that being so, they are to us the most important *facts* in the everyday process of living. Now let us test that by taking the extreme case; let me say, even for the purpose of discussion, that I am a mystic, that I believe in what is called mysticism. I am probably right in thinking that at once Mr. Smith gives me up in despair. Am I right?"

"Well——" said Geoffrey, smiling awkwardly.

"I understand. You would rather not appear to be rude, and if you spoke your mind straightforwardly you might sound very rude indeed!"

The gentle humour was appreciated and Geoffrey laughed.

"Yet consider," said the Dean. "Your mystic is no more an abnormal person than is a great scientist, or a great artist. Like them, he is a person who has gone through a long and difficult training in an effort to achieve certain results. He is a man who has taken the trouble to investigate by personal experience certain psychic processes, and he can tell you, so far as language can communicate to you his meaning, the nature of the results he has achieved."

"And what when his language fails, which seems to be the difficulty?" asked Geoffrey.

"Well, he can't help that. I see you shrug, but think. Assuming you had to explain to a man who was born blind the *redness* of the port in your glass, could you do it? Could you get him to apprehend *redness* as you and I apprehend it?"

Geoffrey was forced to admit that he could not.

"Similarly, if you cannot understand the state of mind the mystic attempts to describe to you, the fault may not lie altogether with the mystic. Now just as the scientist goes on making discoveries about matter, so the mystic goes on making discoveries about the powers of the mind, until he is able to do things with it comparable to what the taking of photographs in a dark room was to pre-Röntgen man. I gather that you are not impressed by Yoga. But what Yogis have achieved in the way of control over the body alone appears to us to be miraculous. Sight, hearing, and smell are enhanced to a degree that to us is incredible. The Yogi can endure extremes of heat and cold. He can sit naked in a snowstorm for days without food and be none the worse. We are astonished at a man seeing a watch-face that is placed outside his visual range, with his eyes shut. But such a thing was a commonplace to certain Indian thinkers, who could see and hear without the use of their senses at all. It is said of some Yogis that they could make their bodies invisible and even pass through doors. Perhaps they had achieved Colonel Brown's fourth-dimensional state! However, I am not going to debate these physical marvels. What I am concerned about is the states of mind that can be achieved by their difficult and exacting processes of concentration. For example, through concentration on what he calls the three-fold modifications which all objects constantly undergo, the Yogi assures us we can acquire the power to know the past, the present, and the future. He knows when he is going to die. Automatically you at once become not merely sceptical but full of active disbelief. You have the feeling that if you were allowed to test these Yogis in your laboratory you would very soon expose them. But that is merely a feeling on your part, a revolt of your mind, automatic and extremely strong, against what you don't want to believe. But that does not dispose of centuries of strenuous development of the mind, of a kind and to a degree new to us and therefore charged with fear of its powers over what to us is the unknown. These powers have yet to be investigated by our psychologists. Such investigation may take a long time, because our psychologists are not sufficiently advanced in psychic experience to assess the evidence. However, this is what I am coming to, and here I am capable of checking results through my own experience—checking them, that is, to a small tentative degree."

Hitherto the Dean had talked with a simple logic out of what was obviously a wide knowledge of his subject. But it was clear even while he was talking that he respected Geoffrey's difficulties and appreciated his revolt, as if he knew that such an attitude on Geoffrey's part was and must be inevitable. But by his very tone it could be seen that these physical marvels, like seeing with the eyes shut or entering closed rooms, interested him merely as by-products of a central and infinitely more important reality.

As he paused his eyes took on a depth, an effect of light, in which there glowed a profound kindliness and understanding. Helen was at once moved, felt herself waiting with a dumb excited expectancy, as if a soft hand had caught upward at her heart.

"Upon a man who has achieved, by effort and struggle, those higher powers of the mind there comes at last a clear consciousness of profound harmony. He realises that there has been added to him an extra dimension of being. I am aware that my words may convey nothing to you, or, at the best, so little that it is negligible over against the reality, so I beg you, in your forbearance, to allow me to illustrate it as best I can. I should put it like this, that the extension of perception that is achieved might be compared with what a blind man has added to him when he first acquires sight. If I say to you that it is as real, as truly a *fact*, as is the blind man's new world to him, I should still hardly be telling the whole truth, because it is, to the person who experiences it, far more real, in the sense that it grasps not mere visual phenomena, appearances, but Reality itself. And I know this with as absolute a certainty as I know that if I put my hand to the bar of the grate there I should burn it, or if I put this glass to my lips I should feel the wine, and taste it, and get its bouquet. The trouble for you lies in my use of a word like Reality. I might illustrate that by referring to the Reality of you as the personality or spirit or whatever you call that thing which inhabits your body and which you usually designate as 'I'. If you could think of the 'I' being extended, transformed, into a universal 'I', into a cosmic consciousness, and if you could think of yourself as coming in contact with, of being permeated by, that consciousness—the spirit within and behind all matter as the 'I' is within and behind the body—then you might vaguely get some sort of parallel. Though I suppose you wouldn't really, because you would still be without the actual experience, as in the case of the blind man and the *redness* of wine. However, let me make one more effort at illustration, for all this has some bearing on second sight in the Highlands."

He paused for a little, and then went on: "There comes to most human lives a period, often perhaps not a very long period, when the senses are enhanced, when the spirit is quickened, and when the very essence of life seems to change in meaning, in purpose, in aim, and in desire.

191

Colour glows. Flowers, trees, the surface of our earth, are seen with what is called new eyes. Over all is a lovely light. The mind is transported. Beauty becomes so heightened that the frail, newly awakened spirit can hardly bear it; in fact, cannot bear it at times, and breaks down in tears, tears neither of joy nor of sorrow, that yet seem to perform a mysterious cleansing or purifying act. The person undergoing this experience acquires a new consideration for humanity, wants to do little acts of kindness, wants all the world to be happy, to be at peace, to be rid of struggle and wrangling and the diabolic horrors of war. Life before this change is seen to have been to a large degree meaningless, because it was without this intense conception of harmony, of a state of being that is recognised—whatever went before or comes after—as the most vivid and thrilling experience or fact that all existence contrived to offer. Many undergo this experience in an extreme degree, that fulfils itself to the highest or loses itself by frustration in the depths. Others experience it much more mildly. But all experience it in some degree. I am referring, as you will have guessed, to that condition termed 'being in love'."

Helen found his eyes on her. They were not questioning, yet she experienced for a moment the extraordinary illusion of holding converse with them, of opening her mind, of accepting their understanding, of saying in some inner region, "Yes", and then, like the neophyte before the master, of bowing. And she actually bowed. Or, at least, her head drooped, and the dark-brown hair, with the straight parting on the left, was towards the Dean, and all the others, turning and looking at her, saw her head like that.

And to them all this silence, by virtue of some inward conviction, was the most eloquent passage of the evening.

"Now that blessed condition of being in love is to a small extent a parallel to that other higher condition," the Dean went on as if the pause had been quite natural, while the others brought their faces from Helen and all their expressions, which each felt to be secret, could be read like the marked stops on an organ. "Just as the physicist discovers absolute harmony in the laws that govern or determine matter, so the mystic discovers absolute harmony in that higher condition to which his mind has won. There at last the psychical becomes supreme over the physical. Always our mind, in science as in everyday life, is trying to conquer matter in some form or other. The materialist is continuously engaged in the fight. *There* man succeeds. On the way to that condition the senses gain a power infinitely beyond, though of the same kind as, the little acts of premonition, telepathy, insight, intuition, silent understanding, identification with another, and with flowers and scents, which characterise human love. In a word, in that final state, which is a state of supreme love, everything is reconciled, all dualisms, all differences and divisions, in a feeling of an eternal Now, of a timelessness in which past, present, and future are fused. You are pervaded by a feeling of light, of bliss, of ease, of having at long last *come into your own.*

"Now I have tried to suggest to you the ultimate condition to which this psychical thinker, if we may so call him, strives to attain, in order that such by-products of his journey, as second sight typifies, may be seen in their secondary and to him quite unimportant light. For as I have said he develops these by-products far beyond anything comparable in the highest experience of human love, so that, for example, he can at last see that which is not within range of his physical eyes or which has not yet come before his physical eyes. And not only in the case of sight, but also of sound, and even of smell. To him these by-products are elementaries, and students are warned against playing with them, as I, a churchman, would warn my congregation against playing with carnal things. To him they were elementaries—over two thousand years ago.

"The strife here is between matter and mind, and mind will win through, because it is more important, more stupendous in its significance, than matter. A boy whistling a tune is a more wonderful phenomenon than the largest inert sun in all the universe, and we know it, and the materialist admits it. At times, matter will predominate and we become estranged from the things of the mind, of the spirit, by the force of external things, by excessive toil, by material greed, by all sorts of sensual cravings and excitements, by intrigues, by tyranny, by lust for power, and by the conjunction of all these in war. Not only does the mystic tell you that, not only the Christian, but even the so-called anti-Christian, anti-mystic, like the communist or socialist, tells you the same thing. Everyone who is for the freedom of the spirit, for its integrity and need for development, must tell you the same thing, and must damn and want to destroy all that which thwarts it and keeps it from its high adventure. Now the spirit will never be defeated. Not because it strives for what is easily called right or moral or religious or equalitarian, but because it does not want to be cheated out of its own fulfil-ment, out of attaining that state of freedom, of delight, of ecstasy, of which once or twice in a lifetime it has caught a glimpse. The materialist, the scoffer, the sceptic, may try to destroy that spirit. He can never succeed. In the struggle it is not the spirit he will destroy, *it will be himself.*"

The Dean paused for a moment. "Don't misunderstand me," he went on. "Science will *help* enormously, more perhaps than any other factor. Already, you see, Colonel Brown is attempting to prove by mathematics the existence of the fourth dimension for the use of our spirit. We are here to-night discussing it. Which in itself is surely a remarkable thing. And always cropping up are these marvels concerning watches and ghosts and funerals and strange prophecies. All these are mere signs, intimations. I have dealt with Yoga because it happened to have been mentioned. I might have dealt with Plotinus, other men, other periods and places. For the spirit is in all men, and it is the same spirit.

"I might even have tried to deal with this land, this very beautiful land, the Highlands; have tried to show a manner of life, a humanism, concerned not with the outward show of material aggrandisement, but with the inward affairs of the spirit, as in poetry and music and good manners, in vanities and jealousies and strife, in a certain vividness, divine or diabolical, of the personal spirit. I do not wish to flatter this spirit. It appears, anyway, to be dying, to be passing out. But it had its day in an environment which forced the eyes at times to stare in contemplation. You have only to listen to their music, to perceive the way in which the finest, most sensitive spirits amongst them still become overborne by its rhythm, to see that what I say is true.

"But I am not going into that, fascinating as the subject may be, linking up rhythm and contemplation with the philosophies of the East, with the fundamental oneness of man. All I want to say is that I am not surprised that in this land in particular there should have lingered on these mental manifestations or marvels, grouped under the name of second sight. And when you examine them you find, as one should expect, that they do not refer exclusively to seeing or to such prophecy as the Brahan Seer's 'Doom of the House of Seaforth'. They also refer to other senses, as in India—though manifestly these simple people of a past age here, who could neither read nor write, had no knowledge of even the existence of Indian religion or philosophy; they refer to the sense of hearing—for example, the hearing of boards being sawn for coffins before they were actually sawn; even a forecasting of events by the sense of smell is by no means unknown. These marvels are in the case of the Highlands merely the manifestations of a spirit in decline—instead of, as they should be, the manifestations of a spirit exploring towards the light. And if I have spoken so much it is merely that I have tried to put them in proper perspective, to give them their elementary place, in this mysterious movement from the simple consciousness of the lower forms of life, through the self-consciousness of man to-day, to that higher consciousness which, I am afraid, I have failed even to suggest."

The concluding words had a note of simple humility, and as the Dean smiled Helen turned her eyes away.

Presently Sir John said, "You have brought the East back to me. There were times often, I admit, when I was disturbed, disturbed more than I might care to say, though always just quite by what, it was difficult to know. You dismiss it, of course. You say, 'Yes, seems pretty marvellous.' You are sceptical, for you have to protect your own mind. But that certain of these thinkers had developed extraordinary gifts there could be no doubt. No question of deceit or fraud. On the contrary, there was a giving up of material things. They acted not for gain but for loss, if one may put it that way. To me they were almost completely incomprehensible, and would have been, I think, quite incomprehensible, were it not for one personal experience. However, I have enjoyed the talk. You haven't lost the old gift for philosophy, David."

"I think", said Mr. Blair, "that Sir John should tell us his personal experience."

Sir John smiled and shook his head.

Lady Marway looked at him and then got up. "I think it is really time we were going."

"No, no, no!" cried Mr. Blair.

But now all were on their feet, and as Lady Marway went up to the Dean, the others got into little talk groups.

Mr. Blair said to Geoffrey, "By the way, did you ever hear or read of the prophecies of the Brahan Seer?"

Geoffrey pleaded ignorance and Mr. Blair turned to a bookshelf. "Read this. Don't lose it. You'll enjoy the curse on the House of Seaforth. Are you fond of that sort of curse, by the way? I have a very good collection of curses. Although I suppose this wasn't properly a curse. But it's quite a remarkable story."

"Is it censored? I mean, are the curses really printed?" Joyce asked, raising innocent eyebrows.

Mr. Blair was delighted with what he took to be her wit.

She became quite struck by this rubicund little man and insisted that he tell the story there and then specially for her benefit.

Marjory said nothing. Geoffrey smiled. George backed up Joyce. "Very good," said Mr. Blair, bowing gallantly and assuming his tortoiseshell glasses; for it was now obvious that Lady Marway, the Dean and Sir John were deep in personal discourse, while in Colonel Brown's corner Harry and Helen were manifestly engaging that clear-headed army man in fourth-dimensional manœuvres.

"This Brahan Seer lived in the sixteen-hundreds. Brahan is near Dingwall. The seat of the Mackenzies, the Seaforths. This Seer made very remarkable prophecies, most of which were fulfilled."

"One moment," said Geoffrey. "Is all the evidence the usual traditional hearsay?"

"Well, pretty nearly," replied Mr. Blair.

"Pardon my interruption. Please go on," said Geoffrey.

"Except in two cases at least, where there does seem fairly clear evidence that knowledge of the prophecies was widespread before the events happened. One was in the case of Fairburn Tower, a thriving mansion house of a local laird. The Seer said that the Tower would fall into ruins and that a cow would climb to a high room and have a calf there. The family decayed, the Tower fell into ruins, and a cow duly climbed the turret stairs and had a calf in a top room. People who had long known of the prophecy came from Inverness to see the cow. They had to let her down by ropes from a top window."

"But what on earth made the cow climb the stairs?" asked Joyce.

"It seems the local farmer had stored some of his straw in the top room. The cow had followed the fallen straws up the stairs."

Geoffrey laughed and was going to ask something when Mr. Blair, turning over a final page, found his prophecy of doom.

"This Seer", he explained, "was disliked by her Ladyship of Seaforth, because he could see too far into her affairs. She apparently was that sort of lady. Besides, he seemed to have had a fairly caustic tongue and was too obviously what we would call nowadays a democrat. So in the absence of her lord she got him tried by the church authorities for being a Satanic agent, and by all accounts the remarkable fellow was burned in a tar barrel near Fortrose. On his way to his unhappy end, he uttered Gaelic words to this effect:

" 'I see a Chief, the last of his House, both deaf and dumb. He will be the father of four fair sons, all of whom he shall

follow to the tomb. He shall live careworn, and die mourn-
ing, knowing that the honours of his House are to be extin-
guished for ever, and that no future Chief of the Mackenzies
shall rule in Kintail. After lamenting over the last and most
promising of his sons, he himself shall sink into the grave,
and the remnant of his possessions shall be inherited by a
white-coifed lassie from the east, and she shall kill her sister.
As a sign by which it shall be known that these things are
coming to pass, there shall be four great lairds in the days of
the last Seaforth (Gairloch, Chisholm, Grant, and Raasay),
one of whom shall be buck-toothed, the second hare-lipped,
the third half-witted, and the fourth a stammerer. Seaforth,
when he looks round and sees them, may know that his sons
are doomed to death, and that his broad lands shall pass
away to the stranger, and that his line shall come to an end'."

"Jehosophat!" exclaimed George. "You are not going to
say next that all that really happened?"

"It did—but not for nearly a hundred and fifty years. The
prophecy got around and people wrote letters about it
before it happened, and credible men who survived the fulfilment of the prophecy told how widespread the prophecy
had been throughout the country in their youth. When the
last Seaforth died, the papers featured it at length. Sir Walter
Scott knew about it. Historically all that seems quite certain.
In fact, there were people who thought that the old Seer, as
generation followed generation, had made a grave fool of
himself. Then there came a Seaforth who had four sons and
the whole affair happened as detailed. Colonel Brown tried
to work out mathematically the reasonable probabilities. The
factors: a laird who would in his life become deaf and dumb
(for he was not born so); four sons; the death of those four
sons before himself; the loss of his lands and the end of his
line; the lassie from the east who would kill her sister
(through an accident, as it happened, while she was driving
a dog-cart); and the four contemporary chiefs with their
remarkable malformities. Colonel Brown said that when you
give odds to each factor and multiply them to get the degree
of probability—or something like that, for I never was a

mathematician—the final odds against the whole happening were so inconceivably vast that coincidence must definitely be ruled out. Do I make myself clear to you?"

"Perfectly," said Geoffrey. "I should agree with Colonel Brown. But—I have not yet agreed with the evidence. When I read this I shall be able to show you its gaping lacunae. For example, in the letters that you assert referred to the curse before it was fulfilled, were those terms that you have read out explicitly stated?"

"Well, I couldn't say as to explicit statement. The trouble in those far-off days was, of course, that no one wrote, or no one thought of writing down facts to stand as evidence. Everything was committed not to paper but to memory. Poems and everything else. That fact has got to be taken into account when it comes to destructive criticism. Evidence was not deliberately or consciously withheld. For example, you will find here many prophecies of the Seer, utterly fantastic things, which never have been fulfilled. Nor, I should say, ever have the remotest chance of being fulfilled—short, perhaps, of a world war that will turn us into primitive barbarians again."

"And that's extremely unlikely the way things are going, what!" said George.

Mr. Blair glanced at him and smiled.

"But tell me," asked Joyce, "how on earth could he see hundreds of years ahead?"

"He could see millions of years ahead," said Geoffrey, "with the greatest of ease, because a million years to a man like that are but as a day."

"Are you trying to be sarcastic?"

"Trying? I'm only trying my best to understand the extraordinary credulity of men who dabble in this sort of thing. If you only understood the terrific fight that science has had to put up against every kind of religious prophet and tribal witch-doctor and cultured dabbler in the occult, you would understand my impatience. And surely to goodness, you know them in London: you know people who go to crystal gazers and diviners of one kind or another, and in particular those loathsome mystics who have west-end parlours, oh very cultured, esoteric, you don't pay—no, no, you just leave something, all in the nature of a religious service, dim lights, incense—oh God, it turns my stomach. The new Messiah!" He laughed.

Mr. Blair laughed also, and then, lowering his voice, "I like your attitude. It's what I call classical. Now, wait! I have an idea. Something has presumably been happening over at your place. Why not carry out an experiment? Why not? If you really have some material to go on. I understand about your laboratory tests and so forth, but after all you can't bring these surroundings and people to London. There is just this about the real second sight. It apparently is an involuntary and unusual exhibit. You can't ask the subject to sit down in a chair and turn on the prophetic tap. You see my point?"

Geoffrey's eyes gleamed. "I am tempted," he said. He gave a small reflective chuckle to himself. "It might be fun."

"I doubt really if we should take any more notice of it," said Marjory hesitantly.

"Why not?" asked George. "Should I like to see it going up in a shower of sparks!"

"What a game!" cried Joyce, and laughed so loudly that Lady Marway turned round.

"Hush!" said Mr. Blair, with exaggerated secrecy. His party nodded. Mum was the word! The air of conspiracy made Mr. Blair very jolly, and when the maids brought in tea trolleys, he had everyone seated again, except Colonel Brown, Harry, and Helen, who seemed to be quite lost in their debate.

Into the involuntary silence came Harry's voice: "But what of the Seer's prophecies that have not been fulfilled? I can see that the mere fact that they have been recorded shows that people in the Highlands knew of them and even wrote them down. But I mean it's so fantastic to expect they ever will happen now——"

"Precisely," said Colonel Brown. "So far as I know here's a point about them that's never been made before.

Remembering that in the fourth-dimensional world—the world, we assume, of second sight—it's as easy to step back into the past as forward into the future, then we may conclude that among the Brahan Seer's visions some in fact referred to the past, though the Seer himself might not know that, and, therefore, be perfectly honest in placing them in the future. For example, he said that boats would one day tie up to a certain rock in Strathpeffer. From lack of knowledge, it simply could not have occurred to him that, as is obvious to us now, the valley between Dingwall and Strathpeffer was once upon a time under water and that boats in all probability have tied up to the said rock in time past. That may be a dubious case. But take...."

Mr. Blair tiptoed to a desk, picked up an old cow-bell, and rang it furiously. Three solemn, startled faces turned round, and then, for a few seconds, there was the gayest laughter.

On the way to their cars, when cordial greetings had been spoken, Geoffrey said to Marjory, "What a show!"

"I think he's a dear old man, the Dean," she replied.

"Of course! But heavens, that old philosophic style! At this time of day! Isn't it remarkable that a man of such obvious intelligence should deliberately let it get fogged in that way? Fogged, moth-eaten. And he went on—heavens, didn't he go on!"

"Hsh!" said Marjory, as Sir John and Lady Marway joined them and they all got seated.

"David seems tired a bit," said Lady Marway quietly to her husband. "He has somehow the air—I don't know what it is—of being world-weary at the back of all his simple, kind ways."

"Yes," said Sir John. "I think the real trouble is that he feels the conditions of the world to-day, feels it is due to the triumph of the material over the spiritual. Really feels it." The car started off. "It's an odd thing, but you'd notice that he never mentioned religion. It's as profound in him as that. Somehow, I felt what he was getting at. I—felt it."

"I did, too."

"I always liked him," said Sir John.

In the second car, Harry said to Helen, as they got seated, "Enjoyed the evening?"

"Yes," said Helen.

There was silence until Joyce, having recovered her scarf, rushed up and slammed the door, whereupon George observed, "I think the way you've been getting off with mine host was obvious enough positively to be offensive."

Joyce laughed. "I say, isn't he a dear old funny old thing! Whatever does he do with himself normally?"

"Breeds parrots, I should say," said George.

"George! And after the amount of his food *and* drink you contrived to stow away!"

"I withdraw. Do you know what I was trying to do that time I choked?"

"No."

"I was trying to catch the wine as it slipped down. It was so smooth, hanged if I could. I wonder where that sort of stuff is grown. Whoops!"

The mist had grown thicker, but presently they climbed out of it into a cloudless night of moonlight and shadows, a night of such serene starry loveliness that, as each car entered it, silence fell on its occupants.

"So lovely," said Marjory on an undertone.

Geoffrey glanced at her, and then fixed himself comfortably into his corner where he could see her without appearing to look at her. Now that he thought of it, she had been very silent to-night. Her fairness in the shadowed moonlight had a quality of gossamer that made him stare at it as at an illusion of beauty. He saw the dark places of her eyes, wondered if they were looking at him, suddenly felt they were, and experienced a sensation of constriction about his chest and throat.

Harry stared out of his window. Helen glanced at him and knew that he was not thinking of her.

Joyce adventured upon the *Barcarolle*—night of stars and night of love—humming it thoughtfully, and sighed.

George sobbed softly and sadly.

They came down into banks of fog again, and then suddenly across the night came strange elusive sounds.

"Stop!" said Harry.

George drew up and as Harry lowered his window they heard remote, muffled, eddying music coming from the hills on their left.

"Isn't it weird?" Joyce caught her breath.

They listened.

"Whatever can be doing it?" Joyce wondered.

"Barrie and Mary Rose and her keening," said George in deep sadness. "They will not have been finding their island yet." But there was no real mockery in his tone.

"Would you mind waiting for me for five minutes? I promise not to be more than ten at the outside," said Harry.

There was astonished silence in the dark car. George switched on the roof light and turned to look at him.

"You don't mind, do you?" Harry smiled to the girls.

They didn't mind, of course, but exactly what was the big idea?

"Here," called George, "don't be mad!"

The door slammed. Harry passed through the spot light. His body grew into a phantasmal shape, grey as the night, then vanished in a moment. George switched on the full headlights and was blinded by a white wall. He swore mildly, but with expression. They listened. No sound—except the eddying music, that wasn't music, but a weird crying out of the heart of the hills, a sad crying, a high insistent note, that doubled and trebled upon itself, fell and rose, eddied away altogether, to come again more insistent than ever.

"Whatever do you think has gone wrong with him?" Joyce asked Helen.

"I don't know," said Helen.

"Oh God, what is it?" cried Joyce.

"Someone playing bagpipes on the hill," said Helen.

"Bagpipes!" said Joyce. She laughed harshly, then instantly was silent.

"I never did understand the things before," said George. "This is obviously their locale."

"I should say so!" said Joyce. "Turns the stomach all queer."

"Lord God," said George, "it *is* like something yearning!"

"What was it that yearned in pain?" asked Joyce.

"A god," said Helen.

Joyce laughed.

"I know," said George, "I know what it is. It's a pibrok."

"A what?" asked Joyce.

"A pibrok," said George. "A lament."

"A lament? Whatever for?"

"Don't ask me," said George. "They get a gold medal for playing it at the Northern Meetings."

"A gold medal!" echoed Joyce, and went off into high laughter. George joined her.

"Though I must say I don't quite see the joke," said George.

"Neither do I," said Joyce.

So they laughed again and felt better.

Into the silence came the insistent playing, deceitful in its movement as the cry of a golden plover, near and far, the moor and the hill, passing over the tops…coming out of the bog, the bowels of the mountain.

"Heavens, I wish it would stop! Where on earth could Harry have gone?" Joyce asked impatiently.

"He'll be back within ten minutes if he said he would," Helen suggested.

And at that the music ceased.

Joyce applauded "And thank you very much for stopping."

At the end of what seemed much more than ten minutes, George looked at his clock. Ten clear minutes later, Harry had not yet appeared. This was getting a bit too much! With all due respect to Harry, this was going beyond the limit!

An argument arose between George, who wanted to sound the horn, and Helen who didn't.

"He's lost," said George.

"He's probably turning round in circles," said Joyce. "Press it hard."

George blew a prolonged blast.

"What's that?" whispered Joyce. Then she collapsed backwards with a groan. The hill music had started again.

"We're lost. We're damned. This bloody spot is haunted," George intoned.

"Oh—shut—up!" cried Joyce. She turned to Helen. "You don't really believe in ghosts, do you, Helen?"

"I do feel one or two moving around," said Helen. "I am beginning to have the awful sensation of being fourth-dimensional."

"Oh God!" groaned Joyce. "You make me crawl with them." Quite involuntarily she brushed her shoulders, and, diving for the wheel, pressed the horn-button.

A seven-foot, ghostly representation of Harry wavered on the edge of the mist and disappeared. The door handle shook. "I'm very sorry," said Harry, entering by the head and slamming the door after him. "I couldn't get away."

"Where on earth were you?" Joyce demanded.

"Corr Inn is just up there," Harry explained. "I had a small debt to pay the landlord for beer. Have I been more than ten minutes?"

George and Joyce turned on him and rent him with their tongues into small pieces. The process lasted the six miles to Corbreac, where they found the first car getting ready to come and look for them.

Harry explained how he had come to owe the landlord a debt, decided he might as well pay it, and take the opportunity of enjoying bagpipes on the hills at night. He was sorry the others had not heard the excellent entertainment. Very sorry if his thoughtlessness had upset anybody.

But clearly none of them wanted to discuss it, though a gleam did come into Geoffrey's eye. Joyce yawned, looking exhausted.

"Are you aware it's midnight?" Lady Marway asked.

"Yes, high time we were in bed," her husband agreed. "I'll see to the doors."

Within a few minutes the room was in darkness.

When Sir John had undressed and washed and was getting ready to go through the ritual of brushing his hair, Lady Marway, from her bed, looking at him, said quietly:

"Do you remember, to-night, when David had finished talking, you said to him that the spirit of the East, with its power of seeing and knowing, would have been quite incomprehensible to you, were it not for one personal experience? I somehow can't get it out of my head. I've been racking my memory. What was it, Jack?"

He looked at himself in the mirror for a moment, and then shrugged slightly. "I'd rather not say."

"I'm sorry. I did not mean——"

"Now, now," said Sir John. "That understanding tone did always make me tell."

"No, please. I merely felt it because I thought that I had forgotten. If I did not know, then I don't mind."

"But you did know. At least I always thought you knew."

"Jack!"

"Well," he said, taking a brush in each hand and proceeding calmly to deal with his tough, dark-grey hair, "the experience was simply my being in love with you."

Chapter Ten

Sir John raised his eyebrows as he saw Geoffrey emerge from the gun-room door ready for the hill. Harry and George showed an equal surprise. Maclean was the first to say good morning.

"Really feeling fit for it?" asked Sir John.

"Yes," said Geoffrey. "Not quite free and easy but exercise should oil the parts."

"I'm glad," said George handsomely, for he would now have to stand down.

"Quite sure?" asked Geoffrey.

Harry offered George his beat and so did Sir John, but George assured them that he had yesterday set so high a standard that he was relieved, for their sakes, not to have to repeat it.

When the beats were gone over and the wind discussed, Sir John asked Geoffrey what he thought was the easiest one for him.

"Benuain, if I may have my choice."

Sir John regarded him with frank astonishment. "But—the climbing?"

Geoffrey shrugged. He would manage all right.

The pony had been sent on. The car would take him round by the public road to within a mile or two. The wind was just right for the west approach.... He would have a bite of breakfast.

George, seeing Joyce come round the corner of the house, went towards her, signalling silence with his face. "Geoff!" he muttered. Then aloud, "Would you care to come with us, while I drive Geoffrey round?" And he marched her off to the garage.

When, at the end of the drive, Geoffrey and Angus got out and good wishes had been offered, Joyce said to George, "Isn't he determined to get something?"

"Something!" said George. "He's going to get King Brude or bust. He was merely in a funk lest Harry or I got him. Odd chap, Geoffrey, in many ways. Fighter and all that; keen and jealous as a schoolboy. Angus will have to watch his step to-day! See, there's the pony coming." George had to go on half a mile before he could turn his car. On the way back they saw Geoffrey's large figure astride the small beast and stopped the car to chuckle.

"Wonder what's in his mind?" asked Joyce.

"Death," said George.

Which was wonderfully near the truth, for at that moment Geoffrey called to Angus and spoke to him, saying that this was not a day for any mistake to be made; if King Brude was on Benuain, then King Brude must die. What was the plan? And as Angus went over the ground, from one spy point to the next, Geoffrey cross-questioned him. There was no laughter in his face. It was grey and grim. There was none in Angus's face, which showed signs of last night's wastage at Corr Inn.

"He may not be there at all," said Angus.

"No doubt. But he is more likely to be there than any-where else in the forest, isn't he?"

"Yes," said Angus.

"You know that the heights of Benuain are his usual ground; that in this weather he'll never be lower down?"

"It's not likely," said Angus.

"Well, what do you mean?"

"I mean that he may not be in the forest at all."

"He may not. He may be in the damned moon, but it's not likely. Unless, of course, he has second sight." He laughed. "He may move in four dimensions." He felt cheered a bit, for he was not in good physical form. "Know anything about the fourth dimension?"

Angus appeared not to hear.

"There's a legend that a lot of you fellows know Latin and Greek. Ever heard of that?"

Angus remained silent.

"Don't you understand a joke?" Then on a more friendly tone, "Why make the idiotic suggestion that he may not be up there? To cheer me up?"

"It wasn't an idiotic suggestion," said Angus. "The rut is on. Last year I know that King Brude had his hinds in Glenan Forest. He was nearly shot there by Lord Starnes in the first week of October. He'll go there this year again."

"How do you know?"

"Because that's the way a stag like him behaves. He goes back to the same place for his hinds."

Geoffrey rode on, trying not to think of Lord Starnes, trying to banish the appalling vision of that plutocratic gentleman shooting King Brude, shooting the stag that was his, Geoffrey Smith's, and no one else's on earth. His eyes gleamed vindictively, his mouth closed.

The first climb was not too difficult, and with a fair wind against them, no great precautions had to be taken. Geoffrey rested occasionally, rubbing a spot in his right side each time. His kneecap, too, felt the strain and had a deceitful tendency to go numb. But he refused to let Angus go on alone, and after an hour's hard work they came to their first vantage point, where broken ground made spying easy.

It was not a corrie but a valley through the hills, a high broad pass, and it lay in the forenoon sunlight very still and silent. Geoffrey got his excitement, however, not from so immaterial a thing as a sense of beauty, but from the reality of red deer that his naked eyes picked out here and there. The sight of them flushed all his flesh, banished pain and tiredness. Not three hundred yards away, some hinds were feeding up wind. A stag, too; a nine pointer, and a heavy beast; and one or two more stags, youngsters, on the outskirts. Feeding quietly, moving forward a step or two, cropping the tender shoots, unsuspiciously, with quiet grace. Occasionally a head lifted and took the air with such extreme sensitiveness that it stopped one's breath. Then his eyes picked out quite a small herd on the opposite side that he had completely missed. The place was alive with them! Positively swarming! He gulped and looked at Angus spying so concentratedly, slowly, and felt impatient to get the telescope for himself.

"Anything doing?" he whispered.

Angus paid no attention until he had finished; then he very slowly slid back.

"There's one really fine beast over there," he said.

"With that lot of hinds?"

"Yes." Angus was slightly excited. The hunt did this to him, tended to make him forget personal vanities and insults, for coming up the hill he had vowed that he was not going to do much for this particular sort of gentleman if he could help it. And he knew the ways by which a cunning stalker can invisibly defeat the consummation of an impeccable stalk.

"Is it King Brude?"

"No," said Angus. "King Brude is not there. I don't know this beast. An imperial—thirteen points."

"An imperial!" Geoffrey got hold of the telescope and picked up the stag. He spied for a long time. Then he slid back and nodded. "Cupped antlers."

"Double cups."

Geoffrey stirred restlessly. Angus said nothing, aware of the internal struggle. Geoffrey began to question him on the chances of this stalk. Angus explained how it was impossible to get at him where he was, but how in course of time, the hinds should reach a certain spot, where approach would be feasible. They would feed on. They might lie down—almost certainly would. It meant a wide detour to come in on them because of the nature of the high ground on the other side. But it should be possible. They might have to give their day to it.

"You think we'd get him?"

"There's a good chance."

The talk went on for some time, covering all possibilities of the disturbance of these deer, of other deer, all the endless tactics and strategy of the forest.

"What do you think?" Geoffrey asked.

"There is no doubt that that is the stalk we should do."

And there was just no doubt about it. A bellow came up from the pass. Geoffrey got the spy-glass trained again. The imperial was chasing away a young stag that had dared come too near the hinds. While he was engaged on this task, another young fellow amorously adventured his presence on the other side of the hinds. The imperial, turning back, saw him, and, with a short bellow, charged. The young six-pointer was properly nimble, however. The old sultan was giving definition to his harem! A heavy, dark-skinned beast, with what would surely be the outstanding head of the season.

Geoffrey snapped shut the telescope. "If we find nothing in the higher corries, we might get him in the evening. We'll go on." His face was slightly congested. Angus said nothing, but about his eyes came an expression of dry sarcasm. Stags had not yet developed the obliging habit of waiting for anyone.

They had to descend again, and work round below the level of the pass on the west side, where the ground sloped steeply. Twice they were troubled by deer, and had to do one long wriggle up a scree that Geoffrey found very tiring. Angus was insistent that they take no chances of disturbing deer higher up. Geoffrey saw the point, but more than once deemed Angus's care excessive. He knew quite well that Angus could take it out of him if he liked. And he was troubled by the consciousness that he should, as a sports-man, have gone for the imperial. There were other rifles in the forest; others who must take similar chances when they came their way.

Angus went on and waited for him, went on and waited, tireless, brown, tough as heather, his large mouth open often and wet, his eyes dark blue and gleaming.

Geoffrey followed grimly, pausing now and then, but never for long. For an hour they did not speak.

"That's the spot," said Angus pointing upward to the edge of a hollow against the sky. "From that knob, that lump, we'll see into the corrie. If you like, I could go up alone and see if he's in it. If he's not, then there's nothing for it but Coireard, and you would be saved the climb here."

Geoffrey stood gazing up. "I'll go with you," he said.

He doesn't trust me! Angus thought. He smiled to himself, with a leftward twist of his mouth. For he knew it was not altogether distrust. It was the man's keenness also, a keenness that surmounted bodily infirmity, that would surmount anything short of utter prostration. And Angus understood that and liked it. He could trust no one. He must be there himself!

All right, let the devil climb for it!

"Here, not so damned quick!" cried Geoffrey in a fierce half-whisper.

"Sorry," muttered Angus, waiting.

"Blast it, can't you see I'm not quite fit?"

Angus saw nothing for a moment but a blinding anger. It passed, leaving the usual moody trace, which also tended to fade out as they finally spied into the corrie, and their voices, in husky whispers, discussed the prospect. There were no less than two heads which any sportsman might be proud of; one in particular with a fine spread and long tines, including both bays—an extremely attractive, an unusual, head, the beast himself being, unlike the imperial, of a deep golden colour. He was far out on the off side. It would again be a longish stalk, but a better chance than in the case of the imperial. Geoffrey snapped shut the glass.

"Come on!" he said. "The High Corrie."

Angus laughed inwardly. He didn't care a tinker's curse now whether the fellow got a stag or not!

The pony-man in the distance was keeping abreast of them. He was an old hand, inured to the hill, but attached to his ancient patch of a croft. It was long past lunch-time.

"We'll see into the High Corrie first," said Geoffrey.

Angus signalled. Not that it mattered whether Lachlan saw him or not. That wise old gillie would have his own "piece" at his own time!

The going now became heavy and complicated. The telescope was often in use. And once they had to go through the whole art of a difficult stalk to get above some beasts that, disturbed too soon, might easily head for the High Corrie and raise the alarm. As they were on the lee side of Benuain, the wind was occasionally fluky. The deer, apprehending no danger from above, more particularly as the wind came down from the heights, were naturally on the alert to danger approaching from below and up wind. Geoffrey and Angus had to keep high, and often projecting rock faces called for careful and exhausting movements, while what should have been fairly easy going on smooth, if steep, slopes, provided the most anxious moments of all from lack of cover. Once, when they seemed completely caught out, Angus proved his skill by rousing some stragglers in the way to a point just beyond curiosity. The deer looked, and looked, and finally, becoming suspicious, moved off along the side of the hill, while Angus made Geoffrey continue to lie low. Not that any compulsion was needed, for Geoffrey was aware within himself that his strength was going.

But he made no complaint, and when at long last he drew up beside Angus, amongst great boulders on a shoulder below the weathered peak of Benuain, he lay flat on his stomach, his brow on his wrists. Drawing out the cylinders of his telescope, Angus heard the heavy laboured breathing. But he had reached Coireard, the High Corrie!

Angus pulled himself forward a yard or two and inspected the corrie. It was a wide corrie but not very extensive. His astonishment was complete when he saw that, except for one immature stag on the off side, it was empty. There was no need to put the glass on it. Automatically he lifted the telescope to his eye and searched the far shoulder. Completely deserted. He had a look at the young stag. One of the antlers was undergrown and had a deformed twist. The brute had got injured some time and was keeping by himself.

"Well?" came the harsh whisper.

Angus had forgotten his gentleman. He now slid back and shook his head. "Nothing."

Geoffrey's eyes pierced into him as if accusing him of some malign trick. It was a brutal fleshy attack. But Angus understood that it really came from the inner places of defeat and desperation, and was automatic and ugly, but not really personal.

"Look for yourself," said Angus, and handed him the glass. "There's just one small stag."

After Geoffrey had spied for a long time, he was about to get up, when Angus stopped him. "Let me have one more look, please."

"What's the damned good of looking?" asked Geoffrey in his normal voice.

Angus, his brows drawn, instantly hushed him to silence and, ignoring his expression, picked up the young stag again. The thought that this young stag might be a toady attendant on the great had occurred to him, not an unusual relationship amongst deer. Yard by careful yard around the young stag, he searched out the ground. Just beyond the stag there were some shallow folds in the ground and tufts of old rank heather, though for the most part the real heather belt was now below them. Growing out of one of these tufts were what looked like the bare branches of a stunted shrub. He concentrated on them: two branches that curved in towards each other, the two final long spikes of each branch "blown" towards the other two. The span, the grace, the Highland arch. O god of Benuain! The glass shook the vision out of focus.

Should he tell him? He tried to steady the glass, but his hands were trembling. There was no need to tell him. No need. He did not deserve it. God damn him, he did not deserve it. A deep potent instinct moved in Angus, darkened by something of fear and myth, of a justice, a rightness, beyond the standards of the world. For this was the spirit of his forest, its incarnation, its reality, its legend, its living truth. For this man—this man—to shoot.

He shut the glass and slid towards Geoffrey, who had turned over on his left side and closed his eyes. But the mouth was deliberately shut and breath came through the nostrils. Their way back was below them. They would simply get up and go, and this man would never know.

Angus sat upright, looked at the grey face, the intolerance of the drawn lips, the material force of the rounded head, the fleshy dominance, and looked away from it across that northern world of moor and hill. The sun was warm and cast shadows. Far as the eye could travel there were mountain ridges, in dark browns, in misty blues, and in the hollows of ultimate ridges stood back the shadowy cones of ultimate peaks. Nothing moved over these vast solitudes, nothing stirred out of that warm timeless sleep.

"Well?"

Angus half-turned but did not look at him. "He's there," he said on a quiet undertone.

Geoffrey's body swung slowly upward until he was supporting it with his palms.

"Who?" His whisper was harsh.

"King Brude," said Angus.

For several seconds there was complete immobility, utter silence. Then Geoffrey scrambled into forceful life and demanded of Angus what he thought he was trying to do.

"I was merely thinking", lied Angus calmly, "of the best way of getting at him."

Geoffrey regarded him with the mistrust naturally born out of lack of understanding. Angus fixed the telescope and handed it to Geoffrey. "Come here."

It took Geoffrey a long time to pick up the antlers, but at last he did. And then he, too, grew quiet. For in his excitement, he could not speak. He plucked a blade of hill grass, gnawed at it, spat it out, and asked, "What do you suggest?"

"It's difficult," said Angus. "We cannot get near enough from this side. And we can't come in from anywhere beyond, because of the wind. The only approach would be across wind from directly behind and above him. And we can't do that because right round that off side is a face of rock. If we went beyond the rock, farther round, then the wind might carry our scent over the shoulder and down into the corrie."

Geoffrey nodded, his brows knitted. "You think we should wait here till he gets up?"

215

"There doesn't seem to be much else. When he gets up he'll begin feeding. If he comes this way, we're in a perfect place, and the chances are he will, because it is now the afternoon and he will tend to feed down to the lower ground." He spoke evenly. "But he might go on up the corrie, across the ridge, and down into the main glen beyond, or perhaps out over the march, for Glenan lies in that direction— though there's no signs on him yet, for the high-hill stag is always a bit later. If he goes that way, we're in the wrong place. I doubt if we could come round on him in time. Though we might."

Geoffrey was thoughtful, the domineering quality in him quite gone. "Are you sure there's no way up behind?"

"Up the rock? I have never done it."

"Has anyone?"

"Alick has done it."

Geoffrey looked at him, but Angus did not meet the look. "Shouldn't we at least see if we can do it?"

"Whatever you say," said Angus.

Geoffrey's look grew sharper. "Angus! What do you mean exactly?"

"It's whatever you say," replied Angus without stress. "He may get up at any time to feed."

"You think we should stay here?" Geoffrey was watching him.

"Yes."

Geoffrey had seen a dour mood at work in Angus before, generally after there had been some too direct expression of opinion on his own part. He could be touchy, but usually got over it before very long, and in the heat of the actual hunt itself there had always been a natural unanimity between them, for he recognised in Angus a hunter as keen as himself. He could never wish for a better stalker, would never want a better, and any temporary differences were to Geoffrey afterwards, when he had won through, a matter for humorous reflection. That a stalker should be independent and express himself in full at moments of stress was "in character", was in the forest tradition. But now there was a mysterious something extra in Angus's mood that Geoffrey could not fathom and that, by force of his own nature, he must mistrust.

"I should like to see this place that Alick can climb and you and I can't."

"Very good, sir." Angus put the telescope in its leather case and slung it round his back. Without looking at Geoffrey, he picked up the rifle and started off.

He went carefully, giving Geoffrey plenty of time. His manner was quiet and efficient. He had every consideration for his gentleman. He brought him across rough ground below the corrie and then on to smooth ground that sloped so steeply that they had to grip the hillside with a hand. Geoffrey found this side-walking very tiring to his knee. The general body weakness he put down to lack of food. When at last Angus brought him under the long curving terrace of rock, all his muscles were tremulous and his brow cold.

He saw that the place to which Angus pointed was the only way up. It seemed to Geoffrey simple enough and he said so. Couldn't be more than fifteen feet high, wasn't perpendicular, and had obvious projections and fissures for hands and feet.

Angus nodded. "Very good, sir," he said. "Would you like a couple of minutes' rest first? I could try it."

He spoke so simply, in undertones, that Geoffrey experienced a slight pang of remorse, and he glanced at Angus with that perceptible goggle of the eyes that implied a chuckle was not far away, if need be. But Angus was apparently still a little on his high horse. So "You sit down for a minute, too. You need it," he said, with consideration.

Angus shook his head and went up the few yards to the foot of the climb and began examining it. As Geoffrey joined him, he asked who should go first.

"You go," murmured Geoffrey. "Then I could catch you if you fall."

Angus's vague smile may have been an acknowledgement of the joke. "It's much steeper than it looks," was all he said. He began to climb.

Geoffrey saw the feet feeling for holds, the fingers gripping. A little to the right. A step or two up. A little to the left.

Was it higher than he had thought? More difficult? He got a crick in his neck and swayed as he lowered his head—and looked below him. The ground sloped very steeply indeed. If Angus dislodged a lump of rock, it would not simply roll down; it would leap and bound and bury itself far below. If his body fell from the rock face, it would get a flying start!

And Angus was having a slight difficulty quite near the top. The rifle, slung to his back, was tending to get in his way. But there he was—up—and over. Good!

Angus faced down. "Don't try it!" he said, in low earnest tones.

Geoffrey was apparently amused. He caught his staff by its bone ferrule and threw it wildly over Angus's head, half losing his balance as he did so and grabbing at the earth. The idea that he could not do what Alick had done! That he would have to admit defeat before Angus! He kept himself amused and tackled the rock.

For there was no need to get excited about a thing like this, and certainly absurd to let fear touch the flesh.

Quite absurd. But it was annoying not to be able always to get a proper grip with the hands. It was impossible to look down and study the next hold for the feet. The sheer pressure on the fingers was at times very great. And that damned knee of his—he hardly dared risk giving it the body's full weight in a straining upward step. Thank God, here at last was a reasonable ledge. When he got both feet lodged on it and one hand with a secure grip, he lay against the rock. But instead of gaining relief, he had the flushing sensation within him of an insidious sickness. He could feel his flesh going weak, dissolving. And in the core of that weakness, panic stirred.

His teeth gritted, he whipped up his will, he looked up, saw that there was barely his own height yet to accomplish, but saw also that the rock appeared to bulge outward. He whipped up his anger to whip his will. His will might last for a couple of minutes.

He heard Angus's voice, low and intense, stinging him on. Here was the bulge of rock. He could not do it. His left foot scraped against the rock, scrambled wildly for a hold. He was going! God Almighty, he was done! The rushing impact of the spaces below began to assail his senses....

His foot was gripped.

"Go on, damn it, go on!"

His foot was being heaved upward. His right hand gripped round a small boss of rock. His belly was on the verge. His feet kicked free. Digging his fingers in, he drew himself over the ledge, lay on his face, and let the breath sob in his throat.

From the ledge to which he had climbed down, Angus looked up at the vacant rock, then let his forehead fall against the cold surface. He was feeling a trifle sick himself and very weak. A late night and too much drink didn't help a temperate fellow! He swore softly to himself. The danger he stood in was a gentle solace. There was no need to hurry.

Geoffrey's voice wakened him. He looked up and saw the face and knew, deep in his bowels, that he hated it. His body felt light as he heaved upward. Geoffrey stretched out a hand.

"It's all right," said Angus, surmounting the verge in his own fashion without help.

"It's steeper than I thought," said Geoffrey.

"It's a bit steep," said Angus.

Geoffrey was constrained in his mind and sick in his body. His eyes were intolerant. He had conquered the rock. He kept his chin up, his mouth shut. He was going to conquer King Brude. He held himself together, his breath noisy in his nostrils. For a stalker to help his gentleman over difficulties was part of his job. That's what he was paid for. The gentleman took it for granted. The stalker had the reward of duty well done. And perhaps the real gentleman did not altogether forget it when it came to giving a tip.

Angus sat waiting for Geoffrey. And after a minute or two, Geoffrey turned for the crest.

It was an easy climb, a walk in fact, until the crest was at hand. Then Angus, selecting his spot, crawled up to it, Geoffrey at his heels and the rifle ready. Angus motioned Geoffrey up beside him.

King Brude had got up and was eating towards the boulders on the other side which they had so recently left.

The distance was still no more than about a hundred and fifty yards, but the shot was difficult because the stag was facing directly away from them.

Angus began to whisper: "Get ready. I'll draw the attention of the toady, if I can. King Brude will then swing round and look this way. Don't waste time. The only chance before he gets out of range."

Geoffrey had no sooner got the rifle trained on King Brude, than that guardian of the great, the toady, whose body was three-quarters on, raised his head and looked directly at him. King Brude paid no attention. The toady made a warning movement. King Brude lifted his head over his shoulder; turned slightly to get a better look.

"Now!" breathed Angus.

Geoffrey fired. There was the splash of the bullet in a pool of shallow water beyond. It had gone just over the shoulder.

"Missed!" said Angus.

King Brude took a prancing stride or two. He was still uncertain, and paused an instant, the great head questing them. The rifle cracked.

Then King Brude leapt into action, and went flashing up the corrie after the bounding toady.

"Quick!" cried Angus. "Quick! For God's sake, fire!"

Geoffrey, on his feet, fired twice, but the shots were wild.

"Give me that!" Angus snatched the rifle from his hands. "Your second got him in the guts." And, turning from Geoffrey, he began running after the deer.

Geoffrey shouted at him, followed for a few lumbering steps, maddened, then sat down, his teeth showing as the lips drew back.

But he was exhausted. And, anyway, it was the stalker's duty to follow up and secure a wounded beast. Whatever happened he, Geoffrey, had shot King Brude! The stag would die. Death might be delayed, but death was certain. The bullet, a little too far back, had merely missed an immediately vital part. Geoffrey experienced a slow-spreading satisfaction, for until Angus had spoken he thought he had missed altogether. He watched his stalker until he had disappeared, then lay back for a little rest.

As it happened, Geoffrey's instinct to trust Angus now was not misplaced. For Angus would follow King Brude, day and night, until one or other of them gave in. And the mood defeated tiredness in his body.

It was a long hunt, for more than once the watchful young stag defeated Angus. King Brude was sick and wanted no more than a quiet place in which to rest.

They crossed the march into Glenan Forest as the late afternoon light threw long shadows. Angus watched them through his glass. If they kept going straight ahead across the moorland, darkness would defeat him that night. But King Brude's growing sickness was clearly too much for the long expanse and he turned towards broken rising ground on the right that lay north-east of the upper reaches of the Corr. Angus deflected his course to come up wind against this territory of which he knew little beyond its general lie or formation. He had no thought of trespass, for the tradition between neighbouring forests permitted the following of a badly wounded deer across a march.

But again, after a careful stalk, the young stag, moving about restlessly, saw him, for he trotted about with consternation, and Angus, acting on instinct (King Brude was invisible), made a movement with arm and head that in an instant turned consternation into panic. Wheeling on his hind legs, he bolted away at full gallop.

Angus lay dead still for a minute, then went forward on his stomach.

King Brude was lying, his back to the rising slope from which his toady had so ignominiously fled, facing down to open country, instinctively trusting the wind behind and his eyes in front. Angus could not get any nearer. The distance was about two hundred yards.

Angus fired and hit him, but not fatally. King Brude staggered to his feet, but not to fly.

Angus advanced, the rifle against his shoulder. The light was not too good. When he fired again, he must kill. For he knew now that the hunt was over. King Brude had turned, as he would turn against hounds, against all mortal enemies: King Brude was at bay.

Noble he looked, too; the great head up; the eyes, against the westering light, full of fire. A superb beast, the power streaming forward from the lean flanks. Angus saw him gathering his power into neck and shoulders, as if to meet death in a last wild charge, the head sinking and rising with a slow terrible beauty.

Angus could not fire at that head. He dared not mar its beauty as a trophy. He must shoot him in the neck. His body felt weak and light and tremulous as grass.

At ten yards they faced each other. King Brude's flanks moved. As he staggered, Angus fired at the neck. King Brude sank to the ground. Angus dropped the rifle and, opening his knife, ran in.

But King Brude was not yet dead, and Angus was very nearly caught in the wild heave of the antlers. The third or tray tine of the right antler grazed his forehead, drawing blood. Death had never been nearer him. King Brude's spasms were now extremely violent and Angus who, in his own madness, had grasped at the antlers, was thrown about like a bunch of grass. He lost his knife. A sobbing violence came into his throat. There was a wild mad exhilaration in the short battle, before the great head lay sideways and yawed in vomit. Angus retrieved his knife and stuck it to the hilt in the base of the neck above the breast bone. The head jerked and fell for the last time. The blood gushed forth.

Angus sat beside the dead stag, drooping forward, gasping heavily. His right hand came up and wiped blood from his eyes. He had been in at the death of many great stags. He had "blooded" more than one excited gentleman after his first kill. Normally an occasion when the stalker smiles quietly and, after listening to excited speech, offers a word or two of congratulation or praise of the antlers.

Angus's head drooped lower. He was very tired. His shoulders began to jerk. He lay over on his face. His fingers dug into the heath. He muttered into the earth, "Ah, Christ!" and wept.

After a time his body grew quite still and lay as if it had fallen asleep. Then he stirred and sat up. His face was disfigured with blood and tears. His manner was now very quiet. He arose and picked up the rifle and, instead of gralloching the stag, climbed back to the high ground whence he had first fired and stared across at Benuain.

The shadows of the hills were towards him. He could see no one. A stretch of horizon in the west was all vivid greenish blue light, against which the farthest ridges were black and clear cut. Gateway and pathway to another world. He should put up a smoke. Instead he put two bullets in the rifle and fired one. The echo exploded in Benuain with the noise of a distant peal of thunder. He listened and thought he heard a cry. He laid the rifle across his knees and sat staring before him, his face growing expressionless, the eyes like hazed blue glass.

Chapter Eleven

"There is no need for anxiety," said Sir John. "If anything had happened during the day, one or other of them would have returned for help long before this."

"Well, I must confess I think it is rather inconsiderate of Geoffrey," said Lady Marway, "for he is bound to know that we must be anxious about him."

The others said nothing. It had been decided a few minutes before not to postpone dinner, and when the bell went, they all got up at once. George was full of ideas at table about the possible nature of Geoffrey's great kill and suggested they should go out to meet him and bring him home in triumph. He himself would go to the spot where he had dropped Geoffrey in the morning and, turning the headlights over the forest, switch them on and off. "Tic-tac, you know. Geoffrey could reply by lighting matches. How far could you see a match?" This was debated, until Harry suggested they could make an S.O.S. flare with a bunch of old heather. "Of course!" cried George. The other car could take the Corr route. Voices grew animated and broke now and then into laughter. This would be a small adventure, and immediately after dinner there was an exodus to the garage, Lady Marway staying behind.

Harry announced that he would tackle the Home Beat on foot, and, catching Helen by the arm, departed there and then, before discussion could stop them.

The sky was clear and the stars brilliant, and soon the eyes got used to the dark. The dying moon would not rise for some time.

"It is more difficult", said Harry, "to get talking to a person alone here than it is in London! I did want to get hold of you after we came back from Screesval."

"So did I," said Helen. "I kept thinking about it—I mean about the Dean and Colonel Brown."

"Did you?" said Harry. "I actually looked at my watch at two in the morning and wondered if you were asleep."

"Why?"

"If I had been sure you weren't asleep, I might have called on you. Or, alternatively, I thought I might have got up and crept downstairs and outside and round to your window and thrown up something. Would you have come down?"

"I was awake," said Helen.

Harry stopped. "Helen, would you have come?"

"Let us go on," said Helen, moving off.

Friendliness was about them and a delicious small excitement.

"Tell me", she said, "why you were disturbed after Screesval."

He walked for a little way in silence. "I got an extraordinary feeling there about Geoffrey. Once, when I looked at him, I saw his face. I saw it coldly, in a queer sort of inhuman way. My mind was cold, I mean. Geoffrey's face was isolated. Just for a moment or so. I didn't like it."

"What did you see in it?"

"I have wondered. I have thought since that you could take three men, a doctor, an artist, and an ordinary man, and each would see something quite different in a face. Remember I was under a certain influence, which the talk of Colonel Brown and the Dean had strengthened. I mean, second sight. You know the common expression: I saw death in his face. Usually that happens when the face has some signs—gone grey or blue or pinched. Geoffrey's face was anything but pinched! I think I must have had a dream or nightmare I have forgotten. I can see Geoffrey's face rigid in death at any moment."

"Harry, how horrible!"

"I know. It shows you what the mind will do once you give it rein. I put no trust in it at all. Only, it left me uncomfortable.

Then on the way home, I stopped the car to go up to Corr Inn. It was pure impulse—or pure curiosity. I felt I wanted to see these fellows by themselves, off guard. Remember in the wood when Angus asked Alick to go to the inn that night? I knew they would be there. They were."

"What were they doing?"

"Nothing much. Just drinking and yarning and laughing. But as I groped my way up, I heard that playing more clearly. It was one of them on the hill-side above the inn, playing to himself in the night above the mist. It had an effect on me. It is the first time that bagpipes ever did have any sort of effect on me, beyond being a loud and unpleasant noise. I thought to myself: what can you make of a fellow who goes up the hill-side and plays like that? Why is he doing it? And oh lord I knew that he was moved, that what he was playing did not come out of his brain but out of his blood. And yet I do happen to know, from reading, that the affair is not a haphazard impromptu business, but a very rigid art, and to become accomplished at it takes a very long time. What do you make of it?"

"When I was eleven I was taken to my first Highland Games. I was then at school and the Morrisons took me. Major Morrison was Chief of the Games. Dad and Mum were in India, of course. I'll never forget the impression I got of the pipe band as the pipers came marching towards us. They seemed tall and splendid and came marching over the world, tall and proud and marching to that awful music, growing taller as they drew nearer and more terrible in their power. It wasn't that I was terrified that they would march us down without seeing us. I don't know what it was. But I remember I had to keep my lips tight shut in case I should disgrace myself by crying out. What remains is that impression of tallness and pride, of figures advancing, growing, in that irresistible march."

"Yes. I know it's potent stuff to march to. But this crying of the pipes on the hill-side in the dark, not in marches or in lively dance rhythms or anything like that, but like a curlew, or heaven knows what, in pain! Oh I don't know. It made me feel uneasy. It hurt me in some way—though why or how, I haven't the foggiest notion. There was no one about. I didn't want to go in, though if I saw anyone I had some sort of excuse, for I did owe the landlord for a drink. Then I came to a small side window and looked in.

"There must have been a score of men there. Where they came from, Heaven knows. I suppose if the inn had had resident guests, they had departed. Their attitudes were confidential, full of free gestures, and a thick rich mirth. Five or six of them were listening to one oldish man, with a heavy reddish moustache and greying hair. Obviously a character of some sort. Suddenly they rocked back with laughter. There was a heated argument in another corner. These were the people we think of as silent and grave! Young Donald was there with a whole pint of beer, the dark smile on his face, still shy a bit, like a man that has not unfolded. The room was crawling with warm life. I began to get the feeling of being a spy on what was hidden and unauthorised. As it was, I felt uncomfortable. Yet it fascinated me beyond anything I can say. A feeling of life gathered into this room, hidden away. When I think about it now, look at it in my mind, it seems to have something symbolic about it. Oh, I can't explain. And all the time my eye would go back to Alick. And all the time that pipe music would whirl about my ears, with its notes drawn out, drawn out, and high and tragic. And I knew these notes were getting into the room, too. You could tell it by the jerk of a head, the glitter of an eye. And you had the feeling that even part of a note was enough for these fellows. Angus forced a violin into Alick's hands. And he started playing."

The grey of the hill road was quite discernible now. They walked on without difficulty, though the darkness hid their faces. Helen asked about Alick's playing.

"It was not the playing so much as the fellow himself. You know how straight he stands, how easily, with his full chest. Well, he was sitting, upright—exactly like a kind of Buddha. Nothing religious, I mean, but that full-bodied simple ease. The violin seemed small. There was never any expression on his face. And he played away, his drink beside him. The tone was not strong, but I should say it was very pure and penetrating. He played Highland dance music. They listened to him for a bit. Then Angus got up and did a *pas seul*, some sort of sword dance affair. They nudged one another. They gave a shout, "Hooch!" Their faces shone with merriment, with a glittering innocence. One or two were getting slightly the worse for wear. They conducted with their arms, did dances in the air with their hands, letting out a yell now and then. Legs were pulled, by way of encouragement. I found myself laughing silently, when suddenly Alick stopped playing, laid down the violin, and left the room.

"I thought it was high time that I beat it. Yet—I stayed. Alick came out and we met. Perhaps he was astonished to see me. I couldn't tell. I explained how I had heard the bagpipes and remembered my debt, but had felt loath about intruding. He was silent, then asked me in that aloof way if I cared to have a drink. I said that I realised how unwise it had been of me to come, lest my presence be misunderstood, and suggested he should come back with me a little way before others came out. We moved down, and now I began to feel that awful urge again to ask him that old question about his vision. I stopped him. I spoke to him simply and candidly. I told him of the talk at Screesval and of how even scientists were beginning to believe that a man who had second sight was merely a normal man with an extra power of vision. I told him about the Dean's philosophy. I wanted to make the whole thing seem natural. Then I told him of Colonel Brown's belief that mathematically interference in some degree might be possible. So, if I could be certain of the person who was 'visioned', I might be able to interfere. Could he tell me finally and definitely if it was Mr. Smith? He kept silent. There was obviously a terrific reluctance upon him, and I think—I am not sure—that he hated me at that moment. I could not say any more. The mere thought of words became a horror. I wished to God I had never spoken. Yet, I waited, and at last he said, 'I think it was. The others were in the way.' 'They were carrying the shrouded body in their arms?' I asked as if I were seeing it. 'Yes,' he said. He stood quite still. I wanted to thank him, to shake his hand. I could do nothing. George shattered the night with his horn. I turned away and left him. I was in sheer misery, and sat down not a great distance from you until I felt more normal."

"What an extraordinary experience!"

They walked on in silence.

"You make me feel uncomfortable. I wish Geoffrey was home," she added more firmly.

"I wish he was in London."

"There is nothing we can do?"

"I have thought of that, too. I am trying to be sensible about it. All this may be nonsense. It *may* be nonsense, despite age-old experience and the East and Colonel Brown's mathematics and all that. But it *may* not, for reasons entirely different from what man has ever imagined. If I could conjure up a way of getting Geoffrey back to London at once, I'd do it. Let me say that I am as uneasy as that. Why take any chances—even with superstition—blast it!"

"I know," said Helen.

"And then there is this other rotten side to it, too, that by some silly process of auto-suggestion we may force on the very issue we want to avoid. We couldn't do that if Geoffrey were reasonable. But he isn't and won't be. On the contrary, he is unfriendly, antagonistic, about this, and you get the perfectly awful feeling that he himself will force the whole issue to an unavoidable end. As if even this business of auto-suggestion was also part of foreseen destiny. That's why I don't quite feel that anything desperate has happened to-day. Angus will save him to-day. As Alick did the other night. We shall all save him. If Geoffrey gets killed, I mean, it will be by defying a stalker, by defying the normal sound practice of the forest. And that *is* possible. Very."

"I have that terrible feeling too. That they will bring him home, and tell the story of how he attempted something he shouldn't have."

"Well, look here, we can do no more. I'm utterly sick of it. I feel for your mother, too. To blazes with him, anyway! Let us forget. Our own minutes are being lost discussing him."

"And yet, in some strange way," said Helen, hesitantly, "with all this talk and feeling and premonition, life has quickened. What lies below the surface comes out—and sees the colours."

"I know," said Harry.

They walked for some way in silence, and the excitement of their personal encounter, that had died down, arose again.

"What are you thinking about?" Helen asked.

"Would you like me to be honest?"

"Yes."

"I have been talking all this about Geoffrey but it is not the real thing in my mind. It is all a sort of unreal vision, a vision of external grotesque things that don't matter finally; for behind them—behind them—I see your head bowed before the Dean. I haven't let myself think of that. I haven't honestly, Helen. I can't be flippant about it. Oh God, I don't know, Helen. I daren't let myself think. But it was all—it was the whole living truth. For better or for worse, it was the whole living truth for me. And lord, here's the end of the grey road. The truth has petered out!" He tried to laugh. His voice was very nervous. "There's only the path now. What'll we do?"

"We have our coats on. Shall we sit down? You must be tired after your day on the hill."

He groped about, and found a seat with a sloping back. Her voice was cool as burn water. His hands shook.

"Did I give myself away before the Dean?" she asked, as she seated herself, drawing her coat over her knees.

"You did."

"In what way?"

He was silent. "I don't know," he said.

"He spoke so well, didn't he?" she remembered. "He understood in a way that I never thought was possible. How could he know? Was he once in love—in that way? He must have been, I suppose. And yet—oh I don't know—it was something in his eyes, so deep. It was a kindness, a loving kindness. You think his eyes are sad, but they're not really.

Not for themselves. But for us. He is like one of the mystics he tried to describe. I have been thinking a lot about it. I was thinking over it in bed and wished I could have talked to you. You see, he is like one who has attained that simple serene state of mind, in which there is that harmony he spoke of, like silent music. He could stay there and be happy for ever, whatever happened. But he must come back, because of all the tragedy there is in the world. Don't misunderstand me, Harry, but I got an impression of all the needless tragedy of the world in his eyes. It is awfully difficult for me to get words for this. And I could never have got one, if it hadn't been that he had spoken in the way he did about love. He showed me my own mind. Love seemed the loveliest thing in the world. Not seemed—ah, I knew it was the loveliest thing."

He was silent.

She gave an uncertain chuckle. "Go on, say I am enchanting you!"

"You are not enchanting me. You are merely making me a bit frightened."

"Harry," she said, excitement catching her breath, "do you not understand that I am making a song? Harry, Harry, don't you know that where delight is the heart sings? Don't you understand that love is delight? Harry, I was talking, talking—because because—oh, Harry!" and she turned swiftly and threw her arms round his neck.

Her embrace was fierce.

He knew a lot more about this girl Helen before they at last remembered that they had to go back to Corbreac Lodge.

"It must be very late," she said, as they strode along.

He did not speak, taking the night on his brows.

For it was a remarkable thing how this girl Helen had changed. She was a new person entirely, a changeling. Remarkable metamorphosis when a fellow tried to think about it. He had known her so well, had known her so long, that the old Helen was like a sister, a dear companion. This one—this one...he couldn't think at all, taking the horizons of the night on his forehead as a ship takes the horizons of the ocean.

She caught his hand, she pulled, they ran until they were out of breath. That helped him a bit, but not very much. Every cell of his body, every cell of the night, was filled with wild honey. He could not taste it properly. He was inarticulate. He stopped.

She was very strong, her lithe body was wary and quick. She broke and ran. He caught her.

"Harry!" she said solemnly.

"What now?"

She kissed him and laughed.

Until at long last they saw the lights of the Lodge, and lights behind it, and manifestly strange ongoings. They paused, wondering.

"Shall we go on or not?" he asked in a deep reluctance.

She looked back along the road they had come, slowly turned her head and looked up into his face. She did not speak.... Then she took his hand without a word and in silence they went down to the place where Geoffrey had arrived, and Angus, and Lachlan with the pony bearing the body of King Brude, the greatest trophy ever brought home to Corbreac.

By the time they reached the larder, Geoffrey and the others had gone in, but Maclean was still there with a lantern, and Alick, and Angus, and one or two of the pony-men and gillies.

Harry met Angus as he was turning away and complimented him, asking about the stalk.

"It was in the High Corrie that Mr. Smith got him," said Angus. After that he answered yes or no.

Harry greeted Alick, who, after waiting a silent moment, followed Angus.

Maclean himself was not much more communicative, as he held up the lantern.

The dead eyes of King Brude caught light from the lantern. The antlers arched in beauty, high points blown inward.

Harry stared at the magnificent head, for in the shadows it had an uncanny stillness, a growing power. He found himself deeply affected, touched with wonder and some primordial sensation of fear. He said something to Maclean and turned to speak to Helen, to find that she was awaiting him near the house. Before he reached her, she went round the corner towards the front door, and, in the hall, he saw her ankles disappearing upstairs.

At once he went into the sitting-room and up to Geoffrey with outstretched hand. "Hah-ha! You have brought the King home! My congratulations."

"Excuse me not getting up," said Geoffrey, accepting Harry's hand. "But it was a long pull." He smiled. "Thanks."

He was enthroned on his epic, a perpetual grin on his face, a readiness to laugh. He could see the humorous side of everything now. He even confessed to the first stag that he should have stalked. His description of the rock climb, with his side "giving me gyp", was quite dramatic and unspoilt by reference to Angus's helping hand.

"I don't think you should have tackled that, Geoffrey," said Sir John quietly. "In your condition, I do not think you should have risked it."

"Had I known it was as bad as it was, I shouldn't," said Geoffrey. "But we are only wise after the event."

"Wise or dead!" said George.

Geoffrey laughed. He had seen the touch of doubt in their faces, of secret fear. He was scoring over Harry all along the line. Harry with his second sight of solemn death, and Geoffrey, like an intellectual acrobat, giving solemn death the slip! It was good fun in more ways than one.

He was fussed over and packed off to bed by the women.

"I think all this hero-worship positively smells," said George.

"Never mind, old man," replied Geoffrey. "You did pretty well yourself yesterday—enough to make some of 'em think! Eh what?" And he winked to George and laughed, as he went out at the door, bent a little over the pain in his side.

Soon it was bedtime for all. Maclean had prophesied rain from the lack of colour in the sky. The weather forecast from the wireless backed him up. Was the spell of good weather at an end, the exhilarating autumn weather?

As Sir John was brushing his hair, Lady Marway remarked, "I think you should say a word to Geoffrey about taking risks. I was really worried until he got back. I think he should show a little more consideration."

"I did try to warn him."

"I think also the way he went after King Brude—after all, it's your forest, and I think you should have had as good a chance as Geoffrey."

"I don't mind, my dear, not really."

"That's why I mind."

"You're merely a little upset. It's all right. Geoffrey has had his way. And if the weather breaks, it will break for days. It always does after such a good spell. There may not be much more hill for Geoffrey."

She said no more. He stooped down, tall and clean, kissed her good night, and put out the light.

Geoffrey was extremely tired. He stretched himself between the cool sheets on the flat of his back, closed his eyes, and smiled in the dark. He had had a triumphant day. There was nothing a man could not do, once he gave his mind to it. A certain type of man, with a trained mind. A superstition had been growing that no one would ever shoot King Brude. He had exploded that superstition—as he would explode others! Good fun exploding superstitions! A wholesome and necessary duty besides. He called on sleep. It came before the smile faded from his face.

Harry did not call on sleep, did not want to lose consciousness.

Neither did Helen.

Joyce always went to sleep very quickly, like a child whose nervous energy was all used up, unless she had overdone things, when sleeplessness made her acutely miserable.

George was just popping off—held back a little by thought of Geoffrey's triumph. He could not help liking that wink

234

Geoffrey had given him; singling him out, as it were. He admired Geoffrey's assurance. Strong character. Wouldn't mind if he himself could act with that definiteness....

Helen was so wide awake that she could hardly think of one thing at a time. Her mind was so wide open, so sensitive, that it was aware of nothing, as a listening ear is aware of silence. Suggestions of emotions drifted through, but she settled on none of them, drew none of them into her thought or into her arms. This was an exquisite game that played itself. Her happiness was so great that she was afraid of it. She got out of bed, and went to the window, cautiously pulled up the blind, and looked out.... The pale night, the stillness; dear God, the beauty of the quiet night in this quiet remote world...

> *Fra bank to bank, fra wood to wood I rin*
> *Ourhailit by my feeble phantasie....*

Harry had no trouble with his mind, for it was in a perpetual astonishment. He was making the supreme discovery that a state of delight is a state that cannot be communicated, and yet, when you have it, is more certain than all else in the world of appearances. All the horrors of the world were seen at a remote distance, the challengings and boastings and desperations of pigmies in a lower world of partial darkness. The Dean's pity was for them, Christ's divine pity, the mystic's pity....

But his astonishment was really far more cunning than that. For its centre was Helen's art of love, that unforeseen, indescribable play of her instincts, grace of her arms and hands, and quick living mouth. He could hardly believe it yet, because in some way it implied he was worthy of it, and his bones and opaque flesh and ordinary mind couldn't quite accept that. Not altogether. Yet what could come out of delight, but acts of delight, when one thought of it? And the more exquisite the delight in the mind, the more exquisite the acts.... Memory of the acts began to get the better of him. If he got up and slipped outside and round to her window?... If they were caught, what did it matter? That night they had been for ever betrothed....

Mairi was in deep sleep, for she had worked hard all day, and worked hard every day. Yet the last night or two she had been restless. She did not require to talk much. The sight of Alick walking, a glimpse of his face, told her more than words could. She had tried to fight against a creeping sense of fatality, of something dreadful about to happen, of a horror that could almost be smelt, but to-night she had given in. What would be had to be. Ina slept also. They tried, if possible, to get to sleep before Cook produced her peculiar short grunt of a snore. It now came through the thin wall like mechanically timed explosions. Cook was a strong-minded woman. That evening she had given Maclean his orders about getting a salmon for the third night hence, when Screesval was coming to dine.

Maclean had not answered her. He had been in a queer dour mood, due to the killing of King Brude by Geoffrey. He had not looked at Angus, who had felt the hostility.

Alick and Angus had gone away together, and Angus had told Alick the whole story of the day's stalk with an extreme bitterness, right down to Geoffrey's regret that he had not his pocket book on him to pay the bribe of two pounds. "Thank God he hadn't. The rifle—the rifle was in my hands." He grew silent, remembering how murder had sat in his head. He added: "I feel like a bloody Judas."

"You merely did your job," said Alick with a strange smile.

The sky was dark, all the blue out of it, and the stars extremely bright and near. A sign of rain. A soft puff of wind came up the birches, through the slats of the larder where King Brude hung alone, round the Lodge windows and chimneys. The fir trees stirred, making the sighing hissing sound of sea-water. The wind came and the wind went on, up the ways to the forest, into and out of the corries, carrying its tale to sensitive nostrils, through the empty High Corrie, round the bald rock of Benuain, over the moors and ridges, by croft houses and inns and shooting lodges, heard by every sleeping ear in that northern land of mixed uneasy dreams, until it got beyond the last peaks and came to the salt, cleansing sea.

On Marjory's sleeping ear it produced a remarkable effect. Between the time that the sound struck her ear and was acknowledged by her brain, in that inconceivably short instant of time, she dreamed a dream that went through hours of slow, detailed misadventures culminating in the horror of being lost in a forest in the Far East. She awoke wide-eyed, and, holding the gulp of her breath, listened. There was no sound in the house. Only the sound of the wind outside.

Chapter Twelve

Geoffrey did not get up until the afternoon of the following day. The sound of the wind and rain had been a pleasant background to his thought as he lay in bed. He regretted, of course, that the others could not get to the hill. Any beast now brought home must be in the nature of an anti-climax. At one stroke he had taken the heart out of the forest, he had exhausted the marvellous.

There was another satisfaction, too. By killing King Brude he had compensated for that first unfortunate, over-long shot, of which Harry had made so much. That incident had rankled more poisonously than he was willing to admit. He could never quite forgive Harry, and would dearly like to take it out of him in some way—and particularly out of that fellow, Alick. There was only one immediate way in which that could be done—by proving them simple, if necessary even honest, credulous fools. Not that he believed Alick was honest. If, by a stroke of vast fun, he could prove Alick to be the sort of native snake that he was, he would at the same time clear up the whole atmosphere that undoubtedly had begun to depress the place. Lady Marway wouldn't like the process, but she would thank him if in the end....

He found Harry alone in the sitting-room. The others had gone out to pay a call or something, Harry explained, with the exception of Marjory, who was somewhere about, he thought. But he did not appear very interested, nor did he brighten perceptibly at the prospect of Geoffrey's company.

Geoffrey turned to the mantelpiece to hide a small smile and helped himself to a cigarette.

"No further developments?" he asked.

"About what?" asked Harry.

Geoffrey offered an amused shrug. "I have never really managed to continue an interesting, not to say a dramatic, conversation with you interrupted a few nights ago. You may remember—about second sight? Have I missed any further developments?"

Harry looked at him. "Not of any particular moment, I think."

"Good. Are you still of the same mind about their importance?"

"Yes," said Harry, "I am."

Geoffrey looked at him. "Really?"

Harry smiled. "Amusing, isn't it?"

"I must say it is."

Harry made no comment.

Geoffrey stood with his back to the fire. Harry, from his chair, had his face turned towards the window. The day was gloomy with hanging mists and curtains of driving rain.

"If I remember, you said something about four men, and even about *you* or *me*. Was that right?"

"Quite right," said Harry.

"But you did not care to mention the names of the four men? That was a pity, because what this sort of stuff needs badly is evidence recorded beforehand."

"Quite," said Harry. "I merely used my discretion in this matter, as, I suppose, people always have done, because it's personal. However, if you can give me an assurance you will not divulge the names, I could let you have them now."

"I promise," said Geoffrey.

"The names are: Sir John, George, Maclean, and Angus."

Deliberately Geoffrey repeated them: "Sir John, George, Maclean, and Angus." He continued to look penetratingly at Harry. "Do you *really* believe?"

"Belief does not come into it yet. It's not a religious topic exactly. I told you what happened. Normally belief waits on proof."

"Quite," said Geoffrey, tilting his head and taking a pull at his cigarette. "Now about the body. You or me. Any suggestion as to which of us?"

Harry hesitated. "No more than a suggestion."

"Am I to interpret that as meaning *me* rather than *you*?"

Harry shrugged. "You may."

"I see," said Geoffrey. "Any statement as to time?"

"No."

"Pity. We may be coming here for years. The grouping you describe may be possible indefinitely. I trust you see my point?"

"I do. Only he saw us—as we are now."

"Naturally. He doesn't know us any other way. Which should explain much. However, surely you at least see a point like this: If, say, George and I left for London at once and never came back together, we could make the grouping impossible."

"Certainly I see that."

"Well?"

"But you're not in London."

"No. But we *could* go at once. And so make what he alleges he foresaw impossible. Here we are *before* the event, and the free will you believe in could be used to circumvent the happening. Do you appreciate the illogical knot you're tying yourself in?"

"Not exactly—if, as Colonel Brown says, a degree of interference with a vision of the future is mathematically or theoretically possible."

"Oh, good God! That sort of mathematical talk in a dream-vacuum! You don't mean to say you were impressed by that?"

"I was. For all I know, his mathematical knowledge may be greater than yours. He has been trained to deal scientifically with extremely practical things. You can fight that out between you. I'm an ordinary engineer, with no particular gift for the higher criticism whether in nuclear physics or

240

metaphysics. I merely try to recognise a situation when I see it. And all I am sure of is that you and George are not in London. You're here."

"But we could go."

"You could both set out for London at once. You could try to get away from here to-night."

"Are you implying we couldn't get away?"

"No." Harry got up. "Look here, Geoffrey. I want to be quite frank about this. You may think me mad. I cannot help that. All I can assure you is that I was never more serious. You are one of this party—usually a pretty happy crowd, and not quite the normal huntin' and shootin' kind. If anything unfortunate happened here, the distress would be pretty acute, particularly to, say, our hosts. In a word, I should be delighted if you did get away. I should like to prove this particular second sight a piece of moonshine. The point is—" and he faced Geoffrey —"*will you go?*"

Their eyes drew out the silence to an extreme tension.

Geoffrey broke it harshly. "Good God!" he said.

Harry turned away.

"Leave here at once!" Geoffrey's voice was hoarse with sarcasm. "Great heavens, what would sane people think of me?"

"You have no excuse like that," said Harry. "It could be arranged quite simply and naturally."

"How?"

Without hesitation Harry turned from the window and said, "I can walk to the telephone now, ring up your chief, Dr. Lester, in London, say to him that you want an excuse for leaving here immediately. Ask him to ring up Sir John in a couple of hours. Tell him to say to Sir John that a very urgent laboratory affair demands your immediate presence. He'll apologise and ask to speak to you. Then at six in the morning I'll run you from here to catch the south train."

Geoffrey gaped at him. "You have worked it out—as far as that?"

"I dallied with the idea of arranging the call without telling you."

241

"Have you gone quite mad?"

"Don't think so," said Harry, holding his eyes.

The door opened and Marjory came in.

"Come in, Marjory," said Geoffrey, "and bring a breath of sanity with you, in heaven's name."

"More arguments?" smiled Marjory, raising her eyebrows and glancing from one to the other.

"Oh, so so," said Harry. "Small private affair. This sort of weather affects the mind."

"What your mind needs is fresh air," said Geoffrey.

"Thanks for the idea," said Harry—"and the tip." With a smile, he strolled out and closed the door.

Marjory looked at Geoffrey. "What's wrong?"

"Come here, Marjory, till I talk to you. This is becoming monstrous. Absolutely monstrous." He took a crippled step or two on the hearth rug. Obviously he accepted Marjory as a natural ally, and the forces held in sarcastic reserve before Harry could now be given expression. He felt angry; he felt vindictive. To score over Harry, to expose this appalling incredible nonsense—at this time of day, not merely amongst superstitious natives, whom one might excuse, but amongst people like Harry and Helen, the so-called educated!—to expose it became imperative, an absolute duty. He spoke to Marjory with considerable heat. "Don't you agree?"

"If it could be done," she murmured hesitantly.

"Done? We'll do it all right! And wouldn't it be a joke if we could frighten the wits out of them? Blow their hocus-pocus sky-high and frighten the wits out of them! And the wits of Colonel Brown *and* the Dean!"

His vehemence disturbed Marjory. "It might. But——"

"Yes. That's what they need! And that's what they'll get!"

"Aren't you taking this too much to heart? I mean——"

"Do you know", he interrupted her, "what he was trying to get me to do just now?"

"What?"

"Clear off to London at once."

"Why?" Her eyes opened upon him.

"Because the poor mut, worked on by that cunning stalker, has gone spoofy."

"But why London?"

"To be out of harm's way. You see they have arranged between them that I am the corpse-to-be." He laughed. "Now if.... What are you staring like that for?"

She turned her face away. "Nothing."

"Heavens, you're not preparing to go temperamental, too, are you?"

"No. Only it's sort of everywhere and—one—well—one——"

"Gets infected. Isn't that what I say? And you are the only really sane person I could ask to help me. I couldn't ask anyone outside the house. And inside—you are the only one. You are sane, Marjory, and balanced. I have always admired you, really. You will help me, won't you?"

"I should like to help you. But——"

"Never mind the buts."

"Frankly, Geoffrey, I would rather you left the thing alone." She looked at him.

He liked her troubled eyes. They were concerned—not for herself.

"You wouldn't like me to score over them?"

He waited as if for an avowal. She stared towards the window.

"Won't you answer?" he asked.

"Yes, I would," she murmured. "But I don't think it's important enough for you to—to risk—I mean, how would you——"

He laughed, quietly for him. "We'll think that out." His eyes were bright with triumph. "I have a working idea. All we need is something to give it a push. We'll think it out carefully. It will be great fun. Give me your hand on it, Marjory!" He took her hand. He was eager as a malicious schoolboy. He squeezed her hand. Involuntarily she returned the pressure, withdrew her hand, and moved towards the window. A quick step after her, and he paused, clutching at his side.

243

"What is it, Geoffrey?" She came quickly up to him, concern in her eyes, her voice.

His face had paled, his lips were drawn taut. He carefully let himself into a chair. He stared before him, like one who had had a stroke, his eyes alive and gleaming.

"Geoffrey!"

He smiled into her terrified face. "Hsh!" he said, holding up his hand. There was the sound of the car drawing up. "Remember," he said, "not a word. And we'll meet later. A cigarette, please." He pointed to the mantelpiece and wiped his forehead. "Don't worry," he added, smiling to her over the match-light. "I'm all right. To-night we'll begin— preparing the atmosphere."

Chapter Thirteen

"Pretty dull, isn't it?" said George, half-yawning and looking around the darkening sitting-room.

"Don't make it duller, for goodness sake," replied Joyce. They were alone.

George got up. "Sunday is such a dull day in the Highlands."

"It isn't Sunday."

"Isn't it?"

"No. It just rained again." Turning over some papers, she picked up the *Tatler*.

"I've seen you read that at least six times," he remarked.

"Wrong again. We've been here three weeks."

"I thought it came out every week?"

"It does. I brought this copy with me."

But George wasn't interested. "Ah well," he said, "thank God winter's coming."

"George!"

His voice gathered some enthusiasm, as he began. "Think of the Saint Moritz run——"

But she shut him up. "Have a heart!"

"All right." He nodded. "Let's think of the rain. I say, didn't it rain to-day! Sheets of it. And dear cousin Helen thought the white sheets of rain—being drawn across the brown and the gold or something—were very exciting. She's a charming child."

"I don't agree with you. I think she is charming."

"That's what I said."

"I thought you said she was a child."

"Oh, I suppose it's her sort of innocence or something."

"Innocence," repeated Joyce.

"You know what I mean—fresh and naïve, so to speak."

"Quite. Being three years older, I am soiled and tarnished, so to speak."

"Great Scott, of course! You're only three years older. I say—what a gulf!"

Joyce looked at him. "You can be a nasty piece of work."

He met her eyes in astonishment, then smiled quickly. "Heavens, I don't mean—I don't mean——"

"No?"

"I mean the opposite. Quite the opposite. Absolutely."

"How clear!"

"Now hold on there! You know jolly well what I mean. Anyhow, don't let us quarrel again. It's this rotten day, with nothing to do. We always quarrel when we have nothing to do."

"I am perfectly content, thank you."

"There you go! You'll nag at me now."

Joyce jumped up. "Nag? Who's nagging?"

"Joyce, hang it all, you know I am gone on you. Have a heart for a fellow. You get me into a sweat until I don't know where I am."

"You said nag."

"A nag is an old horse, like me. Nag, you know. Nag, nig, nog." And with a deft movement he kissed her.

"I think you're a perfect ass," she said, relenting.

"That's better. Ooo! I wish I could hit something. I should have taken my punch-ball with me."

"Don't worry. There will be more talk to-night."

"Then I will hit someone."

"Fine," said Joyce, sitting down and punching a cushion for her head. "You launch your famous straight left. When Harry and Geoffrey go all over clever...." She shrugged. "I wish you could chip in sometimes and dish 'em."

"Not my line," said George. "Besides——"

"Yes?"

"Well, for instance, if they said to me: 'It is predetermined that you are going to do so and so,' I should reply 'What-ho!' and promptly do the opposite. Seems simple enough, doesn't it?"

"Why couldn't you say so?"

"Such a remark is always followed by a gaping void. Have a smoke."

"No—well, all right. Listen." As she lit her cigarette at his promptly produced mechanical lighter, she asked between puffs, "What would you do—if you met a ghost?"

"Met a what?"

"A ghost."

"Oh, a ghost." He lit his own cigarette. "Uhm, a ghost. Hadn't thought of that. Tricky customer, I should say." He blew out the light thoughtfully. "Difficult to land on, by all accounts. Imagine me going up to him and saying: 'Ghost, what?' You know—Mr. Livingstone, I presume? He vouch—vouchsafes me no answer—except perhaps a jolly old moan. I lead one to the point—just to prove he's not celluloid—and then my fist goes right through. It would be pretty upsetting. I mean you'd lose your balance badly."

"I should say you would."

"Yes." With a musing smile on his face George lit the lighter and blew it out—twice.

"Don't do that," said Joyce as he lit it a third time.

"Why?"

"I just suddenly don't like it."

"Blowing out the dear old flame, what?"

"Oh, I think ghosts can be overdone."

"They generally are cooked a bit."

But she was attending to her own thought. "Where do you really stand *re* this absurd story about Harry being with Alick when he saw those ghosts? Really stand, I mean?"

"He may have had 'em, you know. I've known fellows who have had 'em."

"What, ghosts?"

"Oh, the oddest things—complete with pink eyes and what-nots. And of course nothing there at all really. Very odd."

"Oh, you mean the d. t.s?"

"That's the technical term, I understand."

"Don't be funny. Alick wasn't tight."

"When you're tight you're all right. It's afterwards. They climb up the wall and over the ceiling. Even wag their tails at you. It's anything but a joke to the fellow who has 'em. Nasty."

"Do you think there's something brewing?"

"God knows. Wonder what's happened to them all?"

"Seems an unnatural silence about, doesn't there?"

"It's certainly getting very dark. Will I ring?"

The door opened and Mairi entered. George followed her with his eyes as she turned to light the lamp by the bookcase. A very noiseless efficient maid.... But his thought was interrupted by the entry of Sir John, who saw Joyce's arms extended.

"Not feeling bored are you?" Sir John asked her.

She got to her feet. "In this marvellous place!"

"We get days like these. Can't do anything much. No use for the hill or fishing. Have you anything to read? There should be some detective stories about. Real good ones," said Sir John.

"I do like a good one," said Joyce. "I must confess."

Mairi soon had the standard lamp at its full brilliance and withdrew, leaving them to turn up the other lamp if they wished.

Lady Marway came in as they were hunting for the detective stories: "If Marjory hasn't got them upstairs, they may have gone to the kitchen. But I shouldn't think so. I'll get Marjory."

"Oh don't bother, please," said Joyce.

Lady Marway met Marjory at the door.

"Let me think," said Marjory. "You mean the green... yes—I think I know where they are."

As she turned to go out, Sir John asked her, "Geoffrey all right?"

"Oh yes." Marjory smiled. "Purely stomachic, I understand. One moment." She went out.

"Nothing wrong with Geoffrey, is there?" Joyce asked.

"No. Not really," Lady Marway replied. "I remember—you and George had just gone out. He jumped up quickly after tea and then had a moment's giddiness. That was all."

"Oh, that!" And Joyce recalled a girl who got it without jumping up. "Once or twice she passed clean out. Very alarming at the time—but nothing to it really. She had an interesting sequel."

"Yes?" said Sir John, his smile waiting.

"She got married. For some reason he was quite poor. After that she never got it."

"Here you are, children," said Marjory, entering.

"Thanks, grandma," replied Joyce.

Marjory handed the paper-backed novels to George. "Feel you need a bit of excitement?"

"You have no reason to talk," Joyce intervened, obviously alluding to the recently strengthened relationship between Geoffrey and Marjory.

"One for you, old girl!" said George.

"Paying me back in your own coin," said Marjory.

"Rate of exchange par and all that," said George.

"That's rather a good one." Marjory indicated one of the books.

"Oh, I know this johnnie," declared George. "He delivers the body early. I like that. I always like to know where I am with the body. Some of them keep the body too long before murdering it, if you see what I mean."

"Yes," agreed Marjory. "I always think that's not fair. They try to work up an atmosphere first."

"Yes, and that puts you off your stroke," declared George with some animation. "If you are given the murdered body straight away—you know, see it before you on the floor, knife in back, or bullet hole in chest, or gash on head, as case may be, with one leg twisted up under the other thus, and one arm thrown out like that, and the other"—tying himself in a ludicrous knot—"here...then"—undoing himself—"you know where you are and you proceed quite coolly to work out the doings."

He bowed before the applause. "No flowers by request."

Sir John rather agreed with him on the need for a cool procedure.

"That's really what I mean," replied George, encouraged. "Murdered body: proceed coolly. But some writing johnnies clutter it up with stuff like emotion. I once read one—you won't believe this I know—but it's fact. *The detective wept!*... I knew you wouldn't believe me. Incredible."

"I remember," said Joyce, amid the mirth. "It was quite true. He had some sort of crush or other on the murdered body. Frightful bad taste."

"I agree," said Sir John. "It shouldn't be allowed."

"That's what I said at the time," declared Joyce, with no little enthusiasm. "What is a censor for—if he passes a thing like that?... You may laugh, but it is more tiresome than any silly old bedroom scene."

"I must say there is always something original in your point of view, Joyce." Sir John smiled to her.

"Thank you very much." Joyce bowed. "I have often wondered at the fuss over bedroom scenes. I mean, after you have been places."

Sir John laughed.

"What places?" asked Marjory.

"Oh, *you* know you don't need to go to a nudist colony. The other season we were at—what's its name—along from Monte—you know? Frightfully stimulating."

"What was?" asked Lady Marway.

"The sun," replied Joyce with natural innocence.

Harry came into the fun, and Marjory explained to him: "George has been expounding the whole construction and esthetic of the detective novel. You've missed yourself!"

"Now now!" said George modestly. "Draw it mild."

"If ever", declared Marjory, "you want to know what to do with the murdered body—ask George."

"Uhm," said Harry, nodding with exaggerated thoughtfulness. "Very interesting. What's your line of campaign?"

"Oh rot!" said George.

"Go on, George," Joyce encouraged him. "Tell the gentleman."

George laughed with the others.

"He deprecates", Sir John explained, "the introduction of emotion."

"Exactly," said George. "The whole thing in a nutshell. You are given the body: after that the clues. That's what I say. Any fuss—I mean emotional stuff—and it goes sticky and the real clue is oozed over. You must keep a cool head—and carry on. There's the dead body. Quite O.K. It may have a gash: it may not. Though, personally, I think it should have a gash. In fairness, if you see what I mean?"

"What about poison?" Marjory asked.

"There's poison of course." George shrugged. "Though with poison, it's usually some mysterious kind of poison with effects you were never properly told about. No, I must say I like the corpse with a jolly old gash right on the first page."

"How gruesome!" Helen got up.

"What's gruesome about it?" demanded Joyce, proud of the lead George had established in the conversation.

"The corpse—with the gash," replied Helen. "I have tried to get used to corpses—but I can't. The dead body still impresses me."

Joyce held up her palms, the case being hopeless. "Well, of course...."

"I can't see how people can really enjoy reading about murdered bodies and police and—and ugly motives that——"

"Ah, but then," said Sir John, "you have never been a Cabinet Minister, or a scientist, or on the Stock Exchange——"

"Do *you* read them?" Helen interrupted him.

"I have read a good few and enjoyed them very much. As a means of relaxation, of taking your mind off its more important worries—in short, as an anodyne—it has its points."

"A dead body—as an anodyne!" Helen's eyes widened on her father.

"No one *worries* about a dead body," observed Joyce. "That's morbid."

Harry smiled to Helen. "It's a game, like crosswords."

"But why play it with a dead body and a murderer? What makes them play it with those terrible—terrible——"

"Possibly, my dear," Sir John explained gently, "because death, violent death, is the most terrible thing we know."

"So there is something in what Helen says," Harry suggested. "If it is the most terrible thing, then the curiosity underlying the detective story must be morbid."

"To a certain degree, perhaps," Sir John admitted. "But the motive is really one of human cleverness directed towards the ends of justice."

"The ends of abstract qualities do not usually provide a thrill, do they?" Harry asked.

Joyce, who saw George's leadership slipping away, intervened confidently. "What do you say, George?"

"I—I should say I—agree with Harry. You—you can hit a fellow with a marling spike, but you can't jolly well crumple him up with anything abstract. I mean, can you?"

While they were enjoying this, the door opened and Geoffrey appeared, still limping slightly. He was received with cheers and bowed his acknowledgements.

"Feeling all right again?" Lady Marway asked him in the casual friendly tone obviously meant to change the topic of conversation.

"Never better, thank you." Geoffrey smiled all round.

"I think it was the fruit cake," Joyce declared. "Did you have two slabs?"

"I'm afraid I did," Geoffrey admitted.

"So did George. That explains it."

"Explains what?" asked Geoffrey.

"Why George didn't go giddy. He belched."

"Oh I say!" protested George.

"Yes. Right in the middle of a sentence. Oh terrific. And then instead of apologising for such disgusting behaviour, he roared with laughter."

"I thought I heard his voice dominating the scene." Geoffrey was enjoying the fun.

"Now, no more leg-pulls. I've had enough," and George turned to Sir John.

But Joyce wasn't letting him off as easily as that. "Have you ever heard George on dead bodies?" she asked Geoffrey.

"On what?"

"Dead bodies. You know, the dead body in a thriller."

"No, I can't say I have. But there's nothing I should like better. At least George would have the practical realistic point of view, and that should be refreshing—these days." He laughed loudly.

"Been pretty wet to-day, hasn't it, sir?" said George to Sir John.

They were all amused except Helen who replied, "Yes, did you notice the glass?"

"It fell a bump, didn't it?" said George.

"Yes. It's still going down. I've just tapped it."

"Have you," said George. "Rotten, what?"

There was a distant rumble of thunder.

"Ah, after that it may go up again. Do you think there's any chance?" Geoffrey asked Helen with mock seriousness.

She picked up a cushion.

"You don't like dead bodies?" he inquired in a loud confidential whisper.

She threw the cushion at him. "No, I don't. And I think you are all perfectly horrid and callous and disgusting."

Geoffrey appealed to her: "But, Helen, surely you wouldn't think *me* disgusting as a dead body?"

"Geoffrey!" she exclaimed, with a touch of fear.

"Hush, child," said Lady Marway. "Though I must say I think this talk on dead bodies has gone far enough."

"But surely it's the case", Geoffrey explained, "that the more one discusses a subject the more one gets rid of any fear of it? It's the dumb fear, the unexpressed emotion, that's so dreadful a burden. All the psychologists agree on that."

"Possibly," said Lady Marway. "But I am not quite sure that the psychologists understand everything."

"Perhaps not everything," Geoffrey admitted. "I had an interesting conversation with Maclean. I probed him about what happened when he was a boy. They used to gather in what he called a kailee-house or something like that. They

253

would talk and gossip and sing and tell stories. Sometimes, he said, the ghost stories would be so terrifying that grown men would be afraid to go home in the dark. They believed in them."

"Pure superstition, I suppose," observed Harry.

Geoffrey met his eyes. "No. Just ghost stories."

"The ceilidh-house was quite an institution in those days," Sir John explained. "Their sort of school or college."

"And a very good one, too," said Lady Marway. "For work was done there, real work, like spinning and cloth-making— not all talk." She put aside her tapestry frame. "I must see about dinner."

"One up for you!" declared Marjory. "Perhaps I can help," and she went out with Lady Marway.

"What was your point exactly?" Harry asked Geoffrey.

"That they believed in ghosts—but didn't investigate them."

"Naturally." Harry nodded.

"Naturally?"

"Do you investigate everything you believe in?"

"For the most part, yes," replied Geoffrey.

"Oh, I don't."

"You're telling us," said Joyce, picking up a detective novel, for George's leadership would now be lost.

"I wonder how much of what we believe, we ever do investigate?" Helen asked. "All my education consisted in being told things. And——"

"Yes?" prompted her father.

"Well, the best, the most vivid things, I just happened on. I mean—like——"

"Alick's fauna and flora," suggested Geoffrey.

"Yes," said Helen simply.

Geoffrey gave his short laugh. "You're an impressionist. You can hear things in the wind." He paused and they heard the wind whine as if an outside door had opened. "Maclean said there would be stories about the sounds of wood being sawn for a coffin, before ever there was any coffin, of course; ghostly wood and ghostly saws; and ghostly rappings, too, fore-telling a death, until you would get so worked up that on the way home if you heard——" Three deliberate raps at the gun-room door interrupted him. There was a moment's silence, before Geoffrey finished, "You would be so worked up that you would react like George." For George involuntarily started for the door before Geoffrey with a mocking gesture pulled him up. Sir John said, "That's Maclean's knock," and looked at his watch.

"Well, about to-morrow?" Geoffrey asked.

"Well?" said Sir John, pausing, with a smile, "Feel quite fit?"

"Oh, I think so." Geoffrey turned it over in his mind. "Only not the far beat this time."

"We can fix that in the morning, I think."

Sir John turned the knob and opened the door, saying, "Well, Maclean." Then he stopped dead and stared straight before him. "Maclean!" he called. He went into the gun-room, where the bracket lamp was lit. The others crowded to the door. There was obviously no one in the gun-room. Sir John traversed it rapidly, opened the outside door, stood on the doorstep and peered around. The darkness had fallen very early. "Maclean!" he called again. Then he stepped back into the gun-room, and closed the door and wiped the rain from his hair. "That was rather remarkable. I could have sworn it was at that door."

George was looking around at the walls, but there were neither full-length cupboards nor recesses.

As they re-entered the sitting-room, Geoffrey said, smiling, "I could have sworn it was at that door, too, but it just shows you you can't always trust your ear. Sound can travel in the most elusive way. You know how difficult it is to spot where a new sound is in a motor-car."

"Rather!" said George. "I once had the gear-box taken adrift because of a rattle from the fan."

"Must have been the outside door," murmured Sir John. "Probably gone round to the kitchen, whoever it was." Lady Marway and Marjory entered from the hall door. "Did you see Maclean about?" Sir John asked his wife.

"No," said Lady Marway, looking at him and then at the others. "Why?"

"Nothing. It's all right. We thought we heard him knock."

"I can see Helen is still doubtful." Geoffrey laughed. "You see", he explained to her, "that's the way it happens. You're all worked up to the sound of ghostly rappings, and then if a twig touches the window or an errand boy knocks at the wrong door!…"

"But that was neither a twig nor an errand boy, and you know it," she challenged him.

"Very well." He nodded. "Let's investigate. Do you mind," he said to Lady Marway, "if I ring?" He rang.

"But what actually happened?" Marjory asked, glancing from one to another.

"Oh, just that someone knocked," Geoffrey explained to her. "And we assumed it was at that door—simply because we were expecting it there. Isn't that so, Sir John?"

"Yes," said Sir John, with reserve. He watched the door open and Mairi appear. "Is Maclean about, Mairi?"

"No, sir. We haven't seen him yet to-night."

"Did anyone call just now at the kitchen door?"

"No, sir."

"We thought we heard someone knocking."

"No, sir. We had no one." She was obviously quite sincere.

"Is Alick about?" Geoffrey asked her suddenly.

"No, sir."

They watched her face darken.

"Thanks, Mairi," said Sir John.

As the door closed, Lady Marway spoke deliberately. "I really do think it is time I put my foot down. This is getting a bit too absurd. I feel that the peace of the house is deteriorating. And all over silly trifles like coffee cups and window curtains and so on. I do not mean to blame you, Harry, but there is at least one sense in which I think Geoffrey is right. Out of a vague uneasiness, we are working up a situation. Well, I think it is time we stopped it. If someone knocked at a door, then someone knocked. And I am now going to the kitchen to make sure there was no one knocking there—with whatever intention."

Her definite manner had a distinct effect on everyone except Joyce, who said, as if inspired: "What if it was the front door?"

"Jove, yes!" said George. "Let's get a torch and do some spoor hunting outside. Shall we?"

"Right!" said Marjory; and with Joyce and George she followed Lady Marway from the room.

"That's an idea," said Sir John thoughtfully. "If wet feet came in from outside they should have left a mark."

"Now we're getting down to it," observed Geoffrey confidently, as he followed Sir John into the gun-room.

Helen came close to Harry. "What do you make of it, Harry?"

"I don't know. But I have the feeling that it's a deliberate trick. I have the awful feeling that Geoffrey is playing a trick, the fool!"

"That's good enough anyway," came Geoffrey's voice. "Let's ask Harry: he's an authority on ghosts."

"I wonder if ghosts do leave wet footprints," said Sir John, smiling, as he came in.

"Footprints?" echoed Helen.

"Quite clearly," said Sir John. "Wet footprints from the outer door to the inner."

"As the Scotch say," observed Geoffrey to Harry, "whaur's yer ghost noo?"

"Are the Scotch supposed to say that?" inquired Harry.

"Well, anyhow, someone materially solid entered—knocked—and had time to get away."

Harry, still holding his eye, remarked: "So I supposed."

"Oh you did? Good. Merely to clear away all dubiety, then, will you tell us if, in your experience, ghosts leave wet footprints?"

"It's a matter I have still to investigate," Harry replied. "As for wet footprints in there, I seem to remember"—to Sir John—"that you not only opened the outside door but went out on to the doorstep, which presumably would have been wet. You're sure the wet footprints are not your own?"

Involuntarily Sir John felt the sole of his right shoe. "I remember—yes—but——" He went back into the gun-room, followed by Helen.

"Getting a kick out of it?" Harry challenged Geoffrey.

257

"Kick?"

"Don't be a blasted fool. I warn you—stop!"

"I seem to have got you properly going anyhow!" He laughed. "Another few days and you'd have been more neurotic than your stalker. Though I still doubt if he's anything more than cunning."

"Trying to get your own back, flattering yourself you're doing it in the interests of science and not to soothe your own hurt vanity. You think I don't see through you?"

"Steady!" said Geoffrey, his whole expression narrowing vindictively.

"I'm sorry, Geoffrey." Harry pulled himself together. "I really am concerned——"

But Geoffrey interrupted him coldly: "I am only concerned about the difference between what is evidence and what is not, between reality and neurotic humbug. And if I could expose it by a child's trick, I would. Indeed a child's trick would be the most perfect medium."

"Evidence," said Harry with a shrug. "You affect to be moved only by evidence. You think you can put that over on me?"

"No," said Geoffrey. "Even I could hardly hope to do that, for by your own admission you prefer to believe without investigation of any sort."

"At least I am honest," replied Harry. "You know quite well that nine-tenths of what we implicitly believe no one of us has ever investigated. How many thousands of specialists are concentrating on different branches of knowledge? And their results we accept—because we must—without investigation."

"The mass may accept. Quite. But——"

"No, all of us. You, for example. What are the two most important things in the world to you? Your body and your mind. Well, have you ever done anatomy? Have you ever done mental research? Have you?"

"Where's the point?"

"You're hedging. You see the point. You have never done anatomy—yet you accept what the anatomist tells you about your blood stream and your glands and your liver and all the rest of it. I have never done astronomy—yet I accept the astronomer's tale about the dog star Sirius being so many billions of miles away. Well, this is my point. The folk here accepted the man with second sight as you accept the anatomist and I the astronomer—without investigation. They were satisfied with their results or evidence, as we are with ours."

Marjory, Helen, Joyce, George, and Sir John came in from the gun-room while Harry was talking. Their hunt for a revealing spoor on the wet gravelled surface having proved fruitless, their attention was now drawn by the intensity in the argument proceeding between the two men. Geoffrey, who was facing them, appeared actually not to see them and, immediately Harry had finished, replied:

"But, good God, our anatomists and astronomers have left evidence which we can check if we want to. Your second-sight man left none. I can show you at this moment mathematically how to arrive at the distance to Sirius. Can you show me how a ghost walks or knocks on a door?"

Lady Marway came in from the hall and paused a moment.

"No," Harry answered. "We have not yet got the appropriate technique. Meantime you are merely applying logic to something to which it cannot be applied. As if you took a yard-stick to measure colour or music."

"But you *can* measure colour or music."

"Yes, but not with a yard-stick. You measure it in what you call waves. Until you imagined these waves for yourselves, you couldn't measure it. What these waves are, *you don't know.* They are merely convenient for your purpose. All I am suggesting is that here in second sight is a manifestation of a certain power, for which you have not yet discovered the appropriate waves. That's all."

"That's absolutely hypothetical. One can postulate anything."

"But why was this amazing power not developed?" asked Sir John quietly.

Harry looked at him for a moment in silence. "Would *you* like to have the gift of foreseeing the future?"

"Well—I don't know. Perhaps not. But we *should* be equal to our fate."

"As philosophers and mystics, yes. But as we are—could we face up to a *known* fate? Even one mere suspicion that something *may* happen—and we are disturbed and uncomfortable right to our roots. Where would our fun go, our creative effort? We should be haunted. We should lose that feeling that life has a long time to go—an *indefinite* time."

"I'm not interested in philosophy," said Geoffrey. "Let's go back to facts——"

"Oi!" It was a half-scream from Joyce, who with arms extended and head thrown back, looked like a maenad. "Will it never stop? I think we're all going mad!"

For a moment no one responded. Joyce gripped her hair. Then laughter broke out.

"Well, what would you like to do, Joyce?" asked Sir John, brightly.

"I'd like to play a game. Anything."

"Good idea. What sort of game?"

"Something that would clear the atmosphere. And I know a thriller. George is frightfully good at it. Talk about fun and excitement! We must make sure first"—she looked around dramatically—"that there's nothing breakable about, because in the dark you simply have to dash. Put away those glasses, and the decanter, George."

George acted the butler. "Very good, madam."

"Now", said Joyce, "first we put the light out. No, first, someone goes outside. I suggest George—he's such a snappy detective. Then we put out the light. Then one of us murders someone in the room."

There was a burst of laughter.

"You have no idea how thrilling it is," Joyce explained earnestly. "The murdered body——"

The laughter increased.

Joyce was piqued. "Of course I don't mean it's a real murder."

The laughter grew helpless to the point of hysteria. Geoffrey staggered, stopping a bellow with his handkerchief. The stagger got beyond him. It brought him to his knees, both hands pressing violently into the weak spot in his side. Their laughter fading out, they watched him with wild, anxious expressions.

"Geoffrey!" said Marjory, approaching him tentatively.

"Go 'way!" muttered Geoffrey. Slowly he doubled over the weak spot and fell heavily on the floor, his whole body writhing as if it had been fatally struck, then stretching out full length in a final rigor.

"Geoffrey!" called Marjory sharply and got down on her knees.

But Lady Marway was already beside him. "He's fainted."

Sir John immediately unfastened Geoffrey's collar. "Helen, some cold water. Keep back, please." He warded off Marjory with an arm. "Just a faint. It's all right. Some brandy."

The women went to the cabinet. Harry, watching Sir John who was feeling for the heart, asked quietly, "All right?"

"Looks like a fit of some sort", Sir John murmured. "I don't like it."

The cold water had no effect.

"The brandy," said Lady Marway.

But the jaws were rigidly clenched. The face looked like death. Breathing had to all appearances completely ceased. Harry saw that this was no pretence on Geoffrey's part, for no man could act such ghastly rigidity. Certainly it was real. Was this, then, the fulfilment?…

"We can't", said Sir John to his wife, "try to force it between his teeth. It might choke him. We've got to get him to bed."

She put the brandy decanter and glass on the floor behind her and felt Geoffrey's forehead. "He's quite cold."

"Yes. Hot bottles at once. And the doctor," said Sir John.

Lady Marway lifted one of Geoffrey's eyelids, then got up without a word and followed Helen who had already gone to see about the bottles. Marjory took a step back from

Geoffrey's body, her bottom lip between her teeth, in a state of tense emotion. At that moment there came three knocks at the gun-room door, exactly as before. Marjory let out a thin scream. Harry instantly leapt for the door and pulled it open—and was confronted by Maclean.

Harry could not speak. Maclean said, "Good evening, sir. Sir John asked me——"

Sir John had got up. "Uh, Maclean——" He looked into the gun-room and saw Alick and Angus. "Ah, you're all there. Mr. Smith has had a bad turn. We must carry him upstairs to bed. Would two of you——"

"I'm sorry to hear that, sir," said Maclean, beckoning to his men behind, as he entered the room and went towards Geoffrey. Angus followed quickly.

"Just a faint," said Sir John. "But we must get him to bed at once. Well, now. Perhaps you, Maclean, and Angus will take his feet. George, if you give me a hand——"

"No!" said Harry involuntarily. "I'll carry with George."

"We'll manage. It's all right."

"Please," said Harry, firmly displacing Sir John.

"Carefully, then. Now."

Joyce dashed for the door. When the four men carrying Geoffrey and directed by Sir John had passed out and were about to negotiate the stairs, Joyce, looking back into the sitting-room, saw Alick staring straight across at her. Her eyes widened. He wasn't staring at her: he was staring through her, beyond her. Her skin ran cold. "Oh God!" she cried harshly, and departed, leaving the door open. Marjory followed her.

Alick's eyes slowly concentrated in an ironic expression, then began to rove about the room. They saw the brandy bottle and the glass on the floor where Lady Marway had left them. It was a silly place to leave a brandy bottle and a glass. He went and picked them up and placed them on the cabinet, then turned his head slowly to Mairi in the doorway.

"Alick!" she said in an appalled whisper.

He regarded her steadily, the irony burning in his eyes. Her glance leapt from his face to the brandy bottle and back to his face.

"You're wrong this time," he said, "What are you staring at? Never seen me before?"

"Oh, Alick!"

"Well, I'm not to blame." His tone went savage, but not loud. "Dammit, cannot they manage their own little affairs? What have I got to do with them? It's nothing to me."

"Hsh!"

"Hsh! be damned. What's the good of talking like that to me? I'm not fate or God. I can't stop them playing their little tricks. If they think they're cuter than fate or God, why not? Good luck to them. It's nothing to do with me. I am merely the damned fool who gave myself away."

"Alick!" Horror crept into her desperate appeal.

His irony grew harsher. "You don't like me mentioning God?"

She had come within three paces of him. Her eyes had never left him; did not even leave him when she choked back a sob.

His smile softened and he said gently, "Mairi!"

She turned round and went out hurriedly.

Maclean and Angus came in and Alick asked them in a normal concerned voice, "How is he?"

"Very bad," said Maclean, quietly and decently.

"So long as he is alive," Alick murmured.

"Sir John was going to try for his breath on a glass," said Maclean, not looking at Alick.

"Is there anything else we can do?" Angus asked.

"I was just wondering," replied Maclean. "But I don't think so in the meantime. They won't want to come down and be finding us in this room whatever."

They heard George's voice: "I could slip along for the doctor in record time," and Sir John's reply: "No. Wait first until I 'phone. If he's not at home, you could pick him up somewhere."

"Let us go," said Maclean and the three went out.

Joyce, after a look around, came into the room and George followed her backwards, listening to Sir John. "Hallo? Hallo? Is that the doctor?... Oh, good! Could you

263

come at once to Corbreac Lodge? One of my guests has had a fit or seizure of some kind. His body is very rigid, his heart very faint.... No, not epileptic, I think.... No.... I see. You can't say.... Well, is there anything we can do here, except keep him...."

"Thank God he's at home anyway," said George to Joyce. "Pretty sudden, wasn't it?"

"Oh, awful. Must be his heart. Hsh!" She wanted to listen to the telephone. She was striving to appear calm.

"When we lifted him his body was rigid as a board," said George in low tones. "I didn't like it, I must say. Poor old Geoff."

"Must have been coming on this afternoon," said Joyce.

"Yes. Don't you think I should run along in the Bentley and pick the doctor up. He'll just crawl."

"No, you won't!" said Joyce.

"But—it's rotten when you can *do* nothing. I hate standing around."

"Do you think I do? And that fellow—with his eyes—oh God!" said Joyce.

"Steady, old thing!" said George. "Here comes Helen. How is he now?"

Helen was quiet and abstracted like one moving in a dream. "Much the same," she said.

Sir John and Harry came in. Sir John explained that nothing more could be done except wait for the doctor. He went to the bookcase and ran his eyes over the backs of the books.

George turned to Harry. "I was half-wondering whether I shouldn't shove along and meet the doctor, because——"

"Don't you think that's absurd?" interrupted Joyce, her effort at suppressing her voice merely pitching it high.

"I do," said Harry. "Ever seen a Highland doctor driving on his own roads?"

"No," said George.

"Then you have something to learn." But he hardly smiled as he turned his head and watched Helen go to the bookcase, open the bottom door, and bring out a large volume.

Sir John gave a half-apologetic smile as he took the book. "I have found it useful once or twice in the East in an emergency. You couldn't always have a doctor there just when you wanted him." His fingers were sensitive on the edges of the leaves, almost nervous.

Joyce made a brave effort. "I thought doctors warned one against these medical compilations."

"They write them, too," said Sir John.

Helen was looking straight in front, still in her half-tranced mood. Harry gave her a glance. Joyce and George watched Sir John, who read silently. The silence got drawn out unbearably. George, swaying restlessly, sticking his hands in his pockets, unthinkingly brought forth his petrol lighter.

"George!" whispered Joyce. He felt the convulsive grasp of her fingers against his side.

"Sorry!" he said, with a strained smile, and put the lighter back in his pocket.

No one could interrupt Sir John. No one could speak. Lady Marway appeared, came up to her husband. "It seems extraordinary we can't do something to bring him out of that state. Are you sure you asked the doctor?"

"Yes. Keep him on his back, with plenty of fresh air about and warmth."

"Yes, but...." Her quiet manner emphasised her uneasiness.

"You don't think he's worse?"

"It is difficult to say. I thought—for one moment—he was coming round—then——"

"Marjory is with him?"

"Oh yes. I wondered if we couldn't get a drop of brandy down. It would help the heart."

"You can't. You might choke him."

"Oh," said Lady Marway and stood quite still, fallen back into her own desperate thought.

The thought was with them all, the thought that this was death not in natural but in supernatural circumstances. There was an intangible fear in it, and horror. It gripped their hearts, sickened them with its excitement. And there was nothing to do, nothing to do but wait. Joyce could not cry out nor George act.

"Will you come up?" said Lady Marway to her husband.

"One moment," said Sir John, turning over a page.

They waited. The tension was drawn out. A tumbling noise from the stairs made their hearts leap. The door swung open and Marjory entered, wild-eyed and panting. She smashed the door shut and lay back against it, as if shutting out some awful horror. Then with a spasmodic jerk of her whole body and a smothered scream, she broke from the door, throwing a glance over her shoulder, and fetched up in the corner near the gun-room door. She was manifestly in a desperate and very real state of high nervous tension.

"Marjory!" breathed Lady Marway.

But Marjory saw none of them. She was staring back at the door, the full light of the standard lamp on her wide-eyed, terrified face. They all looked at the door. It began noiselessly to open. A raucous scream shattered the hall. Ina's voice. The light in the sitting-room went down, until both lamps were little more than ghostly luminous bulbs. The lamp by the bookcase, which had not been fully turned up, appeared indeed to come into a life of its own. The door swung fully open and the ghostly figure of Geoffrey came through it, taller than in ordinary life, his white winding sheet, faintly phosphorescent, falling to the floor. The face was whiter than they had last seen it; so death-white that its texture seemed frail, almost transparent. He did not look at them but went straight towards Marjory, walking quite noiselessly. She smothered a whining cry. The medical book slipped from Sir John's hands. Joyce let out a harsh guttural sound. Unhurriedly the ghost reached the gun-room door. Marjory cowered away. As the white face looked round upon them the gun-room door opened and the light illumined the face in a pure spirit effect.

There was the clatter of a rifle falling, the harsh sounds of male fear.

"Oh God!" screamed Joyce.

George let out a wild yell, pushed Harry aside, and charged for the gun-room into which the ghost had passed.

He hesitated one moment on the threshold, the light glittering in his eyes, then swept on and in. His voice rose high and challenging. There was a ghostly moan; followed by a smashing blow, lost in Marjory's wild cry:

"George! It's Geoffrey! It's Geoffrey!"

They were all on her heels at the door. The shrouded figure lay stretched out on the floor, solid and quite inert. George, wide planted on his feet, his arms hanging by his sides, like a boxer who had delivered a knock-out and was himself swaying, all in, gaped down at the body, mouth open.

With a cry, Marjory got to her knees. "Geoffrey!" But the body gave no response. She put her hands behind the head to lift it up.

"Wait, Marjory," said Sir John.

Marjory withdrew her hands. They were red with blood.

"What have you done?" she cried. "What have you done to him?"

Lady Marway caught her wrists.

"Stand back!" said Sir John. Maclean helped him to examine the deep wound in the back of the head, at the same time pulling the rifle that Angus had let fall from under his back, Geoffrey's own rifle. Both men saw at once that the wound was fatal. The skull had been fractured by the edge of an iron clamp that supported the rifle rack.

"This floor is cold. Let us carry him in," said Sir John quietly.

They stretched him out on the hearthrug before the sitting-room fire. Lady Marway turned the small wheel of the wick and the light increased normally and flooded the room.

"Is he very bad?" she asked.

"I'm afraid so. Some bandages—quick—to stop the blood." But there was no anxiety in Sir John's voice, no eagerness.

"But it can't really be bad," said George. "I hardly hit him at all. I just hit him on the chin. It wasn't—it wasn't a knock-out. Not really." He wanted to tell everyone this. There was an eager pathetic smile on his face. He looked from one to another. "I never thought!"

"It was not your blow," said Sir John. "It was what he fell on." He withdrew his hand from Geoffrey's heart.

Lady Marway came in with a bandage roll and some napkins. As she got down on her knees, she looked at her husband. He met her eyes. Her head drooped.

Marjory's whisper pierced the room: "He's not dead?"

They gave her no answer. "I'll do this," said Sir John, releasing his wife.

"But he can't be!" said Marjory. "Oh he can't!" Her voice was rising shrilly. "It was a joke! Don't you understand? It was just a joke!"

Lady Marway went to her. "Hush, Marjory!"

"But, you see, but——"

"Yes, my dear." Lady Marway put her arm round her. "Hush, now."

"But it can't be—he couldn't——" She tried to go to Geoffrey, but Lady Marway held her.

"No, no, Marjory. You can't help now."

"But—oh, I told him I didn't want to! At first, I didn't mind, but then I got terrified! Something terrified me!"

"I know, dear. That's why you acted so well."

"He only wanted to prove—that you could be frightened—by nothing!" She was quivering all over, wild-eyed, her fingers still stained with blood, though Lady Marway had done her best to wipe them.

"We understand now, dear. But keep hold—we have all to face up to this."

As if unaware of what she had been saying, Marjory now stared at Sir John, and asked, like a somnambulist, the words dripping from her lips: "Is he dead?"

"Yes," said Sir John.

She turned cold and deathly pale.

"Was it you who turned down the light?" Sir John asked her.

"Yes," she answered. She remained quite still and straight, now and then taking audible gulps of breath. "He made me." She turned to Lady Marway, and spoke as she might in a court of law, out of a dreadful responsibility. "When you left the bedroom, he spoke to me. He had dosed himself with something—quite harmless, he said—for the time being. But when I saw him all stiff—it frightened me. His side was very bad. I didn't want to do any more. I said I wouldn't go. I tried to persuade him. I begged him on my knees. He got angry. He said he could never trust me again. He said if I didn't go—it would spoil all the fun."

Her lips shut tightly.

"Was it you who knocked at the door?" asked Sir John.

She nodded. "I went out at the front door—round to the gun-room—and back. It was—my idea." The heavy gulps of breath were becoming more frequent. "He meant—after appearing here—and going through the gun-room—to hurry round to the front door—and get back to bed. You would have been mystified. He would then—have been in a position——"

She began to sway. Lady Marway caught her; Harry put a supporting arm round her; together they led her from the room. She made a supreme effort at the top of the stairs. "Thank you, Harry," she said, dismissing him. Grasping her arm firmly, Lady Marway led her to her room.

As Harry entered the sitting-room, four men were lifting Geoffrey, Sir John and George his head, Maclean and Angus his feet. Involuntarily Harry started to go forward, but Alick held him back with an arm, to let them pass. As they were going out of the door, the dinner bell began to toll, for when Ina had rushed into the kitchen saying she had seen a ghost, Cook took the opportunity to give her a delayed lecture. As both girls were terrified to go into the hall, she went herself and was thus ringing the bell, which hung from the wall like a ship's bell, when the four men brought the body out and began carrying it upstairs. Cook spoke to Sir John and learned that Mr. Smith was dead.

In the sitting-room, Alick stood looking after the procession, obviously unaware of Harry, Helen, and Joyce. Harry gave him a glance, but quickly averted his eyes. Helen's trance-like expression came to rest on him, then her whole body quickened and her eyes, brilliant with pain, sought Harry.

Joyce, staring through the open door, burst out, "Isn't it dreadful for George?" Her head went up, her arms stiffened. A moan quivered in her throat.

Helen turned to her. "Joyce," she said gently. "George couldn't——"

"I say, isn't it awful?" cried Joyce.

"He wasn't to blame." Harry's voice was level. "He didn't do it. You mustn't worry about that."

Joyce did not hear them. "He's so sensitive he'll——" She caught her lip in her teeth to keep the scream back.

"Joyce, Joyce," said Helen.

"——he'll never forgive himself!" Her voice rose to an hysteric cry. She rushed out of the room.

There was a long pause, then quietly, without feeling, Harry said, "It *is* hard on George, of course."

Helen came close to him.

They could not look at Alick. Harry wanted to say something to Alick. He could not. There was nothing to say. They could not stay there, with Alick beside them.

Harry looked into Helen's eyes. Something in his smile of weariness, of oldness, touched Helen on the quick of the heart. She came alive and caught his arm. He walked out of the room, with the feeling, none the less terrible because it was surely quite irrational, that he was deserting, that he was betraying, Alick. Opposite the dark dining-room they paused. Harry led Helen into it and closed the door.

Alick's eyes had followed them. Then he looked in front again and an expression of irony took on a bitter depth. He swallowed, pressed his forearms against the pit of his breast, and, as if feeling sick or weak, sat down on the soft arm of a chair.

He got up as he heard Maclean and Angus coming in.

"Well, Alick, it's a sad business," said Maclean. The voice was friendly, but with some intangible reserve. He did not look at Alick.

"It is," Alick answered.

There was silence. Angus threw a pained confused glance at Alick. The occasion, the place, made him ill at ease.

"Come," said Maclean quietly. "We may as well go home. There will be no hill to-morrow."

Maclean and Angus went out. But Alick did not follow them. The ironic expression came back. He sat on the chair arm. His head drooped. I'm feeling sick! he thought, as if by gathering his attention on so small a point he could ward off the blackness of despair, the terrible disintegrating blackness that slowly wrenches the mind to bits.

Mairi appeared in the hall door and stood for some time looking at him. When she had conquered the up thrust of her emotion, she closed the door softly behind her and came to his side.

"Alick," she said gently.

His head lifted and looked in front.

"Well?" he demanded drily.

She put her hand on his shoulder.

"Don't do that," he said coldly.

She took her hand away, in no way hurt, as if she understood him.

"I'm sorry, Alick."

"Oh, it's all right," he muttered indifferently.

"Aren't you going home?"

"I'll have to go somewhere, I suppose." There was a pause. "Not much good staying here, is there?" His mouth gave a twist. "They're beginning to avoid me already."

"They don't—mean——"

"No. Oh no." Then on the same level tone but with a sudden intensity. "Damn, I am vexed about it. He was a decent enough fellow." He breathed heavily. "However—that's that."

"They won't hold it against you."

"Perhaps not. But they'll never be able to look at me without remembering. I know all about that." His mouth caught its bitter expression. "Pity, for I like this country well enough. It's good enough for me—perhaps because it is my own country."

"But Sir John wouldn't——"

"No. He wouldn't. He's kind. But he will expect *me* to go." The bitterness found its own humour. "Mr. Kingsley said they were having great arguments about how things in the Highlands were dying out, even things like second sight."

"Alick!"

"He asked me why. I didn't like to tell him."

"Why?"

"We are so sensitive, I suppose." Self-mockery was in his breath. "We must go—and take the things with us. That has always been our small tragedy."

"But—you needn't——"

"No? You think not?"

Then Mairi said, after a little time, in a toneless voice: "Yes, you'll have to go.... Where?"

"South—where I won't be known."

"To the cities?... When?"

"Now."

Very quietly, in the same toneless voice, she said: "I should like to go with you—if you would take me."

"Would you?" he asked indifferently.

"Yes."

"Not afraid of a vision of death?"

"No."

For the first time, he turned his head and looked at her. "What do you mean?"

She held herself against the upthrust of her emotion and said simply: "It would be death for me without you."

His irony became very bitter, very searching. "You think love should triumph over death?"

"It does."

His searching expression broke. "Mairi!"

The sound of her name was little more than a breath of tenderness, but it broke the barrier she had raised against her emotion. She dropped to the floor and buried her face between his knees, clinging to him to stifle her sobs.

"Come, Mairi," he said after a few moments. "We'll go. Come on." He helped her to her feet. "We'll go together."

And they went out through the gun-room door.